A SOLDIER'S BAPTISM

David lifted his rifle, laid it across the log, and clicked back the hammer. War cries resounded in the trees—and then he saw them. For the first time in his life, David Crockett beheld the fearsome sight of on-rushing Indians, warriors who in moments would learn they had been baited into an ambush.

"Now!"

As one, scores of rifles cracked. Indians spasmed and fell, some silently, others with deathly screams. Smoke rose through the treetops. For a moment there was near silence, broken only by the sound of men reloading, and then fully shattered by the crack of Indian rifles and the whiz of arrows sailing above.

Now that the first shots had been fired, David felt very different than before. A sort of wild eagerness for battle came over him, and a thoroughly inexplicable sense of invulnerability.

He had survived the first round of fire, so why not the second, the third, the tenth or twelfth?

CROCKETT
OF
TENNESSEE

*A Novel Based on the Life
and Times of David Crockett*

Cameron Judd

BANTAM BOOKS

New York   Toronto   London   Sydney   Auckland

CROCKETT OF TENNESSEE

A Bantam Book / August 1994

ISBN 0-553-56856-6

Published simultaneously in the United States and Canada

Bantam Books are published by Bantam Books, a division of Bantam
Doubleday Dell Publishing Group, Inc. Its trademark, consisting of the
words "Bantam Books" and the portrayal of a rooster, is Registered in
U.S. Patent and Trademark Office and in other countries. Marca Reg-
istrada. Bantam Books, 1540 Broadway, New York, New York 10036.

PRINTED IN THE UNITED STATES OF AMERICA

RAD   0 9 8 7 6 5 4 3 2 1

*To Joe Swann and Jim Claborn, two who keep
the Crockett legacy alive*

Part 1

POOR MAN'S SON

Chapter 1

Territory of the United States Southwest of the River Ohio, Spring 1794

He left the forest and ran barefoot across the meadow, dodging stumps and calling for his dog. It did not come, just as it had not come all morning, though he had called incessantly. The boy paused for breath, mounted one of the taller stumps, brushed a shock of dark hair from his eyes and scanned the landscape. No dog in sight. His throat was already sore from shouting; now it began to grow tight as well. Tears threatened to rise.

"Painter!" he called again. At age seven, he had a shrill shouting voice. "Here, Painter! Here, boy!"

He waited. No Painter. Drawing in a deep breath, he squatted on the log and looked around. The field was greening in the new spring, the wind was fresh and cool, moist and pleasant. This was the kind of day the boy usually loved, but at the moment he was near to despair and hardly noticed the weather. It appeared that the much-beloved Painter might have left for good this time. The mongrel had vanished from time to time before, as dogs will do, but until today had always returned within a few minutes of being called.

An urgent male voice came filtering through the trees from beyond the forest grove on the far side of the road.

The boy cocked his ear to listen. His father was evidently scolding the older boys for some mistake or another as they worked to finish roofing the new mill. The mill, of the overshot style, stood on Cove Creek in the sprawling territorial county of Greene, and was almost ready for operation now, lacking only a portion of its roof, a final section of millrace, and installation of the grain hopper. Finishing the roof was the day's foremost concern, frenetically pursued under threat of the clouds gathering on the horizon and all the various other signs of rain—low-flying birds, surfacing earthworms, ants covering the holes of their hills—that pointed toward a big storm on the way.

The boy descended from the stump, picked up a stick, and walked through the meadow, swinging glumly at flies and bugs that chanced to come within range. His father's voice wafted to him again—was that his name being called? He wasn't sure, and being in no humor at the moment to labor slavishly with his brothers around the unfinished mill while his dog was still missing, decided to pretend he hadn't heard. He headed across the clearing into the woods on the opposite side.

He had just entered the edge of the forest when he heard the rattle and rumble of a wagon up the dirt road. He turned and watched as a big Conestoga, lacking a cover but laden with crates and casks and bundles, rolled into view. Driving the wagon was a tall, thin man with a narrow black beard, and beside him a young boy who would have been his double with the addition of age and whiskers, and the deletion of a certain coppery skin tone the man lacked.

As the wagon hit a section of the road paved with side-by-side logs laid crossways over a perpetually marshy area fed by a spring, the eyes of the boy at the woods' edge and those of the boy on the wagon met and held for a few moments. The wagon jolted on across the logs, moving recklessly fast, and rounded a bend. As it went out of sight, the watching boy caught a snatch of a song, sung by the bearded driver. It sounded odd and slurred, like the song of a drunk. But it seemed awfully early in the day for anybody to be drinking.

The boy listened to the fading rumble of the wagon, then turned away from the road and went deeper into the woods, calling for his dog as he went. Far away, from somewhere along the horizon, thunder rumbled across the hills.

Another curve lay ahead, and the wagon veered around it and onto a long downgrade. The road was new, full of holes where stumps and roots had been dug out, along with a few stumps that still awaited removal. A particularly large one presented itself unexpectedly, and the driver responded with a shout and jerk on the reins, turning the team and wagon just in time. Bundles and packs shifted and bounced on the bed. The driver laughed. The boy beside him did not laugh; he was struggling to retain his seat, and grew pallid and hollow-eyed as he was tossed around. His left hand was gripped tightly across his middle.

"Keep holding tight there, Persius!" the driver cackled. "A devil of a ride, ain't it!" He reached under his wool coat and pulled out a bottle. He unstoppered it without letting go of the reins, took a swallow, corked the bottle and returned it to its hiding place.

"You're going to kill us both."

"What? You afraid? You're a Tarr, boy! Ain't' no Tarrs afraid of nothing!"

"I'm sick. My belly hurts."

"Howdy do! Look at that one!" The man hurriedly redirected the team again. This time the side of the wagon grazed the stump he had dodged. They came around onto a flat and moved even faster, riding into the wind.

Persius Tarr said, "I'm sick," then leaned over the side of the wagon and vomited. Matter blew back across the wagon sideboard and onto some of the contents of the bed. The driver glowered and swore violently, and pulled the panting, steaming team to an overdue halt.

The boy, gone pale beneath his swarthiness and struggling not to heave again, ducked his head low, staring at his feet, wiping his mouth with the back of a hand. His father's gaze was searing. Silence held until it grew almost too heavy to bear.

"See what you've gone and did?" the man said in a voice that managed to be simultaneously soft and threatening. "Look at that mess you've spit up all over everything back yonder! You see it?"

"Yes."

"No you don't. No you don't. You ain't even looking."

The boy, shoulders hunched, glanced briefly over his shoulder at the soiled cargo, then resumed his previous posture, avoiding his father's eyes.

"Now, what can we do about that, Persius? Who do you reckon ought to have to clean that mess up? You think I should have to do it?"

"No."

"Who do you allow should?"

"Me, I reckon."

"That's right, that's right." The man stopped talking for a few moments in order to take another drink. "That's right. You're going to clean it. And when you're done, I'm going to whup you with a stout stick. You've spat up all over our wagon, boy! Spat up like some puny baby child! You not even big enough to hold down your victuals? Pshaw! Look at you! You're yellow as the janders!"

"I'm feeling bad. I reckon was the wagon bouncing around that done it. And my belly, it's been hurting a lot lately."

His father snorted contemptuously, and clumsily began disengaging himself from his perch on the wagon. In his condition, it took quite some time. Once down, he almost tumbled to the ground until he finally steadied himself into a wavering upright posture. No trace of joviality remained. "You get to cleaning that mess, hear? I'll go fetch a whupping stick. And I'm going to use it. I'm going to whup you. It'll hurt me more than you, but I got to do it."

He turned and weaved off into the forest. The moment he was out of sight, Persius Tarr muttered, with his lip quivering from emotion, "No, sir, I reckon you ain't, not this time!" then leaped off the wagon seat and began running through the forest in the opposite direction, racing as fast as he could go, gripping his aching stomach as he went.

Dusk came early because of the clouds. They spread over the sky, making a low, black ceiling. The wind heightened, then raged, blowing tender leaves off the trees, jerking and tearing at the roof boards of the new mill. In gathering darkness the boy, still without his dog, stood beside his father in front of the cabin, looking at the mill with sorrow in his eyes. A fresh gust of wind grabbed at a roof board, wrestled with it and yanked it free, sending it sailing out into the air and down into the fast-running creek.

A short, homespun-clad woman with bright eyes, a sharp nose, and a belly big with pregnancy, walked quietly to the man's side. She took his arm and smiled. "Don't stand there worrying yourself, John Crockett. A mill roof can be repaired."

Another wild burst of wind came; a second and third roof board jerked loose and joined the first in the water, floating rapidly away.

"Yes," he replied. "But it's more than the roof I worry about." He looked skyward. "Them clouds . . . never seen clouds so black." He fingered his beard. "We could lose it, Rebecca. The whole mill. Everything. I ain't never seen falling weather so fearsome. It's going to be a devil of a thunder gust."

"Look there, Pap. The creek's rising," the boy said.

"That's 'cause it's already raining in the hills. It'll be down upon us soon." The wind regathered and made another sweep. More roof boards flew. John Crockett shook his head, lips pursed. "It'll be on us, and nary a board will be left on that roof by the time it comes. I'd make a wager on it if I had a penny left to wager with."

They stood together, a somber trio, until the first pebble-sized drops of rain began to splatter the ground around them. One hit the boy squarely atop the head. It was so heavy it made him jump.

"That will turn to hail, or I'm an Injun," the woman said. She turned to the boy. "Come inside, David."

"Painter's still out there somewhere. He'll get wet."

"Painter's dead," John Crockett said. "If he wasn't dead, he'd have come back by now."

"John, there's no need to talk so harsh to him. You know how he loves that dog."

"It's the truth, Rebecca. He might as well face it now as later. It's just a dog, anyways, and a puny one at that. Last I seen it, it was a-bleeding out the mouth and whimpering. He's crawled off and died somewhere, most likely. God! Look there—the whole deuced roof nigh blew off that time!"

"Come inside, David," Rebecca Crockett said, tugging the boy away. "Let's get out of the wet."

John Crockett remained outside for nearly an hour, alone in the rain, before he joined his family inside the squat little cabin. Hail rattled the roof; water dripped through in almost a dozen places. Nine unsmiling faces looked at him by the dim light of a tallow lamp.

He spoke spiritlessly. "The creek is up. It will be in the cabin soon. We must leave."

"In this storm?" Rebecca asked.

"Yes. Otherwise we'll be washed out of here like deadwood."

William Crockett, David's older brother by four years, asked, "What about the mill?"

John Crockett turned his head away, blinking rapidly, and David was astonished to realize his father was fighting tears. He answered William very tersely, without looking him in the eye. "The mill's gone. A good piece of it washed down the creek about half an hour ago."

Chapter 2

The family moved together through the darkness, bending beneath the storm and the fearsome lightning. David stayed close behind his father, though it was a strain for his shorter legs to keep pace with John Crockett's wide strides. The forest all around had grown wild and surreal, trees whipping about like ankle-shackled beasts straining for freedom, the sky an alternating display of blackness and hot light, the wind a cold, wet, face-slapping antagonist.

David stopped abruptly. Was that a dog's bark he had heard from the direction of the cabin? "Painter!" he yelled. "Painter! Here, boy!"

"Quiet down, David," John Crockett called over his shoulder. "A dog can fend for hisself. Keep on walking."

David Crockett had already figured out where his father was taking them, even though he hadn't said: a squat little hillside cabin, built many years before by hunters as a station camp, used since by others as a pig shelter and a chicken coop, and now not used at all except as a playhouse for David himself and his little brother, Joseph. David had sworn Joseph to silence, on pain of a thrashing, about their visits to the hut. Rebecca Crockett had ordered her sons to stay away from the place; she had seen an entire nest of snakes there once, and considered it dangerous. David and his brother had played there many times, despite the prohibition, and if there were snakes, they hadn't seen them yet.

They entered the log hut, Rebecca Crockett moaning her alarm now that she saw where they were. The hut stank and leaked and was filled with cobwebs, but David thought it a great improvement over exposure to the open storm. He sat down on the mucky dirt floor and huddled close to his mother, who sat with a hand cupped in unconscious protectiveness over the swell of her pregnancy, and looked around nervously, though it was too dark to see any snakes, if there were any. At the other side of her, cradled under her arm, was two-year-old Jane; Betsy, three years younger than David; and little Joseph. The older children sat nearer the door, beside their father, watching the storm, which went on without diminishing.

"It's Noah's freshet, come again," John Crockett muttered. "And no ark to save the Crocketts."

William asked, "What will we do, Pap? Without the mill, I mean."

A lightning flash limned John's form against the uncovered doorway. He looked fearsome, somehow, against that backdrop. William's question seemed to anger him. "How the devil should I know? I only wish I did."

David felt so sad he was afraid he would cry. Whenever John Crockett was like this, it made David tense and afraid. And he was still thinking about Painter, out there in the storm somewhere, maybe dead, maybe hurt. He felt more and more sure that it was Painter he had heard barking back at the cabin.

On a deeper level of which he was almost unconscious, David also felt alarmed about the family's future, now that the mill was gone. What would they do? How would they live? He was too young to comprehend monetary affairs in detail, but he was cognizant of his family's poverty and the general instability of John Crockett's finances. He had overheard his mother and father worrying together over debt many times. In David's seven years, the family had moved twice. From David's birthplace at the juncture of Great Limestone Creek and the Nolichucky River, a riverside home David had dearly loved, the

Crocketts had moved to a farm some ten miles north of Greene Courthouse. From there they had come, very recently, to Cove Creek, to build and operate a mill in partnership with Tom Galbreath, a Pennsylvania native who had come to Greene County by way of Virginia. David knew his father had counted on the mill venture to provide a lasting security for his family ... but now the mill was washed away, and security with it.

Another hour passed. David dozed against his mother's arm. When he awakened again, the storm had declined significantly. The rain was slow and steady, the wind was down, and there was no more lightning. He slept again. When he next woke up, it was dawn, and he was alone in the hut. He stood, rubbing his eyes, and went to the doorway. John Crockett was standing outside, slump-shouldered, looking around at the devastation of the storm: fallen trees, tangled limbs, runoff springs gushing down the hills and creating great muddy gulleys.

Rubbing his eyes, David emerged from the hut. His bare feet sank deep into the sodden mast covering the ground. He looked around at the faces of his brothers and sisters. No one was smiling; even the smallest ones seemed to sense that the family had been dealt a harsh blow.

The Crocketts marched through the drenched and battered forest until they reached the cabin and mill. The cabin was still intact, except for part of the roof. Water had left its mark high on the cabin wall, making evident John Crockett's wisdom in moving his family out of the place before the flood hit. The water had risen all the way into the cabin, and though it had receded by now, Cove Creek still looked like a river, running far out of its banks. The mill was roofless and enveloped by the muddy current, so that it looked like it had been built, idiotically, in midstream. The wheel was broken and standing at a cocked angle in the water. All the chinking had washed out from between the logs of the wall, and in some places the logs had floated out of their notches.

The Crocketts stood silently, looking it all over. John Crockett's expression was placid, though his heavy brows hung lower than usual over the hollows of his eyes, and his struggle to keep his temper in front of the little ones was transparent even to young David. Rebecca, close by her husband's side, smiled brightly when her children looked at her, but she fooled no one. The young ones cried; even David, who was old enough to believe that tears were for girls alone, wanted to bawl.

Wilson Crockett, about two years older than David, was the first to actually enter the cabin. He stayed inside a few moments, then came out. "David, come here."

David entered the cabin. The interior was sad to see. Though Rebecca had hurriedly placed household items atop the table and single cupboard, hoping to keep them from the flood, the waters had been too deep and forceful. The table had been swept aside, and the cupboard had fallen forward, dumping everything in and on it. The cabin's dirt floor, slightly hollowed in the center by Rebecca's frequent sweeping, now was a muddy waterhole.

"It's mighty bad in here, Wilson."

"It ain't the cabin I wanted to show you. Look yonder in the corner."

David looked and saw what looked like a sodden and rumpled pelt of some sort. Then he realized it wasn't a pelt. It was Painter, and he was dead.

David said nothing, did not move. He felt as if he had been rooted, then frozen, in place. Wilson stepped over to the corner, the muddy floor sucking at his feet. He knelt beside the dead dog and examined it.

"There's blood around his mouth, David. He's been bleeding from the throat."

David tried to swallow the growing lump in his own throat. "What would have made him bleed?"

Wilson stood, shrugging. "I don't know. Sickliness, maybe. Or maybe he et something that cut him some way or another. It looks like he come back home in the storm, after we had already lit out. I reckon maybe the rising water killed him." He glanced at David's face, which was growing blotchy and puffed around the eyes as he fought back tears.

Wilson patted his young brother's shoulder, obviously

enjoying playing the role of older-and-wiser. "Don't cry, David," he said piously. "Heaven has done Painter a great mercy."

"What's that mean?"

"That's just what you say when someone has died in pain. That's what Mama says. The dead one was a-suffering before, and now they ain't, so heaven has done them a great mercy. You understand?"

"You think Painter suffered before he ... before he was done a mercy?"

"Well, he must have. He was a-bleeding, wasn't he? So see? You ought to be thankful. He's been done a mercy."

David held silence. Wilson, looking satisfied at having vented his wisdom so liberally, left the cabin. David went to the corner and picked up his dog's cold body. He held it and stroked the wet fur, tears streaming down his face.

"I'll bury you, Painter. Out in the secret place." He hugged the furry corpse close. "Don't feel bad at being dead, Painter. Heaven has done you a mercy. That's what Wilson says, and I reckon he knows a lot more than me about that kind of thing."

There was a special, secret hollow in the woods a mile from the cabin, a place to which David and Painter had escaped many times to play. He headed there now, carrying Painter's body under his left arm and a shovel in his right hand. The hollow seemed the right place to bury Painter.

David had taken varying routes to his hollow to avoid making a trail his siblings could follow to discover and invade his private domain. Today he chose a route that initially followed the new wagon road, from which he would cut east at the base of the second downgrade to reach the hollow from its lowest side. He was in control of his emotions now, though barely, and his eyes were red from fresh crying.

He reached the top of the second downgrade and

stopped. A stunning sight lay below. At the base of the
slope was a tangle of wreckage. A wagon had gone off the
road and rolled, shattering against a tree. David gaped. He
remembered this wagon; it was the very one that had rattled by so fast the previous day, when he was out looking
for Painter, the one bearing the man and the boy.

David began to tremble. He dropped the shovel, laid
Painter's body gently to the ground, and walked down the
slope, slipping a couple of times in the mud. The former
contents of the wagon were scattered all along the road,
and despite the masking effects of the night's storm, David
could still detect the point the wagon had slid out of control. The horses remained hitched to the wagon and were
alive, though badly hurt. They made sounds of pain terrible to hear, and their eyes were wide-open and wild. David
knew they would have to be shot.

He was looking mostly for the boy he had seen, but
instead he found only the man, beneath the wagon,
crushed by its weight and as dead as a man could be. David stared at the corpse a few moments, then turned and
ran in panic back up the hill, shouting in his high-pitched
voice as loud as he could for his father.

After topping the rise and starting down the far side,
David came to a stop so abrupt that his feet slid from beneath him and he fell on his rump in the mud. He stared
up into the face of the boy from the wagon. The swarthy
boy, looking as if he had weathered the storm without
shelter, had just walked out of the edge of the woods, and
seemed as surprised as David was to encounter another human being. The boy appeared to be slightly older than David, perhaps by a year. His frame was thin and juvenile.
His eyes ... that was the aspect of him that was unsettling. His eyes might have been those of an old man. They
were eyes that had seen too much, too soon, and had been
rendered veiled and hard.

The two boys eyed each other like tomcats for a few
moments. David stood. The other set his lip in a snarl—an
automatic, defensive facial gesture, like the arching of a
cat's back.

"What are you a-gaping at?" Persius Tarr asked.

"I was just . . . I was . . . who are you?"

"Somebody who could whup you in a knock fight."

David wondered if that was a threat. Why was this dark boy so testy? "I don't want no fight."

"Then don't stand a-gaping."

"You was in that wagon, with that man."

"Was. I got out and left. I'm on my own now."

David, naturally enough, misinterpreted that comment to indicate that the boy knew about the fatal accident. "Was he your father?"

"Who?"

"The man under the wagon."

Persius Tarr snorted. "*Under* the wagon? What are you, a fool? My father don't drive his wagon from the bottomside! I reckon he might if he got drunk enough, or if he turned stupid as you." He made a forced effort at haughty laughter, but cut it off suddenly, grasping his belly like it had been kicked.

"You sick?"

"Go off and leave me be." A radical change of spirit had occurred. A gripping pain had driven the fight out of Persius Tarr.

It came clear to David. This boy *didn't* know about the wagon crash, didn't know that his father was dead. The import of it all was overwhelming. David went pale. He had never before been faced with the prospect of giving such tragic news to another person.

"I told you to quit a-gaping at me. I'll whup you if you don't."

David searched for his voice. "Your father . . . that wagon, it's yonder over the hill . . . your father, he's . . ."

The boy's expression grew stony. "What are you babbling about?"

David swallowed. "Your father, he is . . . he has . . ."

"What, hang it?"

"The wagon, it went off the road and turned over, yonder beyond the hill."

The look of defiance left Persius Tarr's face. He looked scared now. "Where's my father?"

"He's with the wagon . . . under the wagon. He's . . ."

David stopped, uncertain how to say it. "Your father fell under the wagon—it rolled over on top of him . . . and heaven done him a great mercy."

In his capacity of Greene County constable, John Crockett wrote down a description of the accident based on what Persius was able to tell him and the physical evidence left behind at the scene. This he would file with the county coroner. But in the meantime there was nothing to do but get the dead man into the ground.

Grave-digging was difficult and messy in the mud, and the bottom of the hole filled with water. No coffin was available, so the late Mick Tarr was wrapped in a blanket, tied with cords, and lowered into the grave as he was. They heaped mud back over him, John Crockett clumsily led a prayer, and it was done.

"You can stay with us a time, Persius," John said without enthusiasm. "You don't have any other place to go, I don't reckon."

"No sir. But I can make it fine alone."

"No. You stay with us, for now."

David was glad to hear that. Persius was a very interesting fellow, and David had a feeling he would like him after he got to know him better. There was something about Persius that spoke of freedom and rugged experience far beyond anything David had known. David sensed he could learn from Persius—learn things, maybe, that his parents wouldn't teach him even if they could. Who could say? If everything went well, maybe Persius would become part of the family, and stay forever. That would be fine, like having a new brother.

David walked beside Persius as they headed back to the cabin. Persius kept his eyes fixed straight ahead and his expression solemn.

"Ain't you going to cry?" David asked.

"I never cry," Persius said.

"Why?" David was taken all at once with an interesting possibility. "Are you an Injun? You're dark enough to be one, and you won't see Injuns crying much."

Persius's dark eyes narrowed. "I ain't no Injun! I'll whup your hind end, you say that again!"

"Settle down there!" John Crockett barked. "There'll be no fighting. You boys hear me?"

"I ain't no Injun!" Persius repeated, this time in a low mumble. "It makes me mad when folks call me an Injun. I don't know why folks always got to say that. Some of these days I'll whup me a few hind ends and see how they like that!"

"I said, settle down!" John repeated. This time Persius obeyed, though he still looked as if he could explode, trying to contain his anger.

David slowed up, letting Persius move ahead. A fascinating, mysterious fellow, this Persius Tarr was . . . but he was sure going to take some getting used to, if he was going to be around for long. One thing was certain to David: he would be very slow to mention Indians around Persius Tarr again.

Chapter 3

Two Days Later, Along Cove Creek

"Reach a mite more, David! Just a mite more, that's all!"

David strained a little farther, grimacing at the effort. He was standing precariously on the side of a storm-felled sycamore that extended like a bridge across the creek. He held to a branch with his left hand and gripped the end of a long stick in his right, probing the stick's other end into the water.

"A mite more, David! There, there! Hurrah! You're almost at it!"

The encouragement came from little sister Betsy, who stood beside the muddy root clump of the tree, which had fallen during the storm. She leaned forward, mimicking with her own thin body the cautious balancing act of her brother. Her eyes brightened suddenly, and she clapped.

"Snared it!" David exclaimed triumphantly, lifting the stick. On its end was a soaked beaver hat, washed down the creek during the storm and lodged in partially submerged branches. David swung it around toward his little sister, who snatched it and began to shake the water out of it. David dropped the stick into the water and edged back to the bank.

Betsy shaped the hat into some semblance of what it must have been before, and put it onto her head. It was far too large, and slipped down over her eyes. David laughed. "Well, you wanted it, and now you have it, and it's big enough to swaller you!"

The little girl took off the hat. Her hair was now as wet as the hat was. Her quick frown just as quickly became a smile. "I can sell it!" she declared. "I can take it into Greene Courthouse and sell it for money! And I'll let you have some of the money, David, 'cause it was you who fished it out for me!"

David laughed at his sister as she turned and darted toward the cabin to show her prize to her mother. He swept his gaze over the broader scene, and saw his father exiting the damaged mill, Thomas Galbreath beside him. It made David wish ironically that getting rich really was as easy as fishing a hat from a creek.

The unfortunate mill partners had been together since early morning, talking privately and intensely, with serious expressions on their faces. For the last half hour they had been exploring the ruined mill, from which the creek waters had receded the day before, leaving it standing in a wide expanse of mud. With the water down, the mill didn't look as devastated as before . . . not until one looked closely.

John Crockett and Galbreath were evaluating whether there was any chance at all of repairing and opening the mill. John had already expressed his belief that there was none, and if the looks David saw on their faces gave evidence of their mutual conclusion, it appeared John's pessimism had been validated.

David brushed the water and fragments of bark off his hands and headed toward the cabin. William, third-born of the Crockett sons and namesake of John Crockett's brother in neighboring Jefferson County, was on the roof, patching it as best he could. Rebecca was inside, where she had been busy since before dawn, doing what she could to make the cabin a home again, however short-lived a home it would be. She had been remarkably successful for such brief efforts in a badly storm-smitten structure, having covered the floor with evergreen boughs gathered by her children and put the furniture back into place. Unfortunately, the stick-and-mud upper portion of the chimney, weakened by rain, had fallen away from the house only this morning, leaving a fireplace that opened directly to the sky and wouldn't draw smoke properly.

When David entered the cabin, Persius Tarr was at the table, eating corn bread and "long sweetening," as the locals called sorghum molasses. David was shocked to see Persius receiving such a treat—Rebecca usually doled out long sweetening with the conservatism of an army commissary officer on short supplies. For a moment David felt resentful of Persius, until he remembered how sad and alone the bereaved boy had looked beside the grave of his father. Persius had no parents, no home, and no possessions beyond what cargo had been in the wagon—though that, he confessed, hadn't really been his father's. It was mostly useless stuff, with little value, and had all been stolen in Washington County. The late Mick Tarr, it seemed, had been a thief as well as a drunkard.

"Can I have some sweetening too, Mama?" David asked.

"Get away, Davy—Persius is a guest, and he ain't et nearly as good as a boy should for Lord knows how long. If I give you sweetening, I have to give it to all your brothers and sisters too."

David glared enviously at Persius, who in turn ignored him, being preoccupied with his food. Persius ate with an enthusiasm exceeding any David had heretofore witnessed. Molasses dripped down his narrow chin—an awful waste of good sweetening, in David's opinion. He stood watching the display, quietly resenting the favored treatment this stranger was enjoying while the Crockett children, Rebecca's own flesh and blood, were excluded. But that was just the way Rebecca Crockett was, doling out her tenderness to anything or anyone who caught her sympathy, and expecting her own offspring to do the same. Life was certainly unfair.

Persius surprised David by suddenly gripping his belly violently and making a terrible face. The motion was so swift and intense that Persius dropped his corn bread onto the floor. Rebecca Crockett noted what had happened and put her hand to her face as she always did when major realizations struck her.

She said, "Why, Persius Tarr, I've been blind as the dead!" David thought his mother's words poorly chosen, considering that Persius's father was just now getting settled in his muddy grave. "I know what's wrong with you, boy! You're eat up with worms!" David winced. Poorly chosen words again.

David backed off three steps. Persius rubbed his stomach and looked concerned. Rebecca swept over and put her arm over Persius's shoulder. "Poor child! Poor, orphaned boy! I can help you. David, head out to the herb shed and fetch me a branch of my dried wormweed. You know which is the wormweed, don't you?"

"Yes."

"Run on, then. And Joseph"—she turned to David's little brother, who was sitting in the corner, poking a captured bug with a twig—"go fetch me some more firewood. I've got some worming to do."

David raced to the shed. He was glad to fetch the wormweed. He himself had been recipient of this remedy before, and so knew that Persius Tarr had quite an experience ahead of him.

The interior of the shed was hung with all sorts of herbs, or "yarbs," as the folks of the region pronounced the word. David examined the upside-down array of fragrant plants until he spotted the pale green, dusty-looking "wormweed." He yanked down a big handful of it and raced back to the house.

Little Joe had already brought in the firewood, and Rebecca was poking up a new blaze in the chimneyless fireplace. Smoke drifted back into the cabin.

"Here's the wormweed, Mama."

"Thank you, Davy."

David watched with interest as Rebecca cut the wormweed into small chunks and mixed these with some of the sorghum. She poured the mix into the bottom of a small kettle, hung it on a pothook that swung out over the fire, and stirred the molasses carefully until it had boiled down to sugary, candylike lumps encasing the wormweed.

At that point she removed the kettle from the fire and left it to cool.

"What will that there do?" Persius Tarr asked in a cautious tone.

"It'll kill the worms in you, boy, and get rid of that bellyache," Rebecca replied. "There's no cause for anyone to suffer from the worms as long as there's wormweed growing on God's earth. That's what it was put here for. It's my belief that for every ailment of fallen man, there's herbs to cure it. It's God recompense for the smiting of the earth."

She went outside to tend to other business then. David scooted up a stool that was really no more than a log section and sat down, putting his elbows on the table and peering into the kettle as the candy cooled.

"You going to eat some of that?" Persius asked.

"No. I ain't wormy. This here's just for folk who's wormy."

"You ever eat it before?"

"Once."

"Did it work?"

"Yes. Yes indeed."

Persius frowned. "I ain't sure I want that weed in me."

"Better than having worms. Worms can kill you if they get bad enough. There was a boy over on Limestone Creek who died of the worms. He was skinny as a post, all white and buggy-eyed. You'd best eat that wormweed. Besides, my mama's going to make you, whether you want to or not."

Rebecca Crockett reentered a few minutes later. She gouged the candy from the kettle with a butcher knife, cut it into squares, and set them before Persius. "Eat. As much of it as you can. All of it, if you can hold it."

Persius began consuming the candy, cautiously at first, then more quickly. "Tastes good," he said.

"It'll purge you out," Rebecca said. "By tomorrow morning, maybe by tonight."

David, chin resting on his folded hands, watched Persius devour the worming candy until the last crumb was gone. When Persius put away the last bite and rubbed his mouth on his sleeve, David grinned at him.

"Can you feel 'em dying in you?" David asked. "Listen! I can hear their death moans!"

"That's just my belly a-rumbling," Persius replied. "I don't feel nothing." He got up and left the cabin.

David followed. He was going to stick close to Persius Tarr for the rest of the day. When that wormweed began doing its job, he intended to be there to see the results. He knew from experience they would be quite interesting.

John Crockett's eyes were fixed on his trencher of pork and corn, so far untouched. His expression was doleful, with occasional flashes of bitterness; that mood also was reflected in the faces of his family. All were present except David, who had headed out into the woods with Persius and hadn't returned, even though Rebecca had called them both several times. At the moment, Rebecca's eyes flickered between her husband's face and the closed door as she waited for her wayward son and Persius to come back.

"The mill can't be rebuilt—Tom and I agree on that," John said. "He hasn't the will for it, and I haven't the money, and that is that. So it seems we'll have to be moving on."

Rebecca's voice had a strained quality, evidencing the worry she still tried to hide. "But where can we go?"

"Well, there's the three hundred acres on Mossy Creek, ours fair and legal by grant of North Carolina," John replied. "Perhaps we could build there, farm it or find some other means of living on it." He studied his wife's face from the corner of his eye; Rebecca usually tried to mask her reactions, but never succeeded. Everyone in the family could read her with ease.

Rebecca's eyes met his, dropped, flickered to the door and back. "I wonder where David and Persius have got to?" she murmured.

"Never mind them boys—they'll be in soon," John

said. "As I was saying, there is the Mossy Creek land. Or . . ." He paused, and during that pause Rebecca looked up in an urgent manner. ". . . or we could move into a cabin that Tom Galbreath has offered to us over in Jefferson County on the road to Knoxville. There's land belonging to a Quaker, name of Canaday, that might give opportunity to enter business of the kind we've talked of before."

"A tavern?" Rebecca asked.

"Aye, yes. It may be the best means left open to us, now the mill is gone. Perhaps the only means."

"How long would we stay at Mr. Galbreath's cabin?" Wilson asked.

"Can't say. Until we could situate ourselves better. Until we could get our feet back under ourselves."

Betsy ducked her head and looked beneath the table. "Our feet is already under us, Pap."

Rebecca smiled, but Betsy's childish misunderstanding seemed to irritate John. "Hush up, girl, till you're old enough to talk good sense!"

"John!" Rebecca remonstrated gently. She put a hand on her daughter's shoulder. "It's just a way of speaking, Betsy. That's all. It means, until we can make a good living for ourselves, and get past our troubles."

Betsy blinked, fighting tears, and scooted closer to her mother. John Crockett could be fearsome to a child when he was angry.

Rebecca, glancing toward the door again, said, "Well, I like the sound of moving to Mr. Galbreath's cabin. I've never wanted to live on the Mossy Creek land, as you well know."

"I know," John said. "Though I've never notioned out just why." He looked over the faces of his children. The anger in him remained, but he felt vaguely sorrowful at having upset Betsy. He strained for a softer attitude and tone of voice. "So what would you think of it, young Crocketts? Would you like to move to a new home? Maybe build a tavern for us to run?"

The answer was a babble of affirmatives. John smiled

and picked up his two-prong fork. "Very well. So it will be. So it will be."

The door burst open as he finished. David, eyes wide and manner excited, bounded into the room. Every face turned toward him.

"Everybody!" he heralded with excitement. "Come see! Persius is outside a-pooting worms!"

John Crockett flipped his spoon over his shoulder and rolled his eyes heavenward in disgust. "Well, that puts an end to my supper! Boy, you think folk want to hear such as that when they're at their food? Lord a'mighty!" He shoved his trencher away so hard the food was knocked out of it.

His children didn't share his disgust. The younger ones erupted off their seats and bounded out the door, shamelessly eager to see the amazing sight for themselves. The older ones departed directly after, though with less haste, trying to preserve some appearance of dignity. Rebecca stared at David reproachfully, but with an underlying sense of amusement. She glanced toward her husband when he stormed up from his seat, stomped over to the mantel and began fumbling with his pipe and tobacco.

Eager to see again the spectacle outside, David turned and scurried out the door into the dark, his bare feet slapping the mud. Rebecca closed her eyes and shook her head.

"That boy! What a thing to come talking about at suppertime!" She chuckled, eyes shifting to her husband, searching for some sign his mood was improving.

John was lighting his pipe, eyeing her back through the puffing smoke. His mood in fact was not improving. "You think it funny, do you? I don't like it. David's got a way sometimes of making me mad. He's gone and ruined my supper."

"Oh, sit down and eat, John."

Muffled, childish exclamations of astonishment, combined with shouts of anger from Persius Tarr, unwilling showman, came through the cabin wall. Rebecca smiled and said, "Poor Persius! I'll call in the children and leave him in peace. I don't think he likes them watching him doing what he's doing, and you can't hardly blame him."

"Leave them outside," John ordered. "God knows I seldom get any peace from having them around. Sometimes I think it would be better not to have children. Eating you out of house and home, ever babbling and getting sick and costing you money and ruining your supper talking about somebody pooting worms—God! I wish I had a good stout drink right now!"

Rebecca hunched her shoulders, lowered her head, as if she was trying to draw into herself. She despised it when her husband was like this. Hated it. To talk of it being better not to have children ... did not such words tempt providence? What if the children should die because of their father's unfettered talk? What if the baby growing within her right now should not survive? Rebecca Crockett lived in a world that was harsh and stern, a world in which such symbolic retribution did not seem inconceivable.

Silence held in the little cabin. John puffed his pipe, pacing and glowering. Rebecca nibbled without spirit at her meal, then shoved her food away. For a time she sat wordlessly, feeling the baby move inside her and saying a prayer of thanks for this evidence of its health. A little later she realized her spirits were on a fast, downward spiral, something that happened often when she was pregnant.

She had no time for moodiness. Standing, she went to the door and called for her offspring to return to supper and leave poor Persius Tarr alone.

Chapter 4

Persius Tarr ran off from the Crockett house the next day, and David was the first to detect his absence. He felt troubled, knowing Persius had probably run off out of embarrassment at what had happened the night before, and out of anger at him for having turned it into a public spectacle. After it was over, he had called David aside and cussed him thoroughly, cussed him better than he had been cussed by anybody in his life, including his oldest brother, who could swear the air blue around him. David had been quite impressed. Here was yet another aspect of Persius Tarr to stand in awe of.

He decided on the spot to track Persius down. Lately he had been trying to make a good tracker of himself, so that he could someday become a great hunter. Here was a challenge indeed: tracking a human being.

Finding Persius's trail proved much easier than he had anticipated, mostly because Persius had made no effort to cover it. He had stomped right through a muddy portion of the cabin yard, out around the woodshed, and into the woods. From the look of the tracks, David guessed he hadn't left more than twenty minutes before.

Fetching a long, curving stick whose shape reminded him of a rifle's, David proceeded into the woods, keeping his eye on the path and picking out Persius's footprints. After a time it hit him that tracking Persius was turning out to be unneccessary altogether; obviously he was keeping to the path. David felt disappointed. It would have been fun to sneak like an Indian through the forest, tracking down an unwary traveler. He lifted the stick "rifle" he carried and smacked it against a tree, breaking it in half. Now the half retained in his hand was a war club, and he was a painted Cherokee warrior on the vengeance path, trailing an unsuspecting but doomed white hunter, soon to be dispatched and scalped. *Aiiieeee!*

Losing himself in his fantasy, David bent slightly and began moving on the balls of his feet, his face fixed in a vicious snarl. Beware, Persius Tarr! he thought. Your scalp will hang on my belt before the sun reaches the crest of the sky!

He anticipated catching up with Persius very quickly, but found his quarry was moving swiftly. After a while the Indian fantasy faded and the chase ceased to be fun. David was growing concerned now. What if Persius really did get out of reach and never returned? He didn't want that to happen; he was growing to like Persius, and see him as a source of companionship far preferable to what his brothers could provide. His brothers, after all, were ... well, *brothers*. They were overly familiar, uninteresting, even dull, when compared to the still-mysterious Persius Tarr.

David was circling up a bend in the trail that led to a fire-balded hilltop when he heard a shot. He guessed it came from maybe half a mile away, and judging from the sound, was probably a light charge of bird shot. Some hunter ... but now he stopped, confused. What was that weird howling coming from somewhere ahead?

That's Persius's voice! Somebody must have shot Persius!

He raced ahead, running until his breath came in ragged, hurting gasps. He slowed when he saw Persius ahead, sitting on a log and examining his left forearm. Sure enough, there was blood on his sleeve.

"Persius!" David yelled. "Are you hurt?"

From the sharp way Persius looked up, David knew he hadn't realized he was being followed. When Persius saw him, he glowered.

"What's it look like? You see the blood, don't you? I been shot!"

David came up close, bent over and examined the arm. It appeared that a load of shot had mostly just fanned across the arm, cutting the skin enough to bleed but doing no other damage. "You're lucky," David said. "That could've hurt you a right smart."

Voices and movement in the ravine that lay off to the right side of the trail caught their attention. David's throat tightened and he stood up straight when he saw Hez Caine, thirteen-year-old resident of a cabin about three miles from the Crockett mill, come striding up through the trees with his three ever-present accompaniments: a smirk on his face, an old hound named Big Tick at his feet, and his little brother Nahum at his side. Both boys carried flintlock shotguns.

"Well, look here!" Hez said in a beligerent tone typical of him. "What's this, Crockett?"

"You shot him, it looks like," David replied. "You fired up the slope toward the trail, didn't you!"

"So what if I did?" Hez glanced at Persius's scratch. "He ain't hurt. You little children-on-the-tit need to keep out of the woods till you're old enough not to get in the way of hunters." He glanced at the stick in David's hand and grinned nastily at his little brother. "Look there ... he's got him a stick to play with, Nahum!" Then he eyed Persius up and down. "Look here: I believe this one's a real live redskin."

"You'd best not talk that way to him," David said. "Persius'll whup you if you make him mad. He's got true pluck, and he ain't a redskin."

"Oh, he'll whup me, will he?" Hez edged up to Persius. "Well, you hatchet-faced coon, get to whupping!" He laughed in Persius's face.

Wordlessly, Persius reached over, took the stick from David's hands, and broke it across the crown of Hez Caine's head. David chortled with joyous surprise. He had despised Hez ever since being bullied by him the first time they had met, months before. Hez grabbed his head and cursed, then raised his rifle and tried to butt Persius with it. Persius grabbed the weapon in mid-swing and jerked it out of Hez's hands. He tossed it aside and waded in, fists hard and swinging.

Out of sheer exhilaration, David launched into Nahum, punching him twice in the jaw before the nine-year-old boy knew what was happening. Though he was older than David, he was very small-framed and hardly any bigger. He swung back at his attacker, but David ducked and put a solid blow into Nahum's belly. Persius, meanwhile, was working over Hez most efficiently, having bloodied his nose and pounded both eyes sufficiently to guarantee they would be black as coal by night.

When the Caine boys were at last on the run, David grinned at Persius. "Reckon we whupped them good."

"Reckon we did."

"Don't go off, Persius. I'm sorry about calling the others out to see you . . . you know. The worms and all."

Persius, panting, considered the apology and accepted it. "Didn't want to leave no how," he said. "No place in particular to go."

"You'll come home?"

"Yes."

David beamed. "I'm glad. I want to be a friend to you, Persius Tarr." And he did want it, very badly. Persius was the kind who didn't hold back—he just did what he wanted to do, not worrying about rights and wrongs or outcomes. Even something as daring as breaking a stick over a head that sorely deserved it.

Persius said nothing, but flashed a quick smile that told David what he wanted to know. His offer of friendship had been accepted. He could hardly restrain himself from laughing joyously right out loud. As far as he was concerned, there was no reason at all that Persius Tarr couldn't become part of the Crockett family, just like he had been born into it. Nothing would suit David better.

David at his side, Persius Tarr walked back to the Crockett place. And for the next several days, he and David were never apart. They fished together, hunted, carved their mark on trees, threw rocks at jaybirds, swam in the creek. From time to time David would see his father watching Persius with a look of concern on his face, but he thought nothing of it. John Crockett was always looking concerned about something or other, and most times it turned out to be nothing worth worrying about at all. Or so it seemed to David.

The young ones slept. Betsy, using the salvaged beaver hat as a pillow, snored in volumes remarkably loud coming from so petite a source. Persius Tarr, sharing sleeping quarters with the Crockett sons, snored too, but not so loudly. Clouds and rain had returned, though lightly, a far cry from what the storm had been. Raindrops sizzled against the banked fire after falling through the open hole where the chimney had been.

John Crockett lay on his back, looking up at the underside of the loft where the boys slept, his right arm around Rebecca. Passing days had lessened the frustration and anger that had caused his outburst at the supper table. He regretted it now, even though he hadn't apologized to Rebecca for it. There was some shortfall in his personal makeup that made him generally unable to apologize in words. He knew Rebecca would like to hear an occasional expression of sorrow from him when he offended her, but it just wasn't possible for him. Surely she knew he was sorry. That would just have to be enough.

Tonight he and Rebecca had been talking quietly and seriously since the children had been asleep. The subject was the delicate problem of Persius Tarr, a problem John Crockett had already made up his mind about, and even taken the first steps toward resolving.

"We can't keep him, Becky," John said softly but emphatically. "I'll be doing well just to keep our own fed. We can't take in stray orphan boys like you'd take in a stray cat."

"Well, it don't seem right that a stray cat can find a home and an orphaned boy can't."

"They ain't the same thing at all, Becky, and you know it. He's a boy, and he'll take feeding and clothing and maybe schooling. I feel sorry for him, just like you do—but we can't take him in."

Rebecca sighed and shifted her posture, making the bedding rustle. "Then what will become of him?"

John paused a moment before answering, knowing she would not like what he was going to say. He cleared his throat. "The Orphan Court."

Rebecca tensed and did not relax. "I knew that was what you would say. It seems so cruel!"

"It's not cruel. It will provide him a chance for a home, and to learn a trade. Lord knows he needs that! From what he tells me, that father of his was a thief and a scoundrel. He's got bad blood in him, and bad blood can't be cleaned up except with good honest labor. That's what my own pap always told me."

"It's so sad that he's alone. I've never asked him about his mother. She's dead, I suppose?"

"Yes. He says he never knew her. She died when he was small."

Rebecca was silent, then sighed. "It's such a sad thing—an orphaned boy, no place for him to go."

"There's many a sad thing in this world, wife. All we can do is firm ourselves and struggle on through them. And he does have a place to go. The Orphan Court will set him up with someone who can take care of him proper. I've already talked to Saul Greer about it, and he's agreed to give me some help."

"It's such a sad thing."

"Sad things are just a part of life, Becky. You get past them and go on. All you can do."

Three Days Later

David Crockett sat beside his father on the hard seat of the wagon, wishing he had been allowed to drive the team today. He glanced over his shoulder at Persius, who sat in back of the open wagon, facing the rear, shoulders hunched sorrowfully. Sadness pricked David again. He had come to like Persius in their brief, shared time, and it seemed a shame that he soon would be gone, probably to some distant corner of the huge county, bound off to someone by the Orphan Court. There he would learn to make barrels or shoe horses or some other such trade so as not to be a burden on society. And the Crocketts would be miles away, in a new home over in Jefferson County. David believed that after today he would probably never lay eyes on Persius Tarr again.

The wagon rolled up the dirt road into town. David sat up straight, looking around. He seldom visited Greene Courthouse, as the county seat was known, and so looked for whatever changes had come to the little town since his last venture here. To David Crockett, Greene Courthouse didn't seem as small as it really was, because he had little to compare it to. He had never seen another town except for Jonesborough, the seat of neighboring Washington County, and a few other local communities such as Leesburg and Rheatown.

Greene Courthouse had been laid out in typical grid fashion some years before, around what folks called the Big Spring, an ancient watering spot at the crossing place of old Indian war trails. In the center of the hamlet was a log courthouse building erected the year before David's birth, and destined soon, talk had it, to give way to a more permanent, larger structure. The courthouse stood directly in the center of the junction of Main and First Cross streets, and until the creation of the Southwest Territory in 1790, had been a governing center not only for the county, but also for the so-called State of Franklin. David knew little about the Franklin state, which had failed politically, though he did think it noteworthy that he had been born during its brief tenure. Though a territorialist, he was by birth a Franklinite.

The wagon passed the courthouse, around which a few men stood, talking and chewing and smoking. Every one of them waved at John Crockett, or called his name. This made David proud. His father was generally liked and respected in his community. John Crockett was much more a denizen of Greene Courthouse than was any other member of his family. Generally he came on official business. He was a frequent juryman, and the county posts of magistrate and constable that he had held—both offices indicative of the esteem with which his peers regarded him—had brought him here fairly frequently. He knew virtually the entire populace of the little town. And he was able to read and write, unlike many of his neighbors, which earned him further standing.

"Well, we're here, boys," John said, pulling the wagon to a halt in front of a wide, low log building with an overhanging porch. The front door stood open; a man exited with an armful of bundles, and grinned and nodded when he saw John.

"Howdy, Caleb," John said. "Pretty day, ain't it?"

"Surely is, John. How are you faring?"

"Not good at all. The storm took my mill."

"No! Will you get 'er fixed?"

"Nope. Closing down and moving over to Jefferson County. I aim to open a tavern, if I can."

"Will you? Good luck to you, John. A tavern! That might be just the thing."

Persius looked around, then tugged on John's sleeve, interrupting the conversation. "This here's a store?"

"Yes. Come on. I'll take you in to meet Mr. Greer." He turned back to the other man. "Caleb, good day to you. If you ever pass through Jefferson County, look me up."

David touched his father's arm as the man walked away. "Pap, does Persius really have to go? Can't he go help us build the tavern?"

" 'Fraid not, David. We don't have the means to keep him. My first duty is to my children and wife. Lord have mercy, boy! We have another baby on the way right now. I can't hardly feed the family I done have."

"I don't want him to go. He's my friend."

"I know that, son. That's why I let you come along today, so you could be with him longer. Now don't get weepish on me and make me wish I'd left you home. This is something that must be done."

They descended from the wagon and entered the building. David blinked as his eyes adjusted to the shadowy interior, dim even in the day because of the light-absorbing effect of log walls. The store interior was stacked, in no apparent pattern, with a marvelous hodge-podge of items, some of them frontier standards and others reflective of the slowly rising standard of living brought on by a higher populace, better roads, and better government. There were hand tools, firearm implements, crates, barrels, smithing tools, jump and coulter plows and plow tongues, earthenware and tinware dishes and pots, mason's chisels, pack saddles, foot warmers, flax brakes, scutching blocks, long-handled waffle irons, fireplace fenders, trivets, hand mills, bake kettles, teakettles, candle molds, and finished furniture of the kind some richer folk had, but which the Crocketts had never seemed able to afford. David walked in, eyes wide as he examined what looked to him to be a kingdom's worth of treasures.

A man in baggy, greasy trousers and a faded blue shirt approached. "John Crockett! So you've arrived!" He put out his hand for a shake, then tousled David's hair. He looked back at Persius, who was glumly slipping in. "So this is the lad you spoke of the other day?"

"That's right, Saul. This is Persius Tarr. Persius, meet Mr. Greer."

Persius crept up and limply shook Greer's hand.

"Mr. Greer is going to keep you here in town with him until the Orphan Court on Tuesday," John said, putting as bright a sound on the words as he could. "He's a good man, and a friend of mine. You can trust him."

Persius grunted a minimal acknowledgment, darting his eyes around the room to avoid looking into John Crockett's face.

Greer said, "That's right, Persius. I'll see that you have a good stay—and if you want to work about the store, why, your help will be welcome."

Persius grunted again, even more softly.

Saul Greer put his hand on John's shoulder. "Come aside, John. There's news I've heard only last night that you'll want to know. I've been looking forward to you getting here so I could tell it to you. An Indian trader from along the Tennessee has told me something I believe pertains to your own kin."

A look of intrigue on his face, John Crockett stepped aside and began talking in covert tones to Greer. David went to Persius. "Where do you reckon you'll wind up?"

"What?"

"After the Orphan Court. Where do you reckon you'll wind up?"

"I don't know. Don't much care."

"Why not? They might put you with somebody mean as a snake. They say orphans get treated bad a lot."

"It don't matter. I won't be there more than a little spell."

David's eyes widened when he realized what Persius was implying. He drew closer. "You'll run off?"

"I surely will."

David grinned. "I've always thought it'd be a jolly thing to run off. Get out in the world and have adventures."

"It'll be a sight lot better'n being an orphan bound to some old blacksmith or pot maker."

"Ain't you scared?"

"Scared? Hah! Why, I was running off from my own pap the day you seen me." He paused, and in a less haughty tone added, "I reckon getting off that wagon saved my life."

"Did your pap look for you?"

"He did. I hid and watched him. He walked all through the woods, swinging a big old stick he'd fetched to beat me with, calling and cussing and saying he was going off without me if I didn't show myself. After a bit of that, he got back on the wagon and rode away. After that must have been when he turned 'er over and killed hisself. If I'd gone back to him, I'd be dead too."

"You're mighty brave, Persius. I'd be 'fraid of running off."

"I ain't 'fraid of nothing. Not me. I'm a Tarr. We're go-ahead folk. That's what my pappy used to say: Tarrs are go-ahead folk."

"Go-ahead folk," David repeated, liking the bravado of the words.

John Crockett came to David, his private talk with

Greer completed. He touched his son's shoulder. "Come on, David. We must go up the street a bit."

David looked up at his father and was surprised at the odd expression on his face. A look of . . . awe? Wonder? And happiness, undeniably; John Crockett looked like he might laugh aloud at any moment. David wondered if it was getting rid of Persius that made his father happy, and felt offended.

"Good-bye, David," Persius said.

"Good-bye, Persius." David's lower lip begin to dance and quiver. A strong impulse to throw his arms around Persius struck him, but he resisted it. Such a display would seem unmanly, and he didn't think Persius would much like it.

He was surprised, then, when Persius advanced and did that very thing, giving David a tight squeeze and hurried release, then turned away and headed over to a couple of plows leaned against the far wall, where he pretended to inspect them, keeping his back toward the Crocketts, whistling in forced idleness as if he couldn't care less about anything that was happening.

David lacked the emotional will of Persius. Tears streamed down his face and he sobbed aloud. Losing Persius was even harder than losing Painter.

Back aboard the wagon, David dried his tears, figuring that his father surely would scold him for crying, as was usually the case. But this time John Crockett had nothing to say. He didn't even seem to notice that David had been upset.

David glared silently, bitterly, at his father, who hadn't lost that strange expression—and who hadn't even shown the good grace to say farewell to Persius.

"Davy-boy, there's a man we must see up at the inn yonder—he has news for me. It's about your uncle Jimmy."

That caught David's attention. "Uncle Jimmy? But Uncle Jimmy's dead!"

"So we've thought, all these years. But it seems we may have been wrong. There's nothing sure about it yet, but he may yet be alive."

John Crockett snapped the lines and sent the team into motion, pulling the heavy wagon along the rutted dirt street. David looked back over his shoulder. Persius was standing in the doorway of the store. He stiffly lifted his hand in parting, turned and walked back inside.

Chapter 5

Events over the next hour helped take David's mind off the sad matter of Persius Tarr. John Crockett drove the wagon to a tavern near the Big Spring and parked it beneath a pale green weeping willow. "You stay here," he told David. "The man I'm supposed to talk to ought to be inside, according to Greer."

David scooted to one side as far as he could, so as to immerse himself in the new willow strands just for the fun of doing it. He tugged and twined them for diversion, but fumed at being left alone to burn with curiosity. He considered walking back to the Greer store to talk to Persius some more. He was afraid doing that would anger his father, though—and besides, he wanted to know as soon as possible what this tantalizing hint about Uncle Jimmy was all about.

"Dumb Jimmy," David muttered in a whisper. Time and again he had heard his father and uncles refer to their long-missing brother by that name. Jimmy Crockett had been given up for dead long ago. If by some miracle he was still alive, it was surely the first time in the fellow's life that fortune had been kind to him.

Even Jimmy Crockett's birth had been "troubled," as John Crockett had explained, and had left him deaf. As a result, he had never learned to speak beyond mouthing a few simple words that he crudely vocalized with squeaks and grunts. Of course, there had been no hope for any kind of normal life for the boy. From the beginning, the Crocketts had assumed that Jimmy would remain with his parents until they died, and then fall under the care of his brothers and sisters. But no one at that time had anticipated what the family now called, in serious tones, "the Tragedy."

The Tragedy had occurred long before David was born, and so of course he had never had the opportunity to meet his uncle Jimmy. David regretted that. He had never known a deaf-and-dumb person. Jimmy would have been interesting to know, simply because he was different.

It was during the revolt against Britain, in the "Year of the Three Sevens," 1777, that the Tragedy occurred. The place was Carter's Valley, north of the Nolichucky region where the John Crockett family now made their home. The actual site of the event was now part of the town of Rogersville, which David had never visited, even though his grandparents were buried there and it was John Crockett's former homeplace.

David settled himself beneath the willow and thought back on the Tragedy as his father had recounted it. According to John Crockett, 1777 had been a particularly violent, bloody year. There was strife between the settlers, who were steadily pushing into the wilderness, and the Indians, who resented the encroachment and had thrown their support to Britain in return for promises of aid. During April of that year, John Crockett's parents, residents of Carter's Valley, were among the first victims of Indian raiders when a band of Creeks and militant Cherokees, called Chickamaugas, attacked their cabin.

John Crockett himself might have been a victim had he not been away at the time, riding with a defensive band of frontier rangers of which he was part. Jimmy and Robert, John's brothers, were home, however, as were both their parents.

The elder Crocketts were killed swiftly by the Indian raiders. Robert fled desperately, saving his life, but a bullet struck him in the forearm, damaging it so severely that it had to be sawed off later. As for Jimmy, his handicap hampered his escape, and he was taken prisoner. He hadn't been seen since, nor heard from, and it seemed natural to assume, given the passing of seventeen years and the receipt of no news about him, that Jimmy Crockett had gone on to the life hereafter never having escaped the captivity of savages. Now it appeared that assumption might have been wrong.

David chewed a willow leaf, spitting out the pieces as he squinted through the greenery at the tavern's open door, trying to see what his father was doing inside. He could make nothing out. He slipped down from the wagon seat and edged around closer. Still he could see nothing. So he crept over to a window and sneaked a look over the sill.

John Crockett was seated at a table, leaning forward and resting on his elbows, fingers interlocked and chin thrust out. David knew that posture; his father sat that way whenever he was intensely interested in something he was hearing. In this case, the interesting something apparently was whatever was being said by a very lanky, rugged-looking fellow on the other side of the table.

David studied the stranger. Unlike many waistcoated, buckle-shoed men one saw in the towns these days, this man had virtually nothing store-bought anywhere on or about his person. His trousers were of homespun wool, made in the old French fly style, and his hunting shirt, equally old-styled, looked like linsey-woolsey to David. He wore moccasins that reached nearly to his knees— and on him this required tall moccasins indeed, because David had never seen a longer-limbed fellow. The man's hat was a felt slouch that remained on his head even though he was indoors. A short, dyed feather stuck into its band was the only visible ornamentation on him. But his buckskin outer coat, which he had draped over the back of his chair, was fringed and beaded profusely. It was a beautiful thing to see. Someday, David thought, it would be very fine to have a coat like that for himself. The man's face was very nearly the color of the coat, raggedly bearded and leathery in texture. His hair was the hue of gunpowder, long, and clubbed behind his head. David wasn't good at guessing ages, but he could see that the fellow was older than John Crockett. Certainly he lived his life in the wilderness. His very appearance suggested forests and mountains and icy streams. A thought crossed David's mind that would have seemed odd to anyone privy to it, though it made perfect sense to him: that man looks just like wood smoke smells on a cold morning.

David couldn't hear what was being said, which frustrated him, but he dared not draw any closer for fear his father would see him and grow angry at him for leaving the wagon. John Crockett was the devil when he got mad and took cane in hand for discipline. And all the worse he became when he had some liquor in him—and at the moment there was an earthenware mug on the table before him, from which he was taking occasional big gulps with enthusiasm bred of transparent excitement. David watched carefully a few seconds more, then made a discreet return to the wagon.

Half an hour passed before the senior Crockett came out. He had a big smile on his face as he came toward the wagon a bit unsteadily, and climbed aboard with much grunting and wheezing through his nose. It never took liquor long to go to John's head. "Let's go home, Davy-boy. I need to talk to your mother."

"Who was that man, Pap?" David asked. He inwardly cringed as soon as the words were out, fearing that by such a specific reference, he had given away the secret of his spying. But his father didn't take note.

"There was an Injun trader in there," John said. "His name is Fletcher, and he's recently seen a deaf-and-dumb captive amongst the redskins—and from the sound of all he says, I believe it really could be Jimmy. The age is right, and the look of him as Fletcher described it. Fletcher, he had spoke of this captive to Greer, who used to trade amongst the Injuns hisself, and right off Greer figured it might be Jimmy, having heard me talk about him in the past." John took up the lines, cleared his throat, leaned over and spat onto the ground, wobbling so much that David almost grabbed at him so he wouldn't fall. "Greer, he's a good man. He's helped this family a sight, son, taking Persius off our hands until the Orphan Court, and now putting me in with Fletcher."

David felt a pulse of irritation, which he kept secret, over the comment concerning Persius. It was ever more obvious that Persius had been nothing more than a burden to John Crockett, a problem to be shrugged off and forgotten.

"What will happen now?" David asked.

"Fletcher's going back among the Injuns soon, and he's going to see what more he can learn. He believes there might be a way to get Jimmy free. Buy him free—if we can fetch up the money or goods. I've told him to come get a-holt of me in Jefferson County once he works things out. We ought to know more later in the year. Lordy! Wouldn't it be a fine thing if it really is Jimmy and we can truly get him free again!"

David sat trying to imagine what it would be like to be an Indian captive for seventeen years. Jimmy Crockett had been scarcely an adult at the time of his capture. David counted it out on his fingers. Jimmy had spent almost as many years in captivity as he had spent in prior freedom. He wondered if Jimmy might have turned Indian himself by now. Many times he had heard tales of Indian captives who refused freedom when it was offered, preferring their life among the savages. Rebecca Crockett clicked her tongue and shook her head at such stories, declaring they illustrated the human capacity to degenerate into savagery. David didn't quite see it that way. He could understand how it might be fun to live free and wild in the forests . . . though Indians these days certainly weren't as free and wild as they once had been.

"I hope Jimmy can get free, Pap," David said. "I'd like to see what he looks like."

"So would I, David." John's voice sounded slightly slurred. He paused thoughtfully, hiccuped beneath his breath. "It's been a slew of years since last I seen him. A whole slew of years."

John Crockett put the team in motion, and turned the wagon across the center of the street. They headed back the way they came, riding too close to the side of the road and forcing David to duck branches. They passed Greer's store, and David looked for Persius, but didn't see him. As they went out of town and back toward Cove Creek, David felt a mix of sadness and excitement, the former because of Persius, the latter because of Jimmy Crockett.

A few days later, the following was recorded in Greene County court records:

> Ordered that Persius Tarr an orphan be bound to Robert Hanks until he shall attain the age of eighteen years to learn the trade of blacksmith, said orphan to be eleven years of age the third day of December next. One dollar paid.

Three weeks passed, and a notice was posted on the wall of the courthouse, with copies on the notice boards of the various taverns and ordinaries throughout the county:

> Notice given and recorded by Robert Hanks of Warrensburg that the orphan Persius Tarr, bound to him by the court, has fled in violation of his binding and is declared delinquent. Reward of one dollar offered by victim for return of said orphan Persius Tarr.

The Crocketts never saw the notice of Persius's flight. By then their cabin on Cove Creek was empty and the old mill was abandoned, to be scavenged by others for its logs. John Crockett had packed his family and goods onto the wagon, set his sons to driving the livestock, and had gone farther west, into Jefferson County, to a new home in a small, borrowed cabin. He had abandoned his dream of being a miller at the same time he abandoned his cabin and ruined mill. He dreamed a new dream now, that of being a tavern operator and innkeeper. As for Rebecca, she was heavy with child and heavier still with the responsibility of caring for those she already had. She had given up on dreams of her own long ago. As long as there was a roof above and food in the pantry, she would ask for nothing else.

Chapter 6

Autumn 1794

Firelight flickered across the hearth and illuminated the brown face of John Crockett, who was seated on a stool, a musket across his lap, and cleaning cloth, oil, and brush at his feet. The musket was a beautiful weapon, a Brown Bess that he had brought back from the King's Mountain campaign in 1780, when he and a rough-hewn army of his fellow "over-the-mountain" frontiersmen had beaten back the threat of Patrick Ferguson and his loyalist force, saving their home region from likely invasion and thus turning the tide of the war in the south. The musket was the one relic John Crockett had brought back, and he had pampered it ever since, though he seldom found it useful.

The Brown Bess was a heavy, smooth-bored weapon, designed in the days when British Redcoats fought from tight ranks, laying down a barrage of simultaneous fire in a battle style that depended more on the sheer mass of fire than individual accuracy. John Crockett had tried hunting with the musket a time or two, then had given it up for his more trusty and accurate rifle. "You have to aim that blasted Bess a good five, six inches above your target to hit it beyond two hundred paces," he complained. "A man has to stand right on a critter to hope to hit it."

Despite his complaints about it, John Crockett truly

loved his musket. Men of the backwoods had few possessions kept sheerly for the pleasure of ownership, and
therefore pampered whatever treasures they had. He regu-
larly cleaned the Brown Bess, shined it up, and hung it
back on its pegs, where it would usually remain untouched
until the next cleaning a couple of weeks later.

David, somnolent from the whirring of his mother's
spinning wheel and the lulling heat of the fire, through
drooping lids watched his father's concentrated work on
the musket. John Crockett's intent expression hazily called
to David's mind some previous time when he had seen
him work with that same exact expression of seriousness.
When had that been? David searched his recollections.
Yes, now he remembered.

It had been at the second of the Crockett homes in
Greene County, ten or so miles north of Greene Courthouse, and about this same time of year, when the wild
grapes were ripe. David's uncle, Joseph Hawkins, brother
of Rebecca Crockett, had come by the cabin about midday,
poking around for a free meal in the midst of a day's deer
hunting. Afterward he had trudged off into the woods
again, rifle over his shoulder, heading across a ridge that
divided the Crockett place from the land of a neighbor.

David was hauling in an armload of firewood when
he heard the crack of his uncle's rifle beyond the ridge.
"Uncle Joe's brought down a deer, Mama," he called into
the cabin. "I seen a whole bunch of them on the ridge this
morning."

Then another sound assailed his ear: Uncle Joe yelling wildly, as if in panic. David dropped the wood in the
doorway. "Mama, something's wrong with Joe."

The yelling continued. Rebecca, dusting cornmeal
from her hands onto her apron, came away from the stove.
"Lord a'mercy, it sounds like he's flaxing toward us right
fast! I hope a bear ain't chasing him!"

David had a fear of bears in those days. He suffered
nightmares about them quite often. Rebecca's speculation
scared him speedily into the cabin, where he stood and
peered out the door from behind her skirts.

Uncle Joe came tearing over the hill, his moccasins

kicking up leaves. "Lordy, Rebecca, oh Lordy! Where's John? Where's John?"

David looked for the bear. He didn't see one. Maybe it was something else that had Uncle Joe so worked up. He hoped so.

Rebecca said, "What's wrong, Joe? I don't know where John is—"

"I've shot a man, Rebecca! I took him for a deer amongst the 'possum grapes. Lord, Lord, I've kilt him sure!"

David's eyes grew big; his mother's face blanched. "Who is it, Joe?"

"I don't know—he was yonder over the ridge, a-picking grapes. . . ."

"David, run for the field there, and see if your father is about."

David took off at a lope, but had not gone a hundred yards before he heard his father's voice calling from the opposite direction. He stopped and turned his head to see John Crockett trotting in from the orchard. David pivoted on his heel and came back.

By now Uncle Joe had told his tale again. David's father's face grew tight and dark-looking. He went into the cabin and came out with a handful of cloth rags. "Take me to him, Joe."

The men headed off over the ridge. David turned a pleading eye to his mother. She bit her lip, faltered, then said, "Go on, then."

He ran over the hill, and found them there. His father had just dragged the shot man out of the grape thicket, and Uncle Joe was standing there looking like he might cry. David thought that quite a novelty; he had never seen a grown man shed tears, and had wondered if that was even possible.

"This is my neighbor—his name's Mortimer Cade," John Crockett said. "He's alive, Joe."

He laid open the shirt. David's eyes bugged. There was blood all over Cade's midsection, bright and liquid and ever replenishing from a hole on the lower left side of his torso. David swallowed; his stomach was making uncomfortable threats. There was blood under the man too, lots of it.

John Crockett brought out one of the rags, a silken handkerchief. He poked it into the bloody hole, pushed it in farther, farther, then put his hand behind and took hold of something. The cloth vanished suddenly into the bullet hole, and came out, bright with blood, on the other side.

"I declare, he's shot clean through!" John Crockett said. "The ball come out the back. I doubt he'll live, Joe."

The memory, almost forgotten moments before, now was stark again. David stirred by the fireside. "Pap, you remember Mr. Cade, who got shot by Uncle Joe?"

John Crockett kept on polishing the stock of the Bess. "I remember him."

"Did he die?"

"No, son. He's yet living, though Lord only knows how he made it through. I was worried about him—he looked nigh dead a-lying there." John smiled slightly. "Of course, you did too, after I pulled that silk through him. You fainted out stiff as a log."

David ducked his head, embarrassed. He had no real memory of having fainted that day. All he could recall was seeing the handkerchief pushed through the wound, then opening his eyes to find himself back inside the cabin.

"Somebody riding in outside, Pap," Wilson said, coming to his feet and laying aside the axe handle he had been whittling.

John stood and set the musket against the wall. He went to the window and looked out, then stepped rapidly to the door, lifted the bar, and threw the door open. "Will!" he called into the darkness. "Is that you I see out there?"

"Why, yes it is, John. How you faring? Hello there, Rebecca!"

"It's Uncle Will!" Betsy shouted.

The Crocketts crowded outside to meet Will Crockett, brother of John and a resident of the Dumplin community, some miles to the southwest. Will grinned and tousled the heads of the younger ones, shook hands with the older ones. He saw the baby bundled in Rebecca's arms, and grinned widely.

"The new one's come! I had nary a notion! Is it boy or gal?"

"A girl," Rebecca replied. "We're calling her Sally."

"She's pretty as a wall picture."

"Thank you."

"Is she hardy?"

"Very fine and strong, thank the Lord."

"Will, what in heaven's name brings you this many miles?" John asked. "Is everything well in your home?"

"Very well. I've come with good news."

"Oh?"

"Yes." Will Crockett turned and called back into the darkness. "Mr. Fletcher?"

A second rider came into view. David recognized him at once: Fletcher, the Indian trader from the tavern in Greene Courthouse.

"I told him to stay back until you knew it was me, us coming in at night and all," Will said. "Mr. Fletcher has come to give good news about our brother Jimmy. Jimmy truly is alive, John, and now in the hands of a French-born Injun trader name of Beaulieu."

John said, "Praise be." He looked past Will. "Hello, Mr. Fletcher."

The frontiersman nodded his greeting.

"How did Mr. Fletcher come to you, Will? I was looking for him to come to me."

"Sheer chance and fortune, John. He come asking about for 'Mr. Crockett' and got hisself sent to the wrong one. If you'll let a weary brother inside your door, I'll be happy to tell it all."

"Come in, come in indeed," John said. "I'm anxious to hear it. Wilson, David, see to their horses, and give them grain. Come in, Mr. Fletcher. Come in and let me see what I can find to put some fire in your bones this evening."

"Sounds right good, Mr. Crockett," Fletcher said. He nodded toward Rebecca and touched his hat. "Good evening to you, lady."

"Good evening, sir. Welcome to our home."

David and Wilson worked as fast as they could with the horses, stripping off the saddles, feeding the horses, and brushing them down in a mad rush. They were eager to return to the cabin and hear the news. An uncle they had never known, an uncle made all the more fascinating by the limitations nature had given him, not only was alive, but was seemingly available for return. It was a miracle, sure as the world. It could be nothing less.

Late December, 1794

The precipitation that struggled down through the bare treetops seemed uncertain whether to take form as rain or snow, and alternated between the two. Mud clotted the hooves of the horses, and a cold wind sliced against the faces of their three riders.

"How far now?" Will Crockett asked Fletcher, who rode at the lead.

"Not quite a mile," Fletcher answered. "We'll go through yonder valley, then north. The post is up on a rise; you'll see it as soon as we pass the hill."

They went on then in silence. John Crockett's coat was threadbare and too thin for the weather; he shivered badly. Will was better-suited and rode in a casual slump, not fighting the cold. As for Fletcher, he was a man who spent much time in travel, and his lean form fit his horse like it had been specially designed for it. He didn't seem to notice the cold at all.

The last half mile was the hardest because the trail was poor and made worse by the weather. The horses strained hard to maintain their pace, heaving and steaming in the cold. Only the single riderless horse, saddled in readiness for the hoped-for Jimmy Crockett, had it relatively easy.

A ridge at their left leveled toward the valley, and when the riders passed the base of it, their destination came into view.

They halted the horses, letting them rest. Will

Crockett leaned over and spat tobacco amber, then squinted as he investigated the conglomeration of hillside structures to which they were about to go. "A man couldn't have built an uglier mess of huts had he set out to do it," he commented. "What slapped that place together, Fletcher? A whirlwind?"

Fletcher said, "Beaulieu throwed it up hisself. He ain't much for pretties and such. Long as his roof will shed water, that's all that matters."

"You talk like you know this Beaulieu right well for a man you never met before the summer," John said.

Fletcher turned a cold eye on him. "You trying to call my word into question, Crockett?"

"Just talking, that's all. Just saying what comes to my mind."

Fletcher scratched his beard, never taking his eyes off John. "If I was a man who judged folk by their manner, I'd say you don't trust me, Crockett."

"I don't know you, Fletcher. All I know is you tell us this Beaulieu has our brother and will sell him free. If that proves out true, then I'll trust you."

Fletcher cut himself a chew of tobacco. "I won't fault that. I can respect caution in a man, Crockett. It can save his hide when the pinch gets tight." He looked up the slope. "Yonder's Beaulieu, peeping out the window at us." Fletcher waved twice in the air, then turned his hand from side to side three times. "There. Now he knows it's me. We can ride on in."

Fletcher took the lead again. John glanced at his brother and signaled him to pause before falling in behind. Fletcher gained several yards' lead, and John said softly, "I don't trust him, Will. I've come to believe he's been lying to us all along."

Will looked puzzled. "You surely seemed to believe him on the front end of it all. What's changing your mind?"

"Little things, like him knowing this Beaulieu better than he lets on. And his way. His look. Rebecca, she didn't trust him the first time she seen him. Told me that herself.

And she's a good judge of a human being. Rebecca can read a man like he was news hung on a store post."

"You place too much confidence in that woman, John. You always have."

Fletcher turned in the saddle. "You'uns aiming to camp back there?"

"We're coming, Mr. Fletcher," Will called up. "Go on. We're right behind."

In single file they plodded up the slope toward the cluster of log buildings, their tired horses moving more eagerly now, in their dim way knowing from experience and instinct that habitations meant grain, water, shelter. They rode to the front of the largest structure. John looked around, brows lowered. Every now and then he came upon places he didn't like from the first look, places that touched his nerves like a cold hand and made him cautious. This was one such place.

"Gentlemen, we've arrived," Fletcher announced. "Let's go have a talk with Mr. Beaulieu."

Chapter 7

A short, plump man came to the door and stepped out, grinning a grin made dark by absence of teeth. "Mr. Fletcher!" he said in a voice that betrayed his French origin. "*Entrez*, good man, and bring your friends!"

"Howdy, Mr. Beaulieu," Fletcher said. "These here is the Crockett brothers."

"Ah, *oui! Enchanté de faire votre connaissance!* We have business, do we not? Much to discuss!"

"You have our brother here, Fletcher tells us," John Crockett said.

"*Oui,* my friends. So I believe. Come in and we will talk our business."

"Where is Jimmy?"

"He is here, you shall see him. But first, some whiskey, no? *Il neige!* Brrrr!" Beaulieu wrapped his arms around himself and made an exaggerated show of shivering.

"We don't need whiskey, just our brother," John said.

Will stepped forward. "No need to be biggety, John. Mr. Beaulieu, we'll gladly share a cup with you."

"*Bon!* I am pleased. *Entrez*, please . . . come in."

"It'd help, sir, if you'd talk American instead of them Frenchy words," John said.

"I beg your pardon, Mr. Crockett. It is a difficult habit to overcome. *Je regrette.*" Beaulieu slapped his brow with the heel of his hand. "I have done it again! You see what I mean, eh? I will try. I will try." Beaulieu entered the building with a grand flourish. The others followed. As they entered, Will flashed John a subtle frown that wordlessly urged a little more concern for diplomacy, a quality John Crockett often disregarded.

The inside of the trading post, so poorly stocked that half its shelves were empty, stank and was dark and damp. Beaulieu waved his hand to display the place, as if he was actually proud of it.

The whiskey was stored in an enclosed cabinet with a store-bought lock. Beaulieu told them he had made the liquor himself, and it wasn't bad. He toasted the two brothers twice, and Fletcher once, grinning widely all the while and still mixing French with his English. After the third toast, John Crockett swiped his hand across his mouth and said, "Well, let's get to trading. We want to see our brother . . . if it really is him."

"Then you shall see him, and know for yourself. But first, concerning the money . . . I have gone to expense and much trouble to purchase this man. The Indians, they like him because he is deaf and dumb, and makes them laugh with his ways. *Dieu!* It was difficult to buy him free. So it is understood, of course, that I will be paid in good faith, even if his identity should prove other than the brother you seek."

"What? I'll make no such agreement," John said. "That's a dotey notion if ever I heard one! I'll not pay you for somebody that ain't Jimmy!"

Beaulieu's brows shot up. His face went red. "No? Then there is no bargain. *Retournez!* Go back where you have come from!"

"Fine with me." John turned and walked out the door. Will gaped in amazement, then followed.

He caught up with John at the horses. "What the devil are you doing, John? You going to walk away from here and leave Jimmy?"

"No."

"Then what are you doing out here?"

"Casting my lots to see how they roll." He flicked his

eyes back toward the trading post. "Like I thought. I believe they've rolled the right way. Here comes them sneaking scoundrels."

Beaulieu and Fletcher appeared at the door. Fletcher
came out. "Mr. John Crockett, don't go riding off. We'll
do this your way."

John nodded. "Take us to Jimmy . . . if it's really
him."

Beaulieu, looking sulky, nodded for the others to follow him. They went around the main trading post building
and into the unordered clump of smaller structures behind
it. Pigs rooted in a muddy pen nearby, sending out a foul
organic stench. In another pen were a couple of horses,
one sleek and healthy—apparently a recent trade—the
other broken-down and thin, being a longer-term possession of the Frenchman.

Beaulieu went to a log hut on the edge of the clearing. A barked log about the thickness of a thin man's leg
barred the door shut. John stopped in his tracks when he
saw it.

"You have Jimmy penned in a hut? Penned like a
common critter?"

Beaulieu frowned. "He has been treated well. Better
than by the Indians, I am sure."

"Lift that log. Let him free now!"

Beaulieu pushed the log up and dropped it to the side.
He reached for the carved handle—and the door receded
from his fingers, yanked open from the inside. A thin,
ragged figure burst out, shoved Beaulieu backward onto
his rump and darted past him. When he saw the three other
men, he stopped, legs spread and crouched, hands extended and ready for battle, and made a guttural, frightened sound in his throat.

"Lord have mercy, Jimmy!" Will Crockett said.
"Lord have mercy, what has become of you?"

John advanced slowly, hand extended. "Jimmy,
Jimmy . . . it's John. Your brother. John." He mouthed the
words carefully, looking straight into Jimmy's face in hope
he would be able to read the words he could not hear.
There was no question that this was Jimmy Crockett, de-

spite the nearly two decades that had passed since he had
last been seen. The face, though lined and weathered and
lean, was the same; the hair, though thinning on the top
and very long on the sides, was the same dark mop that
was common to the Crocketts. Mostly it was the eyes—
intense, dark, small, keen—that more than any other evidence told the brothers they had found their missing
sibling.

Jimmy frowned, looking closely at John. His eyes
flickered over to Will's face, back to John's, over to Will's
again. He straightened, murmured, dropped his hands.
John ceased advancing, letting Jimmy study him.

Beaulieu, meanwhile, had come to his feet. "I'll hold
him for you," he said, coming toward Jimmy from behind.
"He will try to run again. . . ."

Will's expression turned fiery. He looked squarely at
Beaulieu. "Stand aside, man, and don't touch him. If you
lay a hand on him, I'll snap it from your arm. I got good
reason to smite you down anyhow for keeping him penned
in his own filth!"

Jimmy detected Beaulieu then and moved away from
him. John nodded and smiled, and again held out his hand.
"John," he mouthed. "John . . . John. It's me. Your brother
John."

Comprehension slowly but visibly dawned in Jimmy.
He made an odd sound and began to shake. Tears began
streaming from his eyes, and he mouthed a word, vocaliz-
ing as best he could at the same time. Though garbled, the
word came through to John: "Brother."

John went to Jimmy and wrapped his arms around
him, hugging him close, ignoring the stench of him and
the muck that clung to his skin and clothing. Will joined
them, and all three brothers wrapped their arms around
each other, weeping like children. Fletcher watched impas-
sively, and Beaulieu eyed them like a rat spying from a
hole.

"Well, my friends, I see all are *heureux*, all are happy,
I should say? This truly is your brother, eh? *Bon!* So now
there is the matter of *paiement*, no?"

Will broke free and turned toward Beaulieu. He

pulled a sack of coins from under his coat and dug out a handful, which he counted in his palm. He flung them on the ground at Beaulieu's feet. "There's your money, Frenchman."

Beaulieu gathered the coins. "There is only half the agreed amount here!"

"The other half you lose out of treating our brother like an animal. That's our bargain, and there'll be no other."

Fletcher came forward. "I've got a say in this! I'll not be cheated out of what I'm due because you're mad at Beaulieu!"

"Take what you can get from Beaulieu, then."

"No! This is mine, not yours!" Beaulieu said, yanking his handful of coins back against his chest.

"You always were a cheat and liar, Beaulieu. I'll have my money, or your topknot!"

"You want money, take it from them!" Beaulieu waved toward the Crocketts. "It is them who have not kept the *accord*!"

Fletcher produced a pistol, which he leveled at Jimmy Crockett. "Give me them coins, or I'll kill him."

John stepped between Fletcher and Jimmy, reached under his coat and pulled out a small flintlock pistol of his own. He thumbed back the lock and aimed the pistol at Fletcher's chest. "Drop your pistol. I'm grateful to you for helping us find Jimmy, but I believe you're a lying rogue who's been in league with the Frenchy yonder from the beginning, and I'll kill you dead if you don't drop that pistol. And if I miss, my brother won't."

Fletcher looked at Will. He had drawn out a hidden pistol as well. The Crockett brothers had come prepared.

Fletcher dropped his pistol. John advanced and picked it up. "I'll leave it on the trail, where you can find it easy. And now, we'll be taking our leave."

For a long way up the trail, they heard Beaulieu's voice, cursing in French, very loudly.

"If we're fortunate, they'll argue between theirselves long enough to give us a good start on them before they follow," Will said.

"Maybe they won't follow," John replied.

"They'll follow," Will said. "Mark my word. They'll follow."

"I ain't at all certain we've handled this the right way," John said.

"Neither am I. But we've got Jimmy back. That's what matters."

John Crockett raised his head slowly, looking over the top of the boulders that hid him and down onto the darkening trail below. The sun was edging downward in the west, weakening with the waning of day, and the shadows it cast were long. Soon it would be dark, and there would be no point in keeping watch with the eyes; it would be up to ears and instincts then to let the Crocketts know whether Fletcher and Beaulieu had in fact followed.

Surely they had, or would. Fletcher and Beaulieu did not seem the type to be shortchanged and simply ignore it. But John didn't expect them to show themselves until after dark. Fletcher in particular could pose a significant threat. He was an experienced and crafty woodsman, more so than either Crockett brother.

John rose and went back to the camp, where Will was tightening his rifle flint and Jimmy was huddled beside the hidden hardwood fire, which John had built in a recess at the base of rocks, with a flat stone jutting over the blaze as a cooking surface. Such a fire could hardly be seen except close up, and the slow-burning hardwood put out very little smoke.

"No sign of them," John said. He reached into his pouch and pulled out a packet of jerked beef, bit off some and offered another piece to Will, who declined it. John rose then and made the same offer to Jimmy, who grabbed the food eagerly and began devouring it.

"Jimmy, I reckon you were right hungry," John said. "How long did they leave you without food, I wonder?"

Jimmy, of course, could hear none of this, and made no response. John patted his brother's thin shoulder and went back to Will. "I sit here and see him, but I can't get it through my noggin that he's sure enough alive and with us again. It seems a miracle."

"Well, I won't rest easy until we've got him far from here," John said. "Maybe we made a mistake, Will. Maybe we should have give them all the money."

"Not after the way they treated Jimmy. No sir."

Jimmy rose and came to them. He smiled a smile so broad it seemed it shouldn't fit on so thin a face. Looking around surreptitiously, he patted his side and made a sound—in a voice too loud given the circumstances.

"Hush, Jimmy, hush," Will said, putting a finger to his lip.

Jimmy didn't seem to understand. He made the same sound, and patted his side again.

"I think he's trying to say a word," John said. Then to Jimmy, mouthing the words precisely: "What is it? Say it again."

He did, and still they did not understand. Jimmy frowned, looked around again, and pulled up his ragged shirt, revealing a small pouch bound around his waist.

"What the devil is this?" Will asked.

Jimmy untied the strap and removed the pouch. He tugged its ties open and spilled some of the contents into his palm, making the same sound as before.

John's eyes widened. "Is that . . . Lord a'mercy, Will, is that what I think it is?"

"If you're thinking it's silver, by gum, I believe it is."

"Silver . . . that's what he's been trying to say, Will! Silver!"

Jimmy, having read John's lips, grinned even more broadly, and nodded with vigor.

"Where'd you get it, Jimmy?"

Jimmy put the rough nodules back in the pouch and laid it on the ground, then mimed the motions of digging and hauling.

"He mined it, Will! By the eternal days, he mined it!"

"Injun silver!" Will said the words in a tone of awe. "Plain as preaching, it's Injun silver!"

"I've heard stories about Injun silver mines, hid in

the mountains. They say there's some in Kentucky, and down here too."

Will looked squarely into Jimmy's face and spoke slowly. "Do you know where the mine is? Can you find the silver mine?"

Jimmy shook his head, and made motions as if tying a knot behind his head.

"They blindfolded him," John said. "They must have kept him blinded going to and from it."

At that moment they heard a noise in the forest, out in the damp brush, and then a faint click, like that of a rifle lock.

There was no time for words. John grabbed Jimmy and pulled him to the ground as Will hefted up his rifle. From the forest came a loud crack and a burst of flame. A rifle ball smacked into the tree just behind Will, having passed within a foot of his head.

"Lord!" Will exclaimed. "I was nigh a dead man that time!"

"Shoot back!" John yelled.

Jimmy, who could hear none of this but understood what was going on, moaned and wrapped his arms around his head, shoving his face against the ground.

Will aimed into the gathering dark and fired. The burst of smoke and fire hammered John's and Will's ears, and the powder stench was acrid and hot.

Out in the gloom, someone had grunted loudly immediately after Will's shot. It sounded like Beaulieu. There was a mad scrambling, a crashing of brush and breaking of sticks and branches, and then silence.

"Beaulieu!" John whispered.

"Yes," Will replied. "And I believe I've shot him, sure as the world."

Chapter 8

The night hours were long and tense. John and Will kept a long, tiring watch, made more difficult by a tendency of Jimmy's to make sudden and startling noises and movements. Several times the Crockett brothers were certain that Fletcher and Beaulieu were upon them again, but each time that fear proved groundless.

When the first pink light of dawn spread in the horizon, the Crocketts were confident that their antagonists had been put off. It was possible that Beaulieu was dead. The reaction after Will's shot into the darkness indicated that, at the least, he had been wounded.

The three men wolfed down a meager breakfast, mounted, and rode. Still concerned about the possibility, however remote, of being followed, they took a route straight through the forest for the first eight miles, paralleling but avoiding the trail. This slowed their progress very much. After they joined the trail again, they traveled with great caution and frequent hiding, and made only another five miles before darkness forced a halt for the night.

The night passed without incident, and when the Crocketts went on the next morning, they had no more fear of pursuit. Snow began to fall, and by noon was, in Will's description, "shoe-mouth deep." The temperature rose above freezing for only a few minutes in the height of the afternoon, so there was no significant thawing of the hardening ground.

The farther they went from the Indian country, the more interested Jimmy seemed to be in his surroundings. John and Will found him fascinating to watch. And when by the light of the next night's fire they saw him weeping silently, yet smiling at the same time, they were moved. Clearly Jimmy Crockett had never expected to know freedom again, and was joyful it had come.

When they finally reached John Crockett's borrowed cabin in Jefferson County, they were greeted in near silence by John's children, who were overwhelmed by a cautious curiosity about Jimmy. The smallest ones eyed their strange uncle from a distance, while the older ones came close and extended their hands for a shake. Jimmy chortled and made peculiar noises, putting his hand out to touch their faces and laughing. As best anyone could figure, what had him entertained was the novelty of seeing Crockett family traits in so many new faces.

David was among the recalcitrant ones, hanging back from Jimmy. He edged over to his father. "That's my uncle Jimmy? Really and truly?"

"Yes, boy, really and truly. Look at him! Looks just like your brother Wilson in the eyes, don't he! It's a happy day, David. Jimmy's back among his kin, back where he belongs."

David grinned, and screwed up his courage. He walked up to Jimmy and put out his hand. "I'm David," he said. "I'm tickled to meet you."

Jimmy bent over and looked him in the face, very closely, and laughed again. Then he put his hands under David's arms and picked him up, studying him up and down with a big grin on his face. David, slightly alarmed, dangled in space, looking pleadingly at his family. But they merely laughed. No one came to his aid.

"I believe he particularly likes you, David," Will Crockett said. "Don't worry. He won't hurt you . . . I don't believe."

Jimmy set him down again, as lightly as if he were a sack of feathers. For a lean fellow, Jimmy Crockett had more than his share of strength, developed in long hours of labor in a silver mine no other white man had seen.

For the rest of the winter and into the early summer, Jimmy Crockett remained with David's family. Over that time a bond of friendship was forged between boy and man. More than any other of the Crockett children, David came to love his unspeaking, unhearing uncle, and relished every moment he spent with him. Jimmy's handicaps had hindered him from fully joining the society of men, and so he retained a boyish quality of mind that made him a congenial and happy companion for eight-year-old David. Will had been correct: Jimmy clearly favored David above all his other nieces and nephews.

As time passed, David discovered something remarkable: despite his physical limitations, Jimmy managed to communicate fairly well, using a mix of vocal sounds that approximated words, and hand and body movements. Sometimes he would draw intricate story-telling pictures in the dirt. Over many days, David was able to gather with reasonable certainty some of the facts of Jimmy's troubled but interesting past.

He drew several conclusions based on the things Jimmy managed to convey. First, just as his handicaps had kept Jimmy from escaping the 1777 Indian raid that had killed his parents, so too had they helped him escape death. Apparently, Jimmy's original captor had found him interesting, perhaps pitiful, and had treated him relatively well, keeping him for several years within his household. At some point Jimmy had been conveyed to another man in payment of a debt, and there his treatment had been worse. He had been put to work in the hidden silver mine, to which he was taken almost daily, blindfolded going in and coming out. On the homeward treks he would be laden with the ore his day's labors had produced. David tried to picture what it must have been like for Jimmy: unhearing, unspeaking, and with the blindfold, unseeing; trudging some unknown trail with a heavy basket of ore on his shoulder and a gruff Indian captor at his back.

The silver that Jimmy kept in his little pouch, David ascertained, was some he had managed to sneak for himself. Jimmy was quite obsessed with his treasure, and often played with the nodules of silver like a child toying with pretty pebbles. David would sit and watch him, envying him for the silver, but never daring to ask for any.

At night, David noticed, John Crockett also would watch Jimmy and his silver. At those times the look on John's face was not pleasant to see, and David would be reminded of the Crockett family's continuing poverty.

But there was hope for better times. John, negotiating with a Quaker landholder with good commercial property, had completed his arrangements to erect a log tavern and inn on land on the road between Abdingdon, Virginia, and Knoxville. In the spring John began devoting as much time as his farming would allow to building the tavern. It was a log building, on the small side for taverns, bearing with it the promise to the Crocketts of many nights crowded in with strangers.

"It's the wagoners who will provide our business," Crockett explained to his sons. "We'll serve them food, give them shelter, fodder for their teams—and plenty of spirits. Rum, whiskey, cider, gin, wine. If all goes as I hope, we will make a better living than we ever have. As the country grows, my boys, so will the traffic on the roads, and so will our livelihood."

David was happy to see his father growing enthusiastic and optimistic about life—except that his eagerness to advance his plan brought plenty of hard labor to the Crockett sons. David and his brothers were put to chopping trees, dragging logs by horse power, hewing, notching, lifting. There were shingles to be riven, puncheons to be split, foundation stones to be gathered from the creek and adjacent rocky fields, carted to the tavern site, and put in place.

But for David, primarily, there was a well to be dug at a spot identified by a local diviner. Because he was lean and small but strong, he was given much of the initial digging work, and he hated it. Only when his uncle Jimmy helped did he find any pleasure at all in the ceaseless shovel-and-barrow drudgery. Jimmy was very used to digging, after all, and gave David much relief.

But what relief came was largely annulled by the pushing, commanding presence of John Crockett. The man had his good points, but when it came time for labor, he was like a driver of slaves. And because the tavern was the dearest project he had ever undertaken, he drove all the harder. Rain, cold, even snow was not sufficient cause in John Crockett's view to rest from labor. And on one particularly chilly and damp day, the stress brought ill fortune to young David.

The well was down about fifteen feet now. Within its claustrophobically constricting walls, it was very cold and damp. Even so, David was sweating, and felt unusually weak, hardly able to fill the buckets with earth and rock for his brothers to pull up by ropes for emptying. He struggled at the task, his fingers growing cold and numb, his face growing hot—until the next thing he knew, he was lying on the wet ground beside the well, his brothers looking down at him with concern. There were ropes around his chest, very tight, and his father was on his knees, struggling to loosen them. As David closed his eyes and faded into a fevered oblivion, he numbly realized he must have fainted in the well, and been pulled from the hole by the ropes.

The things he was aware of for the next four days were totally beyond his prior experience. Sometimes he saw his family, and the interior of their cabin, but everything seemed distorted and outsized. Other times his perceptions were of unknown faces, of lights, and of odd and miscolored landscapes. At one point he explored a brilliant, flower-filled meadow, warmed by sun and wind, with his dog Painter at his feet, and smiling strangers in unusual clothing calling him by a name that wasn't his. He was at peace, happy and content.

He knelt and put his nose into the flowers, which were amazingly bright in color and headily scented. Their aroma grew stronger, filling his nostrils. He wrinkled his nose, unsure whether the smell was pleasant or bad. Then his perceptions became different. There was a heaviness on his chest. The flowery meadow vanished, and he became cold. Music played in the distance, a tune he didn't know, but which filled him with fear. Struggling, he opened his eyes. He found himself lying on his tick, and above him was the face of his uncle.

"Jimmy has put a poultice on your chest, David." The voice was his mother's. He turned his eyes and saw her face, moving down beside Jimmy's. "He's gathered yarbs and such from the woods, and they'll make you well, God willing. Now, there's something I want you to drink." She gave him a strong-tasting, bitter tea that made him frown and wince, and soon he went to sleep.

After that the strange world David had been living in existed no more. It gave way to the world he had known before. He began to feel hunger and thirst again, and finally to complain about it. His mother laughed to hear it, and David grew angry, failing to understand that it was relief that made her laugh.

He had only one decline, and with it one more strange dream: himself, drenched in sweat, looking out across a murky, moving field; that odd, trumpeting music he had heard before blowing to him on the hot wind. Something about it made him recoil in fear; he put his hands over his ears, but the sound of the music did not lessen. He tried to run and got nowhere, then his eyes opened and he was on his bed, his mother holding to his hand and saying gentle words. Afterward he improved quickly. There were no more dreams.

Only later did he understand how sick he had been. His family had been convinced he would die—all but his uncle Jimmy, who had managed to communicate to the others that he had learned skills in his captivity that could save the boy. He had roamed into the woods, gathering what medicinal herbs and plants the winter hadn't fully decayed, and made free use of the many dried herbs Rebecca Crockett kept on hand. John Crockett seemed skeptical about it, but Rebecca was adamant: it was Jimmy's herbal treatments that had saved her boy's life.

David wanted to thank Jimmy for his help, but this was not possible. A day before the fever left David for good, Jimmy departed. Will Crockett came up from the Dumplin community to take Jimmy home with him. No one knew if he would return; the presumption was that he would not.

Jimmy had left something behind for David. It was a piece of his precious Indian silver, the largest, smoothest, and most beautiful one.

"That's worth something, David," his father said. "You can sell that for good money."

"No," David replied, clenching his fingers around the silver piece. "I'll not sell it, no matter what it's worth. Uncle Jimmy give it to me to keep, and I'm going to keep it."

John Crockett studied his son in silence, unsmiling. His eyes were hollow and hungry, the eyes of poverty that has come early and lingered too long. David felt vulnerable and a little afraid, yet defensive. He clutched the silver more tightly, and his own eyes took on a fire of determination to keep what was his.

John Crockett scratched his beard, gave a little grunt, turned and walked away, mumbling under his breath and seeming older than his years.

Sometimes it seemed to David that there were two incarnations of his father, each appearing from time to time. There was John Crockett the dreamer and planner, always looking for a new scheme, a new way out of debt and trouble. Then there was John Crockett the hollow man—the incarnation present tonight, the one David found repellent and sad.

David decided that he would never let himself become a hollow man. He would be a dreamer, all the time. Dreamers were better, by a long shot.

Chapter 9

"Hold it down, boys, that's right—hold tight there, don't let her fly up on me!"

John Crockett yelled the order to his sons, who were groaning loudly as they strained to hold down the top of a tall, bent-over sapling. At the narrow top of the sapling David clung like a grasshopper to a weed stalk.

David grimaced and struggled to hold his nearly upside-down position. He was the undisputed champion climber of all the Crockett children, and so to him had fallen the task of shinnying all the way up and tying on a rope that his brothers used to bend the tree slowly toward the earth, with David still on it so his weight would help the process. His brothers then waded into the branches, grabbed the tree, and held it down, while John Crockett dragged the carcass of a fresh-killed deer by a rope strap around its neck. He pulled a hatchet from his belt and quickly hacked off the very top of the tree, then slipped the deer's neck strap over the remaining stub. He then added his muscle to that of his sons as they held the sapling down.

"Drop off, Davy, and get them props yonder," he instructed.

David was glad to oblige. He dropped to the ground and rolled aside. The other Crocketts then slowly let the sapling rise until it pulled the deer almost entirely off the ground. John and his sons pushed the tree farther upright, as David scampered over and picked up a couple of ten-foot poles, each with a fork on the end. He put the fork of the first against the sapling and pushed, and with the help of the others worked the tree up straighter and the deer higher off the ground. He set the end of the prop into the earth and repeated the same process with the second prop pole. When it was all done, the deer hung by its neck from the bent and propped-up sapling, its hind feet dangling a foot off the ground. David wedged a third prop in place, and the deer hung in the middle of a very stable tripod.

John Crockett got his breath and evaluated the job. A quick, unsmiling nod showed his approval; he seldom was demonstrative beyond that. He swept back his hair and turned to David. "You still want the honors?"

"Yes, Pap. If you'll let me."

"You killed the deer. You want to skin it, you can do it. Besides, you need the practice. A twelve-year-old boy ought to know how to skin a deer the right way. I ain't seen you do it right yet."

David might have replied that he had never been given the opportunity to show his skills until now. This year alone he had killed two deer prior to this one, but had not been allowed to skin either of them alone. His father, grumbling about the ineptitude of boys, would always intrude and take over the job as soon as David showed the least sign of uncertainty, or asked even the simplest question. Today David intended to have no help at all, but that would mean he could not falter or seem unsure of himself at any point. If he did falter, his father would take over the job, like always.

David took up his knife, freshly sharpened, and placed himself between the forelegs of the dead deer, resting them on his shoulders to keep them out of the way. He probed the knife through the skin on the inside of one of the deer's hind legs and carefully sliced up the inside of the leg to the groin. He repeated the process on the other hind leg, then similarly opened the flesh inside the fore-legs. Returning to the groin, he slowly cut the hide all the way up to the deer's neck. When he was done, the slices inside the legs joined the main central cut like tributaries leading to a river.

He worked the legs out of the skin, then wriggled the tailbone out of its sheath. Then the hardest labor began, as he slowly peeled the deer's body out of its hide, all the way up to the neck. He sliced a circle around the neck, just below the hanging rope, and within a few minutes had the hide entirely loose. The skinned carcass hung glisten-ing in the sunlight, and David stood aside, panting from exertion but satisfied that he had done a fine skinning job.

John Crockett spat tobacco juice onto the ground. He grunted his satisfaction with the job. "Fine work, son," he said. "Now, let's get that skin into the water."

Thrilling privately at his father's compliment, and taking care to keep the furred outer portion of the hide from contacting the meaty underside, David carried the hide over to a barrel full of water. He immersed the hide and topped the barrel with a lid.

Over the next several days the weather cooled sub-stantially and David worried that the water in the barrel would freeze. This didn't happen, to his pleasure, and when he removed the soaked hide at last, the fur was well loosened.

He carried it over to the scraping block, a smooth, barkless log, fixed in place at a slant so it butted up at about half a man's height. David laid the hide over the log, fur side up, and began scraping in an outward direction with the same bone scraper his father had used for years. The sodden fur scraped off in handful-size clumps. David kept at it, working until he sweated even in the cool, and freed the hide of all hair. Then he turned the hide over and scraped away the fats and tendrils that sill clung to it.

David had saved the deer's head, keeping it in the cold, and now he turned to it, opening the skull and re-moving the brain. His mother had heated water ready, and into a bucket of it he plunged the brains, working them through his fingers into a paste.

Next David stretched the hide over a frame and pulled it tight, then tied it in place. Over every inch of the hide he spread the paste of deer brains, then removed the hide from the frame and rolled it up with the brains still on it. A couple of days later he washed the hide in clear water, removing all the brains, and then worked the hide for a long time against the sharpened edge of a fixed hardwood board until the hide was worn and supple. He smoked the hide afterward over a smoldering black birch fire to seal off the pores.

Rebecca Crockett examined the finished article. "That's as fine a piece of buckskin as I've seen," she said. "I'm proud of you, David."

It so happened that on this particular day, one of the Crockett tavern's more frequent patrons was present, and watched David at work. David knew the man only by his surname of Dunn. He was an elderly fellow, spry despite his years, who kept busy shuttling goods by wagon between the settlements.

Dunn approached David as he stood admiring the buckskin he had tanned out. "That was a right fine bit of tanning work, boy."

"Thank you, Mr. Dunn."

"Did you do it alone?"

"Yes sir. I killed and skinned the deer too."

"That's the first tanning you've done?"

"Yes."

"You're quite the young man, ain't you? How old are you?"

"Twelve years old."

"Twelve! Nigh a man, then. You'll do well for yourself, I reckon. You'd make a fine tanner, at the very least. There's always need for good buckskin."

Dunn walked away, going back into the tavern for another round of whiskey. David grinned and fingered the buckskin. Dunn's comments had greatly pleased him. Nigh a man. He liked the sound of that.

"Nigh a man." he said aloud. "Reckon I am at that. Nigh a man."

Early December, 1798

It was nights such as these that Rebecca Crockett hated, as David knew from having watched her at work night after night. She moved through the smoke and noise of the tavern with a dour expression on her face. Every motion, every glance, revealed her displeasure at the revelry and drunkenness all around her—and David noticed that when she looked at her husband, her expression was darkest of all.

John Crockett was in the corner, by the fireplace, drinking and talking intently to a man who had come to the tavern today, driving a big herd of cattle. His name was Jacob Siler, and he spoke with a Germanic accent that David thought was intriguing.

It wasn't Siler who was responsible for the spirit of drunkenness permeating the tavern tonight, but the two drovers who had come in with him. One was a skinny, mean-faced boy, maybe four or five years older than David, who drank like a man twice his age but leered at Rebecca with the lust of youth. That infuriated David, who was growing old enough now to understand such things. It also surprised him, because he couldn't think of his mother as the kind men would stare at. She wasn't just any woman, or some lewd wench—she was his mother! But clearly the drover boy was the type who stared at any grown female. It made David want to yank the dog irons from the fireplace and wallop the young lecher in the head with them.

The other drover, much larger and a few years older than the lecherous one, was the main source of noise. There was something in his face and manner that indicated he lacked a full share of mental capacity. He was engaged in a loud conversation with a stranger, seemingly a vagrant, who was on his way to Knoxville. The two shouted at each other rather than doing the logical thing and moving within easy talking distance. Their initial subject had been something to do with the oddities of weather in North Carolina; now, somehow, it had shifted to the topic of raising chickens, an area in which both men seemed eager to claim superior expertise.

"A man can tell by his fingers which hen has laid the egg," Siler's drover was saying. "You got to feel the lay bones, you see. If a man can lay two fingers between them, there's your laying hen. That's her."

"Why, surely that's the truth, sir, but only if you have checked her the day of the laying of the last egg of the batch."

"Or the day after," returned the other. "You can check her the day after too."

The other fellow must have detected the simple-mindedness of the drover, because he had adopted a crisp, confident tone of voice that contrasted greatly with the other's slurring. "No, no, not in my opinion. The bones, they begin to come together right fast. The day after is too late."

David found the odd conversation amusing. He was sitting in the corner, whittling on a cedar stick, and listening quietly. Wilson was beside him.

"Them men is funny," Wilson said. "I like to listen at drunks a-talking. Don't care what Mama thinks about it. I think a drunk is funny."

"So do I," David replied.

The arguers were getting louder now, and irritated with each other. They had come to a point of violent disagreement, something to do with the best time of spring to cull nonlayers from the flock.

"Pap'll up and tell them to quiet down, once they get to cussing," Wilson predicted.

David expected the same, and looked at his father, waiting for him to rise and quiet the disagreement. But John Crockett didn't rise. He leaned closer to Siler so as to hear whatever he was saying, and then David was surprised when Siler and his father turned their heads at exactly the same moment and stared directly at him. David's eyes met his father's, and their mutual gaze held for a moment. Then John and Siler looked back at each other and resumed their conversation.

David knew they had been talking about him, and it

was very unsettling. He laid down his knife and cedar stick.

"Rebecca," John Crockett said, waving for her to come. She left the fireside, where she had been stocking the blaze, and came to him. David watched with great concern as his father talked to Rebecca, whose face was turned away from him. When she turned and looked back at him, over her shoulder, a solemn expression on her face, David thought he might become ill. Every intuition told him that whatever was being said was not something he would want to hear.

Rebecca went away from the table and back to the fire. David watched her with wide eyes. She kept her back to him, not turning. From time to time she moved her right hand up to her face, as if she was brushing strands of hair off her forehead . . . or perhaps wiping tears off her cheek.

Wilson, who had observed none of this, was laughing and commenting in a whisper about some other absurd thing the drunks had said. David didn't listen. He picked up his stick and knife and walked to the ladder. Climbing to the loft, he crawled onto his tick and pulled the blanket over him. Staring into the darkness, he listened as the drunks shouted back and forth, insulting each other's total lack of understanding of poultry. There was a curse, the sound of something breaking, more curses, and then John Crockett's voice, protesting and calling for peace. Obviously the drunks had, as was inevitable, come to blows.

David rolled over and closed his eyes. Normally he would have been bounding downstairs to see the excitement for himself. Tonight he didn't care.

He sensed that whatever had been the nature of the discussion between his father and Jacob Siler, it was going to affect his life in some way—and he was just as sure he wasn't going to like it.

His mother gave him the news before breakfast the next morning. From the redness and swelling of her eyes, and the pallor and puffiness of her face, David knew she had cried long into the night. He accepted her words with the stoicism of a condemned man hearing the death sentence he knew would come even before his trial began.

"Your father has bound you out to help Mr. Siler herd his cattle, David," she said. "They came to the agreement last night. You will be paid as much as six dollars, if you give good service."

David swallowed before he spoke, to keep his voice from quaking. "How far will I have to go?"

"Into Virginia." She paused. "Hundreds of miles, by the time you return."

David stood in silence. His face revealed nothing, but inside he was struggling hard against the impulse to weep aloud. Bound to Virginia . . . it seemed an infinite distance to a young boy who had never been far from his home, and never away from his family.

He looked up at his mother. It took only a second or so for Rebecca's composure to shatter and for tears to come. She knelt, shaking and sobbing, and wrapped her arms around her boy, hugging her face against his chest.

Part 2

THE WANDERING BOY

Chapter 10

In a lowing, mud-pounding mass, Jacob Siler's cattle moved down the dirt road and around the bend. David Crockett lingered at the curve and waved for a long time at his family, eyes stinging in the cold wind and wetted by the emotion of parting.

There had been no time to gather his thoughts and mentally prepare for this separation. Hardly an hour had passed between the time David learned he had been hired out and the actual departure. He had bid a numb good-bye to his family, his brothers and sisters staring at him, expressionless, like he had become strange, or doomed. He didn't like the feeling that gave him.

Only Rebecca shed tears. John Crockett seemed gruff and cold, and revealed no emotion at seeing his twelve-year-old boy depart. David wondered if his father even cared—until John called him aside and unceremoniously presented him with a long oaken walking stick he had whittled out a couple of years before and had always used himself. David accepted it in silence, keeping his eyes averted from his father's face. It was a brief but meaningful moment, John Crockett's way of saying good-bye and Godspeed.

David was touched, even though one contrary fact still loomed in his mind: his father had made no arrangements to bring him home. He knew it because he had already asked Siler if he was planning to return, and he was not. He was moving the cattle from his former home in Knoxville to a new home in Virginia. David could only guess that in making it home again, he would be on his own.

"Boy, are you coming or ain't you?" Siler yelled from around the bend. David gave a final wave to his kin, turned and loped off, not looking back again because he knew to do so would make him lose his composure.

It came to his mind that this was a moment to remember forever: the moment that David Crockett went from being a boy to a young man out in the world.

To David's good fortune, the labor of cattle herding left little time for brooding, and as the miles dropped away behind him, his sadness lessened.

And there was Alonz Tidwell to distract him too. This was the simple drover who had gotten into the argument about poultry-raising the night before. He was a comical, loud fellow even when sober, and the pain of his hangover did not silence him. To David's amusement, he was still fixed on the very topic that had led him to violence, arguing with the air about chickens and their raising. David gathered that Tidwell had raised chickens on the Piedmont of North Carolina for many years while his farmer father was still alive, and considered himself an unassailable authority on poultry. After a while he grew tired of talking to himself, and fell back to give David the privilege of his wisdom. It was clearer than ever today that Tidwell was mentally deficient. He seemed to David much like a child living in the body of a man. But whatever else he lacked, he did seem to know a lot about chickens.

"You see a fat hen with a scrawny hind end, lazy and poorly at her feed and her comb all colored wrong, and her forevermore taking to the shade in the summertime and the coop when it rains, there's your hen that ain't laying her worth, David. Your name's David, ain't it? Thought so. Well, David, that hen's your next dinner. All she's good for. That fool back at your pap's tavern, he didn't know squat about hens. You hear him, David? Old long tall fool. I ain't seen bigger a fool since the twentieth of last summer. I give him what he had due, by gum!"

"How long will it take us to get to Virginia?" David asked.

"Now David, your no-count hen, she'll be the first to go to roost, and the last to leave it in the morning. I've seen it myself. You know much about hens, David?"

"No. How long until we'll get to Virginia?"

"Long time, long time. It lies that way." He pointed straight ahead. "That's why we're driving the cattle in that direction, you see."

"That makes good sense to me."

"Well, it does, it does, when you think about it. I'll tell you anything you need to know. You just ask me, whenever you want to. Huh?"

"I will."

"Good boy. I like you, David. You're a good boy."

David smiled. Though Tidwell was as odd and mindless a fellow as he'd ever met, he was glad to be in his good graces. Out on the hoof, one never knew when one would need a friend.

It didn't appear likely that David was going to find a better friend among his companions. The other drover—the younger, sparer one who had stared so hard at Rebecca—was named Ben Kelso, and he didn't like David at all. David didn't care. He didn't like Kelso either.

For one thing, Kelso was a dirty-minded fellow, talking incessantly of women in terms David had scarcely heard before. Only David's exposure since early childhood to mating farm animals, older brothers, and a few lewd tales he had overheard wagoners telling in the tavern, enabled him to understand all that Kelso talked about. To hear Kelso tell his own story, no greater conqueror of women had ever walked the earth. He claimed such a breadth of experience with females that David calculated out his carnal exploits, if authentic, must have begun about the age of six. Kelso's boastful lies became even more tiring to hear than Tidwell's chicken chats, but David wasn't bold enough to tell him to shut up. Kelso had a bullying manner that intimidated him.

As for Siler, he was far too much a figure of authority for David to feel friendly toward; besides, he resented

Siler for being the one who had led him into this circumstance in the first place. Had Siler not come to the tavern, he never would have been hired out on a job he didn't want.

David kept his bad feelings about Siler prudently hidden, and as time passed, they actually began to be replaced by a more accommodating attitude. Siler seemed a decent soul for a kidnapper, which was pretty much how David thought of him. The first night of the journey, as they sat beside a roaring blaze, Siler told a little about himself. He lived near Natural Bridge, Virginia, was son-in-law to one Peter Hartley, a fellow early settler of that region, and the man to whose farm the cattle were being driven. Furthermore, Siler was, according to his own assessment, an excellent gunsmith. David wasn't impressed with that claim until Siler brought forth a rifle he had made and let his employees examine it. David was no expert judge of guns, but he recognized much skill in the making of this weapon, a brass-mounted beauty with a Deckard lock and ornamental patterns artistically carved into the gleaming maple stock.

"That rifle is as fine a one as I've done, I reckon," Siler said, running his hand along the stock. "There's only one that I've made better, and that was for an old neighbor of mine in Pennsylvania, name of Squire Boone. You're bound to have heard of his son, Daniel, who made his name to famous up in Kentucky. I knew the Boones well, back in Pennsylvania. I daresay Daniel has fired that rifle I made his pap a right smart bit."

David had heard of Boone, whose name had been lent to his Kentucky settlement of Boonesborough, as well as the later-formed Boone's Station. And not very far from David's birthplace had run Boone's Creek, so-named because Daniel Boone had hunted along it a good quarter of a century before David's birth. Lots of folks in what was now Tennessee had known Boone well, either through meeting him during one of his frequent hunts or during the time he had lived within what was now the state's borders. David was impressed that Siler had known Boone's family all the was back in Pennsylvania. He admired Boone's reputation. Attaining fame almost solely on the basis of exceptional woodsman's skills was a feat few achieved. It seemed to David that fame and greatness would be pleasant possessions to hold.

He certainly found little potential for fame, greatness, or pleasure in the cattle-driving business. This was troublesome work, monotonous when all was going well and grueling when it wasn't. Siler was running about a hundred head of cattle he had fattened on grain and clover pasture during the summer at Knoxville. They lumbered along toward Virginia with Siler guiding the herd behind a steer he led from horseback. David and the other two had to make do with walking, carrying big beech switches with the brown leaves still intact and using them to shoo the cattle along and keep them together on the road. There were a couple of trained dogs that helped herd the cattle too, though sometimes these caused trouble by attracting other dogs along the way, and these would bark and frighten the cattle. Twice, there were small-scale stampedes that sent the drovers scrambling through the woods and fields, regathering the scattered herd.

Here and there along the road were taverns, ordinaries, or farms where the cattle could be pastured and grazed at night for a fee. If Siler happened to be in a good, open-pursed mood, he would put the drovers up in a bed— all three in one, usually—and even pay for grain to be given the cattle. Other times when he was feeling stingy, he would have his drovers sleep outside with the cattle, or would even trade off some of their labor for a few hours the next day to pay his grazing fee. David found himself occasionally performing jobs as diverse as fence-building, hog-slaughtering, and barn-building, all for strangers who had given them board and their herd pasture.

All this continual exertion made changes in David Crockett. The daily walking strengthened his legs, lengthened his stride, bettered his wind. He had been thin to start with; now he became even more lean, but it was a healthy, muscled leanness. He felt light and taut, like he could spring right across a tall fence if he took a mind to. Though he despised much of the work he was involved in,

especially the extra duties done in lieu of paying grazing
fees, he realized he was becoming a better specimen of a
boy because of it.

Often they shared the road with other herds, occasionally cattle, but more often hogs. Massive herds of
swine, several hundred head in size, sometimes a thousand, and once—awesome to see—they came upon a herd
of about four thousand hogs. David had never seen or
smelled anything like it. A swine herd that size was unusual, though such came along from time to time. Hogs
were actually good travelers that held up well on the road,
though they only could make eight miles or so a day,
where cattle could make fifteen or even twenty.

Seeing different country in the company of other than
his kin made him think less about his home back at the
tavern and the gentle arms of his mother. Only when he
contemplated the miles piling up behind him did he feel
significantly homesick. This usually happened at night,
when he crawled into his bedroll. A time or two he might
have cried, if not for fear that Ben Kelso would hear and
deride him before the others.

The closer they came to the end of the journey, the
more impatient David became with the plodding cattle. He
was eager to reach Virginia, get his pay, and head back
home. He anticipated the prospect of returning to the tavern with money in hand and success to his credit. He
would bask there before brothers and sisters, a calm and
enviable young man who had traveled far and seen the
world.

"I wish these cows would sprout wings and fly," he
said to the simpleminded Tidwell. "I'd get a-holt of one's
tail and let him fly me right to Virginia, then I'd take my
pay, buy him from Mr. Siler, and let him fly me back
again."

Tidwell, very easily amused, cackled at the fantastic
words. "A flying cow!" he said. "You hear that, Ben? David here was saying he wished that—"

"I heerd him," Kelso said. "Don't see nothing funny
in that."

David glowered at Kelso, thinking how everything

about the fellow aggravated him, from his voice, to the way his hair stuck up from his head like dried grass in a wintry field, to the way he swaggered and talked and bragged. This kind of despising was a novel experience for David, who never before had met someone whose very presence and manner could anger him so.

One time near the journey's end, when no inn was nearby and they had camped for the night near the herd beneath the open sky, David was lying in his bedroll near the fire, huddled on his left side in his blankets and examining the piece of silver Uncle Jimmy had given him. He was so absorbed in watching the firelight glimmer on the nodule that he didn't hear Kelso sneak up to him. Kelso's hand shot over, and suddenly the silver was in his grip, not David's.

"Well now!" he said. "What we got here? Looks to me like—" He stopped. His taunting tone vanished. "This here's silver! Real silver!"

David was already up, hand extended. "Give that back, Kelso!"

Kelso backed off, looking at the silver with the fire of greed burning in his eye. "Where'd you get this?"

"It's mine! It was give to me by my uncle!"

"Give to you? Well, then it didn't cost you nothing. No real loss if you lose it!"

"Give it back!"

"What do you care if I give it back? It didn't cost you nothing!"

Siler was out among the cattle, out of earshot. Tidwell, who had been asleep, wakened and sat up sleepily. "Something wrong, Kelso?"

Kelso paused, then grinned devilishly. "Surely is, Alonz. David here is trying to steal this silver piece of mine."

That surprised David so much that he gaped silently for a few seconds. "That's a lie!" he bellowed, turning red. "That silver is mine!"

Tidwell said, "That's the truth, Ben. I seen him looking at it before. You better give that back. Mr. Siler wouldn't want you taking it from him."

Kelso sneered scoffingly at Tidwell, but was not willing to defy him. Even if he was sadly lacking in intellect, Tidwell was much bigger and older, and potentially dangerous if he got mad. Kelso exhaled, then turned an angry eye on David. He extended the silver toward him—then yanked it back suddenly.

"Yes sir, I'll give it back to you, David!" Kelso said, eyes twinkling. "I'll put it right over here for you, where you can get it!"

He strode over to the herd and behind a grazing cow. He knelt and picked up a short stick, then deftly he flipped up the tail. Suddenly he inserted the silver into the rectum and poked it in several inches with the stick. The cow lowed and moved forward, resisting this most unexpected invasion, but Kelso kept pace with it, then led it back. He wore a big, smirking grin that sent a cold chill of fury down David's spine.

"There! You want your silver, Dave, you come fetch it! It's tucked right up this here cow fundament, safe and sound!" Kelso laughed uproariously, and tossed the manure-fouled stick at David, just to watch him jump to avoid it. It was too much to take. David couldn't hold back tears. Fury drew them out, a pure and almost holy fury. If he had held a knife in hand right then, he would have murdered Kelso on the spot, whatever the penalty. To his good fortune, the very fury that overwhelmed him also saved him from rash action, freezing him in place as effectively as stark fear sometimes freezes a soldier at the point of greatest danger.

"What are you waiting on, Davy? Come get your silver! Just lift the tail and finger it right out! Easy as picking your nose, and I'll bet you've done that aplenty!"

Tidwell rose, swore, and lunged forward. Kelso's eyes went wide with sudden fear. Tidwell strode over to the cow, pushed Kelso aside very roughly, and with a deft probe of his forefinger brought the silver out again. Then he reached over, yanked Kelso to him, and began wiping the dirtied silver and his equally dirtied finger on Kelso's sleeve.

Kelso cursed and fought, but Tidwell was too much for him. "Now Kelso," Tidwell said, "you know this is only fair. You're the one who's brought it on yourself, you know, by being so sorry and mean to my friend David."

Only when the silver was clean to his satisfaction did Tidwell stop wiping. He pushed Kelso aside and took the silver nugget back over to David.

"You'll want to clean it up some more down at the creek yonder. I cleaned it as best I could for you, but some water would do it better."

David took the silver, sniffing and feeling embarrassed that he had cried. "Thank you, Alonz." He fired a furious glance at the seething Kelso. "I reckon we could clean it by making Kelso wash it in his mouth."

"Well, we could," Tidwell said very seriously. "If you want, I'll do that, David."

David shook his head. "Reckon not. I'll not squat so low as to be on his level."

Kelso looked very relieved for a moment, and then his look of fury returned. He glared with hatred at David, who curled his lip defiantly, turned, and headed down to the creek.

Kneeling by the water, David washed the silver clean and put it back in its pouch. He was rising to go back to the camp when something pounded him hard between the shoulder blades and toppled him into the bitterly cold water. He thrashed and whooped and gasped for breath, struggling to come to his feet.

Ben Kelso stood on the bank, laughing. "That'll learn you!" he declared. "You don't play Ben Kelso for no fool!"

"Boy! Benjamin Kelso!"

The voice was Siler's. Fists clenched and swinging at his sides, he strode down to the creek. "I saw you push him in, boy, so there's no point you denying it. And Alonz told me what you done before. You've crossed the mark. I'll stand for no man in my hire causing a ruction amongst his companions."

Kelso spluttered, then said, "It ain't true! Them two, they're lying to you, trying to make me look bad."

"It don't take lies to make you look bad, boy," Siler said. "The truth does that, with no help. You've had a way of graveling me ever since I hired you on. I've never made a bigger mistake in my life, I don't reckon."

David clambered up out of the water. The cold wind hit him and made his teeth chatter. Siler dourly looked him over, and motioned him back toward the camp. "Dry yourself out by the fire and get to bed, before you catch your death of it. As for you, young Kelso, you'll be on your way in the morning. I'll have no more part of you."

"Old jackass!" Kelso muttered.

Siler raised his foot, kicked Kelso into the water and watched him flounder there. "I'm an old jackass who can still kick, as you can see. I'll give you your pay in the morning, and you can go."

"I'll take my pay tonight!" Kelso yelled back. "I ain't sleeping another night in your camp, old man!"

"Well, if that's your intention, I'd dry myself by the fire before I left, boy," Siler said. "But you'll have to wait until David's done it first."

"I'm freezing half to death!"

"Just half to death, eh? Well, then I reckon you'll pull through it just fine."

Siler turned and walked back up to the camp, David at his side.

"Mr. Siler, if you don't care, I'd like to give Ben his pay," David said.

"You?"

"Yes sir. There's a special way I have in mind to do it."

Kelso came grumbling and glowering and shivering back into the camp some minutes later and let the fire dry him. Silence hung over the camp. Siler was at his supper, eating without talking, keeping his eye on Kelso.

"I want my pay," Kelso said when his clothes were dry.

"Take it. It's over yonder."

"Where?"

David answered this time. "Tucked right up that there cow fundament, safe and sound! Just lift the tail and finger it out! It's as easy as picking your nose, just like you said your own self."

When Kelso stomped away from the camp minutes later, cursing and wiping his finger on his trousers, laughter followed him a long way into the darkness. Tidwell laughed louder and longer than any of them. He was still cackling and chortling when David crawled back into his bedroll. When David finally fell asleep, Tidwell had gone from laughing to talking to no one in particular. David paid no attention to the content of his chatter, but when he dreamed that night, it was of chickens.

Chapter 11

After the Kelso incident, David's feelings toward Siler warmed considerably. He knew now that Siler truly liked him and valued his work—obviously he valued it far more than he had that of Kelso. David felt a sense of being part of things in a way he hadn't felt before. That evening his usual bout with homesickness was notably absent. Siler was no longer a resented authority, but a defender.

"We'll be there this afternoon," Siler announced the next day. "Lord knows I'm ready to be home again."

Indeed, they reached the home of Peter Hartley in early afternoon. Siler had a reunion with his family that David thought was surprisingly emotional, and brought back his own homesickness for a few minutes. That faded, however, when Siler introduced him to his kin and described in glowing terms what a fine job he had done, then made a virtual ceremony out of presenting David with six dollars in pay. Tidwell received only three, but it didn't seem to bother him. David wondered if Tidwell even understood that he had come out with less pay for more work. Tidwell, after all, had been with Siler even before David was bound on at the tavern.

After supper that night, shared with the Hartleys around their big table, Siler called David aside. "I've been generous with you, giving you six dollars for a few miles of herding. Now, I expect, you may be thinking of going

home. I don't want you to do that. I want you to stay on
and work for me here for a time. You're a good hand for
work, and I can use you."

"Well, Mr. Siler . . . I don't know what to say. My
pap might be looking for me, and my mother will worry
if I don't get home before too long."

"They won't worry. They ain't looking for you back
any particular time. I told your pap I might be keeping you
on for an ex-tree spell."

David had heard nothing about this before. He wondered if Siler was lying to him. His impulse was to say no,
that he would go home as planned. But Siler's looming,
pressuring presence made him hesitate to do that. He recalled his father's exhortations about honesty and obedi-
ence. Probably it was his duty to stay on, if that was what
Siler wanted . . . yet David didn't want to. He mumbled
and faltered, fidgeting on his feet.

Siler pressed his case. "Look out yonder at that snow
a-falling," he said. "It would be a fool thing for a young
fellow like you to to set off alone in the wintertime. Your
pap would have my hide if I let his boy set out alone in
such falling weather! You wouldn't want him to think ill
of me, would you?"

David said, "I'll stay for a while," then felt like kicking himself for doing so.

As days passed into weeks, he found further reason to
wish he had gone on. Siler worked him hard, but that
wasn't the problem. What worried David was that Siler
talked about work they would be doing in the spring and
summer, and it became clear that he had no intention of
David going home at all. The warmer feelings David had
developed for Siler after the brawl with Kelso quickly
cooled again. He began to perceive Siler as an imprisoner,
a man who would seek his own advantage in David
Crockett's disadvantage.

David decided that he would have no choice but to
escape. And "escape" was exactly how he thought of it.
As far as he was concerned, he was under legal obligation
to Siler and couldn't leave at will. All he could do was run
off.

But how best to do it? After careful thought, he concluded that the most promising option was to make Siler believe he was happy in his situation, then take whatever opportunity for leaving that presented itself. After all, the roads were heavily traveled with westward-moving travelers. Surely he could take up with one of them. In the meantime, he would make the best of his circumstances and take whatever pleasure he could find in them.

Among those pleasures was a friend—a boy his own age who lived in a house a couple of miles up the road from Siler's place, which was close to Hartley's. Whenever Siler gave David time away from labor, David would trudge the two miles and spend whatever time he had in recreation, playing marbles with round pebbles, using slings to fling stones at unwitting birds, skipping stones on a nearby pond, making and shooting crude bows and arrows, setting rabbit snares, and other boyish pursuits.

On one particular Sunday afternoon about a month after his arrival in Virginia, the day's recreation consisted of fighting with snowballs. A three-inch snowfall had come the night before, and it was a wonderfully sticky snow, the kind that packs nicely in the hand and makes excellent missiles.

David had just delivered his companion a solid shot to the side of the head when he heard the snow-muffled approach of the wagons. He stopped and cupped a hand over his brows, squinting as he looked down the road, because the sun had come out and made the snow blindingly brilliant. His companion came to his side.

"What are you staring at? It's just another bunch of wagoners."

"I believe I know one of them," David replied, squinting harder.

There were three wagons in all, pulled by stout teams. Two were driven by young men, the third one by an older fellow. It was this one who seemed familiar to David.

The wagons rolled up closer, having a harder go of it because of the snow than they would have otherwise. David and his friend stepped aside, letting the first two pass.

The third wagon pulled up closer, then stopped after its driver got a look at David's face.

"Well, howdy there, young man!" the old man said, grinning. "Have you tanned out any good buckskin lately?"

David's heart rose and sang. As he had thought, it was Dunn, the elderly wagoner who had admired his work on the buckskin many weeks ago! He grinned back. "No, sir, not lately."

"Last time I seen you, young fellow, you surely had. That was fine tanning you done on that deerhide." He looked more closely at David. "Have I mistook you? You are the Crockett boy, ain't you?"

"Yes sir, I am."

"You're a long way from home, Mr. Crockett."

David licked his lips nervously. He wasn't the kind to impose himself on others much, but this was a unique situation, and Dunn represented the best chance he might soon find to break free of his bondage. "Maybe I won't be for much longer . . . if you can help me, Mr. Dunn. Reckon I could talk to you in private?"

Dunn flicked his brows, looking confused and slightly wary. "Well, I reckon so. We'll step right over here."

David advanced and talked in low tones to Dunn. It proved difficult to communicate. His playmate, very curious, kept sneaking in close to listen, causing David to further drop his volume, which only made it harder for the slightly hard-of-hearing Dunn to understand him. When he finally did understand, he stepped back, a concerned expression on his face.

"That's quite a request," he said. "I am fearful of entwining myself with the bad side of the law if I fulfill it."

"Please, Mr. Dunn. You may be the only good chance I get for Lord knows how long. I'm pining for home mighty bad."

Dunn fooled with the back of his neck and made funny shapes with his lips, the very image of discomfort. At length he sighed and relaxed.

"Very well. I'll help you—*if* you'll show me you're serious."

"I'm serious. Just tell me what to do."

On the way back to Siler's, David could hardly keep from dancing down the road. Freedom loomed, big as the sky and wonderfully inviting. It was all going to work out. He could sense it. Before the night was through, he would be a free soul again, out on the road and heading for home.

Chapter 12

David walked into the yard of Siler's house at sunset, as snow fell profusely all around him. He looked about in confusion. Usually the Siler place was buzzing with activity, but now it was dark and silent.

"Hello!" he called. "Mr. Siler?"

No one answered. David went to the door and found it open. He walked in, calling again, still receiving no reply. A grin stole onto his face. "They ain't home!" he whispered to himself. "They've gone off on one of their Sunday visits, I do believe!"

Surely fortune was on the side of David Crockett today! He could hardly believe that two strokes of luck would come in such quick succession. First, to encounter Dunn so unexpectedly, and find him open to his plea for help, then to come back to Siler's and find the family gone—this was a fine situation indeed! With the Silers away, he could pack his few possessions and be ready for the night's escape into the welcome custody of the wagoner Dunn.

Dunn had told David that he and his sons would spend the night at an inn about seven miles west of Siler's place. If David could reach the inn by daybreak, when Dunn planned to depart, he would be welcome to join their party.

David gathered his things and bundled then in a cloth,

which he stuck beneath the head of his bed. Hardly had he finished when the Silers returned, talking loudly about the heavy snow and the cold.

He made sure his pack was hidden, then met them at the door. He looked out past them into the night, and his heart sank. The snow was piled up to five or six inches, and still falling fast.

He wondered if he would be able to meet the challenge that faced him. His gratitude toward Dunn took a significant drop. Blast the old fellow! He had said he was willing to help him return home, but the scheme he had laid out would be hard to follow in such a storm as this.

Maybe that was Dunn's intention, David thought. Maybe he had wanted to make it hard for him to get away, just so he wouldn't have to involve himself in spiriting away a bound-out boy. David glowered into the storm, thinking: Well, old Dunn, if that was your scheme, you'll find yourself surprised when I walk up and shake your hand in the morning, and hold you to the bargain!

The Silers had apparently enjoyed their neighborly visit and did not seem eager to retire. David sat and listened to their talk, fidgeting and casting surreptitious glances out the window every chance he got, hoping to see a decline in the snowstorm. There was none. Why, of all times, did such a storm have to strike this very night? Why would providence tease him with such a promising opportunity for escape, only to nullify it with a blizzard? It was terribly frustrating.

David went to bed well before any of the others did, and pretended to sleep. His mind was filled with the images of his family back at the tavern. He longed in particular to see his mother.

At long last the Silers retired and the house fell silent. David lay unmoving, listening until he was sure that all were sleeping. Then he rose and put on his coat and boots, hand-me-downs from one of the older brothers, which were already worn-out when David had gotten them. Silently and slowly, all but holding his breath, he slipped out of the house and into the cold night.

The snow drove down, heavy and stinging cold. David held his pack against himself and huddled inside his coat as he set off, taking high steps over the heaping white at his feet. There was no moon and the darkness was virtually impenetrable by the eye. He headed for the road, moving as fast as he could, hoping that he could make the seven-mile journey without freezing.

By the time he reached the road, there was no trace of its bounds left visible to the eye. Even the rutted tracks left by the wagons that had traveled it through the day were filled, leaving David to judge the road's location solely by the gap it made through the timber.

He set the image of his family firmly in his mind, refusing to think of anything else, and walked as fast as he could. His heart began to hammer under his ribs, making his pulse ring in his nearly frostbitten ears. He walked for the longest time, wondering how far he had come. To his right he saw the house of the playmate he had been with when Dunn's wagons came along.

Two miles. Five more to go. He was seriously wondering if he could make it. Should he return to Siler and try to escape another day? At the very least he would be inside warm walls. He thought of the bed he had abandoned, of its thickness and warmth, heavy quilts atop him. . . .

No. *No.* He would rather risk freezing than remain where he had been. He pushed ahead.

It seemed to him that the trek down the empty road lasted the duration of two nights strung together with no day between them, and though he knew this was an illusion, knowing it didn't ease the trial. Teeth chattering, fingers numb against his pack, he struggled forward.

The snow was rising deeper by the minute. He could no longer feel his feet inside his boots, and that scared him. Once he had seen a man who had lost his toes to frostbite, and it had been an ugly sight. The tracks he left behind began filling with new snow almost as soon as he made them. That, at least, was good. Siler would not be able to follow him. Maybe providence wasn't against him after all.

He was near to collapse when finally he saw the gatepost of the inn where Dunn and his sons had stayed. He was making for the door, figuring he would have to pound it to waken the occupants and gain entrance, when he saw a human figure at the side of the building, where the barn and stable stood. There were horses there too. Maybe Dunn had risen before daylight to feed and hitch his teams.

"Hello!" he called. His face was so frozen he could barely mouth out the word. His lungs ached from breathing the cold air. "Hello!"

"Who goes there?" Dunn's voice! David was overwhelmed with relief. His dangerous trek was over. He had made it.

"It's David Crockett!" he called back. "I've come . . . like I said. . . ."

He fell face forward into the snow, feeling inexplicable warmth wash over him. The snow was soft, not at all chilling. He wanted to sink into it like it was a heap of soft feathers. It was even better than the bed he had been dreaming of.

Smiling, congratulating himself for his successful escape, he closed his eyes.

They poured hot tea down his throat and warmed him by the fire. Dunn hovered around him like a nurturing angel, exclaiming all the while about David's grit and determination.

"I was sure we wouldn't see you, boy, not in this storm," he said. "Why, I can't think of another living soul who would have set out to walk the distance you have in such a mess as this!"

David thought: I'll wager you were counting on me not walking it either. But what he said out loud was: "Will you take me with you, like you said?"

"I will indeed. I wouldn't turn you back for anything, not after all you've gone through, bless your soul! You must be truly longing to see your kin, boy."

"Yes sir, I am."

They ate a good breakfast, and David's cost him not

a penny, because the innkeeper was as impressed as Dunn was, and made the meal a gift of honor. And he firmly promised David he would reveal nothing to Siler, should he come asking. Old Siler never had set too well with him anyhow. Always looking out for himself at everyone else's expense.

The wagons, bound for Knoxville, set out shortly after daylight. No more snow fell, and the temperature rose, slowly transforming the snow into muddy slush. The wagons almost bogged down on the road, and moved far too slowly to suit David, who grew so impatient he began counting the sluggish turns of the wheels and trying to estimate the miles.

He looked behind him often, watching for Siler—though he knew that Siler could hardly catch up to him this quickly, on such a bad road, if he even bothered to follow.

The wagons were slow, but they were steady, and as the day passed David felt more and more secure. He determined that even if Siler caught up with him, he would not go back. Dunn would surely rally to his aid in such a situation.

David closed his eyes and thought about the warm tavern and the welcoming embrace of his mother. He smiled. Home lay ahead.

The teams trudged, the mud-coated wheels turned over slowly, and the next day it was the same. By the time forty miles were behind and they had neared the Roanoke and the house of one John Cole, a friend of Dunn's, David's warm anticipation of home was matched by intense frustration. He was sure the wagons moved at about half the speed he could make on foot, and though he felt deeply obliged to Dunn, he had decided to set out on his own. He didn't want Dunn to think him ungrateful, but he simply couldn't wait. To continue at this snail's pace would surely bedevil him right out of his sanity.

They spent the night at Cole's, then the next morning David set out. Dunn disliked the notion, and begged him to reconsider, but David would not listen. Waving good-bye to his benefactors, he took up his pack and began walking.

He had gone only a short distance when he heard someone coming up behind him on the road. Turning, he saw a man riding on a horse and leading another. When he noted that the led horse was saddled but riderless, he had a fright. Might old Siler have sent this man after his run-away hireling? David thought of running, but decided that would only make matters worse. He could see already that the rider was a stranger to him, and so would not know the face of David Crockett if he saw it. David determined to use a false identity should the question be put directly to him.

"Howdy," the man said when he reached David.

"Hello."

"A cold day to be traveling, eh? Especially on foot."

The question made David suspicious. "I don't mind it."

"Well, where you heading? We seem to be going the same direction."

"Into Tennessee. Jefferson County."

"That right? Well, so am I—well, not exactly. I ain't going to Jefferson County, and I won't be staying in Tennessee. Passing through. I'm Kentucky-bound."

David's suspicions declined, just a little. The man's manner seemed open enough, and his talk of Kentucky didn't have the ring of a lie. That riderless horse still worried him, though. He looked back at it, and the man noticed.

"Fine horse, that one," he said. "All I have left of a herd I sold at market yesterday. The saddle was part of my payment." He rubbed his chin. "In that it seems we're going to be on the same road for a time, why don't you make that saddle useful? Climb up and ride. Rest your feet."

"I don't mind walking."

"I won't hear of it. My name's Wilkerson, by the way. Abe Wilkerson."

David wondered if this Wilkerson was pulling a ploy

on him. "I'm Persius Tarr," he said. For some strange reason, it was the first name that came to mind.

Wilkerson gave him an odd look. "Tarr?" He paused, seeming confused or troubled. A moment later, however, his expression warmed again. "Tarr! Now, there's a good and rare name, and a rare name, like a rare jewel, is all the finer, eh? Pleased to meet you, Persius."

David shook Wilkerson's hand. A decision faced him, and he made it quickly. He would risk a little trust and accept Wilkerson's offer, even though his doubts were far from settled. After all, if Wilkerson proved treacherous and tried to take him back to Siler, all he would have to do is leap off and run. He was fleet; he could outrun this fellow on foot, and take to the brush if he tried to follow on horseback. And if Wilkerson proved to be no more than the helpful soul he purported himself to be, well, traveling by horseback beat walking any day.

David mounted. It felt deliciously good to spread his aching legs across the saddle and rest his feet in the stirrups. With Wilkerson's help, he tied his pack behind him, and they set off, heading toward the Roanoke River.

The horses crossed the cold river and plodded up the far bank. Abe Wilkerson sang a drinking song, then a hymn, then another drinking song. David relaxed. He trusted Wilkerson far more now. If he had been sent by Siler to bring him back, he wouldn't have taken him across the river.

They traveled steadily and without incident. Entering Tennessee, they took a route through Blountville and on into Carter's Valley and Rogersville, where David wished he could seek out his grandparents' graves. He could not, however, without revealing that he had lied about his identity, a fact of which he now felt ashamed.

They went on until they came to a point six miles from the Holston River. Beyond the Holston, David would have only another eight or nine miles to go to his home. He could hardly wait.

The point of parting had come. Wilkerson's road led to the north, David's across the Holston, on to Cheek's

Crossroads, then to the tavern. He said a sincere farewell to Wilkerson.

"Persius," Wilkerson said, "there's one thing I must know, and I know no other way to ask it than straight out. Were you the horse thief I heard talk of at the market?"

David gaped. "Horse thief! No, no. I've never stolen a horse—I've stolen nary a thing!" Why was Wilkerson talking this way? Was he going to turn on him here at the end?

"Well, I believe you, if you say so. I've never been one to confuse gossip with gospel. But you might want to know that there's much talk in Virginia of a Persius Tarr who stole a fine Chickasaw horse from a farmer on the James River. He's said to be a lone sort of thief, who run off a couple or so years back from a blacksmith he had been bound to by the Orphan Court."

"Run off . . ." This was the first David had heard of Persius's flight from bondage back in Greene County.

Wilkerson went on. "Now, Persius Tarr ain't a name I'd expect to find on more than one human being in any given century, but if you say that ain't you, then I believe you. But you take care, hear? There's others that might not be so quick to take your word as I am."

"I'll be careful."

"Good-bye, Persius. Maybe our paths will cross again someday."

David watched him ride away, marveling that news of his old companion Persius had come so unexpectedly. Not good news, to be sure, but news still.

He was glad to know Persius was still alive. Of course, he might not be alive much longer, if he had truly turned horse thief. Frontier justice, both formal and informal, had little patience for a stealer of horseflesh.

David drew a deep breath, turned toward home and began striding across the wintry countryside. Fifteen miles to go—a long trek by most standards. To David, with hundreds of miles behind him, it seemed like no distance at all.

Chapter 13

The David Crockett who returned from Virginia was not the David Crockett who had left home months before. Trials of the trail had matured his mind and hardened his body. He was taller and leaner, making him look gangly, disguising the increased strength of his muscles.

His parents seemed proud of his safe and successful return. John Crockett was pleased most of all by the money David brought home. He had had spent very little of the pay Siler had given him. John claimed it all and applied it to one of his many debts, which, along with taxes, plagued the man like fleas on a dog. Sometimes he was able to pay off what he owed, many other times not. The three hundred acres he had owned on Mossy Creek, and to which he had briefly considered moving after the mill disaster, had been sold by the sheriff in 1795. And in 1798 one Gideon Morris had gone to his grave having never collected the payment for thirty-five bushels of Indian corn John Crockett had bought from him on credit all the way back in 1783. John Crockett had a propensity for falling in debt to any neighbor kind enough to extend him credit.

But he had one admirable trait—though David came to think of it more as troublesome. John wanted to see his sons educated. Belief in the value of education was typical of the Scots-Irish from whom he had descended. John had a full share of the mixed Scots-Irish nature: ruggedness, freedom from tradition followed solely for its own sake, occasional suspiciousness and intolerance of those who were different, clannishness, adaptability, loyalty, dislike of too much government.

In the fall of 1799, David found himself sent off for an education. East of nearby Barton's Spring, a man named Benjamin Kitching had set up a school, and to and from this school the Crockett brothers trod each day. David found education a hateful, stifling affair. What need did he have of book learning? He had already traveled in the world and made his way on his own. Besides that, certain of the other scholars in Kitching's school had a way of getting on David's nerves.

The main problem was one Andrew Duff, who began as David's friend and quickly became his enemy. Duff was the biggest, oldest, and perhaps the most intelligent of Kitching's pupils, and his favorite. To Kitching's face he was unctiously respectful, almost worshipful; when Kitching's back was turned, he would imitate the man's rather peculiar crumpling smile, which was generally described among the pupils as making Kitching's round, wrinkled face look like a "dried-up tater." Duff could mimic the smile to near perfection, and used his skill to inflict a tormenting amusement on the other students, who of course didn't dare laugh out loud for fear of alerting Kitching.

At the time David entered Kitching's school, he was of a frame of mind that placed a high value on cleverness. This resulted mostly from the reaction of his brothers to his story of how he had gotten his colorful revenge on Kelso in the incident on the trail to Virginia. He related the tale on the way to the first day of school, and his brothers thought it uproarious and praised David profusely for his cleverness. For the first time, David realized that wit could do more than entertain. It could win a person the respect of others.

He was thinking about that when he saw Duff's mimicry of old Kitching the first time. It was like a moment of inspiration. In Duff he instantly perceived a worthy mentor.

When the school turned out for the midday meal, David made a point of meeting Duff, and with toe scuffing dirt and eyes on the ground, mumblingly told him of his admiration. Duff accepted the praise with haughty satisfaction, and allowed David to share his company while they ate.

Their friendship, born quickly, died the same way. David had proudly seated himself beside Duff in the little classroom, while Duff looked appropriately indifferent. The day's lessons began, Kitching went through his usual lectures and gestures, and David waited for his chance. Kitching eventually gave it to him. He came to David's seat, asked him a language question—which David failed utterly to answer—then turned away. David glanced at Duff, then did an imitation of Kitching's smile, just as Duff was about to do the same.

Duff's eyes became cold as gray iron. He gave David a look of astonishment that rapidly evolved to anger. At the same time, a quiet gasp of admiration whispered through the class. David's mimicry of Kitching's smile had been even closer to the real thing than Duff's best effort of the past.

Kitching heard the murmur and turned. His eye, guided by schoolmaster's intuition, swept to David. "Mr. Crockett," he said, "are you providing some sort of—of diversion for your fellow scholars while my back is turned?"

"No sir."

"It ain't true," Duff said. "He was mimicking you, Mr. Kitching."

"Oh?" Kitching replied, brows lifted. "Is this true, Mr. Crockett?"

"No sir," David said. He was stunned. Duff, whom he so admired, had betrayed him!

Duff's small-boned little sister, who sat in the back of the room and who was known to adults for miles around as "a fine young woman," and who had been extolled from three local pulpits as an incarnate example of decency and honesty, raised her hand. "That's not true, Mr. Kitching. He did do it. I saw him."

David turned and gave her a silent snarl. She looked at him down her nose, with brows arrogantly lifted.

Kitching advanced. "You will spend an extra hour in this schoolroom today, Mr. Crockett, after everyone else has gone home. I'll remain with you, and you may work on the additional assignment you will receive as a special gift from me to you."

After that, David Crockett had no more use for either Kitching or Duff. His hatred festered and seethed, and the desire for vengeance—particularly against Duff—burned like fever.

The next day he found a seat far across the room from Duff, and spent the morning lost in dark plans. Kitching strode about and lectured, but to David he was merely a noisemaking, moving mass of dull color. By midday David had made up his mind about how best to deal with Duff.

There was nothing subtle or witty about his plan this time. Duff deserved a straightforward thrashing, nothing less, and David intended to provide it.

During the afternoon spelling period, David found his opportunity to escape. Kitching was occupied with some of the older students, including Duff, and while his back was turned, David slipped out of the classroom and headed toward the outhouse in the yard. He did not return, but instead slipped down the road and hid himself in the roadside brush. He knew Duff's daily route homeward. He would pass this way.

The next thing David was aware of was awakening suddenly to the sound of voices on the road. He had dozed off in the thicket. He sat up on his knees, rubbing his eyes, then peered out through the brush. It was Duff! He was coming down the road with his sister at his side. David stood, clenching his fists, tensing his muscles, trying to quickly regain the sense of determination that sleep had taken from him.

Duff let out a yell of alarm when David emerged from the brush in a leap. The girl screeched and dropped her books. "I'll whup you, horseface!" David shouted. The girl screeched again and hid her face. "Not you!" David clarified. "Him!" And then he tore into Duff, fingers spread like a wildcat's paws, and raked a long, bloody series of scratches down the left side of Duff's face.

Duff howled and fell back, grappling at his own face. His sister wept in the background. David lunged forward again, pounding his fists into Duff's belly, then followed up with a punch to his chin. In the meantime, others of Kitching's scholars were coming up the road and discovering the violent spectacle. In moments David and his foe were surrounded by a circle of yelling, cheering boys, urging on the fight.

In truth, it wasn't much of a fight. By all objective standards, Duff should have won, having superior height, weight, and reach. What he lacked was the will and the skill. He was a joker, not a fighter, and within two minutes he was on his back, David straddling him, raining blows onto his face and chest, Duff crying and trying to cover his nose to keep it from being broken.

"Make him say uncle, Davy!" one of the onlookers urged.

"Say uncle!" David yelled.

"Uncle!" Duff shouted.

"Uncle who?"

"Uncle Davy!"

"I can't hear you!"

"Uncle Davy! Uncle Davy!"

David exhaled slowly. Great dollops of sweat dripped from him. "That's good. That's fine. You've been whupped, Duff."

He got up, panting for breath, and brushed himself off. His clothing was disheveled and he was covered with dirt. Immediately he was surrounded, his shoulders pounded in admiration, his hands grasped and shaken vigorously. David grinned. He was a victor, and it felt good. Duff rose and limped away, his weeping sister giving him ineffectual comfort.

David straightened his clothing as best he could and washed himself off at a nearby stream. By the time he was home, his exhilaration had faded. He prayed his parents would not somehow detect he had been fighting. Lately his father had been drinking quite a lot, and growing more stern than ever. David didn't want to think about how John Crockett might react if he found out what had happened.

He was fortunate. John was busy through the late afternoon, and drinking in the evening, and took no notice of any of his children. Rebecca gave David a strange look or two, but said nothing.

The next morning David awakened with a sobering realization. Surely Duff would make sure that Kitching learned every brutal detail of the fight. Given Kitching's affection for his favorite pupil, David knew full well that all he had to look forward to at school was retaliation of the fiercest variety.

He discussed his fears with his siblings on the way to school, and received no comfort. "There's only one thing for you to do," Wilson said. "You'll have to lay out."

"What do you mean?"

"Stay out of school until old Kitching cools off. None of us will tell Mama or Pap ... will we?" He looked around at the other Crocketts.

All gave their pledge of secrecy, and David headed for the woods, where he idled away the day. The next few days were the same. David began enjoying this life of leisure and woodland recreation. By gum, he had won his vengeance over Duff and gotten away with it!

And then it ended. He returned home with his brothers one afternoon and was called aside by a solemn and bleary-eyed John Crockett, whose breath carried the heavy smell of alcohol.

John held up a piece of paper. "This here's a note from your schoolmaster, asking me why I ain't sent you for schooling the last six days. 'Pears to me you got some explaining to do, David Crockett."

David blanched. His mouth fell open but no words emerged. Kitching had counterstruck, and David had been utterly unprepared for it.

"You been laying out, ain't you, boy?"

"Yes sir."

"Why?"

"Because I know old Kitching will whup me if I go back."

"Why would he whup you?"

David's throat felt very dry. "Because I had a knock fight with another fellow."

John shook his head. "I should have figured it. You've got mighty airish and biggity in your ways, David. You think that because you trailed to Virginny and back you're a full-growed man. Well, you ain't. You're a boy, and you've done wrong, and I want you to turn tail right now and head back to that schoolhouse with me to tell Mr. Kitching what's been going on."

"Go back? But Kitching ain't there. School's out for the day."

"If he ain't there, we'll find him. Let's go."

David was beginning to get mad. His father, drunk and drooling and stinking, disgusted him. The idea of being forced back by a sorry drunk to face a sorrier schoolmaster was more than he could handle.

"I won't do it!"

"What? You're defying me, boy?"

"I won't go back to Kitching. Call that what you want to call it, you old drunkard!"

John's eyes widened, red and hot as the apocalyptic lake of fire. "You disrespecting little poot, I reckon you're due a little bringing down!" He staggered off to the side and hefted up a heavy hickory stick from the stack of firewood beside the tavern. "Turn around and take your whupping like the man you seem to think you are!"

David did turn, but not for punishment. He took off at a dead run. John Crockett cursed and shouted for him to halt, but he kept going. John began to chase him, waving the hickory stick.

It was a long and frantic chase, and David led it, very deliberately, in the direction opposite the schoolhouse. He was astounded that his father was capable of such a run. A half mile of ground fell away behind his racing feet, then three-quarters, but still John Crockett kept up his end. About the mile mark, David saw a hill rise before him. Spurred by inspiration, he crossed it and ducked sideways off the trail and into the bushes. He lay very still, trying to control his panting, and watched the road from hiding. A half minute later John Crockett came puffing and gasping over the hilltop, and continued on, hickory pole in hand.

David closed his eyes. His ploy had worked. When his breath returned, he rose and headed deeper into the forest. There would be no returning home today. Maybe not ever. He had defied his father and disputed his authority. To go back now would be to take a beating even more severe than the one he had escaped.

David was glad for his escape, but saddened and sobered as well by an understanding of what this meant. Once again he was on his own—but this time he had no paying work, no protective guide, no prospects, not even a pack of clothing or food.

David Crockett was alone in the world, and any way he made in it, he would have to make entirely on his own.

Chapter 14

At first David just walked for its own sake, having no idea where to go or what to do. Eventually he forced himself to a halt, sat down on a stump and called to mind something his uncle Joseph Hawkins had once advised him: "There's nothing gained in going if you ain't figured where it is you're going to."

David reasoned it out. He couldn't return home; that much was clear. In his boyish mind the prospect of his father's wrath loomed monstrously. But neither could he simply set out across the country with no provisions, no work, and no destination.

For a quarter of an hour he sat there, pondering, his elbows on his knees and his chin resting in his hands. Then his expression brightened and he stood with resolution. He had a place to go after all, and perhaps even a way to escape his father's domain, and Kitching's, long enough for tempers to cool.

The walk that followed covered several miles. When David reached his destination, he felt edgy and nervous. He had come to Cheek's Crossroads, a major landmark that almost every traveler through the area passed through and often lingered at. It was possible that his father, surely by now having ended his chase with the hickory pole, would figure out that he might come here. This was a busy place, a natural spot to which people on the move migrated. So David looked carefully about before making his appearance in the yard of the man he had come seeking, Jesse Cheek, who lived at the crossroads named for his family, and operated a large, well-known store there.

The first person he saw, however, was his own brother James, a handsome, strong man of about twenty. When James saw David, he looked startled, put down the saddle he had been about to lift onto the back of a tethered horse and ran to meet his younger brother.

"David? Is something wrong back home?"

"I reckon there is!"

A look of dread came over James. "Oh, Lordy! Somebody's dead?"

"Not yet. But I'll wish I was dead if I go back, or if Pap catches me here. I've run off, James. I had no choice, or Pap would have beat the fire out of me with a hickory pole."

He told his puzzled brother the story about Duff, the fight, the hooky playing, and finally the chase. Jesse Cheek came around the house about the time David began, and heard most of the tale. James listened to it all with an increasingly dour expression, but Cheek laughed loudly at several parts. David was almost offended. He felt like his life was in the balance, and Cheek was laughing! David gave Cheek no indication of his offense, however, because it was Cheek who would rule on the request he was about to make.

"I want to go with you and James, Mr. Cheek," David said. "I've herded cattle before, all the way to Virginia, and I can do the work."

James cut in. "David, that's fool talk. There's nothing for you to do but to head back home and face up to what's due you."

"I can't go back! Pap'll flay the hide off me!"

"You've earned it, if he does."

Jesse Cheek waved his hands. "Peace among the brethren!" he extolled. "David, step over yonder and finish up saddling that horse for James. Me and him, we got some man-to-man talking to do."

David saddled the horse while watching the men con-

verse, their backs turned toward him, their voices low and
inaudible. From the way James was waving his hands and
talking, David surmised that Cheek must have indicated a
willingness to take him on against James's wishes. That
was encouraging. Cheek was a persuasive and stubborn
man, whereas James could be worn down with only a little
argument, and it seemed Cheek was giving him plenty.

David finished his job, squatted beside the horse and
waited for the verdict. When Cheek turned around with a
grin on his face, David leaped up, beaming. He knew he
had been accepted even before they told him.

James shrugged in surrender. "It appears you're coming with us, David. I suppose it won't matter in the end.
I'm too big for Pap to whup, so if he gets wrought up, no
harm should come of it to me. Don't know about you,
though, David. Pap will hold that thrashing in store for
you a long time. He holds to a grudge like a mud turtle
holds to a toe, and you'll have to come home and face him
sooner or later."

"I like the sound of later," David replied. "I want to
give him time to get over being so mad. I'm afraid he'd
beat me near to death if he got his hands on me just now."

They drove the herd through the wintry countryside
of eastern Tennessee, moving up the well-trodden road toward Virginia. Along the way they met many travelers,
ranging from emigrant families on their way to home-
steads farther west, to trains of wagons laden with cargo,
and even one string of fourteen belled packhorses, a sight
seldom seen now that the roads were fit for wagons.

David watched the string of beasts pass, each laden
with two hundred pounds of salt and other commodities on
wooden packsaddles, as well their own feed of dried corn
and beans. At the head of the train was a buckskinned
frontiersman, wearing a felt slouch and looking at the
world through eyes that were crinkles in a face of old
leather. He might have been a long hunter from decades
past, or a scout for some frontier army of the days of revolution. The image of that frontiersman, a breed already

fading, would remain with David through the years, an image from a time when the wilderness was still king and men still knew it, and respected its authority.

From Tennessee they headed into Abingdon, once known as the Wolf Hills because of the wolves that would howl there by night, then on to Lynchburg and Charlottesville, through Chester Gap, and finally to Front Royal, their destination. Cheek sold his horses to a man named Vanmetre, and there the party divided.

James Crockett remained with Jesse Cheek and the balance of the other drovers, planning a later return, but one of Cheek's brothers, eager to get back home because of pressing business, made an immediate start back toward Tennessee, and David was sent with him, mostly because James urged it. He had begun to worry again about how his parents would react when they found out he had helped his little brother run off.

Unfortunately, David's companion was a surly character who hadn't warmed to the young interloper throughout the entire journey, and he made little effort to be friendly. Worse, he took only one horse with him, riding it himself and never offering to let David ride at all.

After three days David had enough of this, thought back to his prior journey homeward, and told his partner that he would return on foot independently. The man seemed glad to hear it, even volunteered to give David some food and money to see him home again. David was cheered by this until the man handed him the paltry sum of four dollars, along with some dried-up biscuits, a hunk of hardened cheese, and a bag of partly molded jerky. David knew better than to ask for more, and graciously pretended more gratitude than he really felt.

He went on, leaving his companion behind. Near Lynchburg he decided to exchange some of his cash for food, and sought out a trading post.

He took off his hat as he climbed onto the porch of the store. Someone pushed open the door and walked out past him. At once David's thoughts were thrown back to that trading post in Greene Courthouse, where he had said good-bye to Persius Tarr. The sights and smells that came

through that opening door were much the same. Persius
. . . he wouldn't mind seeing him again, assuming he was
still around to be seen. He remembered the report of
Persius having made himself a reputation as a horse thief
not far from this very place. Persius could easily be dead.
Horse thieving was serious business, and could put even a
young fellow at the end of a noose just as quickly, or
quicker, than committing murder.

David had a light step developed in hunting and stalk-
ing, and always walked in the straight-paced Indian fashion, which he had found worked best for the long
cattle-driving treks of which he had already become a vet-
eran. He was far from clumsy, and so was very surprised
when he walked through the door and immediately fell
prone on the dirty floor. A rumble of masculine laughter
rolled through the building. Anger waved a hot hand
across David's face, leaving it red.

He came nimbly to his feet, furious. The thing he had
fallen over was a human foot, thrust out across his path.
He might have seen it had his sun-dilated eyes not been
adjusting to the shadowed store interior when he walked
through. He had been tripped, apparently for the entertain-
ment of the store patrons.

He wheeled to face the man who had tripped him.
Seated on a barrel just inside the door, the culprit was a
round-bellied, dirt-caked sack of flesh whose eyes had the
oddest, hollowest of glitters. The man was already grinning when David faced him. The smile was all gums and
tongue, no teeth there to show.

"You tripped me, you old jackass!" David yelled into
the broad and grinning face. "You think that's right funny,
I reckon, tripping up somebody for sport?"

More laughter came from the other side of the room.
David looked. There were six men there, a couple of them
behind the long counter, which pegged them as the store's
operators, the others either customers or, more likely, loiterers. All were laughing. David gave them his harshest
look, which had no effect at all. At age thirteen he was not
very intimidating.

The man by the door was still grinning, but not

laughing. He said nothing at all, staring at David in an infuriating but also disconcerting manner. David balled up a fist, thinking of striking the man ... but something made him hesitate. He looked closer into the face.

"That's right—calm down, young fellow," one of the men behind the counter said, seeing what was about to happen. "Can't you see that man is simpleminded? He didn't mean to trip you. He didn't even know he was doing it."

David stepped back, cocking his head. Birdlike, the man did the same, keeping the same silly grin on his face. In an unconscious reaction of surprise, David swept his hair back with his right hand, and the man on the barrel imitated the gesture.

"Ever seen a traveling show with one of them monkeys in it that'll do whatever he sees somebody else do?" asked the man behind the counter. "That's what this poor gent is like. You do something, he'll do it back at you. He wasn't trying to trip you, boy. He don't know what he's doing."

David's anger dissolved. He felt great pity for the man. "Well, I reckon there's nothing to be mad about."

"That's right, son. That's the Christian way of thinking. Can I help you, now?"

David bought the goods he had come for, mostly crackers, cheese, and other traveling foods, and stowed them here and there around his person. Meanwhile, the man by the door began to sing, loudly, in a language David didn't know.

"Listen at him!" one of the loiterers exclaimed. "He's a-going at it again!" He laughed loudly.

"I don't see what's so funny about some fool singing babble," one of the others said.

"It ain't babble," said the storekeeper. "That's French talk. I've heard it aplenty down in New Orleans. Don't you know nothing, Eli?"

"Does that man live here?" David asked.

"No, no. He was brought in here maybe an hour ago by a long-legged old lean fellow. Asked us to keep an eye on him while he went for some liquor. What was that you said about that long-legged fellow, Reuben?"

The indicated man cleared his throat and put on a proud expression. "I said, 'Look at them long legs! That there long-legged feller, he ort to file a lawsuit against the town for laying out the street too far below his hind end.' That's what I said, precisely."

The other men laughed until they were red-faced. David smiled politely. He had heard variations of the same line several times back home at the tavern.

The joker beamed at his audience and said, "Yes sir, I says, 'That feller ort to law-sue the town for laying out the street too far from his hind end.' Said it right off. 'The town has surely laid the street out too far below that fellow's hind end. He orta file a lawsuit.' Them was my exact words."

"Shut up, Reuben, shut up, before I shake my bowels out a-laughing!" one of the others pleaded, suffering in great fits of mirth.

David, far more amused at the men themselves than at the purported witticism, headed for the door. He paused in front of the man on the barrel. "I don't know if you can hear me or nothing, but I'm sorry I called you a jackass," he said in a low voice, so none of the others could hear.

The door burst open suddenly, making him jump back to avoid being struck. He looked up and blanched. Standing before him, clad in his distinctive beaded coat, was Fletcher, the old Indian trader who had taken his father and uncle to bring home Uncle Jimmy. John Crockett had shared the story of the resulting adventure many times, and the tense little battle in which the Frenchman trader named Beaulieu, who had treated Uncle Jimmy so animalistically, apparently had been hit by Uncle William's blind shot into the brush. . . .

David spun to face the man on the barrel again. *Beaulieu!* Who else could it be? He noted a scar on the wide forehead—a scar like a rifle ball would leave, entering the skull.

So now it was confirmed. Uncle William's shot had indeed struck Beaulieu, damaging his brain—and the pitiful result even now sat drooling and grinning before David's eyes.

"Out of the way, boy," Fletcher said, pushing David aside and going past him. He strode toward the counter, where the men had abruptly stopped laughing, now that the object of their mirth was present. Fletcher took three steps, then stopped, spun on his heels and looked sharply at David.

"Don't I know you, boy?"

"No sir. I don't reckon so."

"The devil you say ... you're the son of a Crockett, or I'm a son of a whore!"

David headed out the door on a dead run. Fletcher, cursing and yelling, chased after him, his long legs gaining ground despite David's best efforts. Panic began to set in. No, David thought. Fear will make him win. Fight back, no matter what. Always keep fighting back.

He ducked quickly to one side, wheeling and swinging down his hand to pick up a loose stone about the size of a large hen egg. Fletcher was no more than twenty feet from David when he let the stone fly. There was hardly time to aim; he threw almost totally by instinct.

The rock took Fletcher full in the forehead. He stopped like he had run into a wall, teetered, and fell sideways, blood streaming down both sides of his nose.

David laughed, not in taunting, but in the sheer joy of an unexpected victory. New energy rose inside him, and his legs churned at twice the speed they had moved before, taking him around the bend and out of sight in the woods. Fletcher, who surely by now had learned it did not pay to dally with a Crockett, would not catch him. Another David had met his Goliath, and the stone had flown as true for the latter-day David as it had for the first one.

Chapter 15

He heard the rumble of the wheels, smelled the horses, and finally saw the wagons. A long line of them, laden with casks, crates, and sacks, rolling slowly toward him.

David Crockett shifted to the side of the road and kept a steady pace, passing the wagon train. All the wagoners were strangers to him, but friendly enough, calling and waving, perhaps thinking it odd to see so young a traveler on foot alone.

David went on past; the train of wagons receded behind him. A glance at the sun and a rumble in his stomach told him it was nearly time to eat, and it crossed his mind that had he remained closer at hand, the wagoners might have offered an invitation for him to share their food, allowing him to stretch his own provisions further. It was a selfish thought, to be sure, but a young fellow with less than four dollars to see him through hundreds of miles had to think selfishly to survive.

He decided to turn back and catch up with the wagon train, even though that would temporarily take him away from the direction he needed to go. The pretext of looking for a dropped knife would serve the purpose, he figured.

David's hopes were fulfilled. The wagoners had stopped for their meal by the time he reached them, and several friendly voices called for him to join them. There proved no need to invent a story about a lost knife.

David was seated with trencher on his lap and bread in hand when a short, round fellow with a big grin splitting his ruddy face came to him, bearing his own laden trencher. With a grunt and mumble he settled his plump body down beside David, then stuck out his hand.

"Myers, Adam Myers," he said.

David swallowed a bite of bread. "David Crockett."

"Crockett! I once met a Crockett in my hometown. What was his name? John, I think. A constable or magistrate in Greene County, over in Tennessee. That's where I hail from. Greene Courthouse."

"John Crockett is my father."

"Law of Moses! What do you think of that? Where is your father these days? Bad fortune with that mill venture of his a few years back . . . I heard he had moved."

"Yes. He's in Jefferson County now, running a tavern for wagoners, not too far from Cheek's Crossroads."

"Well, I'm throwed, running across you out here. Alone and all, and young as you are."

David sensed that Myers was curious about his business, and volunteered, "I came with my older brother and some other folks, herding cattle. I'm on my way home; they'll be coming later."

"Oh. A cattle drover, are you? Have you ever worked with wagons?"

"I rode with a wagoner named Dunn for a short bit," David said. Myers nodded and lifted his brows, apparently assuming David meant he had worked with Dunn. David saw no need to correct the misunderstanding. He was beginning to catch the scent of a coming offer, and though he hadn't come looking for one, it couldn't hurt to hear out all the options.

Myers vindicated David's anticipation with his next sentence. "Young Mr. Crockett, perhaps you'd like to join my train," he said. "We're going to Gerardstown and after that will be returning to Tennessee. It wouldn't be much out of your way to come with us, and I'd pay you decent. I could use the help."

David weighed the possibility, and rejected it. "Thank

you, Mr. Myers," he said. "But I reckon I'd best be getting on home."

As David walked on a half hour later, his stomach nicely full, he told himself that he had gotten out of Myers all he had hoped for: a good, free meal. Still, Myers's invitation lingered in mind. And did he really need to get home, after all? Wouldn't it be as his brother had said: John Crockett holding his anger like a snapping turtle holding a toe? The drove to Front Royal had moved along at a fast clip, and David was making an even faster return journey. At this rate he would be home long before John Crockett had let go of his anger, and probably be worse off than before. And old Kitching would certainly have a thrashing of his own held in store for his wayward pupil.

David stopped, thought for a few moments, then turned. Myers's offer was seeming more enticing the longer he considred it. A side journey to Gerardstown would buy more time for tempers back home to cool, put an extra jingle in his pouch, and give him company and protection on the homeward journey, even if it did delay it.

He loped back to the wagon train. Myers greeted him with a grin and handshake. He seemed a jolly soul, the kind of employer who was a goodly companion as well.

David was sure he had made the right decision. He caught himself thinking that his father would be proud of him . . . but there was something uncomfortable about that idea, considering that it was his father he was running from, so he put the thought out of his mind.

"Well, I wonder who them folks are?" Adam Myers asked.

David was beside Myers on the wagon, shielding his eyes with his hand and peering hard at the approaching riders. "I can tell you who they are," he said. "That one on the roan horse is Jesse Cheek, and the fellow on the big black is my brother, James."

James Crockett wore a big smile by the time he was close enough for expressions to be visible. He had always been keen of eye, and had recognized David on the wagon while still far away.

"Dave, it's fine to see you," he said. "I ain't rested easy since you took off."

"I've done well enough," David replied.

"So I see—riding on a wagon instead of walking."

"Where's my brother?" Jesse Cheek asked.

"Way on toward home by now," David said. "We parted ways."

"You had a falling out?"

"No sir. Just parted ways." David didn't want to tell Cheek how his brother had hogged the saddle and left him to walk.

David introduced Myers to the others; hands were shaken on all sides. Myers said that he remembered having seen James back in Greene Courthouse when he was a much younger fellow. James said that Myers looked familiar to him too, then turned to David.

"Looks to me you're heading the wrong direction to go home," he said.

"I ain't going home, not yet," David responded. "I've hired myself out to Mr. Myers to go to Gerardstown. After that, we'll be coming back to Tennessee."

James frowned. "I don't know about that, David. The family will be fretting fierce over you by now. And if I go home and tell them it was me who helped you run off to begin with, and then that I let you head out with a bunch of wagoners—no offense to you, Mr. Myers—why, Pap'll probably take that hickory pole after me instead of you."

James's obvious intent was to stir David's feelings back toward home, but his mention of the hickory pole didn't help his case. David deeply feared the beating he was sure to receive.

"I've made Mr. Myers a pledge to work for him, at least as far as Gerardstown," David said.

"That's right," Myers added. He didn't seem so jolly now. James's attempts to lure away his employee apparently annoyed him.

James went at it hard. He reminded David of the time he had been away from home already, with none of the home kin knowing what had become of him. He talked of their sisters and mother, describing the tears they had surely shed over him and the prayers they must still be sending up for his safe return.

David was deeply affected by James's words and, to his own shame, began to cry. A great homesickness stirred in him—but each time it welled up, the image of John Crockett and his hickory pole arose to counter it. No, David decided. He could not return, not yet. He told James to give word that he was well and would be home as soon as his new work would allow it.

At last James accepted the inevitable, hugged his brother close and patted his shoulders with both hands. He hurried away quickly, trying to hide his tears, but David saw them and was wrenched.

He looked over his shoulder and watched James and his companions until they were out of sight. The wagons lurched forward, and David turned his gaze ahead.

At the moment, being a wagoner and far from home didn't seem to have much good about it at all, the threat of John Crockett's hickory stick notwithstanding.

They reached Gerardstown and disposed of their load. Afterward Myers sought a return cargo and could not find one. Eventually he heard of hauling work in another town, and went there. David did not follow, but remained in the Gerardstown area, working for a farmer, plowing and doing general labor, for twenty-five cents a day.

When Myers returned, David asked him if he was ready to return to Tennessee as planned, and discovered to his shock that Myers's scheme had changed. He still could find no return cargo to Tennessee, but he had located a profitable back-and-forth route between Virginia and Baltimore. For now, going home to Tennessee would have to wait.

Myers made the Virginia-Maryland run several times. David, in the meantime, continued laboring for the farmer, and saving his meager pay.

Spring came. David bought himself new clothing,

sought out Myers and asked if he could accompany him to
Baltimore. Myers had such a run planned, it turned out,
one that would require only two wagons. He agreed, and
David set off, seven dollars in his pocket, on a journey
that would take him farther from home than he had ever
been. Myers warned him of the dangers of the big city—
theft on every hand, scoundrels who could spot a newcomer at a glance and fleece him of his money in
noments. Might not David feel better about his seven dollars if Myers kept it for him? After all, Myers said, he was
a businessman, accustomed to keeping and guarding
money. David thought about it, and handed over his treasure.

An accident along the way caused damage to a
wagon, and very nearly injury to David, who was almost
crushed between the barrels of flour that made up the
cargo. After shifting as many of the barrels as possible to
a second wagon and making arrangements with a local
farmer to store the rest until they could return to get it,
they limped the rest of the way into Baltimore and took
the damaged wagon in for repairs that would take at least
two days to complete. They went back and fetched the
barrels they had stored with the farmer.

Then there was nothing to do but wait. David found
himself with more time to explore the city than he had anticipated, and set out to do so alone. Myers, who had
grown moody since the accident, had seen it all before,
and cared nothing about touring the town again.

Baltimore was a marvelous place to the young frontier boy. He had never seen so vast an expanse of buildings, nor so many people in one small area. He roamed the
streets, gaping openly, seldom noticing the knowing grins
he generated from the seasoned city folk who had seen
such rural types blow through their town many times before.

What intrigued David most was the wharf and the
great ships that lay in dock there. He stood in awe, staring
at the tall masts, the intricate roping, the lapping water, the
sails lined magnificently against the sky.

He watched as one particularly impressive ship sailed

in and docked. Settling himself in a warm, sunny place, he watched the crewmen and dock hands emptying the holds. Curiosity arose, and he looked for and found an opportunity to slip aboard, very carefully, taking care to draw no notice.

Exploring the ship provided David more fun than he had experienced for the longest time. What a life this must be! He tried to imagine being aboard ship in the midst of ocean that stretched endlessly on all sides. Looking up the masts at the conglomeration of ropes and sail attached to them, he wondered what it would be like to crawl like a spider among it all, swaying and swinging high above the waves.

"And who may you be, young man?"

David wheeled and faced the speaker, a stranger dressed in a manner that marked him as the captain of the vessel. David's heart rose, pounding, like it was trying to emerge from his throat. He assumed he was in great trouble.

"I'm . . . I beg your pardon, sir. I'll leave."

"What a voice! You have the sound of the western hills about you, my lad!"

The captain, on the other hand, had the sound of the Scottish hills in his own voice. That he was foreign only made him more intimidating to David. He backed away, turned and headed for the ramp.

"Wait there, my boy," the captain said. "Let me have a look at you." He came closer, eyeing David evaluatively. "You're lean, but stout. I'd wager you can climb."

"I don't know, sir."

"Tell me about yourself. What work have you done?"

David, puzzled by the attention, briefly and rather clumsily mumbled a list of his various jobs. The captain rubbed his bearded chin thoughtfully, then said, "Might you consider a voyage to Liverpool?"

David was very taken aback. Was he being offered work? It certainly sounded that way. He was beginning to learn something about himself: he had some sort of natural quality, inexplicable to him, that made him appealing to others. He wondered if the captain was making a serious offer, but felt shy about asking. A misinterpretation would be embarrassing.

"Well, lad, what of it? Would you like to be a seafaring man?"

So he really *was* being offered a job. He didn't know what to think about such an unexpected, momentous proposition. He stammered and looked around—and a great sense of excitement rose all on its own, unanticipated and intense. His mind filled with images as big as the ocean itself—crashing waves, great and strange fish leaping from the water and descending again, dark shores coming closer, and cities filled with people whose faces and clothing and language differed from anything he had encountered before.

He looked up at the captain and nodded. "Yes sir. I believe I would."

Chapter 16

The captain's name was McClure. He talked further with David, asking him about his parents and seeming pleased to learn they were far away in Tennessee. Did David mind the thought of being miles from his homeland and kin?

No, David replied. He had gotten past his homesickness, and wouldn't mind sailing all around the world if he got the chance. And as he said it, it was fully true. In the tearful parting with his brother weeks before, he had passed an emotional milestone. He still loved his kin, still felt fondly about his homeplace, but having made the break, he didn't feel as bound to it as before, especially considering a prospect as exciting as this one. Right now, the idea of being a seafarer was on him as strong as if it had been a lifetime ambition instead of a totally new notion.

McClure instructed David to go fetch his clothing and goods, and to return as soon as possible. Burning with the thrill of a new way of life—an ocean voyage! Liverpool!—David raced back to the inn where he and Adam Myers had taken lodging.

He found Myers half drunk and thoroughly transformed because of it. When David entered, Myers turned a glowering red face to him. "Where you been, boy?"

"To the wharf. I spoke to a ship's captain—he's offered me work on the ship. He says I can sail to England. . . ."

Myers paused, taking it in, then snorted in contemptuous laughter. "England, is it? You? Why, they'd tire of you so fast they'd feed you to sharks before you were out of sight of land! You wouldn't know how to do a seaman's job!"

David was startled and puzzled by this new, dark side of Myers now revealing itself to him. "Well, whatever you think about it, it's what I want to do. I've come for my clothes and my money," he said.

"Have you? Well, you'll have neither."

"They're mine!"

"And you are in my hire, and under my care. You can put aside any notions about ships and ocean voyages. You're going nowhere but back to Tennessee. I've got a return load at last, ready to be hauled out as soon as the wagon is fixed."

David was crestfallen—then, in mounting stages, angry. "You're not my father, nor my owner. I want my money!"

"Well, you ain't having it."

"Give it to me!"

"I'll give you the back of my hand!" Myers groped around. "Where's that dratted bottle? Ah, here she is!" He took a long swig.

David raised his fist. "Where is my money? Give it to me!"

"Maybe I done spent it."

"You lie!"

Myers stood, wobbled toward David, and took a swing that missed.

"I want my money!"

"No—now get yonder into that bed, and stay where I can see you."

"No!"

Myers reached down to his boot and pulled out a knife. He waved it toward David. "Get into that bed, so I can keep a watch and make sure you don't sneak off on me."

David knew enough about drunks to realize it wouldn't be wise to challenge Myers while he was armed. Further, his anger was fading into despair, and he was losing the will even to argue. He went to the bed and fell into it, thinking of the ship, and the waiting captain, and his disappearing hope of a voyage to Liverpool.

It was late afternoon, and by the time the sun was setting, David had fallen asleep. When he awakened, Myers was slumped in a chair beside the door, the knife still in his grip. David stood and thought about trying to slip past him, but Myers lifted his head and looked straight at him in silence. Perhaps it was a move made in the midst of sleep, or perhaps not. David crawled back into his bed.

Myers kept a watch over him very closely all the next morning, and then throughout the day. David had hoped that as Myers's drunkenness went away, so would his ill will. This didn't happen. It seemed that Myers meant it when he said he considered David his personal charge.

A day later the wagon was fixed. David and Myers loaded up with the wares bound for Tennessee and set out, David's wagon in front where Myers could keep an eye on him at all times.

Days passed. David's anger at the way Myers had treated him, and cheated him out of his money, lingered and grew, and he longed for escape. No opportunity came. Myers watched him doggedly. His harsh attitude clung to him, and David wondered what was wrong with the man. Had he encountered some sort of trouble in Baltimore that had soured him, but which David knew nothing about? It was a mystery David Crockett would never solve. Whatever the reason, Myers was now as gruff and unpleasant as he had been jolly in the past.

Early one morning, well before daybreak, David rose, gathered his clothing and a little food, and set out on foot. He had no money, nothing of value at all except the little scrap of silver his uncle Jimmy had given him. If it came to it, he decided, he would exchange the silver for food and goods—but only if there was no other way to survive. The token remained precious to him in a way that outstripped monetary value.

Alone, cheated, and sad, David Crockett walked silently through the darkness, going nowhere but away from Adam Myers. His mind was miles away, aboard a tall ship, crossing the vast ocean toward England—a place that now, he was confident, he would never have the chance to see.

Pale sunlight streamed over the rolling Virginia landscape. David Crockett, crouched among dogwoods beside the road, looked out cautiously at the scene before him.

Another wagoner, it appeared. A small-time one, judging from the fact he was alone and had but one wagon. The load had shifted, jarring a barrel free from its ties and dumping it out on the road. The wagoner was in the process of climbing down from the driver's seat, muttering and complaining underneath his breath. David was astounded when he got a good look at him. He was perhaps the biggest man he had ever seen, at least five inches above six feet, and built like one of the barrels he was hauling.

The wagoner mumbled so badly that David could pick out only snatches of what he was saying: mutterings about a "world of sorrows," and "deuced loose barrels," how a "man can't make a living with such as this" and how jolting a barrel loose from a wagon was such a fine way to start the day it made him "want to sit down and read the Bible for thirty minutes."

Despite his complaining, the problem really was very minor for the big man. David watched admiringly as the fellow flexed his muscles, lifted the massive barrel with hardly a strain, and set it back into place with a grunt.

"You stay there now," the man said, dusting off his hands. "You fall out again and I'll kick you to splinters and take the loss."

David sneezed. It burst from him without warning and couldn't be stifled. The wagoner turned and looked right toward where he was hidden.

"Who's there?"

David stood and stepped onto the road. He felt so dejected and hopeless that he hardly cared that he had been revealed. So what if this wagoner proved to be the same sort of heartless, guileful type David perceived the world to be full of? What further harm could come to a wandering boy who had already lost his money, and the chance to be a sailing man?

"Well, where'd you come from, boy?"

"The woods."

"I can see that. What's your name?"

"David Crockett."

"You come from around here?"

"No. Tennessee."

"Well, you're a ways from home."

"I'm going back. I've got nowhere else to go. I was going to be a sailor and go to England, but that was took away from me."

"Is that right? Well, I can't take you to England, but if it's Tennessee you're heading toward, I can get you part of the way there. I'm going west a ways. Not all the way to Tennessee, but I can take you off your feet for a time."

The man seemed friendly enough, and David was longing for friendship right now. He felt utterly alone, utterly used up. But he was hesitant to accept this offer, recalling how Adam Myers had been so kind and jovial to begin with, but so harsh and dishonest at the end.

The wagoner stepped forward, hand outthrust. "I'm Myers. Henry Myers."

Myers! That was all David needed to hear. He had dealt enough with wagoners named Myers already! Without even shaking the proffered hand, he turned and began walking quickly down the road, leaving the big wagoner looking confused.

"What's wrong, boy? Have I made you mad?"

David felt a wave of sadness and stopped. He turned. "No, sir, it's only that . . ." He began to cry.

The wagoner stepped closer. "Son, it looks like your day has commenced even worser than mine. Is there anything I can help you with?"

David was full to overflowing with his sorrows, and began spilling out his tale to Henry Myers. When he was done, Myers's face was red and he was storming and fuming, infuriated to learn of the treachery of David's prior companion.

"The worst of it is, he's sullying up the good name of Myers," Henry Myers said. "I'll not stand for that! David, you take me to this Adam Myers, and by jings, we'll get you your seven dollars, or I'm a hop-toad!"

Adam Myers moaned and wailed and repented with a fervor seldom seen short of the church-front mourner's bench. Henry Myers towered over the deceitful man and forced him to admit his crime. Yes, he had taken David's money under false pretense, and had spent it. He couldn't pay it back at the moment, but would gladly do so once he reached Tennessee.

David knew this would never happen. Probably he would never see Adam Myers again. Even so, he felt satisfied. The scoundrel had been shamed and punished, and that would have to be good enough.

David had a grin on his face when he and Henry Myers rode off together on Henry's big wagon. They left Adam Myers cringing and defeated, and when David glanced over his shoulder at the first bend and saw his friend-turned-enemy in such a state, he thought it a fine sight indeed.

Henry Myers made good company, but David took a careful attitude toward him still. His experiences had shown him that appearances were not always to be trusted, and that if a fellow was to be cared for, the only sure way was to do the caring for all on his own. From here on out, David Crockett would blindly assume the honesty of no one.

He remained with Henry Myers several more days, moving farther west, and Myers gave him no reason to doubt his goodwill. At length they reached a sort of ordinary or inn where wagoners frequently stayed—this was a much larger, nicer inn than John Crockett's tavern—and put in for the night.

David was dead tired, and dozed in his seat at the big table, around which a half-dozen wagoners moved and drank and talked loud and coarse, as was typical of their breed. There were others there too, travelers or stage riders or perhaps locals who frequented the place.

The next morning, Henry Myers informed him that he had made a deal with one of the other wagoners and would be heading north briefly before continuing on. Would David want to remain at the inn and then continue with him when he returned?

David thought it over and decided against it. Though he didn't say so to Henry Myers, he feared that perhaps Adam Myers would show up here, in that wagoners apparently knew and frequented the place. No, he said. He would go on as before, on foot, and carry with him gratitude for all Henry had done.

Just before he left, Henry gave David another cause for gratitude. He went among the other wagoners and described David as a homeless, straggling little boy, alone in the world and mistreated by a previous companion who was "not worthy of his last name." Perhaps the good men in the inn could throw together a few cents to help a young traveler in need?

The appeal worked to the tune of three dollars, and David set out better off than when he had come in. Using his money as sparingly as he could, he went as far as Montgomery Courthouse, and there found himself destitute again.

He sought work and found it with a farmer named James Caldwell, who paid him about a shilling a day until he had accumulated five dollars after a month of labor.

The end of this employment found David in the midst of another spell of disinterest in an immediate return home. He bound himself to a hatmaker named Elijah Griffin, working for him eighteen months, until Griffin abruptly absconded. Like David's father, he was prone to debt, and when he left, David had not received any of the pay he had been promised. It was yet one more lesson for the young Tennessean on the selfish ways of men.

It was early in the year 1802, and fifteen-year-old David Crockett was in a sad condition. He had no money, and his clothes were little more than rags. Lacking any other recourse, he looked for more work, and found it only in fits and spurts, here and there. He was tempted to sell his silver piece, but resisted. It was the only tangible link he had to his earlier days and home.

At length he turned toward Tennessee again, astounded that what had begun as an impulsive flight to avoid a beating had turned into such a lengthy and colorful journey of life. He was much different now than when he had begun. Physically he was almost a man. His voice had deepened, his shoulders had broadened.

He was beginning to look something like his father. He wasn't quite sure how to feel about that, just as he hadn't always been sure how to feel about John Crockett.

Chapter 17

The night was stormy and wet, hammered by a relentless wind. David paused on the road, drenched to the skin, trembling and miserable, and gazed helplessly across the tumultuous New River, despairing of finding a way to the other side.

He looked behind him, into the dark. He couldn't have counted the number of times he had done that in the last two hours since he left a rugged little tavern in which he had taken shelter from the worst of the storm. That stop, he had quickly learned, had been a mistake. Inside he had found a big crowd, including a gang of six men who had been working on a nearby road; they too had been driven to shelter by the weather. Or so was the pretext. From their actions, David believed they hadn't so much been driven in by the liquid raining down from the sky as drawn in by the liquid they were pouring down their own throats in prodigious quantities.

Something about him seemingly hadn't been to the liking of a couple of the drunken road workers, who set in to harassing him, poking at him, trying to make him fight. After twenty minutes of this, David decided that the storm would be far more pleasant company than the drunks, and left the tavern, grateful he had escaped serious trouble.

Ahead he saw a little dock with some boats tied, and a small hut from which light spilled and smoke rose from the chimney to be whipped away by the wind. David went to the door and knocked. He asked the man who answered if he might purchase a ride across the river—and the man cursed him for a fool and told him that anyone who crossed the river with such whitecaps rising and lightning flashing was asking for an early death. He slammed the door, and no amount of knocking would bring him back.

David returned to the road, more determined than ever to find a crossing. That was when he first realized he was being followed.

It was tremendously unsettling. Who would follow him on such a night, except for unfriendly reasons? He wished he hadn't entered that tavern. Someone in the place must have decided he would be an easy robbery victim, and followed him out to do the job.

David headed down the road all the faster. Now he *had* to get across the river, else he wouldn't feel safe at all. He would rather risk capsizing and drowning than the stabbing point of a highway robber's blade.

Ahead he saw another house, boats tied to a covered dock beside it. He went to the door, knocked, and was again rebuffed. This time he argued more vehemently. If only he could buy use of a canoe, he would make the crossing himself, and would tie the canoe on the far bank. At last the man relented, and charged a price far higher than was justified. David turned over the money with an ache of regret. Considering everything, however, he did not feel he had a choice. He lashed his pack as securely as possible in the canoe and set off across the churning water.

Never would he forget that crossing. His canoe was turned and battered, half filling with water, and moving with the current much faster than it traveled across it. By the time he struck the far bank, he was nearly two miles downstream from where he had set off. He tied up the canoe, offering a prayer of thanks to the heavens for his survival, thinking too how furious the canoe's owner would be to find it so far from his home. But that was his problem, David thought. He had plenty of his own to worry about.

He lifted his pack and was turning to go when a lightning flash illuminated the river, and he saw another canoe out there in the darkness. From what little he could see in such an infinitesimal moment, it appeared there was only one occupant in that canoe.

Now there was no question about it. He was certainly being followed, by some very determined person. But why? Surely no common robber would risk the danger of the river crossing merely to take what meager gleanings he would find on such an obviously impoverished pilgrim as David Crockett.

David went on, looking for light in the darkness, sniffing the air for wood smoke, seeking any sign of shelter. A mile, then two, then three, fell away behind him. Still no shelter. And still the sense of being followed lingered, actually grew.

Then, through the trees, he saw a light. Heading for it, he made out the outline of a house. He went to it and knocked, and found a grizzled, skinny old man, as ancient and gnarled as a virgin oak, looking back at him.

"I'm looking for shelter for the night," David said. "Could I find it here?"

"Come inside, boy, and warm yourself," the old fellow said, and more welcome words David had never heard.

The fire was hot and soothing, as was the liquor the old man poured into his cup. David's tension, and his nervousness at being followed, diminished. The log walls around him were thick and sheltering, shutting out danger.

The old man laid him a pallet on the loft upstairs, where the rising heat from the fire made ideal sleeping conditions for a young man who had been chilled clean through. David slept very soundly, hardly stirring all night.

When he awakened the next morning, the first thing he noticed was that his little pouch containing the silver piece was gone. He sat upright with a jerk and groped around him. It wasn't there. He hadn't lost it in his blankets. It had been taken.

David climbed down the loft ladder, ready to accuse the old man and get back his silver. At that moment he hated the whole of humanity. Was there no one on the earth who wasn't a thief or scoundrel?

At the base of the ladder he stopped. The old man was there, by the fireside. Another man was with him, this one much younger, and a stranger. David lifted his finger, intending to aim it into the old man's face and voice his charge—then he looked again at the stranger.

But he wasn't a stranger. David had seen that face somewhere before, though he couldn't place just where, or what name had been attached to it. . . .

The newcomer lifted his hand and opened it. On the palm lay David's silver piece.

"I thought you would want it back," he said. "It was took from you in the tavern by some of them who was being rough on you. I was there, and seen it happen. It took some doing to get it back, I'll tell you, but I ain't worried. I didn't cut him too deep. He'll live. But I tell you, I thought I'd never catch up with you. 'Specially crossing that river."

David took the silver and closed his hand around it. He smiled.

"I'm grateful," he said. "That silver was give me by my deaf-and-dumb uncle." David put out his hand for a shake. "It's fine to see you again, Persius Tarr."

Persius shook the hand. "Not nearly as fine as seeing you, David Crockett. It's been a long spell, ain't it? Just little children, that's all we was. But I ain't never forgot you. And I ain't forgot your mother. She was kind to me. Is she still living?"

"Yes . . . or I believe she is. I ain't been home in a long time."

"Why not?"

"It's a long story, Persius. I'll tell it if you want to hear it. And I'd sure like to hear yours, if you'll tell it."

For days they were together, traveling and talking, moving closer and closer to David's home. Persius's story was every bit as fascinating as David had anticipated, and every bit as gritty. It was, without question, the story of a criminal life. From the time he had fled his court-imposed bondage in Tennessee, Persius had been a youth on the run. He had found some legitimate work, but mostly he had stolen. Everything from pigs and saddles to bread cooling on windows, and from money to horses. Persius made no apologies, and as best David could tell, no attempts to hide his sins. He did note, however, that while in Virginia he never used his true name, because he was known there as a horse thief.

David recounted to him the story of how he had himself commandeered Persius's name while traveling home from his first droving venture, and how he had unexpectedly picked up news of Persius's infamy because of it. Persius laughed heartily, and told David he was fortunate that his companion had been so easygoing. Many would have quickly turned "Persius Tarr" over to the nearest constable or magistrate, or worse, simply strung him up or shot him.

To David, the most remarkable aspect of all of it was that Persius Tarr still held interest in someone he had met for only a few days in childhood. The strength of that interest was evidenced in the amount of trouble Persius had put himself to, following him across the whirling New River.

David was interested in Persius in turn, just as much as when he had been a sprout on Cove Creek, looking up to the dark-eyed young stranger as a devilishly exciting, worldly taster of the forbidden fruit. Had David possessed more of a philosophical or theological bent and a touch more maturity, he might have speculated about fate or predestination linking their two lives. As it was, he contented himself with enjoying this reunion as an unexpected, happy gift given by circumstance.

In Sullivan County, Tennessee, David thought of his uncle Joseph—not the Uncle Joe who shot the grape picker back in Greene County many years ago, but a brother of John Crockett. Joe Crockett lived in Sullivan County, and David figured he could find the place with a little effort. Money was running low; he feared it would be only a matter of time before Persius suggested thievery, and David wanted none of that. Joe could get them well-fed, maybe even give or lend a little money to see them the rest of the way home.

Joe greeted his nephew with delight, and was friendly to Persius. David was not surprised to learn that his family in Jefferson County was at least half sure he was dead, him having been gone so long and not having followed his brother home from the cattle drove. Rebecca Crockett was particularly suffering, he learned.

This news made David more determined than ever to get home, but he stayed with his uncle several weeks, partly because Persius fell ill and couldn't travel for a few days, but mostly because he happened to reach his uncle at a time when he needed farm help, and David felt obliged to give it. At length, the time to leave came around. Joe stocked both travelers with food enough to see them home, and they set off.

"Your folks may not recollect you right off," Persius said. "You've changed a right smart, I'll lay odds, from when they seen you last."

The comment set David to thinking. An idea came to mind, rather idle and playful, but interesting enough to be worth trying.

They reached the Crockett tavern late in the day. It was a busy night, seemingly; more than the usual number of wagons were parked outside. David's heart hammered fiercely. He was home! The knowledge of it was enough to make him shake like a man mortally scared.

Persius eyed him wryly as they neared the door. "They'll take you for a drunk or figure you have the ague, with you trembling so."

"I can't help it."

"Why don't you just out and tell them who you are?"

"No, no. I want to see if they'll know me."

John Crockett himself took David's request for lodging, and for David it was the oddest of conversations, because his father talked to him as he would talk to a stranger. Once he did give a probing, frowning glance at the grimy young face, and looked closely at Persius too, who was even dirtier, so much so his face was coated with an earthen rind. When John turned away, it was evident the sight of them had tugged at his mind, but not yet jogged loose recognition.

David and Persius kept to themselves in a corner of the tavern, speaking little to anyone, with David doing his best not to stare at his kin. His brothers and sisters all looked very changed; he wasn't sure he would have known each of them had he met them anywhere but inside the walls of home. Because the tavern was crowded tonight, neither David nor Persius drew any particular attention from any of the Crocketts, so by mealtime David still sat unrecognized among his own.

His first sight of his mother came when she entered the rear of the tavern, having been in the kitchen house behind the main building, preparing the evening's supper. David struggled against tears of emotion when he saw her, and it was all he could do to keep from revealing his identity. He was on the verge of rising to do that when Persius put out a hand and stopped him.

"Wait until we're at the table," he said. "You've carried it out this far—you might as well keep the wheel a-rolling all the way to the end."

Rebecca's voice called for all to come to eat. Amid kin and strangers, taken for one of the latter himself, David sat at the long table, passing the bowls as they came to him and glancing around at the faces of his family members.

It was in his sister Betsy's eyes that he first saw the flicker of recognition. He locked his gaze on hers and smiled slightly. Betsy's eyes widened, her mouth fell open, and she rose, rounding the table to throw her arms around him.

"It's my lost brother! It's David, Mama! It's our own dear David!"

The explosion of emotion sparked by Betsy's revelation almost smothered David. The Crockett family surrounded him, pressing in, patting him, hugging him, touching him. When he looked at his father's face, he saw tears of joy and relief, and then David could not hold back tears of his own.

And over it all, Rebecca Crockett's voice exclaimed, again and again, "My David, my David, my wandering boy, my boy has come home again!"

Meanwhile, Persius Tarr, grinning around big mouthfuls, helped himself to an extra slab of pork while no one was looking.

Part 3

PANTHER CREEK

Chapter 18

Near the Headwaters of Panther Creek, Spring 1803

Through the forest came the muffled voices of agitated men and the yellow lights of torches, hanging and bobbing like over-sized fireflies beyond a wide belt of newly leafed trees. David stopped, panting, wiping a sweat-sodden shock of hair back from his forehead, and shifted about in search of a clean view of the mob. No use. The foliage was too heavy. He must draw nearer. He took in a deep breath and pushed on.

His mind raced at a pace far faster than the dark woodland obstacles would allow his feet. Don't let it be too late, he mentally pleaded. Persius, don't let them get their hands on you, whatever happens. They'll kill you if they do.

He could tell that the band of torch-carrying men were assembled on a little wagon road that angled north to south through the forest. As he came closer, he could hear their voices clearly. The name of Persius Tarr was spoken several times, spat out like the monicker of a particularly deplorable devil.

He halted and crouched in the brush when he heard a new sound, from farther up the road: the baying of dogs. They were bringing in hounds! David felt a strange thrill of horror. The torches, the hounds, the very atmosphere surrounding the little mob, confirmed the terrible thing old John Canaday had told David about an hour before, when David had returned from a long afternoon's hunt: Crider Cummings was readying to search for Persius, and to hang him as soon as he was found.

The gentle old Quaker Canaday had told David how Persius Tarr had on this very day beaten Henry Cummings, Crider's younger brother, into unconsciousness during a fight apparently spurred by mutual drunkenness. The injured man had been brought to Canaday's house, which stood within a mile of the still house where the fight occurred. Now Henry Cummings lay senseless on Canaday's own bed, his fate uncertain, and his brother Crider, who had left the bedside about two hours earlier, had sworn to gather help and get his revenge on Persius Tarr. Crider already considered Persius a murderer, even though his brother hadn't yet died.

As soon as he heard these things, David had set out to find the Crider Cummings mob. Now that he had succeeded in doing so, it came to him with rather stunning ironic impact: there was really nothing he could do here to help Persius. His urge to locate the mob had been unfocused and desperate, an impulse that had outraced common sense. Now he saw that if he was to do any good, it could best be done by finding Persius himself, warning him of what was happening, and helping him flee.

But this presented a glaring problem: Where was Persius to be found? Since coming to Jefferson County with David, over a year ago now, Persius had lived here and there, in the woods, in woodsheds, in empty, decrepit cabins, even in a cave for one month, and for another in the cellar of a building now used as a church. David had tried to persuade Persius to settle down somewhere, but his friend had staunchly refused. He liked life as he lived it. And a fellow who wasn't above thievery was best off not being tied to one spot anyway.

David tried to think of the most likely places Persius would go on the run. Maybe he could investigate them, one by one, until he found him . . . but no. That would be too difficult, too time-consuming. And it was just as likely that Persius would not be hiding at all, but running, trying to get out of the area before being chased down. If so, David knew he couldn't hope to find him before Crider Cummings's mob and their hounds.

There was only one other hope, and it hung in the hands of fate. He could go back to Canaday's house and help the Quaker try to bring Henry Cummings around to the living again. If that could be done, and if Crider could be notified, then he could no longer regard Persius as a murderer. Maybe his fury would be tempered, and Persius spared vengeance, at least the full, lethal form of vengeance Crider had in mind.

David rose and backed away into the forest, regretting that he hadn't sooner considered matters more logically. In his unthinking zeal, he had come into a place of danger himself. Settled uncomfortably in the back of his brain was the fact that his friendship with Persius was well-known. Should Crider find him here, he might force him to lead the mob to Persius. David couldn't do that, of course, but he might find himself very ill-used before Crider finally accepted that fact.

The baying grew louder and closer; the men in the mob were looking back up the road, waiting for the hounds to come into view. Snatches of conversation revealed the dogs were being brought by Solomon Overby. David knew of these hounds. They were trained to find men and had hunted down many a fugitive on behalf of the local constables. Overby was justly proud of them.

Turning, David headed back the way he came—and fell. A root, unseen in the darkness, had caught his foot. The forest floor was soft and the impact of the fall didn't hurt him, but the noise he had made ... .

"Hear that?" someone on the road yelled. "Right in yonder—come on, let's go!"

Men plunged into the woods. Pure fright gripped David; he knew at this moment what it was to be a fawn when a wolf pack catches its scent. He leaped up and ran blindly into the dark woodland, men coming after him. David's fear was of the mortal strain. Running without the tether of reason, it told him he would die if he was caught.

But David had one advantage derived from his up-bringing as a frontier boy. From early childhood one central fact of survival had been pummeled into him by his father, his uncles, his older brothers, his neighbors: fear is a man's worst enemy. It's fear that makes a man in the forest watch the ground for snakes, only to advance headlong into a low-hanging hornets' nest. It's fear that makes a man waste his shot by firing too soon at a wounded and advancing bear, leaving himself to be mauled, when a moment's wait would have given him a clean kill. It's fear that makes a man fight the water and drown, rather than let it support him so he can swim out and live.

David stopped and turned. He couldn't outrun them, could only make his situation more dangerous by trying. Lifting his hands, he waited for the men to come close.

"I'm unarmed," he said. "I've done nothing—I won't fight."

Three men seized him; one shoved a torch into his face. "Oh, yes, I know you. You're the boy who's bound out to Quaker Canaday, ain't you?"

"Yes, sir. My name's David Crockett."

"Crockett, aye, yes. Why did you come sneaking, boy? Why did you run?"

"I was looking for you. I've come from Canaday's to tell you that Henry Cummings has come around. He didn't die. He's calling for his brother Crider." It was a desperate lie, but what else could he say? At least it would buy time. Crider would be obliged to investigate the story, and meanwhile Persius could put more distance between himself and his pursuers . . . *if* he was running. Persius might have been too drunk to realize what he had done to Henry Cummings, or too drunk to flee.

"Henry's woke up, you say?" The man tugged his beard and frowned. "I don't believe it. You're lying. I know for a fact you're a friend of Tarr. It was you who brung Tarr into this county, early part of last year."

"That's right," said a second man. "Besides, boy, if you were looking for us, why did you run?"

David had no answer. He had been outfoxed, and his face showed it.

They dragged him back to the wagon road and the mob, which had just been joined by Overby and his hounds. The big dogs strained at the ends of long rope leashes. David could all but taste the blood hunger of these men. He wondered if Persius, wherever he was, realized what danger he was in.

"We didn't find no Tarr, but we sure enough found his friend," one of David's captors said.

Crider Cummings, whom David knew from having seen him a time or two at Canaday's house, came closer, bearing a torch. He held it close to David's face, so close it scorched the skin, and frowned. "Canaday's bound boy!" he said. "Tell me, boy, where's Persius Tarr right now?"

"I don't know."

"I don't believe you. You're his friend. Whole blasted county knows it."

"He says Henry's woke up and is asking for you, Crider," one of David's captors said. "He says he come looking for you, to tell you—but he was running from us when we caught him."

Crider put his nose almost against David's. "You say my brother's awake?"

"Yes sir."

"Why did you run?"

"I . . . I got scared. I heard the dogs and I thought they was mad dogs in the woods."

Crider laughed. "Why, you little squat, if you're going to lie, at least tell a good one! Mad dogs, I reckon!" His face instantly became a cold, frightening mask. "I'm sending George Watkins back to Canaday's, just in case you're telling the truth. But in the meantime, you're going with us, Crockett. You're going to help us find that murderer you tomcat around with, and you're going to help us hang him."

"I don't know where he is. I can't help you."

"We'll find him! Them dogs will sniff him out. I got a bit of his shirt, you see. Henry ripped it off while they was fighting; it was still in his hand."

"I'll not go with you!"

"Boy, you ain't got a choice."

Crider walked away and talked to George Watkins, who immediately headed back through the forest toward Canaday's. David's heart sank. Even if by some miracle Watkins did find that Henry Cummings had recovered, it probably would do no good. By then the mob would have moved on, and might be unreachable with the news.

Two men tied David's hands behind him and shackled his feet with a rope, leaving it long enough for him to walk but not run. The treatment let David know just how serious Crider was about this business. He wasn't even the culprit sought, yet he was being treated like a criminal! He could only imagine how harsh they would be with Persius, if they caught him.

Someone poked him in the small of the back, pushing him forward. The hounds, having sniffed the fragment of Persius's shirt, surged ahead, and the mob followed, torches flaring and flickering in the night.

As the mob progressed, David felt increasingly distressed, because he was beginning to form a suspicion about where Persius might have gone. Crider kept harping at him, nagging him with questions—"He got a place hereabouts? You ever knowed him to camp about this ridge? You ever hunted with him along the Holston?"—and David kept evading and lying, even though every step the dogs led them along the path further confirmed the accuracy of his developing suspicion.

Persius sometimes lived in a small, previously abandoned log hut that stood at the base of a cliff where a spring bubbled out from a cave. Though no one but David knew that Persius sometimes lived in the hut, the existence of the hut itself was known to most who lived in the area. Any time now someone in the mob would realize it was to this hut that the dogs were leading them.

David grew angry at Persius. How could he have been so foolish as to go to such an accessible place after beating a man nearly—maybe completely—to death? It indicated to him that Persius was either very drunk or very foolish.

"I know where that scoundrel is!" someone in the mob declared. "The old hut, down by the cave spring, just over yonder rise!"

Others voiced their concurrence. David winced. Now there was nothing he could do to help Persius. They were within shouting distance of the hut already.

Shouting distance ... maybe there *was* something he could do after all, even if it was no more than a warning.

"Persius! It's me, David Crockett—run, Persius, they're coming to—"

A blow across the mouth cut off his shout. And it had been a loud one, as loud as he could make it. Crider cursed and lunged back toward David, rifle butt uplifted. He brought it down hard on the side of David's head. David crumpled and fell. Crider kicked him. Someone hit him with a torch. Bits of flaring pine knot stuck to his skin and burned him.

"Tie him to that tree there, and make sure it's tight enough to hold him," Crider ordered one of his fellows. David was dragged off and bound very firmly to the trunk of a big sassafras.

Then they moved on. David watched the mob head on across the ridge. On the far side was the cliff, the spring, the hut. He hoped his yell had reached Persius in time to help. Even so, the help would be minimal. The mob was so close now that Persius couldn't hope to outrun them.

David struggled with his bonds but could not loosen them. He heard voices from across the ridge, shouting, angry. The dogs were barking violently. They must have found Persius. Tears welled in David's eyes and overflowed. He thought: If they kill him, I hope they'll do it quick, and not make him suffer.

The shouting grew louder. David pulled at his ropes again, so hard that the skin on his wrists chafed and burned. Then he stopped, frozen, and turned his head.

Someone was coming, following the path of the mob. He had no idea who it could be. Was it merely some straggling member of Crider's mob, or someone else of similar ill will? Or was it someone who might help Persius, or at least keep the mob from murdering him?

"Here! Up here!" David called.

There was a scrambling of feet, a tumult of motion. More than one person—David could tell it.

"Right up here! Come help me—I'm tied!"

With the torches gone, borne off by the mob, David could not clearly see the faces of the three men who came over the little hump and to his side. One of them knelt and leaned close.

"David, what have they done to thee?"

It was John Canaday. David laughed aloud. The Quaker's arrival was as welcome as an advent of avenging angels come to rescue him and Persius. He had already developed a strong affection for his kind employer; now he felt a fierce love, and a less-than-rational conviction that Canaday's arrival would somehow stop the mob.

"They're over the ridge, Mr. Canaday," David said. "And I think they've found Persius."

Chapter 19

John Canaday straightened his spine rather creakingly and looked across the ridge while hefting his trousers, which always had a tendency to sag too low beneath the ample belly that age and hearty eating had given him. "God grant we are not come too late," he said, wheezing slightly with exertion.

Despite the darkness, David was now able to see and recognize the two who had come with Canaday. One was Cyril Andrews, a local constable. David was overjoyed. A constable might be able to stop this unlawful reprisal. But an even greater wave of happiness swept over him when he recognized the man standing beside and partially supported by Andrews. It was Henry Cummings himself, not only alive, but walking! David thought that he was surely witnessing an authentic miracle.

Canaday dug a folding knife from somewhere under his plain broadcloth coat and dropped it within David's reach. "No time to free thee, my boy," he said. "I'll leave that to thee. We must off over the hill, good men, and be hasty about it!"

With the corpulent Quaker in the lead and Andrews struggling to keep the wobbly-footed Cummings upright and moving forward, the trio advanced on to the ridgetop and then across. David, meanwhile, had managed with bound hands and teeth to get the knife open, and began sawing at the ropes, all the while straining to hear what was happening across the ridge.

It seemed the ropes would never give way, and David cursed the dull knife as he sawed vigorously. At last he was free, and he stood, made a lunge to begin his race up the ridge, and fell flat, having forgotten the hobbling of his ankles. He dropped the knife when he fell and had to feel around in the dark for it, which took up some two more minutes. The sounds from across the ridge were less audible during that time, possibly because the wind had shifted, or maybe because the arrival of Henry Cummings had led to change in the violent mood of his avengers.

David's groping finally unearthed the knife. He sawed his rope shackles in two, so that halves of it trailed behind each of his feet when he raced up the ridge.

He stopped at the crest to examine the scene below. There stood the mob, gathered around the mouth of the cave from which the spring ran. By the torchlight David made out the figures of Canaday, the constable, and Crider Cummings, who stood facing his brother, hands extended and resting on the latter's shoulders. Henry, standing in a slumped, weak posture, seemingly leaning much of his weight into Crider's hands, spoke and gestured limply. David watched as Crider led his brother back to a nearby boulder and sat him down. Still talking, Henry gingerly rubbed the left side of his head, apparently where Persius had laid him the strongest blow.

But where was Persius? David scanned around and could not find him. Rubbing his wrists, he descended to the clump of people below. Several hostile stares from among the mob greeted his arrival, but he detected a general dearth of interest in him now that Henry Cummings had showed up. He wondered if any of these men were embarrassed, having been ready to hang or shoot Persius Tarr for murder, only to have the supposed murder victim walk right into their midst.

David passed the Cummings brothers and the constable, and went to Canaday. "Where is Persius?" he asked in a near whisper.

"Nowhere to be found," Canaday replied in equally

soft tones. "There are signs he has been here very recently, but he is not here now. The hounds have been bewildered, sniffing around the spring. And there are tracks, leading into the water. These men were ready to head down the creek to follow when we showed up with Henry Cummings, which seems to have changed their plans."

David looked down the spring, then back to where it ran out of the cavern . . . and then he knew where Persius was. His mind clasped around the knowledge like a hand, and held it fast and hidden. Despite the pain that throbbed through his skull where Crider's rifle butt had struck him, a faint smile tugged around the corners of David's mouth.

The constable cleared his throat. "Men, every one of you should get on home now. There's been no murder, as you can see with your own eyes. And Henry Cummings says the fight was mostly his own fault. He holds no grudge against Persius Tarr for it. So there's nothing to be done but to put all this behind, and be grateful you didn't find and hang a man for a crime that ain't even been committed."

Crider turned and spoke. "There may be no crime in your eyes, Constable, but there's one in mine! Persius Tarr is a nuisance and a blight on this community, and he ought to be got rid of."

"Leave it be, Crider," Henry said in a very weak voice.

"You should listen to your brother, Crider," Andrews said. "If you do harm to Persius Tarr based on no more than your own grudge, it may be *you* facing the charge of murder. Now move on. Get on home with you all."

"Why are you defending Tarr?" one of the others asked. "He's a scoundrel and thief, and you know it."

"I do, and the first chance that comes to prove that he is, I'll jail him with a smile on my face for the privilege. I ain't defending Persius Tarr. I'm defending the law, and doing things as they ought to be done."

Crider said, "I ain't forgetting what Persius Tarr did."

"It wasn't his fault so much as mine," Henry said, but his voice was so low and tremulous that his words carried no weight to break the wall of resentment Crider had built around himself.

Slowly, though, the group dispersed, many grumbling that they hadn't had the chance to look downstream. Surely Tarr had run there, keeping to the water to confuse the dogs. The constable left with the Cummings brothers; David figured he wanted to keep his eye on Crider for a while longer.

"Well, David, I'm pleased no violence was done here," Canaday said. "But where, I wonder, is Persius Tarr?"

"I believe I know," David replied. He went to the mouth of the cave and knelt. He called back into the darkness. "Persius! You in there? This here's David—it's safe for you to come out now. They've all gone away."

David stood and backed off, eyes on the cave, the mouth of which was no more than three feet high, and which grew lower farther back. Within a few moments the water moved strangely and it seemed some giant fish was trying to squeeze its way out. But it was no fish, it was Persius. After a time of struggling and splashing, bubbling and blowing, he was fully out of the cave. He rose in the spring, looking for all the world like some water spirit separating itself from the stream that incarnates it, and stepped, shivering and soaked, onto the bank beside David.

"It pools up into a little room back inside there, you know," he said. "I could stand up in there. I knowed about it before I went in. A fellow like me's got to have him a hiding spot or two handy from time to time, so I always search out a place or two like that. God! I'm cold. That water's still winter-chilled."

"Did you hear me yell the warning?" David asked.

"Warning? I didn't hear no warning. At first it was like I could feel them coming, you know. I went up on the ridgetop, and came a-scrambling down here at first sound of them. Then down into the cave."

"Oh." David was a little let down. Persius probably was already safe in his watery cave even before he yelled. It didn't seem quite fair. He had taken a rifle butt in the head, not to mention several hard kicks, for daring to give that warning shout.

"Persius Tarr, I'm pleased that no harm has come to thee," Canaday said.

The darkness hid Persius's features, but David could easily imagine the expression they held in response to Canaday: one of uncertainty, caution. Persius didn't feel comfortable around the Quaker, with his odd dress, antiquated speech, and easy talk about the "Light of Christ" and the "divine presence" that he believed lived inside each person. Canaday had always been kind and respectful to Persius, ignoring his reputation and treating him as if he was the equal of any man. Perhaps it was that, as much as anything, that bewildered Persius.

"How did you know where to come with Henry Cummings?" David asked.

Canaday laid out the story. With much gentle care, washings with cold water, and very fervent exhortations and prayers, he and his family had managed to bring Henry Cummings back to consciousness more quickly than had initially appeared possible. Henry hadn't been hurt nearly as badly as had been thought. And his ordeal must have cleared his head, because he was quick to take blame for the fight with Persius Tarr, and horrified to learn that his brother had already set out to avenge his supposed murder. With effort, he had managed to get up and walk. He believed he knew where Persius could be found, he had said. Lately Persius had mentioned in passing that he was staying at the "springside cabin." Canaday had saddled his horse, and with Henry riding behind him on the same mount, arms around Canaday's broad middle to keep from falling, they had set out toward the most likely springside cabin either of them knew about. To their good fortune, it had been the right one.

"Did George Watkins meet you?" David asked.

"Aye. And when the good man saw our injured friend had been resurrected, he turned tail and ran back the way he came. I didn't understand why. There was no time to ask. We went on until we reached this place."

"I'm grateful," Persius mumbled.

"Give thanks to our heavenly father, Persius," Canaday replied. "I was nothing but his servant."

David explained the odd actions of George Watkins. "By the time he returned to the road, Crider and all of us had already gone on, I suppose. He may not yet know what's happened. It serves him right for tying himself in with such a fool as Crider Cummings."

"Don't speak so of another man," Canaday said. "It is not seemly nor right."

Persius shook Canaday's hand. "It was you bringing Henry here that saved me. If you hadn't done that, they would have kept searching until they found me. Somebody would have figured out about that cave. I owe you a debt."

"God has given much cleverness to thee, my friend. To hide in the very bowels of the earth! Hah!"

"Persius, there may still be trouble for you," David said.

"I know it. Crider has it in for me. He'll still have it in for me, no matter what his brother tells him."

"Why'd you two fight?"

"I don't remember. We was both drinking. Wasn't nothing much, whatever it was. I reckon I shoved him too hard. He knocked his head on the corner of the table, and I just walked out. It never come to me till later that he might have died, or that somebody might come after me over it. I'm sorry it happened. Henry's a friend of mine. I never wanted to hurt him."

"You'd best be scarce for a while, I believe."

"I will. I'll head off somewhere."

"You come back, though. Sometime. I don't want you going off for good, Persius."

"I'll come back."

Canaday said, "For now, come with us, my friend. I can offer thee a hardy meal, and whatever victuals that can be spared. My house is a safe house, and I extend thee my welcome."

Persius scuffed his foot, shivering in the wind. "I thank you," he said. "I am right hungry. Let me fetch my possessions out of the cabin, what few of them there be."

Chapter 20

Persius Tarr's discomfort in the presence of John Canaday was not shared in the slightest by David. He always felt relaxed around the old Quaker, even though there was little in common between them.

Foremost among their asimilarities was the fact that Canaday was sixty-two years old—for his era, quite an old man. He was seldom perceived to be as old as he was, however; he was so hardy as to hide his years well. Many took him for ten or fifteen years younger than he really was. He was respected widely, and known for his honesty and adherence to his religious beliefs. His religiosity made his Scots-Irish neighbors wary and cautious sometimes, but generally he won them over by the sheer goodness of his ways.

And by now Jefferson Countymen were simply accustomed to Quakers. Plain-dressing Friends had lived in the county since 1784. In 1797, two years after Canaday's own move to Tennessee, the local Quakers had formalized themselves into the Lost Creek Monthly Meeting of Friends. The Quaker population had grown steadily, though the prior year had seen the beginning of what would be a massive migration of Quakers to parts of the country north of the Ohio River.

Canaday was one of the most distinguished members of the Meeting, perceived by many as a patriarch. He had been equally respected back in Guilford County, North Carolina, where he had been part of the New Garden Monthly Meeting on Cane Creek, and from where he had migrated west into Tennessee, settling in the vicinity of the Panther Springs community, some miles west of John Crockett's tavern.

As owner of the land where John Crockett had built his tavern, Canaday was John's biggest creditor. David had not realized the extent of his father's indebtedness when he first approached Canaday for work. If he had, likely he wouldn't have approached him at all, for by that time David had taken his fill of working to pay off John Crockett's obligations. Such labors had filled his time almost fully since his return from wandering.

Shortly after his homecoming, David had been sent to work for one Abraham Wilson, who ran a tavern near the Panther Springs settlement, owning land on the main Holston Road and a road that led to Bean's Station. John Crockett owed Wilson thirty-six dollars, and it had required six straight months of David's labor to work off that debt. When that time was up, David left Wilson's employ, though he was vigorously invited to stay. He disliked the seedy character of many of the drinkers and gamblers who frequented Wilson's tavern—a shadier lot than John Crockett's patrons. Several times David had brushed up against trouble from some of these ruffians, and had not enjoyed it at all. This was more Persius Tarr's kind of situation than his—Persius, in fact, spent much time at the tavern, enjoying it as much as David hated it. David left Wilson's employment with a great sense of relief.

He had met Canaday a time or two during his work at Wilson's, and went to him asking for hire. Canaday took him on, for two shillings a day, on trial, and at the end of a week offered him full-time employment. The Quaker laid out his offer: if David would work for room and board for six months, Canaday would discharge John Crockett's remaining forty-dollar debt. In the meantime, David would have a good and safe home, and be treated well. Would he do it?

He probably wouldn't have, if not for Canaday's win-

ning ways and excellent character. That character had a
good effect on David; simply being around the kind man
made him want to do good things, to improve himself, to
become fine and admirable. Under this influence, it
crossed his mind, fully to his surprise, that it might be a
noble thing to work off another of his father's debts, this
time without John Crockett even asking it of him. He
imagined his father's face when he handed him the paid-
off note; he imagined the sense of camaraderie and close-
ness that such a gesture would bring and that had been
generally lacking between himself and his father. This
might be the best opportunity he would ever find to make
his father truly proud of him, to remove the grudging quality from John Crockett's affection.

And so David had accepted Canaday's offer, and
taken up lodging in a gable of the Quaker's house. Come
summer, John Crockett's note would be paid off, and David planned to carry it to his father himself, just for the
pleasure of surprising him. He was looking forward to it—
and in the interim, he was happy in the home of John
Canaday. As happy as he had been anywhere in his life.

Canaday, David, and Persius reached the farmhouse
and entered. There they ate a fine meal, and Canaday
packed Persius a big bag of food.

"We would be pleased to have thee stay the night,"
Canaday offered Persius, but the latter declined.

"Reckon I'll be going. I thank you, sir."

"Good-bye, Persius," David said. "Keep yourself out
of trouble."

"I will. I'll be seeing you, David. 'Bye."

He walked off into the darkness, the sack of food
slung across his shoulders. Out in the night he began to
whistle on old Irish tune. Not until the last strains of it had
faded out of hearing did David close Canaday's door and
climb up to his gable bed, thoroughly worn out and aching
for sleep. It took a long time to come, however, because
his head throbbed where the rifle had struck it, and he
could feel every place he had taken a kick.

One of these days, he might just have to settle the
score with Crider Cummings, who had treated him mighty

ill. Just because David Crockett lived with a pacifist Quaker didn't mean he had to be one himself. John Canaday might have a cooling influence on his fiery Scots-Irish blood, but not even he could chill it completely.

Summer 1803

For about half a year David Crockett had not laid eyes on his family, though John Crockett's tavern stood within a relatively easy ride from Canaday's house. David had made himself several excuses for his failure to visit: he was too busy; he owned no horse; he didn't want to risk the chance of John Crockett asking him about his pay, ruining a certain great surprise David had in store for him when the note was worked off. Only the latter reason had much validity. There had been many occasions when David would have had time for a visit home, and Canaday would have loaned him a horse anytime he needed it. The real reason he hadn't returned home, as he knew but didn't like to admit to himself, was that he was happier at Canaday's house.

Today, however, he *would* return, bearing in his hand the note Canaday had held against John Crockett. It was a defunct note now, paid off by months of steady labor, and David was eager to put it in his father's hand. This was the surprise he had long planned to give his father.

Canaday loaned him a horse, and he set out. Odd, how nervous he felt, heading home again after being away so long. He had sent no announcement of his impending visit. He anticipated the moment of arrival with a mix of eagerness and dread. Would it be difficult to talk with his parents? Just how far away from them had he grown while at Canaday's?

It was Sunday, a day David had grown up calling "the Lord's Day," as his mother had always termed it. Over his time at Canaday's, that habit had been broken. Typical of the Friends, Canaday didn't accept Sunday as the "Lord's Day" above any other day of the week. Every day was the Lord's, he declared. There ought not be an hour of the week when a man wasn't worshiping, if not outwardly, at least deep inside himself.

The day was warm but not hot, and the steamy humidity that was the annual torment of Tennesseans was lower than usual. Time on the road passed swiftly. By the time David was within a mile of the Crockett tavern, his nervousness had faded to a pleasant tingle of tension, as his anticipation of handing his father the note grew.

When he reached the tavern, he saw three wagons parked outside, and several horses lodged in the stables behind the place. A new woodshed and smokehouse stood near the stables, additions made since he had been here last. There was no one outside when he rode in. He was dismounting in front of the log building when the door opened and his youngest sister, Sally, now about nine years old, appeared and eyed him up and down. A big smile erupted, and she yelled back into the tavern. "David's home, Mama! Pap, come quick—he's come home again!"

David smiled and knelt as his little sister ran to him. He swept her into his arms and hugged her close. By now others of his family were emerging. His mother, her hair much more gray than it had been last time, was the next to wrap her arms around him. Her shoulders quaked as she began to weep.

"Mama, Mama, don't go crying on me! I want to see you smile!"

He patted and loved her for a few moments, then lifted his face and found himself looking into his father's eyes. John Crockett had aged even more visibly than Rebecca; he looked more weary than David was accustomed to seeing. David gently broke free from his mother and went to his father, hand outstretched.

John Crockett took the hand, and held it rather than shook it. His fingers explored the calluses, felt the leathery, hard texture of the palm. "That's a working man's hand," John said. "It tells me you've done well what you've been doing. Is the Quaker pleased with you?"

"Yes, I believe he is."

John nodded, smiling with one corner of his mouth. He pulled David closer, put his arm around his neck and gave him a rough embrace. "Welcome home, David. I've missed you, son."

David had to fight back tears. He hadn't expected such a show of affection from his father. "I've missed you too, Pap." He had come prepared to say such a thing as a mere politeness. As he said it, he realized it was true. Even though life at Canaday's house was easier and better for him, part of him *had* missed his family and home. Even his father.

A loud, gruff voice called from inside the tavern, asking for more peach brandy. A second voice cried for a replenishing of biscuits. John Crockett, grinning widely, yelled back, "Keep your patience, hang you! You'll have your fill! My boy's come home!"

Together, the Crockett family entered the tavern, and David thought that of all the homecomings he had known, this was certainly the finest—and the best part was yet to come.

John Crockett's eyes became hollow and sad when he looked at the piece of paper David had just handed him. The meal was long past; the family and the patrons had all gone to their beds. Only David and his father remained awake, seated by the big stone fireplace. Midnight was approaching.

"His note ... God. I reckon he's sent you to collect it."

"He handed it to me before I left," David replied.

John's hand dropped; the note slipped from his fingers and fluttered to the floor, where he stared at it. "I can't pay it, David. God help me, I can't, much as I wish I could. There's no money to speak of, no more than there ever has been." John slumped and looked older. He gazed over into the corner like some grizzled ancient in his dotage.

"Pap. Pap, look at me a minute. I want to tell you something about that note."

John Crockett's gazing eyes didn't flicker. The presentation of the note had put him into a brood.

"Pap," David said again. This time the sad eyes, surrounded by weathered crevices, shifted up. No other part of the man moved at all.

"Pap, I didn't bring that note for collection. It's a gift for you. It's paid in full."

"Paid . . ."

David grinned. "That's right."

John sat up straighter. He bent and picked up the paper again. "But how—"

"I worked it off for you, Pap. Just like I worked off that note Abe Wilson had on you. Mr. Canaday agreed to let me do that. That's what I've been doing these past months. Working off that note."

"But I never asked . . . why did you . . ."

"I did it because I wanted to. I knew you needed it paid, and with me right there, able-bodied and all, it just seemed the right thing to do."

"You've worked half a year just because . . . you've been working for no pay, son?"

"Well, I reckon I was paid. It was just put against the note instead of into my pocket, that's all. I can go back now and work for straight money, if Mr. Canaday will still have me."

John held the note in both hands like it had become some rare treasure. Silently, he pivoted in his seat and dropped the paper into the cold fireplace. "Paid off," he said. "Paid off, by gum!"

"Know what you ought to do, Pap? You ought to strike fire to that thing. Watch it burn."

John nodded, grinning. "Yes indeed. Yes indeed I should."

He took down his powder horn and sprinkled a few grains onto the paper, then took down his precious Brown Bess musket, which hung in an honored position above the wide mantel. He cocked back the flint and fired a spark onto the gunpowder, which flared brightly, setting the note on fire.

Father and son watched the note curl in flame and

crumble to ash. When it was gone, David glanced sidewise at his father, and saw tears streaming down his face. The feelings toward his father that David had in his heart at that moment were perhaps the most tender and affectionate he had ever known. All the sweat, strain, labor, and personal poverty he had experienced in Canaday's employ seemed minor and unimportant. His father's happy tears were the best wages he had ever been paid.

David slept well that night, and all his dreams were good ones.

Chapter 21

David did not linger at the tavern. He had an unarticulated fear that to remain would risk allowing some unhappy word, a minor disagreement, or the odd case of bad humor on someone's part to come between him and his father. He wanted nothing between them. His working off the note had done much to bridge the distance that had always gaped between father and son, and this was a bridge he wanted to stand forevermore.

Rebecca was quite unhappy to hear David was leaving so soon. But he explained to her his financial need, running his hands over his clothing, old and very tattered. "I ain't had a new suit of clothes in Methuselah's age, and I ought to go work until I can afford me some. I'll come back again to see you, soon. Maybe I'll even be able to buy me a horse before long. Then I could come right steady."

"I wish I had something to give you," John Crockett said. "After what you done, I feel I owe you."

"You don't owe me a thing."

"What did David do, Pap?" Sally asked.

"We'll talk about it later," Rebecca said. "For now, I want to put a good meal into my son's belly."

A finer breakfast couldn't have been found in the dreams of a starving man. David put away biscuits and pork and gravy and apple butter in great quantities, and as soon as his plate was empty, Rebecca would refill it. At last he pushed away from the table, waving off her continuing offers, and made ready to go. There was more tears at his parting, but they weren't bitter, instead were loving and prideful. David rode away, feeling very much the family hero.

It so happened that a traveler who had spent the night at the inn had also left, traveling the same way as David, though with almost an hour's lead. David noted his horse's tracks on the road before him. They looked steadily fresher as he advanced, indicating he was catching up on the man. This wasn't surprising. The man had been tremendously fat, and rode a swaybacked horse that looked too old to still be among the living. A poor beast, laden with such a bulky human cargo, could hardly be expected to move very quickly.

So David kept an eye out for the man as he went on. A few miles from the tavern, he was surprised to see the swayback horse, still saddled, come meandering back toward him on the road. Strapped to the saddle was the fat man's bag, and a rifle wrapped in cloth. The fat rider was gone. David pulled to a halt, sensing something was wrong.

Dismounting, he stopped the swayback, stroking its mane and talking softly to it. His hand touched wetness in the mane; when he pulled it back, he was shocked by the sight of fresh blood. Aghast, he wiped his bloodied hand in the dirt and brushed off the clots, then looked more closely at the horse's mane.

No question about it: the horse was not itself injured. The blood must be human, no doubt that of the rider.

Tethering both his horse and the swayback, David began walking up the road. He had not gone an eighth of a mile before he found the fat man lying on the roadside, very still and unquestionably dead. Blood had streamed from his nostrils and was beginning to dry in a crust around his mouth and on his chin and neck. David backstepped away from the corpse. Unceremonious loss of the big breakfast his mother had served him was a distinct possibility at the moment. When he had a better grip on himself, he advanced again and knelt beside the body.

He couldn't figure out what had killed the man. The blood made him wonder if someone had struck him across the face, but the nose didn't seem damaged and there was no bruising. It seemed he had simply started bleeding and died. David had heard before of people who died from bleeding inside their heads. Probably that was the case here.

Fright suddenly gripped David. What if someone should come along and find him with the corpse? They might think he had struck and killed the man. He stood and ran back to his own horse, and leaned against it, very shaken up and panting for breath. Glancing around at the swaybacked horse, he pondered what to do. Surely he should tell someone about it . . . but what if they didn't believe him? What if they thought he was trying to cover his own guilt? He hadn't ever dealt with anything like this before.

Just then he noticed again the rifle tied to the swayback's saddle. Despite his fear, David became very curious. Lately he had developed a fascination with rifles, and longed to own one. The fact that the peaceable Canaday didn't think too highly of firearms only made rifles seem more alluring.

David looked back and forth. No one on the road . . . surely it wouldn't hurt to look at the rifle. He could always put it back just as it had been. Moving quickly so he wouldn't have time to change his mind, he went around the horse, loosed the rifle from its ties, and laid it down on the road. He unwrapped it, and what he saw made him whistle softly in admiration.

This was a rifle indeed! Big-bored, brass-mounted, with a gleaming curly maple stock . . . it was remarkably beautiful, a weapon to take a man's breath away.

David picked it up, admiring the heft of it in his hand. David lifted the rifle to his shoulder and looked down the long barrel. The feel of it was perfectly natural. With a rifle like this in a rich patch of forest, a man could bring down an abundance of mighty fine game.

He lowered the rifle. A feeling of sick dread waved through his belly as he remembered the corpse; the rifle had so distracted him that for a moment he had forgotten it. Despairing and uncertain, he knelt to wrap the rifle again, then paused.

A most unexpected and enticing temptation loomed before him. It would be so easy to take the rifle and simply ride away. No one would ever know, and he would have a fine weapon that otherwise somebody else would probably steal anyway. It wasn't right, but . . .

For the rest of his days, David Crockett never revealed to anyone the facts of that morning. But when the struggle with temptation was done, temptation was the victor. David rode on, leaving the unknown dead man on the road and the swayback horse wandering. He took the rifle with him, as well as a powder horn and shot bag he found in the saddlebags.

It wasn't really stealing, he rationalized to himself. After all, the man was dead. He didn't need a rifle any longer. And David Crockett did.

Canaday lifted a brow in silent displeasure when he saw David bring the rifle in. At best, Quakers considered rifles a necessary evil, and ornamented, fancy rifles such as this one did not seem fitting to them. Muttering a disdainful comment about a "decorated instrument of death," Canaday asked David where he had obtained it.

"There was a man at my father's tavern who sold it to him a while back. Pap was so grateful for me working off his note that he gave it to me." Remarkable, how hard it was to lie to John Canaday. David felt that the old man could look right through his eyes into the heart of the falsehood.

But maybe not, because all the Quaker did was purse his lips firmly, exhale loudly through his nostrils, and say, "If I find thee are taking part in shooting matches, I will not be pleased."

David waited several days for news of the dead man, and for the truth to somehow come creeping out of the shadows to reveal his taking of the rifle. It never happened. For a time his conscience bothered him, but eventually that faded too.

Word came later of a man found dead along the road, apparently the victim of bleeding in the brain. A natural death; no suspicion of murder. No one had known him, though inquiry revealed he had spent a night recently at the Crockett establishment, and nothing was found among his few possessions to identify him. He had been buried in an unmarked grave near the place his corpse was found.

For a few days David worried that someone would come along looking for the man, and recognize the rifle. After a couple of weeks passed and nothing like this happened, David's worry eased. Then he found a new one: What if his father should show up for a visit and ask about the rifle in front of Canaday? David's lie would be revealed. In time this concern faded too. Why, after all, should he expect his father to come visit him? He had never done anything like that before.

Then, one day, a wagon rolled up in front of Canaday's house. David was outside at the time, chopping and stacking firewood. He stood, sweating and breathless, and stroked the hair out of his eyes as he watched. For a moment all his fears came to life again; he felt sure that this arrival was linked somehow to the rifle.

The driver of the wagon helped the lone passenger climb down. David couldn't see the passenger clearly from where he was, so he stepped around the woodpile and took a look from there.

The passenger turned, and he saw the face clearly. His knuckles tightened to whiteness on the handle of his axe and a strange, hot feeling surged through his entire form. He instantly forgot all about the rifle.

He did not realize it at the time, but David Crockett had just taken the last step from boyhood to manhood, and his life would be different from now on.

She was a stunning beauty, perhaps the finest female David had ever seen. Her name was Amy Sumner, and she had come from a place called Chestnut Creek in Surry

County, North Carolina. She was the daughter of John Canaday's half brother, and a Quaker . . . though around this latter status there hung some mysterious scandal that David was not privy to. All he knew was what he overheard by eavesdropping: the Westfield Monthly Meeting of Friends had "disowned" her for some offense that in the Canaday house remained unspoken.

David, naturally, was curious about this mysterious offense, but not especially so. He was no Quaker, after all, and Quaker problems were not his concern. It was the young lady herself who had him intrigued.

In other times he had known bursts of mild infatuation, quivers of excitement in the presence of attractive young female neighbors, and so on—but never anything to compare to this. Amy Sumner, with her wide, dark eyes, her thick, deep brown hair, and pale, freckled face, was a permeating, devastating, thrilling presence in the household of John Canaday. David could think of nothing else. In his imagination he played out scenes of walking with her, holding her hand, running his fingers through her hair, kissing her upturned lips, feeling the bright heat of her admiration for him, her deep love. . . .

Reality, to his sorrow, was quite different from his fantasies. Amy showed no signs that she disliked David. In fact, she hardly seemed aware of him. That was the problem. He hungered for her attention, and she seemed content to let him starve.

He became acutely conscious of his appearance, and of his ragged clothing, which he attempted to mend with a needle and thread borrowed from the Canadays. He washed his hair and tried to keep it neatly swept back, and when no one was looking he would rub his face to accentuate the natural redness of his cheeks, a feature others had praised in the past. None of it made any difference. Amy Sumner was blind to him, except on those rare times he managed to force her attention by speaking to her.

Even that was difficult. David couldn't make sense of it; he had never had much trouble making conversation before. Around Amy, however, his throat would grow tight, his voice almost as shrill as it had been in childhood, and his mind numb. Everything he said to her sounded ridiculous as soon as it was out, and before long he would be slinking away, ashamed he had even tried.

Further muddying the waters was the odd way Canaday and his kin acted around Amy. They had little to say about her, and seemed protective, secretive. Sometimes David had the impression that big plans were in the works, but nothing was ever confirmed to him. Many times before he had actually felt like part of the Canaday family. Circumstances at the moment, and the closure of their ranks around Amy Sumner, with him on the outside, reminded him he was not really part of them at all.

This made for unpleasant feelings, and for the first time since his coming to Canaday's, David began to think that perhaps he might be better off going somewhere else. The thought never progressed very far. As long as Amy Sumner was here, so too would be David Crockett, watching her longingly from the shadowy land of exile into which her inattention had banished him.

Frustration grew and blossomed into a sense of self-disgust. Soon it was evident to David that he would not be able to put aside his deep feelings for Amy Sumner. He was sick of his own inability to convey those feelings to his intended—because by now she was nothing less than that. He loved her so deeply he couldn't imagine not making her his wife. After all, he was freshly turned seventeen years old, a man by most frontier standards, and certainly old enough for a wife.

For two days he readied himself. Out in the woods, far from public view, he rehearsed his speech to her, from the gestures to the inflections, even the light laugh he figured to use at the close of several very clever jokes he had come up with.

She was walking at the edge of the woods beyond the stable when he approached her. The time had come; it was do or die. Struggling with a tendency to tremble, he approached her, said his hello, and launched into his talk.

Amy watched him, and listened closely, and was polite enough not to smile when he finally reached the culmination of his presentation: he felt deep affection for her. He wished, with her permission, to have the privilege of. courting her.

"Mr. Crockett," she said, "I'm very happy you are so pleased with me. My heart is warmed. But the truth is, I've become engaged to be married to my cousin, Robert Canaday. It was a family decision, but I have agreed to it. So you can see my affections are already given to another."

David's legs almost failed to hold him up. Robert Canaday! John Canaday's own son . . . David had not had an inkling. He felt tremendously foolish, and could no longer meet her gaze.

"I . . . I wish you well," he said, eyes on his feet.

"Thank you, and . . . well, thank you."

Maybe she smiled. David never knew. He had already turned and slunk away, feeling the unequaled pain of a heart that had been laid bare before it was trampled.

Chapter 22

For a long time David had wanted new clothing, but now that he had purchased some, the garments felt stiff and scratchy and he couldn't get comfortable in them, no matter how he twisted and tugged. He was engaged in such a dance as he stood before the front door of a cabin about a mile and half away from John Canaday's place, awaiting an answer to his knock.

The door opened, and a man with a strong resemblance to John Canaday, both in features and manner of dress, stood looking back at David. This was Bowater Canaday, one of the old Quaker's sons, and keeper of a small and informal school that operated in his home. He greeted David with a wide, close-lipped smile, and said, "Hello, my friend. I've been waiting for thee. Please come inside."

"Morning, Mr. Canaday." David walked in, slipping off his slouch hat and resisting the urge to tug on his cuffs. "I'm grateful you're willing to speak with me this morning."

Bowater had him sit down, and settled his own rather ample form on a stool in front of the visitor. "Now, I understand it is the desire for some schooling that has brought thee here."

"Yes, sir, it is. I'm in dire need of an education. I'm willing to work for it. I'm a good worker."

"Indeed. My father has been pleased with thee, and has recommended thee to me."

They talked for a time about the motives behind David's request, though David wasn't fully open on the subject. He declared that he was convinced a man couldn't advance in the world without knowledge, and that he had come to believe it was a "God-ordained duty" for every male who could to fill his mind with "as much truth and such as it will hold." He threw that in to put a religious tone to his request, knowing Bowater would like that. Indeed he did seem pleased with such talk, never guessing that David's motives were in fact a touch less lofty than he was letting on.

The truth was that Amy Sumner's "jilting" of him, as he perceived it, had led to much introspection about his flaws. Why hadn't she accepted him? Perhaps it was his poverty, or his poor clothing, or the fact he wasn't a Quaker—but finally he decided the real problem was that he was just too ignorant for her. Females, he concluded, were attracted to men of learning, men with that confident air that comes from abundant knowledge. He could understand that. Men with fuller minds often had fuller purses. He had dwelled on such matters until the desire for learning had become overwhelming. The simple truth was, David Crockett wanted an education because he believed it would help him find a woman.

Talk continued, and David was very gratified with the agreement finally reached. He would work for Bowater Canaday two days a week, and attend school four. In addition to teaching, Bowater would provide lodging and meals. David stood and shook hands with his new tutor, and left to go fetch his few belongings from John Canaday's place.

For the next several months David's life was utterly different than anything he had known before. Bowater was a slow-moving but persistent teacher, and bit by bit David adjusted to the life of a student. He learned to write and read, and to do basic mathematics. This was not at all like Kitching's school. Bowater was far more gentle of manner and patient. David was different too. This time he really wanted to learn, and discovered to his surprise that learning could actually be pleasant. As the weeks passed, he became increasingly proud and more sure of himself.

Half a year went by speedily, and David neared the end of his education. By now he had learned about all he had anticipated learning, and felt ready to reenter the world at large. Women bore stronger on his mind than ever. He hadn't fully forgotten Amy Sumner, though she was unavailable to him, but he had grown hopeful he could find someone else in her place.

It was the final day of David Crockett's education when John Canaday showed up at Bowater's cabin, looking very solemn. With minimal greetings he walked up to David and said, "Come to my home at once, David. Persius Tarr has come to my doorstep. He has suffered much and is in a sorrowful condition, and much changed. To see thee, I think, would do him much good. Come, please. I fear greatly for his welfare."

"Changed," it turned out, was too mild a word to describe the altered condition of Persius Tarr. David was struck by it as soon as he walked into the little gable room that had been his own sleeping place before he went off for education, and which now was given over to Persius. The face that looked back into David's was that of a person who had undergone an experience of life-altering horror. All that David knew about what had happened to Persius was what John Canaday had told him on the way here, and what his eyes now told him: Persius Tarr had been hurt, and seemingly shaken to his heart.

"Hello, David," Persius said softly. "I'm hurt, you can see." He threw back the covers and showed a bandaged arm and side. "I'm hoping my arm won't go putrid and have to be cut off. Mr. Canaday says he believes I'll be able to keep it."

"What happened to you, Persius?"

"Some men tried to kill me. They almost did."

"The violence of men is a stench in the nostrils of God," Canaday said.

"Is that how you got hurt?"

"Aye."

"He has already told me part of the tale," Canaday said. "It is worthy of the hearing. My friend, I'll tell it for thee, if such would give thee a rest."

"I can tell it," Persius said.

David listened as Persius unfolded his story. He was weary and in pain; often he would have to stop for a few moments before going on. Canaday was right. Persius's tale was worthy of the hearing.

Here are the details of his story:

After the incident with Crider Cummings and his band, Persius had decided that the more distance he could put between himself and the immediate area, the better. He migrated north, across Clinch Mountain and into the wild country along that river. There were caves in the hills. Persius found them, and in a small, snug one a quarter of the way up a mountainside, sheltered from the weather and hidden from view, he made a temporary home. When the winter came, he warmed himself by a fire kept almost continually burning at the cave's mouth. He ate fish gigged, trapped, or hooked from the river; rabbits snared in their runs; and whatever small game he could capture beneath deadfall traps.

Lacking a rifle, he resorted to an old skill taught to him by his father and made himself a crossbow from black haw and poplar; a bowstring of long threads from his clothing, woven into a strong, thin cord; and arrows from straight-grained hickory. The latter he tipped with sharpened flints, some of which he chipped out himself, others found in finished form, the work of ancient Indians who had hunted the same mountains long before the Cherokees came, long before the Crusaders journeyed to liberate Jerusalem from the Moslems, even long before Mary gave birth in a Bethlehem stable. The crossbow Persius made was crude but deadly; many a frontiersman had used this ancient weapon to bring in game when powder or lead was in short supply.

It was a lonely existence, but Persius enjoyed it. In the company of people, he either found trouble or it found him. Alone on his ridge high above the Clinch River, he was at peace. At times he actually felt grateful for the incident that had driven him out of Jefferson County and into this reclusive life. There were occasional flashes of something like an underconsciousness, a hazy, half-remembered awareness of a life like this in his past . . . but it couldn't be *his* past. He had never lived like this before. He could only suppose that some ghost-memory resident in his blood was being stirred to life by this solitary existence. He was remembering not his own past, but in some unexplainable way, the past of long-gone ancestors who had struggled for sustenance in a raw, primitive world.

His peace ended on a day that he had believed would bring him good fortune. Hunting several miles away from his cave of residence, operating out of a temporary camp, he wandered along the river in the waning afternoon. He had spotted a mussel near the water's edge, and inside it he found a gleaming, bluish freshwater pearl. It seemed to him an omen of good fortune if ever he had seen one. Few mussels actually contained pearls. Finding one surely indicated that today was a day of luck.

When Persius returned to his camp, examining his pearl and not being as observant as he normally would, he discovered to his shock that his privacy had been invaded. Two men were seated by his fire, hunters, from the look of them, rifles across their knees and smiles on their faces. Each resembled the other, though one was quite a bit older. Father and son, Persius guessed.

"Howdy," the older one said.

"Howdy."

"Crossbow, eh? I ain't seen one of them since my grandpap was yet living."

"Where'd you come from?" Persius asked. He eyed their rifles and wished he had nocked an arrow into the crossbow before coming back into camp.

"We was on up the river a bit. Doing a bit of hunting, you know. We smelled your smoke last night. Knew there was somebody hereabouts." He paused. "Never expected to find us an Injun."

Nothing changed in Persius's face, though he detected an ominous tone in the man's voice. "I'm not an Injun."

"You surely do look it. Don't you think he looks it, Felix?"

"I ain't an Injun."

"Why, it wouldn't make no difference if you was!" the younger one said. "Pa and me, we'll sit down and eat with darkies of any color. We ain't proud."

To encounter hunters, trappers, or travelers in the forest wasn't particularly uncommon, especially given the steadily growing population. The custom in such chance meetings was to be open and friendly, to share what fare one might have. Persius knew that, but something in him balked. These men were disturbing; he wished they would go their way.

But the custom had to be followed, or he would be asking for trouble. "I'm glad to see you," Persius said. "I ain't got much to share, just some venison, but what I have you're welcome to."

The older one said, "That's mighty friendly of you, Mister . . ."

"Walker. Henry Walker."

"Henry Walker. That's a fine-sounding name. My name is Marcus Jefferson. This handsome young man here is my son, Felix."

Persius brought out his food and divided it, noting that the Jeffersons appeared to have well-stuffed pouches. Food of their own? Probably so, but if it was, they made no move to share it.

Persius devoured the meal nervously, hardly tasting his gulped bites. Afterward, pipes came out and the Jeffersons sat observing their uncomfortable host. Their small, vaguely mocking smiles, shaped around the stems of their pipes; their piercing, laughing eyes—all worked together to make Persius feel only more unsettled.

"So where you been living, Mr. Walker?" Marcus Jefferson asked.

"In a cave. Long way from here. I just wandered this way a-hunting."

"A cave! Well, we've been living in a cave ourselves. It ain't far—why, you ought to come see it. Spend the night in there, you know. Looks like it could rain. We could return your hospitality like good folk should."

"I'll get by. I don't mind a little rain. Thank you, though."

"Come with us. Take a look at our cave. We fixed it up fine as a house. I give you promise you ain't never seen so fine a cave as ours is!"

Persius had no desire to go, but the Jeffersons pressed him, and he began to grow afraid that continuing to turn them down might anger them. Beneath their veneer of friendliness was a threat that he could all but smell. And to his displeasure, Felix Jefferson was right about the coming of rain. The sky was full of clouds, and thunder began to rumble. There would be a storm before midnight, a major one, if Persius had to guess. It became harder and harder to find pretexts for resisting the Jeffersons' invitation, and at last Persius reluctantly gave in.

They walked through the darkness for less than a mile, until they reached a tall bluff overlooking the wide river below. The elder Jefferson led the others down a narrow path and edged out into a ledge against the edge of the cliff. A few yards out it widened greatly, and the dark mouth of a cavern opened back into the hillside.

"Here it is. Fine cave, eh?"

Persius mumbled heartless agreement. Meanwhile, the younger Jefferson knelt and struck a spark onto punk, then started a small fire. The older man went to the side of the cave's mouth and, out of a hole, pulled a pine torch made from long splinters of pine heart tied together. He lit the torch in the fire, and when it was blazing brightly, grinned at Persius.

"We always keep a good supply of pine torches made up. Come on in. I'll show you our place here."

Caution reared in Persius like a frightened horse. He knew something was amiss. He couldn't go on pretending otherwise. "No. I won't go in there."

"What? Ha! There's naught to be worried about. Just a cave, that's all. Let me show you where we live."

"No. I'm obliged, but I'm going now."

Jefferson stripped away the pleasant expression he had worn like a mask. "No, redskin. No you ain't."

Then Persius saw a flash of fire and felt a jolt of hot pain in the back of his head. The younger one had worked his way behind him, unseen. Persius went down, mind spinning, skull throbbing with pain. He felt hands grasp him, and he was dragged into the cavern, the light of the pine torch playing against an ever-rising ceiling. Father and son were talking in voices devoid of their prior friendliness, calling him Indian, cursing him as Indian, declaring they would rid the world of him as Indian. He tried to struggle and could not.

"In you go, you red coon," the old man's voice said in his ear. "You just found your way to what my dear departed old pappy liked to call Injun hell."

He went up, out—no hands grasping him now. He spun and turned in the air, falling into blackness. Hands flailing, he screamed, and then he struck, back downward, on rock. His breath was knocked from him, and pain tore through his side and arm.

The yellow light above him arced out and down. They had dropped the torch into the same pit they had just thrown him into. He knew why. They wanted to see him down there, to enjoy the results of their treachery. He heard their voices but could not understand them. One of them laughed.

Groaning, he rolled onto his side. The torch still burned, several feet away from him, and its light revealed heaps of shattered, yellowing bones, empty rib cages like upturned grasping fingers, and skulls with mouths open as if in silent screams.

Chapter 23

At this point in the story, Persius stopped speaking for a few moments.

David said, "Them bones . . . they were bones of animals?"

"No," Persius answered. "Not animals. Men."

"God!"

John Canaday had not heard this part of the story before. He shuddered visibly. "How did they come to be there?"

"They was murdered. Injuns, you see."

"Murdered by Injuns?" David asked.

"No, no. The bones were bones of Injuns, murdered by the two who had throwed me down there, and by the old one's father before him."

"How do you know that?"

"They told me so. Hollered it down at me from above . . . mocking at me. Telling me how they had killed more redskins than they could count, how Injuns had died in that cave for nigh to thirty years. And how fine it would be for me to bleed or starve to death down there amongst the remains of my own kind."

"What? They took thee for an Indian?" Canaday interjected.

"Yes. They ain't the first who have. There's been others before them. You can see I'm dark of skin and hair, and have a countenance a mite like a redskin. It's been a bane to me all my days."

Canaday gave Persius an evaluation. "There is more than a mite of resemblance. Is there Indian blood in thee, Persius?"

Persius looked squarely into Canaday's face. His eyes, hollow and sad throughout his recounting so far, now flashed hot with life. "No. I'm no Injun, not in any part. I'm a white man, through and through."

"I meant thee no offense."

David remembered the time years before when he had asked Persius a similar question and received an equally hostile response. Persius had always seemed unusually touchy about the subject of Indians.

Canaday asked, "Could the scoundrels see thee down in the pit?"

"Yes, at least a little. By the torchlight. I figured out right quick that I'd best sull where I fell, like I was hurt too bad to move, else they'd likely shoot me from above. So I flailed some with my arms and moaned out, cried out my back was busted and my legs wouldn't move . . . and that give them a good laugh."

"God forgive them . . . how can evil be so great?" This from Canaday, a quiet musing.

"How did you get out?"

"They left after a time, once they was persuaded I was mortal hurt. By then that torch had near gone out, but once they was gone, I fetched up and got the flames burning brighter again. And then I looked for a way out . . . walked among them bones." Persius's eyes seemed to peer back into an ugliness his mind was already trying to veil. His voice softened. "There was still skin and hair on some of them, and pieces of their clothes. They was years old, most of them, pretty much crumbling to dust. There was a score of dead down there if there was one. Like stumbling around in hell, that's how it seemed . . . I could see where some of them had tried to climb out and just died with their arms up. . . . God, God!"

He lowered his head, trembling. David had never

seen Persius with so little of his usual self-protective veneer of bluster.

Canaday patted Persius's shoulder. "God bless thee, my boy. God bless thee. All is well now. Look for the light of Christ within thee. Let it give thee comfort in thy times of sorrow."

"There is no light, none that I've ever seen," Persius said bleakly.

"There is, there is. Seek it."

David asked, "How did you get out?"

"There was a way to the outside besides the way we had come in—it took a long time to find it. The torch burned out; I sunk down and just laid there amidst them bones. I was hurting, afraid I was dying. Then the morning finally came, and I saw light shining in through a hole in the rocks, way up high. I climbed to it. Don't know how I did it, with my arm hurt, but I did, and I got out."

"What about the men who had done it? What happened to them?"

Persius paused, then said very flatly, "I don't know. They was gone, and I didn't go looking for them. I went into the woods and washed my wounds, and started straight toward Jefferson County. I don't care if I never set foot along the Clinch River again."

Persius's situation gave David much to think about. Canaday was certainly right: the young man was much changed. His experience in the cave had done more than injure him physically. Somehow, it had fundamentally altered his spirit; like a soldier who has survived his first battle, he did not seem the same person he had been before. Whether this was to be a permanent change, David could not guess.

Because of Persius's altered personality, David was not particularly surprised when Canaday proudly announced about a week later that Persius was becoming a Quaker and sought admission into the Meeting. Already David had surmised that Persius's experience had forced upon him an awareness of his mortality; it was only a short jump from there to religion.

What *did* surprise David was one accompanying bit of news: Persius had also agreed to bind himself to Canaday under a work contract for a year. Persius, tying himself to long-term duty and labor? Truly he had undergone a major transformation. He had always shunned such commitment before.

And this brought up a point David found puzzling. The experience Persius had described in the pit of bones had been chilling and dreadful . . . but he had come out of it safe and alive. The event had been horrible, to be sure, but was it horrible enough to have turned a pugnacious thief into a pacifist Quaker; a freedom-loving vagabond into a bound boy, especially when Persius was in his young manhood, a time when most wouldn't desire an extended bondage of labor?

David concluded that surely there was more to Persius's story than he had yet told. He could find no other answer that covered the facts. Something further had happened to Persius along the Clinch River, something bigger and of more import than two scoundrels throwing him into a pit of bones. David's curiosity raged white-hot—but he did not ask. Instinctively he knew it would be useless. If he was to know, it would be only when Persius Tarr decided to divulge it, if ever.

In the meantime, there were other matters to occupy David's attention. With his schooling and work at Bowater Canaday's place behind him, David returned to John Canaday's house and worked alongside Persius, sharing the little gable sleeping quarters and taking great enjoyment in watching Persius struggle to replace his "yous" with "thees" and his oaths with blessings. It was quite a battle. David began to have doubts about the thoroughness of Persius's conversion.

David did nothing to make it any easier for the fledgling Friend to hold true to his new faith. David had been practicing much with his rifle, and became an excellent shot. He slipped out at every chance to attend target practice and turkey shoots and any other kind of marksman's match that came up . . . without John Canaday ever knowing, of course, because he strongly disapproved of such frivolities. Naturally, Persius was expected to feel the same way, now that he was a convert, but he had a hard time of it. His heart just wasn't in abstinence from fun, and within a few weeks Persius began slipping out to the matches with David. Soon he was a Quaker only in the presence of John Canaday and his brood. When he was alone, he was more and more the natural-born scoundrel he had been before.

But not entirely. There was still something that ate at Persius, that kept him turning at night, sometimes talking unintelligibly in his sleep, sometimes sitting bolt upright with a yell. *What's the matter?* David would ask. *Nothing,* Persius would answer. *Just a bad dream.*

David pondered the mystery and became increasingly sure there was more to Persius's story than had been told. Though he had no new facts, a theory slowly began to develop in his mind; he had an idea of what the untold portion might be. It was disturbing enough that he hoped he was wrong.

He had shot well today, better than ever before, and won a dollar for it. David shifted his precious rifle to his left shoulder and sauntered casually along the roadside, whistling beneath his breath, idly tossing Uncle Jimmy's old silver nugget in his right hand. No need for caution today; old Canaday was gone off to Cheek's Crossroads and wouldn't be around to catch him coming back from a forbidden shooting match.

David relived the event in his head. Too bad Persius hadn't been present to see and envy his excellent marksmanship. Persius was not a particularly good shot himself, even using David's fine rifle; David relished the knowledge of Persius's unspoken jealousy when they competed at matches. Persius would have eagerly taken part in today's event had not Canaday assigned him the task of splitting rails.

David stopped and stepped off the road, hearing a

wagon behind him, approaching the bend he had just rounded. Its rumble certainly was odd, as if something was wrong with a wheel—and then came a loud slamming noise, a cracking of wood, and a man's voice shouting an alarm, followed by two feminine screeches.

Even without having seen anything, David knew what had happened, and to whom. The wagon had lost a wheel and cracked its axle, and the man who had yelled was William Elder. His voice was distinctive and booming. David's family and various branches of the Elders had known each other for years. William Elder now ran an inn near the Dandridge community, just north of one of the bends of the French Broad River.

Elder stood beside the wagon, scratching his head and looking sour, when David came back around the bend. Elder looked up. "David Crockett! I'm jiggered! Fancy running into you here."

David shifted his eyes to the young ladies with Elder—Margaret and Annalee, two of William Elder's daughters. Feeling in frisky and bold spirit today, David narrowed his left eye when he looked at Margaret ... enough of a wink to be noticed, but not enough for her to be sure he had intended to do it. Margaret gave him a brief, uncertain smile in return. Beautiful girls, these Elders. David wondered why he hadn't really noticed that before.

"Looks like you're bedeviled with wagon trouble today, Mr. Elder."

"Yes indeed. That deuced sorry wheel! And now my axle is splintered."

David knelt, Elder beside him, and examined the damage. The wheel lay on its side, pinned beneath the wagon, and the greasy wooden axle had splintered at its end.

"That will take some time to fix," David observed.

"Yes. I'm afraid it will."

"Come on ahead with me to the Canaday house. There'll be help for you there."

David walked beside Elder the rest of the way in, talking over the news and bragging, loud enough for Margaret to hear, about his success at the day's shooting match. She was walking directly behind her father, and when David turned his head just right, he could catch a glimpse of her without being obvious about it. When he saw her glancing back at him with big doe eyes, he felt warm from head to toe.

Persius was happy to put aside his rail-splitting and join David and a couple of neighbors in fixing the damaged wagon just enough to roll it to a neighbor's house for a more permanent repair. The Elders then returned to the Canaday house; by now it was late, and John Canaday had returned. He invited the Elders to remain until their wagon was repaired, and they accepted, much to David's delight.

And to Persius's. David noticed that Persius seemed quite fascinated with Annalee Elder, and strutted about before her in a manner most unseemly for one purportedly a Quaker.

John Canaday must have noticed it too, because the next day he sent both David and Persius to work on the most distant portions of his extensive property, sending them out before dawn, before the Elders arose from their beds. When they returned that night, the Elders had already gone back to their home.

David wasn't angered by Canaday's obvious ploy; he had already made an arrangement that rendered it moot. "It appears I'll have to go calling on Margaret Elder tomorrow evening," he said to Persius after they crawled into their sleeping gable. "Somehow or another that silver piece of mine has managed to go missing. Seems I recall seeing it fall out of my hand into her pocket. Reckon I'll have to fetch it back from her."

Persius grinned. "That's a long stretch to their place."

"Ten miles, at least."

"A man needs some company on so long a journey. I suppose it'll be up to me to provide it."

David smiled and nodded. "They're mighty pretty gals, Persius. I swear, that Margaret's prettier than Amy Sumner. Why in the world I never noticed it before I can't figure out."

"Annalee ain't no slouch herself," Persius replied. "I might have to start calling on her, if she's willing."

"As long as you leave Margaret alone."

"I will. I promise. And the same goes for you and Annalee."

They pledged to respect each other's romantic fields of conquest, rolled over in their blankets, and fell asleep at once. Canaday might not have succeeded in diverting their minds from the Elder girls, but he had succeeded in thoroughly exhausting them.

Chapter 24

John Canaday could hardly understand it. For weeks now both Persius Tarr and David Crockett had been going through unexplainable spells of weariness. At least once a week, sometimes twice, they trudged through their working day in a state of listlessness, moving like worn-out ancients instead of the strong and virile young men they usually were. He wondered if they were ill.

But that theory didn't cover the facts. If illness were causing their mutual torpor, it would do so consistently. Their odd condition was sporadic, and occurred in both young men at the same times. Therein lay the most mystifying aspect of it.

And then there was that long, stout pole Canaday had found of late, leaned up against the gable of the house. He had moved it to the edge of the woods three or four times, and each time it had returned. It was downright puzzling. No one in the household seemed able to explain it, David and Persius included.

John Canaday accepted the shrugs and denials of everyone in the household—except David and Persius. Something was up with those two. The reappearing pole beneath their window, the bursts of weariness—he was certain these mysteries were connected, though he had not a clue as to how. It bothered him to think his workers were deceiving him. Not so much where David was concerned;

he expected a certain amount of deceit from David. But Persius shouldn't lie about anything. After all, he was a convert to the faith; dedicated to honesty, labor, and the simple, good life. Unless, of course, his conversion hadn't gone quite to the bone. But that was an idea that Canaday, with an idealistic streak age hadn't erased, wasn't prepared to accept.

They moved in silence, shifting about on bare feet, avoiding the floorboards that tended to creak. By the light of a single grease lamp they dressed themselves in their best clothing, then opened the window and shinnied down the long pole they had quietly wedged into the corner formed between the chimney column and the house. When it was placed just so, it reached right to the window of their sleeping quarters, and made a dandy substitute for a ladder, and both had gotten adept at descending and ascending by it. Persius went down first, David next, after pausing at the top of the pole to carefully close the window again while he clung to the pole like a squirrel.

"Think they heard us?" Persius whispered when both were on the ground.

"No," David said. "I could still hear the old man snoring when I closed the window."

They went to the stable and quietly saddled and bridled two horses. They didn't mount immediately, but led them well down the road from the house, walking them in the soft, sound-muffling grass instead of on the hard-packed dirt road. Only when they were out of sight and sound of the house did they mount and ride. They would not dismount again until they had traveled upward of ten miles, all the way to the Elder residence. There they would spend most of the night romancing the Elder sisters, staying as long as they could, allowing themselves just enough return time to ride the ten miles back home again, put up the horses and tack gear, and climb back up the pole to their window and into their beds. The next day, naturally, would be an agony of labor done without sufficient rest—but the Elder sisters were worth the sacrifice.

This had been going on for many weeks now, and so far they hadn't been caught. But David worried about John Canaday, who seemed suspicious and had asked uncomfortable questions about the pole. They dared not tell the truth about it. Canaday wouldn't think highly at all of two young men spending time with attractive young ladies after dark, unsupervised, and without the knowledge of the girls' parents. And in particular he would disapprove of Persius, nominally a Quaker, fraternizing with a girl who was not a Friend. David was well-aware that Canaday still prided himself in having led in Persius's conversion. Ironically, he was the only person who had not realized that Persius's "conversion" had backslid itself into nonexistence long ago.

Still, David hoped Canaday wouldn't find out about these nocturnal outings—not that it would make much real difference if he did. He intended to court Margaret Elder—he had taken to calling her Maggie lately—whatever the old man thought about it, and more than that, he intended to marry her. There was no doubt in his mind he had found the woman with whom he wanted to spend the rest of his life.

Keeping company with Maggie in broad daylight was a rare and delightful privilege, and David Crockett enjoyed himself immensely as he strolled beside his beloved in one of the meadows nearby the Meeting House of the Quakers. This was much easier going than courting on the sneak after midnight. On this day the very air seemed lighted with a glow that spoke of happiness and the goodness of life, as if some portion of heaven had fallen to earth and been absorbed into the countryside. And it was all because of Maggie.

This was a wedding day—not for David Crockett, but for his former infatuation, Amy Sumner, and Robert Canaday. David and Maggie had both played a part in the now-completed marriage service and celebration, serving as attendants to the bride and groom. This was the first wedding in which David had participated, and he thought it had been a grand experience ... so grand that he was ready to take part in such a ceremony again, as soon as possible. And not as attendant, but bridegroom.

Maggie's hand in his own felt small and feminine, wonderful to caress. It was not a delicate hand; the continual labors of frontier life had put strength in her grip and and calluses on her palm. David didn't care. He had never known any other kind of girl, and wouldn't have known what to make of an uncallused hand. He could conceive of no finer or more appealing female than the one walking at his side.

At that moment, he was in the midst of what he considered the most important conversation of his life, one he had been waiting for the right moment to take up. This time, in the soothing afterglow of the Canaday-Sumner wedding, had seemed that right moment.

"... and you know I've done a right smart bit of striving to be with you, coming out at night and riding ten mile in and ten mile back and such as that."

"I know," she said.

"Now, a man don't do such as that if he ain't got a strong desire to be with his intended—"

"Intended?" Maggie repeated, casting her glance sidewise toward David.

David felt flustered. He hadn't really meant to use that loaded a word just yet, though in fact it went precisely to the point he was aiming toward.

"Well, yes ... intended. And that's what I'm trying to say to you. I've got intentions for you. I ... love you. I want to make you my wife."

By the time the words were out, he felt he would have choked had he been compelled to add another one. Never had he forced out a more difficult series of sentences. He had laid his heart and his plans at Maggie's feet. He awaited her response.

"Wife ..." she said. "Why, David, you surprise me!"

Surprise? David didn't like the sound of that. How could she be surprised, considering all the time and effort he had put into romancing her? He saw at once that this wasn't going to come together as readily as he had hoped.

"I've never had a marriage proposal put to me before," she went on. "Why, I hardly know how to think!"

"Just say yes. That's all you need to do. I'd make you a fine husband, Maggie. I'm poor, I know, but I'm strong and educated—by a Quaker! You won't find no finer a teacher than a smart Quaker, I'm here to tell you. I love you, Maggie. And I believe you love me too ... don't you?"

"Well, I *think* I do. . . ."

"Don't you know your own heart? We'd make a fine married couple, you and me. Think of the stout family we'd raise! You're the woman for me, Maggie. I'm certain of it."

And yet still she resisted. It was very exasperating to him, the way she hesitated and sidestepped. After a time he began to think she was toying with him. She *had* to have realized long ago he was serious in his intentions. All this display of surprise and uncertainty was surely a pretense. And so he pressed her all the harder for an answer. He wouldn't be put off by girlish coyness, not with the depth of feeling he had for her! The conversation went on another hour, a human, verbalized form of what would have been a ritual courtship dance in the animal or bird kingdom. David pushed, cajoled, begged, and she resisted—a little less, a little more, than less again, and less ...

A few days later, David Crockett rode to the courthouse at Dandridge. When he left, the following was in his pocket, with a copy on file in the clerk's office:

> State of Tennessee—Jefferson County: To any licensed minister of the gospel or justice of the peace—Greeting: I do authorize and empower you to celebrate the rite of marriage between David Crockett and Margaret Elder and join them together as husband and wife. Given at my office in Dandridge, the 21st day of October, 1805. J. Hamilton, Clerk.

David Crockett had never known a greater happiness in his life. The finest woman in Tennessee, a specimen superior even to Amy Sumner herself, had agreed to become his wife. They had even set a date. Nothing stood in their way now . . . nothing but the technicality of asking her parents for their blessing on the upcoming union. It was a custom David felt bound to follow, though he dreaded it badly. After all, William Elder and wife didn't even know their daughter had been seeing David Crockett, much less that she had engaged herself to marry him.

David pledged himself to get that difficult duty out of the way as soon as possible . . . well, nearly so. There was still a little time he could put it off. Surely, he argued to himself, he needed to consider his words carefully, to put it to them in just the right way. And besides, he could use a few days to gather a bit more worldly wealth. Lord knew he had little enough—a fact Maggie's parents were certain to note.

He needed money, and quickly, if he was to obtain their blessing. And short of theft, there was only one way he could think of to obtain it.

No need to rush, David reminded himself. Don't let them distract you—just aim at the nail head, very carefully, and then squeeze, not hard, not fast, just enough to trigger off the shot . . .

The lock snapped the flint forward, sparking the powder in the pan, which in turn set off the charge in the barrel. Even as the ball hurtled invisibly through the great burst of smoke that exploded out of the barrel, David knew that the shot was true. Sure enough, for the third time in succession, lead ball struck nail head, driving the home-forged spike even deeper into the target post. David lowered his smoking weapon and grinned crookedly as cheers rose all around.

Persius Tarr punched him on the shoulder. "You blasted that one like hell-blaze Dave!" he declared in a most un-Quakerish way. "That gives us the match!"

"I know," David said, still grinning. He was proud of himself. He had shot better today than ever before, and the prize was a good one: a beef. Strictly speaking, the beef was only half his, because Persius had been his shooting partner in the match and had an equal share in the prize—though in fact it was David's shooting that had carried the day. Not that Persius had done badly. In fact he had shot a better match today than David had ever seen him shoot before.

A tall man approached David with his hand outstretched. He had a hook nose and a pate rendered hairless and smooth as an eggshell from some long-ago bout with the scalp condition known as "scald head." This was the sponsor and overseer of this particular match, and he had just examined the target and certified that David had indeed hit the nail head three times in a row—a most remarkable bit of shooting. "The beef is yours," he said. "You are free to take it with you, or to sell your share for money."

"I'd prefer the money, I believe," David said. "I'm to be married soon, and I can hunt down meat a lot easier than money."

"Ain't that the truth! Congratulations to you on your marriage." He leaned closer and spoke more softly. "Mr. McGraw yonder will gladly buy the beef from you, I believe. Before the match he asked for the right to make an offer to the winner. I'd be inclined to take his offer, if I was you. He's going to pay with chink."

David went to the indicated man and held a brief discussion, then shook hands and made the exchange. When he came away, he had five dollars in his pocket, and as promised, it was payment in gold coin.

Persius opted to keep his share of the beef, believing he could strike an even better bargain later. He fell in beside David. "Reckon you're as good fixed-up as you'll ever get for marrying."

"Likely."

"When you going to talk to her pap?"

David held silence, not liking the topic. Persius had asked about that quite a lot lately, and David had always put him off by saying he would talk to them as soon as he had a little more money. Now he had some money, yet the prospect of going before them didn't seem a bit easier to swallow.

"I don't know. I need to get it over with. I told her sometime back I'd be stopping in to see her today."

"When's the wedding day?"

"This coming Thursday."

As David said that, he was struck by how close his marriage really was. Time had flown by. He really shouldn't delay any further about asking for Margaret's hand.

He said, "I'd best go have a word with her pap right now."

"Why, if you've waited this long it can't hurt to wait a few hours more. Look yonder! There's a liquor jug making the rounds. This may turn into a prime frolic yet! Stay for a bit."

David was tempted. He loved a good frolic as much as any man, and staying for a time would put off his dreaded duty a little while. He grinned and nodded. Persius slapped his shoulder again, and together they headed toward the liquor.

It was about noon, on a Saturday. The frolic went on through the afternoon, picking up steam and participants. At nightfall David was still there. He had forgotten entirely about fulfilling his pledge to visit Maggie. He was drunk, contented, and filled with fun. There was no room in his mind for any thoughts beyond those of the present moment.

The night grew old, and the party continued. A fiddler showed up, and everyone danced, with or without a partner. By now David was so mentally numbed he could hardly react to anything. So when he saw Crider Cummings stride into the clearing and glare coldly toward Persius, he failed to consider the significance and potential volatility of the event.

At last David, his head fuzzy and spinning, reeled off to the edge of the woods and flopped into the leaves. He writhed and turned a few moments, then fell into a deep, drunken sleep.

Chapter 25

Every step made his head throb. David tried to ignore it, tried to act as if all was well and last night's revelry hadn't so badly wrecked him mentally and physically. When he had awakened on the hard ground this morning, the first thought through his mind had been of Maggie and his failure to fulfill his promised visit. Now here it was, Sunday morning, and David was worried. Deeply worried. How would Maggie receive him, and what could he tell her as an excuse?

Even more significant: How would Maggie's parents react? What if Maggie had cried and complained to them about his failure to arrive? Would they deny him her hand?

This was all Persius Tarr's fault. If Persius hadn't lured him to stay at the frolic, this situation wouldn't exist.

A thought passed through David's mind: Maybe I ought to rid myself of Persius, so his bad name doesn't rub off on me. A man has to watch out for his reputation in the community, and Persius ain't doing mine a bit of good.

The unfriendly thought might have shocked him, had it not come so easily and passed so quickly, and had he not at that moment come to a wagon road that led to the house of one of Maggie Elder's uncles. He stopped, eyeing the cabin. Maybe he should stop by there first and gauge their reaction to him. If he was inhospitably received, or note was made of his hung-over condition, he could know whether it would be more prudent to go on to Maggie's or withdraw.

He went to the door, where he finger-combed his dark hair and gave a couple of rubs to his cheekbones to return some look of life to his features. As he knocked and awaited an answer, he contorted his face into a smile so that at least he would look pleasant when the door opened. The actual effect was to give him a ghastly appearance. Feeling unsteady, he leaned on his rifle.

He was surprised when Annalee Elder answered his knock. Clearly, Annalee was equally surprised. David noted that her hair was loose and very thoroughly combed out, so that it hung straight down her back and over her shoulders. Usually she kept it tied back.

She looked at him evaluatively. Blast it—he could tell from her expression that she saw something was wrong with him.

"David. Hello. What brings you here?"

"Just a sociable call on your uncle . . . is he about?"

"No, not right now. He'll be back later, him and the family."

"Oh. Why are you here?" He had the question asked before it came to him that maybe it wasn't his business.

Annalee blushed. "Aunt Sal, she was working on my hair some," she mumbled. "She's good with hair."

"Is she? Well, I see." He felt embarrassed that he had been so nosy—an embarrassment compounded by the realization that Annalee had been afflicted with a case of head lice, and had come here for a treatment of the herbal-and-root concoction her aunt was famous for making, a mixture that would kill lice right down to the nits.

A quick change of subject was called for. "Would you care if I come in?" he asked. "I'm thirsting for some water."

"Come in, if you want," Annalee said. She went to the back of the cabin and dipped a cup into a water bucket. David accepted the water and sipped it slowly. It made his head hurt merely to swallow.

He sat himself on a three-legged stool and leaned forward, elbows on knees. "Are your parents at their house?" he asked.

"Yes. They are home." She said it in a quick, snippy way, not like she was angry, but as if the subject was delicate. Things weren't looking good.

"Is everything well at your house?"

"Yes, yes."

"Well, is Maggie there? I'm thinking that I'll stop by and see her. To tell you the truth, I was supposed to call yesterday, but I took a little sick spell and ... Annalee? What's wrong?"

She had burst into tears. Burying her face in her hands, she cried vigorously. David stood.

"Annalee, has something happened to Maggie? Is she sick?"

"No, no, not sick ... oh, David, it's hard for me to tell you! She's deceived you."

"What does that mean?"

"She's to be married."

David was confused. "Well, of course she is. On Thursday. I'm the bridegroom, remember?"

"No," she said, looking up at him with red eyes. "She's marrying tomorrow. And you won't be the bridegroom."

David took it in. A sick feeling squirmed through him. "She's getting married ... who to?"

"I'd best not say. You might hurt him."

"Hurt him? Right now I don't have the spirit to hurt nobody." His shoulders slumped and he wished he could lie down. He contented himself with sitting back down on the stool again and lowered his head. "It's really true?"

"Yes."

"So I'm jilted."

"I'm mighty sorry, David."

"Why did she do it?"

"She got frightened. She says you talk so much of frolics and shooting matches and such that she feared you'd be a neglectful husband. You never asked our parents for her hand, and lately another man came courting her. When you didn't show up yesterday, she took to thinking you were having doubts, or maybe felt ashamed of her. . . ."

"Ashamed? How could she think—" He stopped. Now that he considered it from Margaret's viewpoint, he could understand, however grudgingly, that she might have begun thinking that way. He searched his memories for warning signs she might have given out that he had missed. Had she been more distant the last time he had seen her, and had he been too distracted to notice? Maybe so.

"I'm mighty sorry," Annalee said again.

Suddenly he felt sick of it all. Sick of this talk, this family, of fickle women, of the thought of marriage. Sick of life itself. Without another word he rose, grabbed his rifle, and stormed out the door. Annalee followed.

"David, you ain't going to hurt nobody, are you?"

"No."

"Oh, I hope you won't. Maybe you should go to see her. Maybe you can make her change her mind. Our parents think highly of you."

"Don't believe I care even to try right now," he said. He strode away, wishing he had a horse to ride. If he did, he would ride right out of the county, the state, and not stop until he was in a country he had never seen before, where nothing could remind him of Maggie Elder and a marriage that now would never take place.

But he had no horse. There was nothing to do but trudge the long distance home. His rifle felt awfully heavy.

First Amy Sumner, and now Margaret Elder. The sting had probed deep, then deeper. No more, David swore. He would go through life single, and rejoice in his freedom. Women were pliable, deceptive, self-centered creatures, more given to torturing a man than the wildest savage.

Undressing for bed that night, he wondered where Persius was. He hadn't returned from the shooting match. John Canaday, who didn't even know where Persius had gone in the first place, was very worried. David would have worried too, except the memory of

Crider Cummings's arrival at the frolic had left his mind, preoccupied as he was with his romantic loss.

When David finally managed to fall asleep, Persius still was not home.

Two Days Later

According to the story commonly spread around the community, Crider Cummings's body was found covered in leaves about a hundred yards from the road. There was evidence of a scuffle; the body was bruised and scratched, and there were traces of bloody skin beneath the fingernails. He had been stabbed to death, his chest pierced three times.

The murder knife was found nearby, apparently dropped by the killer in his haste to flee. Several people were able to identify the knife as property of Persius Tarr.

And Persius Tarr himself was suspiciously absent. From the time he had left the shooting-match-turned-frolic, no one had seen him. But they had seen Crider Cummings, who arrived at the match just before Persius left. Crider had ridden out in the same direction minutes later.

Even David, who desired to give the benefit of the question to Persius, couldn't seriously doubt what had happened. Persius and Crider had fought, Persius had stabbed him to death, and then fled. Considering Crider's grudge against Persius, it was likely the killing had been done in self-defense. But certainly the fact that Crider's body had been dragged away from the road and hidden in leaves, and that Persius had then fled, did nothing to enhance his situation.

This tragic turn of events greatly added to David's depression. And it devastated John Canaday. All the deception he had been under concerning Persius Tarr's conversion was swept away very rudely. For a time he began acting and looking his true age. David actually worried that the old man would take sick and die.

Canaday eventually got over the worst of the shock,

and bound out another boy in Persius's place, which seemed to distract him. The fellow's name was Jed Gilford. David wasn't particularly happy to be sharing his sleeping loft with a stranger, because he had become accustomed to brooding, something always done better in private. He thought about leaving, but never followed through. He was too used to living away from home to consider returning there for good, and he had no means of making a living or keeping a roof over his head apart from staying on with Canaday. And so he stayed, and eventually got used to the new bound boy, who was about a year his junior.

David spent much time hunting, and continued to go to shooting matches. As far as he could see it, this would be his status for the rest of his days: living as an unmarried man, contenting himself with fields and forests and shooting matches, and having nothing at all to do with women.

Chapter 26

Though the name given her at birth was Mary, most called her Polly, and now the nickname was more hers than the real one. It was how she thought of herself, and the name by which she would soon be introduced to David Crockett, if all went according to plan.

She licked her lips for the twentieth time, and for the thirtieth smoothed down the front of her skirts—movements inspired by nervous tension. All around her was festivity; the event was one of the common frontier celebrations known as a reaping. Long planned, this one was to last three days, and it was here that she was scheduled to meet David Crockett, about whom her friend Kirsten had told her so much.

Polly Finley was excited about meeting this fellow, but also cautious, because he was said to be devoted to good times, and a young woman had to be careful around such a young man. From all she had heard about David Crockett, it seemed appropriate that she was to meet him at a party. He reportedly seldom missed a chance for celebration, and was reputed to be one of the finest shots around, almost never missing a shooting match. There would be shooting here today, and dancing, eating, drinking, and games for the children. A likely kind of place for David Crockett, judging from his reputation.

A more serious concern stemmed from Crockett's

well-known friendship with the notorious Persius Tarr, presumed killer of Crider Cummings. Tarr's name was anathema for miles around. It was a little worrisome that the fellow she was to meet had been his friend, and in fact was said to have been the one who brought him to Jefferson County to begin with.

"Polly!"

It was Kirsten's voice. Polly turned and smiled as her Dutch-ancestry friend approached. Kirsten was the nicest of young women and the most devoted of friends. Polly had nothing but high regard for her, and was frequently angered by the cruel comments people made about Kirsten's appearance. True, she was far from beautiful, not even pretty. Her teeth were a distant memory, and a bout with skin trouble had left her hair very thin, so that her scalp showed through. But what did that matter? She was a fine person, and it was to Kirsten's credit, in Polly's opinion, that she held no bitterness for the lack of physical beauty that made it unlikely she would ever have a man of her own. Polly was made slightly uncomfortable by her awareness that Kirsten actually had quite an attraction to this Crockett fellow herself, yet was, in effect, handing him over to her. Kirsten was a realist, Polly supposed. She knew that because of her looks she would never have him for herself, and so was giving that opportunity to her best friend.

"He's here," Kirsten said, taking Polly's arm. "Come meet him."

Polly held back. Now that the moment had come, she felt very shy. What if she didn't like his looks? What if he didn't like hers?

"Come, my dear," Kirsten said. "He ain't going to bite you! Though I'll tell you true, I wouldn't mind him biting me!"

Polly followed Kirsten through the crowd. Off to the side a gourd fiddle squeaked out ragged music, and a handful of dancers reeled and bobbed. Elsewhere a wrestling match was under way, and on the perimeter of the crowd a gang of boys were cruelly engaged in throwing rocks at young ducklings in a pond. Polly's eyes probed through the crowd, trying to see this David Crockett before he saw her. That way, if she didn't like the look of him, she could always withdraw before matters became awkward.

"He'll be tickled with you," Kirsten said. "He come to my house and set hisself down, making a sociable call on my mother, you see, and I told him, 'There's the prettiest gal I can show to you, the prettiest gal you'll ever hope to see—all you need to do is come to the reaping, and I'll make certain you meet her.' He didn't fight me long, even though he swore at the first that he wanted nothing more to do with women, having been jilted here a few months back by Margaret Elder."

"Yes, I know," Polly said. Kirsten had told her this story three or four times already. Obviously she was very proud of having arranged this meeting.

"When he lays eyes on you, he'll never give another thought to Margaret Elder," Kirsten said.

"Where is he?" Polly asked. "I want to see him before he sees me."

"Too late for that," Kirsten said. "There he is now, yonder. He's looking right at us—see that grin!"

Polly had already picked him out. All her fears of not liking his looks vanished like birds into the sky. As for her concern about his friendship with the hated Tarr, those were forgotten in the rush of pleasure she felt at this first sight of him.

David Crockett, standing with rifle in one hand and hat in the other, was a fine-looking young man indeed. His eyes were keen and bright, his face healthy and full, with ruddy cheeks. His dark hair was long and tucked back behind his ears, hanging down the back of his neck to the top of his shoulders. Labor had rendered him firmly built, lean but strong. He struck her as tall, though that impression was perhaps created by the easy straightness of his posture. His rather thin lips were curved in an appealing smile, and when her eyes met his, he nodded in greeting.

"David Crockett, this here's the gal I told you of," Kirsten said. "Polly, come shake the hand of the finest man you'll meet."

Polly blushed; Kirsten's frank way of speaking put her ill at ease. It didn't seem to bother David Crockett, however; he smiled all the more and thrust out a powerful hand.

"I'm pleased to make your acquaintance, Polly Finley," he said. "I'm David Crockett."

His grip was strong but restrained; she liked the feel of his hand. Despite her deliberate effort to restrain herself, a smile forced its way onto her face. "I'm pleased to meet you, Mr. Crockett."

"David, David! I don't take to being a mister."

Kirsten smiled, showing her gums. "Why, with you two taking on like this, we'll have you married and bedded down together before the week's out!"

Polly's face turned red as a blaze. David blushed a little himself, but laughed easily. It put Polly at ease. She felt drawn to him. And it seemed he was drawn to her as well. The afternoon was bright; the music of the gourd fiddle was beginning to sound remarkably fine, scratchy or not.

It was going to be a good day.

David rolled over and slowly opened his eyes. The dim light of a newly borning dawn spilled through the window. He felt drowsy and happy. Why? Sleepily, he strained to remember, and then her face appeared in his mental vision. Polly Finley! Energy began to surge through him, sweeping away the torpor of sleep. He sat up. Across the little gable room, Jed Gilford grumbled and rolled over in his bed, dreading the day as much as David anticipated it.

Whistling softly, David rose and dressed, then descended to the main level of Canaday's house and out through the front door. Every morning since the reaping, he had taken these walks by the light of dawn, mentally replaying the hours he had spent with Polly Finley and blessing the name of Kirsten the Dutch girl for having brought them together.

What a day it had been! And to think that at the beginning he had felt hesitant to meet Polly, not trusting that the homely Kirsten would know what a real beauty was if she was face-to-face with one. How wrong he had been—and Kirsten had been right. As she had promised, Polly Finley was the most appealing, earthily pretty young woman he had ever seen. It crossed his mind that he had thought the same at first of Amy Sumner, then Maggie Elder . . . but he dismissed the thought. He didn't want to think about them now, only about Polly.

At the reaping he had danced a few reels with Polly—she was quite good at it, he was pleased to find—and afterward they had talked for the longest time. Polly was an interesting conversationalist, intelligent and soft-spoken, with the most pleasing and musical voice he had ever heard.

He had met her mother, a talkative old Irishwoman named Jean, a Kennedy before she married William Finley back in 1786. David took it as a good omen that Polly's parents had come together in the same year he had been born. Maybe providence had already been looking out for him, making the necessary arrangements to bring this human angel into his life all these years later.

Jean Finley, though, was certainly an interesting character, and the only aspect surrounding the Polly Finley matter that made him in the least bit uncomfortable. For one thing, the old Irishwoman had laughingly referred to him a time or two as her "son-in-law." Whether she said it with jovial intent or otherwise he could not say.

In any case, he had put about as much effort into winning over Jean Finley as in trying to win her daughter. It was a case of salting the cow to catch the calf, as his father might have put it. He felt it had worked, because neither Jean nor Polly had seemed eager to part from him.

The reaping had continued through the night. Children were there in abundance, enjoying the rare privilege of playing instead of sleeping the night away. David and Polly had joined their games, leading the children through dozens of old "play-party" activities played by generations before them in distant European lands and brought across the water to the New World. It was nearly day when finally the celebrating ended and David told Polly good-bye.

He walked now through the forest, listening to the morning song of the birds, thinking about Polly. He badly wanted to see her again—but he had no horse of his own, and John Canaday's stock of horses was down at the moment, and he rarely had one to spare for David's use.

He was thinking over this situation when he heard the call from the house for breakfast. It was during the meal when a chance reference by Canaday to his son Robert, now husband of Amy Sumner, suggested to David a possible solution to his problem.

Later in the day, David went to Robert Canaday and struck a bargain with him for an aging, cheap horse he possessed. David offered to work for Robert Canaday two days a week for six months in return for the animal. This would still give him sufficient time to perform his labors for the senior Canaday. Robert was agreeable, and hands were shaken.

David grinned all the way home. The horse he had bargained for might be old and decrepit, but it was a means of transport. No man could court without access to his intended. Two days' work a week was a reasonable price to pay for access to Polly Finley, no question about it.

Much to David's frustration, it was nearly five weeks before his circumstances allowed him the chance to call on Polly at her home, fifteen miles away. When finally he did ride out to see her, it was in a panic of fear. In this time she might have been courted and won by some other. Five weeks seemed an eternity of time; certainly it was sufficient for some rival to move in and edge him out.

His fears were not allayed when he found Polly wasn't at home. Her parents welcomed him kindly, Jean chattering on as before, and William Finley playing the backwoods gentleman to his young guest. But where was Polly? David hated to ask it straight out, fearing that would seem rude to the Finley parents, who seemed to assume he had come to visit them. So he sat there in an agony of ignorance, wondering if he would see Polly today at all.

At last he heard the approach of people outside. He stood, his heart leaping at the sight of Polly entering the doorway, then falling again when a young man of about his own age followed her. From the way the Finleys greeted him, it was clear he was not of the family. A suitor, just as David had feared! He shook the fellow's hand upon introduction, hating him all the while.

The next two hours were among the most difficult and most straining David had ever spent. His perception of the fellow as a rival proved accurate, and he had to hand it to him for effort. Right before David's eyes he wooed and praised Polly, holding her hand, telling her of her beauty—all the while casting bitter glances at David, clearly wanting him to go. David would not go. He had come for Polly, and with Polly he would be.

Yet even his staunch will was about to break when finally Polly began to show encouraging signs. Her movements, her words, her manner began to indicate she was tiring of her original suitor and wished him to leave—but like David, he was stubborn. Finally she turned to him and told him outright to go, and he slinked off like a kicked dog, his eyes boring into David like augers.

David remained at Polly's side until late in the day, and accepted an invitation from William Finley to stay the night. There were plenty of quilts and such they could pile into a makeshift bedroll near the fireplace. David accepted gladly.

But it was odd. Something was different, and it took him some time to figure out what it was. It was Jean Finley. No longer did she chatter to him like a parrot, no longer did she praise his looks and manners. Evidently she had developed a preference for one of her daughter's suitors above the other—and the preferred was not David Crockett.

The devil with her, then, David thought. It's not Jean Finley I want, it's Polly. And nobody—not her, not any rival, nor even heaven or hell—will stop me this time. I've lost twice in love, and I'll not lose again.

• • •

He left the next morning, a Monday. Half a mile away from the Finley house, his rival stepped out onto the road before him, anger written across his face.

"Reckon it's me or you," he said.

"Oh, no," David replied. "It ain't me or you. Just me. That's done been decided."

"You think so, do you?"

"Why, that's what I said, ain't it? Now step aside."

"No. I ain't stepping aside for the likes of you. I know who you are, Crockett. You're naught but the white coon of a Quaker, and the friend of a murderer."

"Persius Tarr, you mean?"

"That's right. He's a murderer. He murdered Crider Cummings."

"I ain't no friend of Persius Tarr no more. Why, I'm way too disappointed in him to stay his friend."

The other fellow looked confused. David went on, enjoying himself.

"You see, Persius didn't kill Crider Cummings with style, if you know what I mean. Three little old stab wounds! Pshaw! That's nary worth doing." He reached to his waist sash and drew out the long butcher knife he usually carried. "Now, us Crocketts, when we kill a man—say for courting a woman we've got our eye on or some other such offense—we do it right. Lay him open from his privates to his chin, and clean out the tenderest of his innards to feed our dogs. That way there's nary going to waste, you see, and there's no question that the killed feller's as dead as he's going to get. Why, with no more than three little stab holes, I wager it took old Crider a half hour to figure out whether he was dead or not. Us Crocketts, we don't leave such questions unsettled. We're the bullies of the hill and third cousins to the Philistines. We name our baby girls Jezebel and our boys Beelzebub. We carry the sharpest blades, the meanest dispositions, and grudges longer than the moral law. Toward the lovely ladies we have hearts as soft as butter, but let an enemy come 'round, and they turn hard as an iron skillet. Yes sir, let a fellow get on the bad side of a Crockett and he'll find his eyes gouged out and ate for grapes and his tongue cut out and tanned down to a razor strop. We eat our enemies for Christmas dinner and make combs for our women from the bones. And we never run from a fight. Never. 'Specially not a knife fight."

David turned the knife back and forth, running his finger along the sharp edge and wincing to feign a cut. He put the supposedly sliced finger in his mouth and eyed the other, letting silence hold while his prior words sank in.

"I believe I'll be heading home now," David said. "If I was you, I'd do the same."

He heeled the old horse into motion. His challenger stepped aside and let him pass. Not another word was said. When David was about to round the first turn in the road, he glanced back. His rival was already out of sight.

Chapter 27

In a great wave the wolf hunters swept through the forest, rifles ready, dogs racing ahead, sniffing the earth. David loped along with the gradually spreading line of hunters, a grin on his face. He had hunted wolves before, but never in such a massive group of hunters. It appeared that at least half the able-bodied men and boys from within a hundred square miles had converged here, with dogs and rifles, to scour the woods in attack on one of the most ancient enemies of man.

It promised to be great fun, enhanced by the fact that David hadn't hunted in this particular stretch of forest before. Sport in strange country was always more challenging and gratifying. And this area gave him a warm, positive feeling: it was not many miles from Polly's home. David's intention was to drop by and pay a call after the hunt was over.

The farther the line of hunters went, the more distance spread between them. David plunged ahead on a straight course for a long way, until the forest became hilly and rocky and lined with streams, so that he was forced to divert to the side. He looked around. Nobody nearby him now. His companions, strangers to him, had wandered off without his noticing.

A ridge rose ahead of him, with a swag at the top. He climbed and went through the swag and into a rugged valley beyond, through which a creek ran. Following the creek, he went a mile or more, then turned north and went through a gap between two wooded hills, down a long draw and across another mile of broken country, where the forest was thicker than before.

Thunder rolled in the distance. David stopped, surveying the sky. Clouds were thickening and rain seemed likely. He listened for sounds of other hunters and heard none. How far had he come? He grew concerned, and chided himself for inattention. He had wandered from the others, obviously, and now had not a notion of where he was. Suddenly hunting in strange country didn't seem quite so fun and novel.

He sat down on a log and dug some jerky from his pouch. As he ate he evaluated his situation, trying to figure the best way to get back. How many gaps had he passed through? Had there been one ridge and swag, or two? When his meal was done, he hefted up his rifle and headed back the way he had come, hoping he could remember.

There—the gap was ahead. He grinned. At least he would be able to get back to where he started, even if he was pretty much out of the wolf hunt now. He went between the hills and on another half mile, then stopped again. Something was wrong. This terrain didn't seem familiar at all. Had he come through the wrong gap? Obviously so.

Now he truly was lost, and the weather was worsening quickly. The wind kicked, clouds hung low and heavy, and the air tasted damp. Blast it all! David was very angry with himself. He was too experienced a woodsman to have an excuse for getting lost.

He traveled on, covering five miles, then six. Still no rain had started, but the clouds remained threatening, and he figured that the heavens had turned against him and were saving up their fury for after it turned dark, just to torment him worse. And dark it would be, very soon.

Muttering an oath at bad luck, he crossed a small ridge and stepped out onto a leaf-strewn level spot. Then he stopped. In the dusk he had seen something quite remarkable: a young woman, racing through the forest as if the devils of hell were at her feet. And it sure as the world appeared that . . . no. It couldn't be. That would be too odd to be true.

He took three great steps forward, ready to run after the girl he had seen. If she was in trouble, maybe he could help her—or maybe she could lead him back to familiar territory. He took a fourth step, and the earth tilted beneath his feet, sending him tumbling until it seemed the ground itself had swallowed him. He sent out a loud yell of alarm and vanished into darkness.

She was afraid, no denying it, and despite a near full day of increasingly panicked exploration and a dozen false hopes, she was no nearer to finding her way home than she had been when she first became lost. In terms of finding her way home, she might as well be in the dark forests of Europe. Hunger gnawed at her, despair its partner. Darkness was falling. She dreaded the thought of spending the night here in wolf country, all alone, without food, without a clue as to how to extricate herself from her situation come morning.

And so she ran. What else was there to do? If she could go far enough, surely she would encounter some trail, some road, some cabin. And yet she knew the country here was sparsely populated. She might be running into nothing but endless wilderness. But run she continued to do, feeling driven.

What was that?

It sounded like the shout of a man. An alarmed shout . . . somewhere not far behind her. She stopped and looked into the gathering gloom. She saw nothing. A chill made her shiver. She thought of the stories her father sometimes told, of ghosts that roamed the woods and screamed, the dead calling out to the living, warning them that soon they would be living no more, and their own wraiths would be dwelling in these dark groves.

Frowning, she scolded herself. Wraiths? That had been no wraith she heard, but a living person. Maybe someone who could help her. Steeling her courage, she strode toward the place from which the yell had come. Where could the man have gone? She looked around, then down.

A wolf trap! That explained it. Whoever had shouted must have stepped on the stone-balanced, pivoting trapdoor that opened above the eight-foot wolf pit, dug bigger around at the bottom than at the top so that wolves that fell into it couldn't climb out again.

"Hello?" she called into the hole. "Is there a man in there?"

A long pause, then a tentative reply: "Polly?"

That shocked her. How could he have known her? "Who's down there?" she asked.

"It's me—David Crockett! Polly, that *is* you! I can tell your voice anywhere!"

She grinned. "Even in the bottom of a wolf trap?"

"I feel the fool for falling in here, but I'm well enough. I'm glad you come along ... can you run a pole or something down here and help me out?"

"David, what are you doing out here?"

"Wolf hunting. I got separated from the others, and lost. I ain't proud of it, but it happened. Then I saw you flitting through the trees and tried to follow, and that's when I stepped into this trap. But what are you doing roaming around in the woods at dusky dark?"

"Pa sent me to find some lost horses of his, and I ended up getting lost. I've been trying all day to find my way home. I never would have dreamed that I'd run across you here, miles away from where either one of us live...." She paused, taken with how remarkable this meeting really was. Surely chance alone couldn't explain the miraculous bringing together of two people who were growing so fond of one another. Destiny's hand was at work here, sure as anything! It was thrilling, even eerie.

"Can you help me out of here?" David asked again.

"I'll run fetch a stout stick," she replied.

When David was out, skinned and bruised but otherwise not injured, they walked together in the darkness, neither of them afraid now, nor even all that eager, except for their hunger, to find a way out of the vast forest. Hand in hand they traveled in the night, remarkably comfortable together, each convinced that this meeting had to be a sign they were intended to be together.

At long last they found a path and walked along it, knowing it had to lead somewhere. They saw a light through the trees, and followed the path to the door of a little house, in which they found living the very man who had played gourd fiddle at the reaping where they had first met. Another sign! What else could explain it?

David Crockett never forgot that night for the rest of his life. The fiddler was a nocturnal soul; he told them he often sat up the entire night, playing his fiddle and feeling as rested by that the next morning as if he had slept soundly all through the dark hours. He played for them tonight, soft old songs that were minor and haunting and beautiful in the darkness. Polly held David's hand, and let him kiss her more than once, and together they sat up all night, Polly sometimes dozing against David's shoulder, while the fiddler made his music. It was a magic night, the kind never to be forgotten, the kind that cannot be planned, but must happen on its own.

The next morning David walked Polly home, following directions given by their fiddling host. Then he set out for his own home, knowing now that he could not rest until Polly Finley was his wife.

He intended to return very soon, and this time he would not make the mistakes he had with Maggie Elder. He would ask William and Jean Finley for their daughter's hand—and he would take it whether they granted their permission or not.

Never had David seen a more savage-looking face than the one Jean Finley presented to him at this moment. Her countenance was something out of a childhood nightmare. There was no questioning it now: she truly had taken a dislike to him.

He wondered if the rival he had intimidated on the road sometime back had gotten word to her of his treatment. Whatever the reason, he didn't expect to hear her making jokes about him becoming her son-in-law during this visit!

And that was too bad, because it was the prospect of becoming Jean Finley's son-in-law that had brought him there. Polly had already agreed in private to become his wife, but she had warned him that her mother preferred her other and former suitor to him. Her father, on the other hand, liked David; if all went well, he would be able to persuade his wife to the right side again.

"Mrs. Finley, Mr. Finley," David said to the couple, who sat facing him, "I won't squander around about what I've come to say. The fact is I've been took in deep affection by your daughter, and I aim to marry her. She's done agreed, but I'd be appreciative of your blessing on the union."

Jean Finley stood, her face growing red. "Would you? Well, I'll tell you what I'd be appreciative of. I'd be appreciative if you'd drag your skinny bottom out of this house."

William Finley gaped. "Jean!" He stammered around, unable to find words. "How can you ... what a thing to say ... why, I can't see how ..."

"I'll not see our Polly marry this rooster," she said firmly, her eyes never leaving David's face.

David could see he wouldn't succeed in overcoming her resistance through nastiness; in fact, such a thing might risk stirring Polly's father against him as well. So he gave Jean Finley the most kind and gentle smile he could muster after such an insult, and kept his voice quiet and even.

"Mrs. Finley, I don't know what I've done to turn you against me so. I recall how once you called me 'son-in-law,' long before I ever thought of wanting to become that. I took that as a compliment, and was grateful for it. Now, you might have come to think it an ill thing to have me for a son-in-law, but I'd be honored if you was my mother-in-law. I truly would. I'd brag about it, and treasure it in my heart. So I'm hoping your anger against me will cool, and you'll see that it's all for the best that your daughter marry herself to a man who loves her dear and will cut off his own arm before he let any harm come to her."

"There's the door," she said. "Use it to let yourself out. And don't never again use it to let yourself in."

Polly, standing by the fireplace and listening to the tense exchange, burst into tears. David saw there was to be no defeating this woman's will. He allowed himself the luxury of becoming just a little bit angry, enough to show, but not so much he couldn't control it.

"Very well," he said. "If I can't convince you, I can't convince you." He turned and faced the weeping Polly. "Polly, I'll be here on Thursday with a horse, and I'll take you-to my father's inn. We can get married there; Lord knows we can't marry here. You be ready, now. I'll stop by the justice of the peace on the way home, and set it up for him to marry us."

Polly kissed David, right in front of her parents, as he headed out the door. He didn't turn to look back at William and Jean Finley, but he was almost sure that from the corner of his eye he saw the woman reaching for the rifle above the mantel, and her husband holding her back from it.

One thing seemed certain: married life was going to be interesting where family relations were concerned.

The justice of the peace, also a magistrate, was named Henry Bradford. He was a resident of the Long Creek community. David presented his request and the planned date of the wedding. Would Bradford be so kind as to conduct the ceremony? He agreed readily, and David headed home.

Much remained to be done. He arranged for word to be sent to the Crockett tavern of the upcoming marriage, and went with his friend Thomas Doggett to sign for his marriage bond. And there was one other arrangement to be made too: he had to find some alternative way to obtain ownership of the horse he had been working for. There wouldn't be time now for him to finish out the agreed work term. He went to Robert Canaday and offered the only bargain he could, and Canaday accepted.

The bargain caused David to make quite a sacrifice, but he didn't begrudge it. Polly's troth was worth whatever sacrifice it took.

John Canaday had a very serious look on his face as he and David talked on the porch of his house. "Marriage is a great leap for any man to make," the Quaker said. "I wonder if this is truly understood by thee?"

"I understand. I'm a man now, Mr. Canaday. I'll be twenty years old in just a few days. I'm ready to do whatever it takes to be a good husband. I love her a mighty lot."

"That is good, that is good. Love is required for any marriage to succeed as God intends."

"You still look worried."

"I see thee as still a boy, not a man," Canaday admitted. "I wonder if this marriage is being done in too great a haste. I ask forgiveness, if this doubt seems an insult to thee."

"There's nothing to forgive. I have only respect and affection for you, Mr. Canaday. You've done much to help me, made me almost like one of your own."

"I have much regard for thee, David Crockett."

"Thank you. Don't you worry. I'm ready to be a good husband. I've already done all I can to ready ourselves for marrying. I've signed my bond, traded my rifle for a horse—"

"Thy rifle? The one loved so dearly by thee?"

"Yes sir."

Canaday smiled slowly and nodded. "If David Crockett is willing to part with so beloved a gun, then indeed David Crockett is ready to be married," he said. "I extend thee my best wishes, David. May thy marriage be blessed and thy house filled with children."

"Thank you, sir." David was deeply touched by the old Quaker's sentiment. John Canaday was in some ways more like a father to him than John Crockett.

"Where will thy house be?" Canaday asked.

"There's a cabin at Finley's Gap I've made arrangement to rent, along with some land. It's not much, I reckon, but it will suffice to begin with."

"And sufficiency is enough for any man. May God bless thee and thy young lady in this new home, David Crockett. I'll never forget the time I have spent with thee, and my house is always open to the Crocketts."

David was a little distressed to feel his eyes growing hot and red. Canaday's words, spoken so sincerely and kindly, stirred his emotions. He realized what a great transition in his life was taking place.

"Thank you, Mr. Canaday. I'm obliged for your words, and for all I've learned from you and your family. I'll not forget you, no matter where I go or what I do. I promise you that. I promise."

Chapter 28

Thursday morning dawned bright and clear and found David filled with a mix of joy, anticipation, worry, and simple nervousness. All preparations were made; the Crockett tavern stood ready to receive the couple, and Justice of the Peace Bradford was on hand, as promised, to conduct the ceremony.

In the company of his brothers Wilson and John, along with John's wife, sister Betsy, and friends Tom Doggett and James Blackburn, David mounted and rode toward Polly's house. The group brought one riderless but saddled horse; this would be for Polly. David's intention was to fetch her back to the Crockett inn; certainly he didn't want to get married at Polly's house, given her mother's attitude toward him.

About two miles from Polly's, David was surprised by a group of other friends who had gathered to help him celebrate his day. Following local custom, David's brothers and sisters, along with Tom Doggett, headed on to the Finley house, leaving the others to wait. Tom Doggett carried with him an empty bottle; this would be presented to William Finley to be filled with wine or liquor, symbolic of his acceptance of the impending marriage. The beverage would then be returned to the waiting wedding party for consumption.

Waiting was intensely difficult for David. For all he

knew, his prospective mother-in-law's hostility might have won the day in her household. The bottle might come back empty. Even so, David fully intended to go ahead and have his wife today . . . but better to have her without a battle, if possible.

He was relieved at the sight of Tom Doggett and company returning, smiles on their faces, and Tom waving a filled bottle above his head. David advanced and accepted the bottle.

"What did you find?"

"The old woman is still mighty savage in her disposition about you," Doggett said. "I thought she'd turn dogs onto us, sure as shooting. But the old man was of much better spirit. He come out and filled our bottle, as you can see, and told us to come on."

"Did you see Polly?"

"Not directly, but John says she was peeping out a window."

David unstoppered the bottle and took a swallow. Poking the stopper back into place, he said, "Let us proceed, ladies and gentlemen."

They went on, David's nervousness growing with each pace, but no more than his determination. He was comforted to know that William Finley, at least, was on his side. And he knew Polly was—she would come with him no matter what her mother said or did.

They came into view of the house; David noted the stocky form of Jean Finley in the doorway. She withdrew inside the house and closed the door as soon as she saw them.

David did not dismount, but rode directly to the door, leading the riderless horse. "Polly Finley!" he called. "Your bridegroom has come to fetch you! Are you ready?"

The door opened and Polly emerged. David drew in his breath. Never before had he seen her looking so beautiful. She wore a dark blue homespun dress, with a brilliant red kerchief draped appealingly around her neck. He eyed her up and down and smiled.

"You're a beauty, Polly. More a beauty than the finest sunrise I've ever seen."

She blushed, smiling. David looked beyond her into the shadowed interior of the house. There was Jean Finley, looking bitterly unhappy, and William beside her, arm across his wife's shoulder, hand patting her gently, placatingly. David caught his eye; William gave him a quick nod.

"Climb up, Polly," David said. And she did. David doffed his hat and saluted Polly's parents, who had moved up to the doorway, and he and his bride-to-be turned their mounts and rode out of the yard and onto the road.

"Wait!" William Finley called. "Just a moment, please!"

David stopped his horse and turned in the saddle. William Finley left his wife in the doorway and walked up to David.

"Stay," he said. "It would surely be pleasing to see Polly married in her own home."

"Well, sir, the truth is that I ain't been made to feel much welcome in this house. It don't seem right to have a marrying here when there's still such strong feelings against it." He glanced significantly toward Jean Finley.

"I know your meaning," William said. "Pay no heed to her. She's like any woman—too much tongue, too little sense and respect. She'll not stand in the way of a marriage here, if you're willing."

David studied the face of his wife, and saw an expression of hope. Obviously she would prefer marriage here instead of at the tavern. How could he deny her? He didn't want to—but it seemed to him that one barrier yet needed to be removed.

"I'll gladly marry here, if your wife will ask it with her own lips."

William scratched his chin. "Well . . . well, sure she will. Just give me a minute to have a word with her."

He returned to his wife and they withdrew into the house. Five minutes passed; David could occasionally hear loud voices coming from inside, but then the volume lowered, another minute passed, and the door opened again.

Jean Finley walked out, paused on the doorstep, then walked up to David, looking up at him in the saddle. "I believe I've been a fool," she said softly. "And I ask your pardon."

David smiled. "It's already given. And I've never thought you a fool."

"Thank you, thank you. But a fool I've been. You must understand, Polly is the first daughter I've seen go off to be married, and it's a hard thing to let her go into . . . into poverty." She paused; this clearly was a delicate subject for her, as it was for David. But he couldn't deny the truth of what she was saying. He *was* a poor man, just as his father had been and still is. Suddenly he understood a little better the way Jean Finley had acted. The Finley family knew the bitterness of want, and Jean had not been eager to see her daughter move into a marriage that might be unable to provide her anything better than she had known through her growing-up years. It was difficult to fault her for that.

Jean Finley went on. "It's clear that Polly loves you much, and if it's you she wants to be with, then I want nothing less for her. Stay here, David. Have the wedding right here. I don't think I can bear to see my girl carried away like this."

David nodded. "Very well, then. I'd be glad to marry here . . . if that's what Polly wants."

"It is," Polly said. She looked like she might cry in happiness at any moment.

"I'll send my brothers to the tavern to give word of the change," David said. "Polly, this will put some delay in our plans."

"I don't mind it."

"Then neither do I."

David spoke to his brothers, explaining the situation, and they set off at once to carry the news back to those waiting at the tavern. Meanwhile, David and Polly dismounted and went into the house with the Finleys.

David marveled at this turn of events, and was grateful. He sensed that Jean Finley still bore her worries in secret, but it really seemed she was changing her attitude. And far better it was to enter a marriage with good feelings surrounding it rather than open bitterness. It gave him a sense of increased hope for the future, and anticipation of a happy life with the woman he adored more than anything else in the world.

They were married beneath the open sky. David could not recall a finer moment in his life than the one that made Polly his wife. Their first night together was spent in the Finley house, with little privacy—but they had expected none in any case. It was the frontier custom to send newlyweds to their marriage bed with much joking and banter and attempts to rouse embarrassment. David and Polly made the best of it, and waited until at last the rest of the household was asleep before turning to one another and entering the intimate marital embrace both had eagerly awaited.

The next day they and the entire wedding party rode on to the Crockett tavern, there to celebrate further. Awaiting them were yet more well-wishers—such were abundant at weddings, if for no other reason than plenty of free food and special "fixings" on hand.

Polly sat happily in the light of torches, still wearing the blue homespun dress she had sewn herself for the wedding. The gaiety and revelry all around made a happy backdrop for her thoughts of the future. She considered her new name: Polly Crockett. To her it had a musical ring. She loved her new husband even more intensely than she had before. They were poor, true enough, but what did that matter? The future lay wide open and bright.

At the moment, David was seated over near the door, distracted by a gaggle of boys while little Mahlon Gilbreath sneaked a twist of tobacco toward David's cup of coffee. Polly almost yelled a warning—coffee was a rare treat that David greatly loved—but held her peace. Let the boys have their joke. This was a time for good humor and fun. And when David lifted the cup to his lips and found the tobacco thrusting up out of it, she laughed right along with the boys. David put on an appropriately entertaining show of exaggerated reaction, then laughed as well.

The memory of the celebration lingered in Polly's mind long after it was past. Particularly gratifying was the way others continued to show their affection and support. Her mother surprised her by giving them two healthy cows with calves. And John Canaday showed up with an order for fifteen dollars worth of merchandise at a local store, to be filled in whatever way the new couple chose. Fifteen dollars went a long way, and Polly was thrilled to be able to outfit her new home with much more than she had anticipated owning so early on.

But still the couple was poor. Unable to buy acreage, they rented land and a rather dark and dismal pine log cabin in the Finley's Gap area, between Bay's Mountain and the old Indian war trail, and within a few miles of David's kin. The cabin was built of saddle-notched unhewn logs, chinked and daubed with mud, and had a single hipped chimney made of mud and sticks, protruding past a roof made of clapboards. The Crocketts' cabin had only two rooms, a pair of doors leading to the outside, and—to Polly's dissatisfaction—no windows at all. The oppressive interior darkness took much adjustment and often depressed Polly, who had grown up in cabins with many windows and much light, but she made the best of it. She passed much time spinning cloth. When the weather was warm, she moved the wheel outside.

Rent was high and farm work difficult, but David and Polly persevered. Months passed, and with each one David promised better things very soon. But the better things never seemed to actually come about. Except for one good thing, the best that Polly could have asked: the family grew.

Their firstborn came along in the summer of 1807. They named him John Wesley. William was born two years later, the Crocketts still living in the Finley's Gap cabin and David still talking of finding a better place and a better life.

William's birth gave a clearer focus to his dreams, however. If the family continued to grow, the cabin would be far too small for comfort, and their meager earnings on high-rent farmland too insignificant to pay for their needs.

David did other work as well, anything to make a dollar. He split fence rails for neighbors, bartered and traded, bought and sold anything of commercial value he could put his hands on. But he never made much money. There was no real danger of starvation; as long as there was room for crops and game in the forests, David could provide meat and vegetables for the table. But they wanted more than mere survival.

David kept eyes, ears, and mind open for any promising news of other areas where a hardworking young couple might thrive. He explored as well, going down into Alabama in hopes of finding prospects there, but this came to nothing. At times the couple felt they were destined to live out their life on rented land, struggling against all odds to get ahead.

Word began to drift in of new settlements along the Duck and Elk rivers, farther west. David and Polly took stock of their situation. They had two sons, an aging horse, a couple of two-year-old colts, and little else.

Then came William Finley with a proposition. If David truly was interested in the new country he talked about so often, he would help him move there. David accepted the proposition at once. His parting with his family back at the tavern was difficult and tearful, particularly for his mother, and David was on the verge of backing out. But he couldn't, not if he wanted the best for his own growing family, and so, with possessions laden on the colts and the old horse, the David Crocketts headed west. The year was 1811.

They settled on Mulberry Creek, a tributary of the Elk River, in the county of Lincoln, on a hill known as Hungry Hill. In the first months the new location looked promising, particularly because game was abundant. David virtually hunted for his family's living. As time went by, however, this became more challenging. There was small game aplenty, but the larger and more rewarding game, especially bears, were ever more scarce.

So in 1813 the Crockett family said farewell to Hungry Hill and moved on to neighboring Franklin County, where they settled on Bean's Creek, north of the beautiful

Cumberland Mountains. About ten miles to the northeast was the town of Winchester, and elsewhere in the vicinity the communities of Maxwell and Old Salem. Here they moved into a hilltop home that David named Kentuck, in anticipation of a future move northward to Kentucky. This was a fine and beautiful place, watered by a good well.

They were content. This, David felt certain, was the place where he and Polly would settle down for a long and increasingly successful and bountiful life together. They were young and strong. Nothing could stand in their way now. Nothing could go wrong. David was sure of it.

Part 4

THE CREEK WAR

Chapter 29

Pups stirred and barked feverishly outside the cabin walls. Polly Crockett stood, laying aside the pair of trousers she was stitching together for her oldest son. Three times the pups had barked in as many minutes, and from the intensity of the barking, it was evident they did not herald David's return from the day's hunting. Now the hound, mother to the puppies, sent up a loud baying, confirming what Polly already suspected.

Something was nearby the cabin, out in the dark. Something that alarmed the dogs. Maybe a bear or deer or 'possum. Even a human being. Indians? The thought came with a chill, but Polly didn't put much stock in it. Even though there had been some minor raids and fights between Indians and settlers in past months, Polly had seen and heard of nothing more like that since settling here. Her intuition was that there was no significant Indian danger to Franklin County, despite rumblings in the south.

But David and most of the other local men she knew seemed to think differently. Not that they had much reason to do so, as Polly saw it. When challenged, David could present no facts to prove that danger was immediate. Yet war talk was rampant. It seemed the local men had worked themselves into such a fever that only warfare would cool it. Polly found it maddening, especially when she thought about David's participation in the near-hysteria. She had never seen him like he was now, ready to ride off at the slightest nudge to face the perceived "great savage threat," when in his heart he knew as well as she that the threat probably wasn't great in their area. If David really believed Indian danger was as immediate as he claimed, he wouldn't go off on hunts that sometimes lasted two or three days.

None of this mattered at the moment, however. Even if not an Indian, *something* was outside the cabin, stirring up the dogs. Polly went to the gun rack on the wall and hefted down the Brown Bess musket that John Crockett had given to David as a parting gift when they first moved away from Jefferson County. She checked the loading and priming, went to the window and peered out past the corner of the shutter.

She remained there a long time, looking into the dark. The dogs settled, then stirred themselves into another frenzy. Polly closed and latched the shutter, then went to the boys' beds to reassure herself they were all safe and asleep. Of course they were; even so, she needed the assurance of actually seeing them.

Drawing a deep breath, she headed for the door, not at all certain it was wise to go out, but knowing she was going to do just that. Wondering and fearing was too much of a strain. Polly had little by way of a conscious, systematic philosophy of life, but one truth she had learned: a fear confronted and understood was almost always lessened. Left unfaced, it might be anything infinitely terrible; faced, it was at least reduced to being no more than it was.

Carrying the musket, she went to the door and out. The dogs were still barking, noses pointed to the west and a dark alley that ran between a woodshed and the smokehouse. "Who's there?" she demanded, raising the musket and aiming into the darkness. "Show yourself or I'll shoot."

"No need to harm me, ma'am," a male's voice said.

Polly jumped back a yard. She had known something was there; she had not known for certain that it was human.

"Who's that?" she said. "Show yourself!"

The figure that emerged was that of a stranger. He had hair hanging to his shoulders, and a beard that covered much of his face. He wore a wide, floppy hat. From what she could see, she could not determine his age. His form was lean and straight, clad in a coat of buckskin, a pair of old wool trousers, and tall boots. Into the sash binding his coat around his narrow waist were thrust a pistol, belt axe, and knife. His right hand lightly gripped the barrel of his squirrel rifle, standing butt down on the ground.

"Why are you hiding outside my house?" Polly demanded.

"Mighty sorry, ma'am. I seen your husband wasn't home, and I was a bit uncertain about coming on in without him there."

Polly felt more alarmed. He knew David wasn't here—yet he had lingered. Or did he really know? Maybe he was asking in order to judge her reaction.

"My husband is here," she said. "He's sleeping inside—been feeling puny, and I didn't want to stir him out. You'd best get on away from here, right now."

"I'll not harm you, ma'am. I come to see your husband."

She could tell he knew she was lying. "Now ain't a good time for it," she mumbled.

"So I can see. I'll come again. Tomorrow evening, maybe." He touched his hat, nodding. "Evening to you, ma'am." And then he turned and was gone.

Polly went back into the cabin, rechecked all the latches and bars, and stood the musket in the corner so it could be reached more quickly, should she need it. Then she settled herself in a chair and took up her sewing again, determined to remain awake and alert until David was home.

She was hardly aware of being picked up and carried to bed. For a moment she perceived herself a child again, being carried by her father. A familiar kiss touched her cheek, and a soft voice whispered its good-night into her ear. Not her father's voice, but David's. She smiled and reached out to him, half unconsciously.

When morning came, she remembered the strange visitor of the prior evening, and told David about him.

"You're sure he wasn't an Indian?"

The question annoyed Polly, considering the general obsession with Indian fears at the moment. "You think I wouldn't have said he was an Indian if he had been? He was dressed like a white man, and talked like one."

"What about his face?"

"I couldn't see it in the dark. He had a hat and beard."

"You didn't know the voice?"

"No. He didn't volunteer no name, and I didn't demand one. I wanted him gone, that's all."

"It worries me. I don't like men coming around when I'm away. I'll stay close for a time. Them deer I killed today will be enough to keep us fed for a long spell."

"It was you he was asking after. I don't know why."

"Likely he'll show up again, if there's any importance in why he came."

The next day David stayed close to home. He puzzled over the unknown man who had frightened Polly. It concerned him, even though there were a hundred possible reasons for someone to come calling, and if this visitor had come with bad intent toward his family, he would have taken his opportunity the prior night.

About sunset the dogs set up a barking outside that drove David from his chair at the supper table and over to the rifle rack. He went outside, armed, and saw a man coming in from the west on a chestnut horse. Shielding his eyes against the swollen sun, David watched the limned figure approach.

The rider came within thirty paces, dismounted and tethered the chestnut to a fence rail. "Hello, Davy Crockett."

"Hello, Persius Tarr. I wasn't looking to see you this evening. How you been?"

"As well as could be expected, considering." He

leaned over and spat a cud of tobacco out of his mouth, then pulled a twist from his pocket and the knife from his sash, and sliced off a fresh chew. He thrust the twist toward David, who accepted. The tobacco was hot and flavorful.

"I met your wife," Persius said. "Pretty as a kitten."

"Thank you. She is. Her name's Mary, but she goes by Polly. A Finley before she married me. She told me you came, though she didn't know you. I got something of a bone to pick with you about that, Persius. You not giving a name scared her. She didn't know what you wanted."

"You think if I had told her my name she wouldn't have been even more scared? She's from Jefferson County, ain't she? Everybody in Jefferson County knows Persius Tarr is the man who murdered Crider Cummings."

David had to admit that Persius had a point. Polly would have been horrified had she realized it was the infamous Persius Tarr she was facing off with. And David wondered if Persius had just indirectly confessed to the killing of Cummings, or if his comment had been waggish. He had used the word "murder" in a disturbingly casual way.

The question would have to be asked . . . but not now. Cordiality required other things first.

"Polly's setting the table for supper right now," David said. "There's pan-fried fish, corn bread, beans, sweet taters—"

"You don't need to say no more," Persius said. "I accept. I'm as starved as a lost dog. Besides, I want to meet your wife and family proper."

"Come on in," David said. "Polly will be happy to have a guest."

The truth was, David really doubted that Polly would be at all happy to have *this* particular guest. He winced inwardly in anticipation of the complaints he would surely get from her later tonight: a scoundrel and probable murderer, seated at the same table as her children! Now Polly, he would say, he's an old friend of mine. I couldn't turn him away. And she would scowl and complain more . . . and he wouldn't be at all sure she wasn't right.

Supper was a tense and difficult time, at least for the adult Crocketts. Polly reacted exactly as David had anticipated, maintaining an icy politeness to Persius and firing angry glances at her husband every chance she got. David suffered from being in the middle of the situation, balancing Polly's anger with the need to be friendly to his old companion.

The Crockett boys, typically, were fascinated with their guest. Little William loudly asked David if Persius was an Indian, and David's negative reply was quick and forceful, for he remembered how feverishly Persius had resented such questions in the past. This time Persius didn't grow angry, for which David was grateful, because certainly the little boy had intended no insult.

Persius's own tensions, if he felt any, were undetectable. David studied him closely, taking care not to make it obvious. Persius looked much older: because of the heavy beard, because of the deeper lines around his eyes, because of the intangible callous quality that inevitably inscribes the countenances of those who have lived a life too full of trial and trouble. He had changed, but David considered that maybe the change wasn't solely in Persius, but in himself too.

Conversation touched on many things in general, and nothing in particular. They talked over of the Crocketts' home life, of funny things the boys had said and done, of how the Canaday clan was doing at last contact, of David's and Polly's parents and siblings. Persius revealed nothing about his own experiences since his flight from Jefferson County, and when the conversation steered in his direction, he deflected it deftly onto some other course.

He was reluctant to talk, and David wanted to respect his wishes. But he couldn't entirely. He was a family man now, with a wife and children to be considered. If Persius was to be welcomed here, there was one thing he as host would have to know, even if Persius didn't like being asked about it.

Chapter 30

After the meal David rose and walked outside, knowing Persius would follow. The boys followed as well; David sent them off to play on the far side of the house. He and Persius cut and settled in fresh cuds of twist tobacco, and chewed and spat without words for a minute or so.

"Persius, I want to ask you something straight out," David said.

"You don't need to say the words. I already know. You want to know if I really murdered Crider Cummings."

"Well . . . yes. I do."

"I killed him. But it wasn't murder. If I hadn't killed him, I wouldn't be standing here talking to you today. He'd have cut my throat."

"So you was defending yourself?"

"Yes."

"Then for God's sake, why did you run off? It made you look guilty. There ain't a jury that could be rounded up in Jefferson County that wouldn't find you guilty now!"

"Think about it, Dave. Is there a jury that wouldn't have found me guilty even if I *hadn't* run? You know my reputation. I'd have been convicted and hung within a week, and you can't deny it."

"All I know is, if a man ain't guilty, he shouldn't flee. It's as good as a confession in the minds of most folks."

"That's fine and easy talk, when the man doing the talking ain't the one who would hang. If you'd been in my shoes, with the kind of name I had, you'd have run like a rabbit too."

David spat, thought it over, nodded. "Maybe you did what you had to do. I ain't been in your circumstance before."

"Now you answer me straight out: Do you believe me when I tell you I didn't murder Crider Cummings?"

"Yes. I know how he felt about you. I have no trouble believing he would provoke you into killing him. I can generally tell when a man's lying to me, and there's plenty of them that has. You ain't lying."

"I appreciate that. You've always seen the best side of me when nobody else would."

"There was a time when you seemed to see the best side of yourself, back with John Canaday, and you turning Quaker and all."

"I meant it when I tried that change, David. Truly I did. Wanted to be different and put aside my old ways. Somehow I just couldn't make it hold, you know. It slid away on me, and I was the same old sinner I've always been and always will be."

David had no advice for his friend on that kind of subject; theology was beyond his scope. Religion was a part of his family heritage, but he hadn't picked it up in a very significant or personal way; his attitude, felt rather than articulated, was that churchgoing and formal religion were more for women than men, unless the men were of the rare and admirable breed of John Canaday. But Persius's words did harken up an old question in David's mind, and offer the chance for him finally to verbalize it.

"Persius, there was something about you during that time I never could quite figure. The story you told about what happened to you on the Clinch River . . . I have a notion there was more than what you said at the time. I've wondered if . . ."

Words became halting, and Persius eyed David with lifted brow. "Go on and say it. I'm in no humor to hold it against you, whatever it is."

David cleared his throat and scuffed his right foot. "I've wondered if maybe you went back and killed them two who had throwed you into that pit of bones. Maybe it was killing them that stirred you so bad that you'd do something as, well, extreme as turning Quaker. You were mighty changed, Persius. More than I could account for from what you told us had happened to you."

Persius's eyes narrowed as David spoke, and his lips made a hard line. But there was no anger in his voice when he responded. "No. There's but one man I've killed in my life, and that's Crider Cummings, and him I killed because I had no choice. That's the truth. I hope you'll believe it."

"I do," David said. But his conviction wasn't settled. He truly could tell, most times, when someone was trying to deceive him, and he strongly suspected that Persius was deceiving him right now. But there was no more to be said about it at the moment.

"Where did you go, after you left Jefferson?"

"South, into Georgia, then Alabama."

"Alabama! Where all the trouble with the Creeks is going on?"

"That's right. It was the Injun trouble that sent me back to Tennessee again. I seen more than enough of what them bloody savages do to white folks. I want to see no more of it."

"What do you mean?"

"I was at Fort Mims when the massacre happened. I seen it all, and I'm hellacious lucky to have come out alive."

"Fort Mims!" David exclaimed. "God bless us all! You were at the very massacre?"

"Yes. I scarcely survived it. The Red Sticks came within the breadth of a hair of finding me and doing me in."

"Finding you? You mean you . . ." Words became halting as David realized the delicacy of what he was asking. "You mean you . . . hid yourself from them?"

"Yes. But don't look at me that way. It wasn't on purpose. I fought them hard, but they struck me senseless, and somehow I wound up with some dead folks falling on top of me; their bodies hid me. I woke up lying under corpses in brains and blood; at the first I thought they was my own."

By now the details of the bloody attack on Fort Mims were spreading like a blaze across the country. A runner had passed through Franklin County a few days before, giving the terrible news.

Fort Mims, created as a defensive outpost near the Alabama and Tombigbee rivers, had fallen in late August after an attack by a warlike Creek faction known as the Red Sticks. Though the fort, which enclosed an acre of land, was only a few miles from the Gulf of Mexico, and some three hundred miles distant from the area where the Crocketts now lived, the massacre there was so horrific that it had done more than anything else so far to stir local anger and fear. The local militia was already gathering in preparation to go to war against the Creeks.

The trouble that led to the Mims incident had a partial origin in the hostilities between the United States and Britain that had broken out in the summer of 1812. The British desired support from the Indians; the United States, of course, desired to thwart this, and Fort Mims was a potential tool toward that end. But the main cause of the Fort Mims attack had more to do with Spain than Britain. The Spanish, resisting the Louisiana Purchase of West Florida, were vending arms to the Indians through Mobile and Pensacola. In the summer, a band of soldiers had attacked Indians who were caught hauling arms and other supplies out of Pensacola. The Indians were killed in an ambush at a creek called Burnt Corn. No one doubted that retaliation would result. And so in the shadow of fear cast by Burnt Corn, Fort Mims was built.

The fort's primary mission was to help protect settlers in southern Alabama, including many who had intermarried and bred children with Creeks. Its walls protected not only the garrison of soldiers, but hundreds of civilian men, women, and children, some of them of mixed white and Indian blood.

Intermarriage and peaceable coexistence with the ever-growing white population were far from the universal ideals among the southern Indians. The Creeks were feeling squeezed by steady encroachments of white settlers onto lands reserved by treaty for them—settlers such as David Crockett and family, who lived on lands that technically were still Indian territory. Such intrusions were stirring much unrest among the Indians, who were divided as to how to deal with it.

Stirring the waters in a different way was the great Shawnee chief Tecumseh, who traveled among the tribes and urged unity against the encroachers. Only by working together, he said, could the Indians hope to stem the white flow. Some Creeks were inspired by Tecumseh's words, but on the whole most were wary of the notion of unity. Indians had been fighting among themselves far longer than they had fought the white men.

And among the Creeks, many prominent men were inclined toward peace with the whites. One such, ironically, had been William Weatherford, or Red Eagle, Creek leader of the Fort Mims attack. Weatherford had made a strong but futile attempt to argue down any violent response at all to the Burnt Corn killings. After his arguments failed, he accepted the next best course: a symbolic attack against Fort Mims. Symbolic was all it would be, of course; the fort was far too strong to be overrun. The Creeks could attack, fire off some noisy shots, and withdraw with anger expended and political point made. Weatherford could please the firebrands among his own people, maintain his own stature and reputation, and do little damage to relationships with the whites.

One thing Weatherford had failed to count on: the ineptitude of Fort Mims's commanding officer.

Fort Mims had received warning of impending trouble, had even been told to strengthen the fort in every way. Yet when Weatherford and his Creeks approached the fort, they were stunned to see the front gate standing wide open, and virtually no sign of a guard. And there, in the open gateway, stood the commander himself, looking very surprised. He rushed to the big gate and tried to close it single-handedly, but sand bunched before it and clogged its course.

Weatherford's eyes gaped almost as wide as the gate, amazed and horrified with the realization that in one fateful moment, control of the situation had slipped beyond his grasp. There would be far more than mere symbolism in this attack after all.

It was going to be violent and bloody, the very scenario that he had hoped to avoid, and the irony was that there wasn't a thing he could do about it.

Chapter 31

The Creeks, one thousand strong, attacked Fort Mims with a wild and unrestrained glee. The commander fell first at the sand-bound gate, and after that the Indians invaded the stockade unimpeded.

Incredibly, the officers were found playing cards, blinking almost stupidly as they saw the horde of Indians falling upon them. As for the soldiers who had been declared ready for battle, many were dancing with a group of young women and girls.

The butchery began at once, and continued for several hours. The Indians paused to plunder for a time, then burned much of the fort and resumed the killing. When it was done, nearly five hundred people were dead. About a hundred of the dead were children. Only a few score, many of them blacks, were taken prisoner.

With his eyes fixed on the dark line of the forest, Persius recounted in a quiet, steady voice how his path had led him to Fort Mims.

After fleeing Tennessee, he had gone into Alabama. Not by design, not for reason. His footsteps had simply carried him that way, and there he had stayed. He worked some, stole some, gambled whatever he made, however he made it. It was a fitful existence, sometimes pleasant, sometimes miserable—the life he was accustomed to.

He was heading for Mobile before the brunt of an angered fellow gambler when he met scores fleeing for security to Fort Mims. They told him of Indian trouble and urged him to join their flight. He did so.

At Fort Mims he gambled with the soldiers, and won more than he lost. Fate had been kind to lead him here, he came to believe. The cards were lucrative, and surely, he reasoned, the Indian troubles must not be all that severe, considering that the soldiers were openly lax and the gate usually not closed.

Then came the attack. Early on he took a head blow from a war club, and when he came to, covered by blood and corpses, he struggled out, commandeered a free-roaming horse that had belonged to one of the officers, and rode it hard toward Tennessee. Out of sheer arbitrary choice he made for the town of Winchester, and while there was astounded to hear mention on the street of the name of David Crockett. Inquiring, he found out David had moved here, with a family, no less.

"I knew I had to see you. I'm sorry I scared your Polly so."

"It appears destiny throws us together quite a lot, Persius."

"So it seems. Not that I believe in destiny. Whatever happens, happens. Ain't nothing to it beyond that."

"Maybe so. But I'll say one thing: if there is a destiny, it must have it in store for you and me to become Injun fighters. There's a militia gathering up to head into Alabama to avenge Fort Mims. After the savagery you watched, I know you'll want to be part of it even more than me."

Persius looked at David as if he had gone insane. "If I had wanted to fight Injuns in Alabama, I'd have stayed down there instead of coming to Tennessee, wouldn't I?"

David's face went blank. Something like a bad taste burned the back of his tongue. Persius was running from a fight, a fight that David believed every capable man had a duty to take part in—especially one who had seen first-hand the carnage that had sparked the war.

"It's our obligation to go," he said.

"I don't believe in obligation no more than I believe in destiny."

"You'd turn and walk away while savages kill decent white folks?"

"Why not? Every time I've been among 'decent white folks' for any time at all, somebody's up and wanted to shoot me or hang me for something or other."

David felt a surging impulse to tell Persius Tarr to climb back on his horse, ride away, and never return. Persius's conscience-free, unapologetic freedom, so alluring and awesome to David in his childhood days, took on a different aspect now that he viewed it from the perspective of an older, more responsible man. Persius had no principles, no sense of duty.

Only his long friendship with Persius kept David from sending him away in rebuke. Living with John Canaday had influenced David Crockett more than he knew: like Canaday, he was looking for something salvageable inside Persius. He wouldn't give up on him just yet.

"Persius, I want you to mull on it awhile, if you would."

"Mull on what?"

"On going with me to fight the Creeks. There's women and children who'll die if we don't stop the savages. Little girls. Grandmothers. Women like my Polly, and boys like my sons. You say you don't believe in obligation, but I ain't so foolish a fish as to bite that hook. Somewhere inside you is a soul and a conscience. Stay the night with us, think on things awhile, and in the morning you can give your word."

"I ain't going to change my mind. I done seen enough dead women and children at Fort Mims. I don't want to see no more."

"You'll see plenty if the Creeks ain't stopped. This Injun war will spread if it ain't squelched. Don't run off from your duty, Persius."

"I don't believe in—"

David cut him off. "Don't say no more. Mull on it tonight. In the morning, do what you want to do. Me, I'm riding in and putting my name on the line. I aim to fight me some Creeks, before it's my wife and children lying dead."

Back in the cabin, David's boys brought out clay marbles and began a lively game before the fireplace. David watched musingly, being in a serious mood, but Persius joined in the game, making a real show of it and prompting abundant laughter from his juvenile playmates. Eventually Persius's clowning and wry faces had David chuckling too, and then even Polly joined in. David wasn't surprised that Persius was beginning to win her over, bad reputation or not. He had a certain charm about him that couldn't be denied.

After the boys were in bed, it was Persius's turn to grow quiet and philosophical. David knew his old friend was considering the challenge put to him earlier. He dared even to hope that maybe Persius was beginning to see the reality of duty after all. It was important to David that Persius go along on the Creek campaign. Running from duty would only make Persius harder, colder, even more estranged from the society of men. And it would mark the end of Persius's friendship with him; this was something David had already decided. He could not keep fellowship with a man who would witness such an atrocity as the Fort Mims massacre, then run away without response.

The next morning revealed Persius in a serious but friendly mood. He smiled easily and seemed at peace. After a generous breakfast of venison, Persius motioned for David to go outside with him.

"I've made up my mind to go with you," he said.

David was honestly surprised. He smiled and shook Persius's hand. "What made you change your mind?"

"Well, two or three things. Your boys was part of it. I got to thinking how bad it would be if the Injun trouble was to spread this far . . . and I thought some too about what I seen at Fort Mims. A man can't see such as that and—" His voice became choked and emotional, surprising David. Persius rarely unmasked his feelings. "I want to tell you the truth about something, Dave. I wasn't senseless the whole time I was beneath them corpses. I came awake, and saw some of the killing with my own eyes. Women and children all around me was murdered. Them Injuns, they had no mercy about them. They . . . God, I hate them, hate the very souls of them! I'll be damned to hell before I'll run or hide from one of them again. I want to kill as many as I can, David. I want to knock the brains out of them like they did all them innocent folks at Fort Mims. Yes sir, I'll go with your militia! I'll go and kill every redskinned devil I can put a ball or blade into!"

Persius had become very wrought-up. Hatred poured from him like heat from a fire. David wanted to back away from him, and for a moment wondered if the fiery, virulent, hateful Persius Tarr standing before him now really was preferable to the selfish and cowardly version of the previous day. Persius had made a transition of attitude so tremendous that David wondered if he was stable of mind.

But there was nothing he could do but pat Persius's shoulder and praise his change of view. After all, it was he himself who had encouraged it.

Polly was displeased and sad when David announced that he and Persius were riding into Winchester to join the force being raised there. But she did not argue; all her arguments had been voiced before, and she would not waste her time with more of it. As for the boys, they were excited and proud, declaring they wished they were old enough to go fight Indians themselves. Polly listened to them with a very sad expression on her face.

David and Persius rode away to Winchester, and there found a great collection of men gathering for the fight. They joined the queue and put their names on the line, though Persius used the false surname of Campbell. He was very mindful of the murder suspicion against him over in Jefferson County. Their enlistment term was for sixty days.

The volunteers paraded and heard speeches from a lawyer named Francis Jones, who was being touted as the likely commanding officer of the volunteer force. Then David returned home to ready himself for the coming departure to Alabama. Persius declined the invitation to come with him. It would be better for him to remain in town, he said, so as not to impose upon Polly's hospitality any longer.

David waved his good-bye; Persius turned and vanished into the crowd. As David rode back toward his home, he wondered if Persius would even be there when he returned, or if he would change his mind yet again and run from this obligation as well. Persius could change quicker than a March wind; there was no predicting his actions.

Departure was on a Monday. The day prior, David said farewell to his wife and sons and rode away from home, bound for war. Polly put up a strong front for the sake of the boys, not shedding a tear.

"We'll need to work hard and be strong while your pap is away," she counseled the boys. "We want him to be proud of how we've taken care of ourselves when he returns."

She sat up late that night, feeling very alone, crying very softly so the boys couldn't hear, and praying for the safety of her headstrong husband.

Chapter 32

Persius had not fled, and showed no signs of having wavered from his resolution. He had gathered some extra clothing for himself, by what financial means, David did not know and did not ask. All the Tennessee Volunteer Mounted Riflemen, as they had dubbed themselves, had been advised to pack light. Their term of service was to be short, and heavy packs were a hazard in Indian fighting.

With Francis Jones in the lead, the contingent traveled in very high spirits toward Alabama. They cheered when they crossed the state line; eagerness to chastise the Creeks was as high as it could get. Plodding on, they reached a point south of Huntsville, called Beaty's Spring, and there encamped to join their unit with a larger assembly of volunteers. Here they were to await the arrival of regular foot soldiers under Andrew Jackson, Major General of the Tennessee Militia.

David came to Beaty's Spring expecting nothing but the usual military practice of rushing about madly, all the sooner to settle in and do nothing for a long time. It was not to be. A second major named John H. Gibson approached the captain of Crockett's group and asked who were the best riflemen and woodsmen in the band; a small group of capable scouts was being rounded up to make an exploration beyond the Tennessee River to look for signs of Creek activity.

"There's the finest bear hunter in Franklin County standing yonder," the captain said, pointing squarely at David. "He'll do the job for you, and keep pace with you or any other man."

"Then he's the man I need." The major approached David. "What's your name, private?"

"David Crockett, sir. I'm pleased to meet you, and would be right honored to serve as scout if you desire my service."

"I do. Now, pick yourself some companions, private. There'll be a dozen or so of us altogether."

David's selections were Persius Tarr and one George Russell, son of Franklin County militia major William Russell, an early settler well known by David. George Russell was quite young; he looked extremely boyish standing there with rifle in hand. David didn't worry about that at all; he knew the kind of marksman and woodsman that Russell was. David was, however, concerned about Persius, who wasn't nearly so skilled and whom he had selected because of friendship. He held out hope that Persius would protest his selection and try to get out of the dangerous job, and was secretly disappointed when he stepped forward readily, looking eager.

Major Gibson, meanwhile, was eyeing George Russell. "This man's hardly a man at all," he said. "This is no job for smooth-cheeked boys."

David felt a surge of iritation. Had he not been given authority to choose whom he pleased? "With all respect, Major, it ain't his beard that interests me, but his skill. If it was beards we were judging by, a goat would have the best of a man."

A muffled chuckle passed through the group. Major Gibson did not laugh. "Private, you stand on the brink of impertinence . . . but I'll overlook it, given the good report I've heard of you. Very well. I'll accept your selections. We'll set out in the morning, so get some rest. The others are already selected and waiting."

• • •

Fourteen in number and led by Major Gibson himself, they rode by morning light to the river, where they crossed at Ditto's Landing and went on. David liked the feel of being part of a small and elite group, though he was equally aware of the danger they were all in. The danger would heighten the farther they advanced toward the Creek nation. In any event, they found no sign of Indians that day, and seven miles south of the landing put up to camp for the night.

They had just completed their supper when the posted watch sang out that a lone man approached. The camp came to its feet, taking up arms, and watched as the guard ushered in a smiling woodsman with keen black eyes that flashed from face to face, the smile never fading. David noticed that when he looked at Persius, he held his gaze a little longer than on anyone else.

He said his name was John Haynes, and he was a former Indian trader in this region—an announcement that made Persius start noticeably, rousing David's curiosity. Did the group need a knowledgeable "pilot" to lead them in this unknown country? Major Gibson quickly accepted. The scouts resettled themselves, smoking and chewing and keeping their eyes on the night instead of the fire, so no one could catch them light-blind. All took time to appreciate the heat and comfort given by the fire, knowing that future camps would probably be cold ones, once they were so close to the Creeks that fires would be too risky.

Haynes and Gibson talked for a long time, off to themselves. David and Persius lounged near the fire, Persius smoking a pipe and keeping his eye on Haynes, David chewing a willow twig.

"Did you notice how Haynes looked so hard at you?" David asked Persius.

"No," Persius said. "He didn't look at me no different than at anybody else." His slightly petulant tone belied what he said. David puzzled over it. What did this newcomer know of Persius Tarr, and why was Persius reluctant to acknowledge him?

A minute later Haynes and the major parted, and the former headed straight toward David and Persius. Persius came to his feet. "Old bladder needs a draining all at once," he said quickly, walking away into the woods.

Now there was another curiosity! There was no misperception about it: Persius didn't want to meet this old Indian trader . . . which only made David want to meet him all the more.

"Howdy, sir," he said, standing and putting out his hand. "I'm David Crockett, private. Volunteer."

"Pleased to meet you, Private Crockett. John Haynes, at your service."

"Glad to have along a man who knows this country. It's all strange to me and most all of us."

"Yes. Tell me, wasn't there another man here with you a minute ago?"

"There was. He headed into the woods for a leak. Why? You know him?"

"Well, I don't know. I'm thinking I might have known some of his kin in the past. He surely puts me in mind of a man I knew many a year ago. His name was Tarr. Mick Tarr."

It took much restraint for David to maintain a blank countenance. "Tarr, you say? Well, my friend's name is Campbell."

"Oh? Well, he for certain bears a strong resemblance to old Mick Tarr. It's been a long time since I seen Mick. For all I know, he's dead now. Last I heard of him, he was heading north up into Tennessee or maybe Kentucky. I don't remember which."

David's mind was racing as fast as his heart. For all the time he and Persius had spent together through the years, Persius was still largely a mystery. Where were his roots? What kind of life had he lived? Just who was Mick Tarr, and what kind of man had he been, apart from his most obvious trait of having been a terrible father to his son? What had been his trade? Who had been Persius's mother? David sensed that he was just now being handed the opportunity to learn the answers to these kinds of questions. But he would have to proceed carefully, in order to preserve the secret of Persius's identity.

"Tarr," he said. "That's a peculiar name. I've found that peculiar names generally go with peculiar folk. That true in this case?"

"Oh, yes indeed. Mick Tarr was a case, I'll tell you! Why, I could tell you tales about him and his woman. . . ."

"Well, I wouldn't mind hearing them. I enjoy a good tale."

John Haynes was gone and David Crockett was deliberately snoring in his blankets, pretending to sleep, when Persius returned from the woods. Squeezing his eyes tightly closed, he felt Persius approach, sensed him leaning over to look at him. It was remarkably hard to feign sleep with Persius examining him so closely. In a few moments Persius went away to his own bedroll about fifteen feet away, and David relaxed. He did not want to be faced with talking to Persius just now. Not with what he had just learned from Haynes.

When he was sure Persius was asleep, he rolled over, his back toward Persius's sleeping place, and opened his eyes. He had the answers he had so long wanted, and now that he did, he felt troubled. The things that Haynes had revealed made him understand Persius much better than he had before. And made him feel as well that he had been very wrong to draw Persius into this war. Very wrong indeed.

David wanted to shake Persius awake and tell him to go, to take no further part in this campaign. This was not properly his fight. He did not belong here.

But David couldn't do that, not without revealing to Persius that he had probed out the truth of his most personal secret. All he could do was lie there and feel revolted at what lay ahead for his friend, and guilty for having delved into questions that would have been better left unasked.

It was another hour before David's pretended sleep became the real thing, and even then he didn't rest well.

• • •

The next morning, Persius stayed well away from John Haynes, which was not difficult because the man was thoroughly engaged in conversation with Major Gibson, and did not have time to query Persius in any case. David felt better about matters than he had the night before—funny, how the combination of great weariness and heavy darkness can make a train of thought seem to carry so much more import than they do by daylight. When Persius pulled David aside and told him that from the woods he had observed him talking to Haynes, and then asked him what Haynes had told him, David returned an innocent grin and a shake of the head. "Nothing but idle chatter about bear hunting. That's all. Why you asking?"

"No reason," Persius said. There was a veiled look of relief on his face.

David heard his name called by Major Gibson. He joined Gibson and Haynes, and was told that the little group was dividing. Gibson would lead one band to the house of a Cherokee named Dick Brown and gather intelligence, while David would lead the remaining men, including Persius and Russell, to the house of Cherokee Dick's father. Later in the day the two groups would join again at a designated crossroads and share whatever information they had been able to pick up from the Cherokees.

The groups formed themselves—Persius avoided Haynes and stuck close by David—and went to their destinations. The senior Cherokee had a half-blood Cherokee named Jack Thompson at his home, and Thompson agreed to join the group of scouts; he would meet them that night at the crossroads where they were to rejoin. David and Thompson agreed on owl calls as their signal, and the group proceeded to the crossroads. It was not yet dark, and Gibson had not come. At length David determined that their position was too dangerous with darkness approaching, and led his men deeper into the woods. About ten o'clock he heard Thompson's owl call, and called back, and within ten minutes the Cherokee had joined them. But David was worried; Gibson still had not returned.

Morning came; still no Gibson. David mulled the situation and decided that nothing was gained by standing still. He announced to his men that Gibson or no Gibson, they would continue with the mission on which they had been sent. No one disagreed, and with Thompson guiding the way, they advanced in stages toward the Creek nation.

The first leg took them to a Cherokee town, where they remained a short time before advancing to the home of a white man, married to a Creek woman, who lived on the very edge of the Creek nation. Though distracted by his duties, David did pause to note Persius Tarr's obvious discomfort in this house.

The man's name was Radcliff. He was an able farmer and had an abundance of corn and potatoes, which he shared freely with his visitors and their horses. But though friendly, he worried openly, reporting that only an hour before a band of some ten warriors, painted for battle, had passed his house. Should they return and discover the scouts there, they would kill them all, and Radcliff's family too.

Thompson informed David of a settlement of friendly Creeks some miles ahead. David did not want to remain and endanger Radcliff, so on they went again, heading for the Creek encampment. It was night, but the moon was full. Travel was almost as easy by its light as it would have been by day. They had eight miles of ground to cover, Thompson estimated.

Some miles along, David lifted his head and signaled a halt. He had heard something ahead; now, by looking closely, he could make out forms as well. Two men, riding Indian ponies and armed with rifles, were coming right at them.

These were almost certainly Creeks—and it was too late to avoid meeting them.

Chapter 33

But they weren't Creeks. They were two black men, very big and strong—brothers who had been stolen out of the slavery of white men and thrown into the slavery of Indians. They had managed to escape, however, and now were making with all due haste away from the Creek nation.

Because both had the advantage of speaking the Creek language, David asked the brothers to stay on with his band of scouts and serve as interpreters. They discussed this among themselves, and asked for a compromise: one would remain willingly, if the other would be allowed to go on toward Ditto's Landing. David saw no fault in this plan and agreed.

The larger and older of the two brothers opted to remain, maintaining that his skill in the Creek tongue was superior to that of his brother, and besides, as the elder, he felt if either were to remain longer in this dangerous country, it should be he. His name was Buford, and David was impressed very favorably with him.

At last they reached the friendly Creek camp that Thompson had advised them of, and were made welcome. Though weary, Crockett and company were relieved to be in the camp at last, and amused themselves with some of the Indians by holding shooting matches with bows and arrows. Judging from all appearances, these Creeks were glad to have their company. But Buford approached, called him aside, and informed him differently.

"They are afraid, having white men in their camp," he said. "They fear the Red Sticks will come and kill all of us, and them along with us."

David looked around. He was circled by somber, coppery faces, waiting for his word. He scratched his chin, thought a moment, then said, "Buford, tell these folks that if a Red Stick dares show his face here tonight, I'll peel the hide off his skull and make myself a moccasin from it."

Buford smiled, then turned and translated. The Indians looked from one to another; slowly, smiles spread over their weathered faces, and laughter came. David grinned. They would be allowed to stay, at least for the duration of the night. He was glad; the prospect of leaving and camping alone in this grim country was enough to put fear into the bravest man.

They tied their horses with saddles and bridles still in place and lay down with rifles in their arms—just in case. The danger of a Red Stick attack was nothing to take lightly. David lay on his back, looking up at the sky and noting how fast his heart was racing. This was a tense time, and with the responsibility of his men's welfare on his shoulders, it was difficult to relax. He hadn't known leadership of this degree of importance before. Its mantle didn't fit his shoulders without some measure of discomfort. But on the other hand, it had its pleasant aspect as well. He was gratified to have been given charge of this little band, and pleased that his authority had been accepted by those in his charge. And so far he hadn't failed them. They were successfully scouting the territory, and as of yet, no one had attacked them.

He closed his eyes and drew in a deep breath. When this Indian campaign was done, he intended to take a good long look at himself and evaluate his future. It might be that the impoverished son of hard-drinking old John Crockett could make a leader of himself. A military leader, maybe, or perhaps a leader in politics. Now there would be a bit of authority worth having! If his own father, with all his lackings and weaknesses, had successfully served as a constable and magistrate in earlier days, why surely David Crockett, smarter and more educated than his father ever could have hoped to be, could make a prime mayor, state senator . . . governor?

David was mulling over such self-aggrandizing fantasies and feeling sleep slowly steal toward him when a loud, piercing scream ripped through his ears like a jagged arrow, and he bolted upright in his blankets, hands squeezing tightly around the stock of his rifle.

"What the devil—"

Buford was already on his feet. "I'll go see, Mr. Crockett."

"I'll come with you."

"No. The way things is, you'd best wait. They'll talk to me better than to you, sir."

David knew Buford was right, and waited with impatience, looking around into the darkness. All the others were up now; Persius came to his side. "I ain't sure I trust that darky. He might be working with the Creeks."

"We got to trust him, Persius. Without him we could hardly even communicate with these folks."

Buford returned, looking very somber. "An Indian has come in, saying a big war party of Red Sticks has been crossing the river at Ten Islands all day. They're going to fight General Jackson."

"God a'mighty!" Persius said.

"That's the kind of intelligence we've been looking for, though I hate the news," David said. "Men, we've got to move like foxes with tails afire and get this news back to Ditto's Landing."

Sixty-five miles lay between them and their destination. Along the way back they stopped at Radcliff's for rest and food, but found his home ominously empty. From there they traveled to the Cherokee town; it too was empty, yet with fires still burning. Fear tightened every throat. Such signs of swift flight indicated they were in great danger.

At length they came to the house of the father of Cherokee Dick Brown, and were given food for themselves and their horses. From there they pushed themselves again toward the main camp, and at mid-morning reached the encampment of Colonel John Coffee.

Weary, trail-dirty, but fiercely proud of the success of his scouting band, David dismounted and headed straight for Coffee's headquarters. A sentinel stopped him.

"State your name, rank, and business, soldier."

"My name is David Crockett, private, volunteer with the Tennessee Volunteer Mounted Riflemen under Captain Francis Jones. I was sent out with Major Gibson to scout for activity of the Creeks, and I've come to report urgent findings to Colonel Coffee."

The sentinel's expression did not change. "I'll convey this information to the colonel. You wait here, Private Crockett."

David fidgeted outside the little thrown-together log headquarters while the sentinel was inside. A full two minutes later the sentinel emerged and motioned David inside as if his mission was no more important than a water boy's. Irked, David deliberately jostled the sentinel as he went past. "Beg your pardon," he mumbled.

He found the colonel inside, lounging back in a chair behind a desk made of boards across barrels, cleaning beneath his nails with a sharpened twig. David walked up before the desk and saluted.

"What is it, private?" the colonel asked, yawning.

"My scouts and I have detected the approach of a large Creek war party, sir, intending to battle General Jackson's forces."

"Have you?"

"Yes sir."

"Well, fine. Tell me more. How did you discover this?"

David outlined events since his departure with Gibson's scouts. The colonel listened, continuing to clean his nails. David was mystified by the man's casual manner. It was as if Coffee didn't even believe him.

Coffee asked a few more questions, and in the end sat

up straight in his chair and jotted down a note or two. Then, for the first time, he looked up into David's face. "Is there anything else, private?"

"No sir. I've told you all I know."

"Thank you. You may be dismissed now."

Five minutes later David had pulled Persius aside to tell him of Coffee's mystifying lack of responsiveness to what surely was important news. David had begun growing angry while talking to the colonel, and now as he recounted the tale, he grew absolutely furious. "What does he think I am, some kind of babbling fool? Is he going to sit there on that fat corposity of a rump of his and let the Injuns run all over us? Hell's bells, Persius! I've got me half a mind to go tell him what I think of him!"

"You can't do that. He's a colonel, and you're just a little private. When the little man takes on the big one, he gets squashed like a tater bug."

"I know it, I know it. Makes me so mad I could burst into flame, though, Persius. Here we risked our lives and come nigh to being run over by a redskin band, and what does he do but sit there picking the dirt out from under his fingernails!"

"I tell you what I been thinking about," Persius said. "What's happened to Gibson and his group?"

David had no answer. He had wondered the same thing himself.

"I believe they might have been killed," Persius said. "Otherwise, I think they'd have come back by now."

The failure of Gibson to return seemed to have more impact on the camp's upper echelon than had David's news itself, toward which David detected a palpable and sniffish indifference on the part of the superiors. A double guard was posted for the night, but it was made clear that this was more to look out for Gibson than to watch for advancing Indians. Neither Indians nor Gibson arrived in the night, and by morning all were near certain Gibson had died.

But later in the morning, who should arrive but Gibson himself, with his men. He went straight to the colonel's quarters and gave a report; when he emerged, the colonel was at his side, barking orders for creation of a quarter-mile-long breastworks, and the sending of an express to General Jackson, who was at Fayetteville, urging haste in his advance to this spot.

David was glad to see action finally taking place. But he was simultaneously enraged, especially when he learned the details of what Gibson had reported. They were virtually identical to what David himself had communicated the day before—yet not until Gibson of the regular army conveyed the information was it really believed and acted upon by Colonel Coffee.

It was a lesson in military realities that David would not forget later in life. Regular army stuck together; irregulars were on the outside. To the trained military man, they had no credibility.

What had been the point of risking his life to scout for the army when the army didn't even believe his report? The longer he thought about it, he madder he grew.

General Jackson arrived the next day after a difficult forced march. David Crockett stood leaning on his rifle and watched the lean, angular-featured major general of the Tennessee militia come riding by at the head of a force of weary soldiers with aching, blistered feet.

"So that's Jackson!" he said to Persius. "Looks right tired, don't he? He could have saved himself a forced march if old Coffee had been willing to listen to a simple little volunteer like me."

"You might as well let it drop, Davy," Persius said. "I've discovered that you can save yourself a lot of heartache by figuring from the outset that the right thing ain't going to happen. Very few times will you be disappointed."

Jackson's troops were weary from their march and were ordered to take their rest that night. Watch was stood by the volunteer forces. David was among the sentinels. He stood his post with an odd, queasy feeling in the pit of his stomach. Now that Jackson's troops were here, the prospect of battle seemed much more real than before. He realized that he could get killed. Lifting his hand before his face, he tried to picture it pale and still, the hand of a corpse. Try as he would, he couldn't quite picture it.

Well, he comforted himself, maybe that's a good sign. An omen that death isn't yet hovering around David Crockett. He put the image of his wife and sons firmly into mind, and for the rest of his watch staunchly refused to think of even the possibility that Crockett of Tennessee would ever fall in battle.

Chapter 34

Eight hundred strong, a force of the volunteer army advanced through the river country, crossing the Tennessee and proceeding through Huntsville, then on to Muscle Shoals and Melton's Bluff. Here the river stretched wide and treacherous, running over an uneven and rocky bed.

"It'll be a devil of a job to ford here," George Russell said to David. Both were mounted, paused beside a river that looked endlessly wide. "I hear there's rocks under there that'll cut a horse's hoof like a blade, and cracks that'll trap them tight."

"Well, I don't aim to get my horse trapped there," David replied. "I'd look mighty askance on fighting the Creeks with no horse. Foot soldiering don't suit me."

"Me neither," Russell replied. He sighed loudly. "Well, here we go! I'll wish you luck if you'll do the same for me."

The volunteer force that made its slow way across the vast river had been sent along this route apart from the rest of the force. Jackson had divided his army, placing David and his fellows under the command of Coffee and sending them roughly along the same route David and his scouts had followed earlier. But though the terrain was now familiar to David, the movement of this sprawling force was in stark contrast to the quiet reconnoiter he had led before. The great mass of humanity and horses infiltrated the river, rousing much noise and thrashing and cursing. Many times horses and men went down, crashing into the water, sometimes with such force that pinkish stains of blood afterward spread through the current.

Russell was right about the rocks. All around, horses became lodged, their hooves driving into unseen crevices in the riverbed and fixing themselves so firmly that the beasts could not draw them out again, even with the help of straining men. David felt breathless all the way across, hoping his own mount wouldn't fall victim, and when at last he splashed out on the far side, he grinned in relief.

Looking about, he saw that most of those immediately around him had also successfully forded, including George Russell and Persius Tarr, who were several paces behind. But plenty of others hadn't been so fortunate. Abandoned horses stood helpless in the river, trapped by the hooves and doomed to remain where they were until someone else came along and managed to free them, or until exposure or predators did them in. It was a sad sight, but David knew nothing could be done. This was an advancing army, and they could not pause here long for the sake of a few unfortunate mounts. The unhorsed soldiers would simply have to go ahead on foot, leaving the horses to their fate.

On the other side of the river the atmosphere was far more charged. The force was bound now toward Black Warrior Town, a village at the headwaters of the Black Warrior River, a long, southwesterly waterway that spilled into the Tombigbee miles away. Here, every soldier knew, was the prospect of a true battle. David felt a cold chill of fear that he didn't want to admit even to himself, much less reveal to others.

Persius rode to his side, smiling. David stared at Persius like he had sprouted a third ear or second nose. What was there to smile about, with battle looming?

"I'm ready to skin me off some redskin topknots," Persius declared loudly. "I hope to gather me enough to make a winter coat."

David had nothing to say to that. He thought it remarkably odd that Persius, who had required a lot of prodding to volunteer for the Creek campaign in the first place, now was so showy in his anticipation of bloodshed. Which Persius Tarr was the real one—the coward or the eager warrior? David had no idea. Only the test of battle would answer that question.

Shouted orders spurred them forward. The wet and somber band of volunteer troops moved in a dark mass toward the headwaters of the Black Warrior.

David allowed himself the pretense of disappointment that the town was deserted. Good thing for the Indians that they had fled! he said to himself. We'd have whupped their backsides and made widows of their women, yes sir.

The town was large and widely spread out. A great field of corn stretched out nearby; even now soldiers were harvesting it feverishly, and raiding the full cribs scattered about the town. This food was needed, because already the army's supplies were very low, and had no edibles been found, it was doubtful the soldiers would have had a full supper to look forward to. There was a hidden supply of dried meat discovered as well, evidence of the haste in which the Creeks had abandoned their homes. No doubt the river crossing had been observed, and word carried by runners in advance of the approaching army.

When the raided supplies were in hand, the burning of the town began. David took part with no hesitation, but with little pleasure either. It was an odd thing, but as he put the torch to house after house, his mind kept going back to Cove Creek and the night the mill washed away. Impoverishment was a harsh demon to have brought down on one's head, whether by the hand of nature or the hands of an army. David had little more affection for Indians than did most others; still, he couldn't help but feel sorry for those unknown Creek people who were losing their homes to the torch this day.

He looked up and saw Persius Tarr setting fire to a large house. Persius's stance was taut and eager; he glanced up and saw David watching him. He smiled widely. "By God, Dave, I wish every house was stacked to the roof with them damn savages!" he yelled gleefully. "I'd roast me a few dozen and eat 'em for supper!" He turned away and entered the empty house, setting the torch to its meager contents. David was vaguely sickened. Persius was a hateful and ugly creature today, and David honestly regretted he had talked him into becoming a soldier. It was unpleasant to see him like this, especially in light of what he had learned from Haynes.

Leaving the town burning behind them, the soldiers rode and marched away and made camp. There they cooked and ate what foods they had remaining from their own supplies, entirely devouring the seized dried beef and making a big dent in the Indian corn as well. They parched it by their fires, ate part of it, and stored the rest of the dried kernels in pockets and pouches. On such fare a man could subsist for a long time, but that was about all. No one considered it good eating.

The next day there was no meat at all in the camp, and David, stomach already rumbling in hunger, went to Coffee and asked his permission to hunt as the force advanced. By bringing in a few deer and such, he could keep the men at least partially fed. Coffee agreed, though warning David to be careful.

Immediately David set off to hunt, and was pleasantly surprised when he discovered a deer already killed and skinned. It was so freshly done that steam from the hideless meat still rose. This was a stroke of luck indeed— assuming the hunter who had killed and skinned this game wasn't too close by. No doubt that hunter was an Indian, probably frightened away by David's approach.

Cautiously looking about and keeping his rifle at ready, David crept up to the carcass and knelt beside it. After satisfying himself that no ambush was about to entrap him, he laid his rifle aside long enough to carry the deer back to his horse and lay it across it. Fetching his rifle, he mounted and rode back to camp.

Making his way through the camp, he was surrounded by men looking at the fresh meat with nearly lustful expressions. He carved off a piece of meat big enough for a meal for himself, George Russell, Persius Tarr, and his handful of other mess mates, then bit by bit gave the rest of the meat away. His fellows cheered him, pounded his arms and sides gratefully, grinning up at him as he grinned back. It was a good feeling to be admired by one's peers. Flickering through his mind were the same kinds of thoughts he had pondered while on the earlier scouting venture.

Maybe, when this fighting is over, I ought to take a good hard look at becoming an elected man. Maybe that's David Crockett's calling. Why, if a man can buy himself a grin and handshake with the gift of a bit of beef, couldn't he just as easy buy himself a vote with the gift of a slug of tobacco or a swallow of whisky? It's giving a man what he wants when he wants it—there's the secret.

A new face appeared, looking up at him. "Howdy," David said, glancing—then he looked again. He knew this face . . . somewhere he had met this man. And from the expression now crossing the man's own features, he knew this fellow was having similar thoughts about him.

"Mister, I swear I believe I know you from somewhere," David said.

"Well, I been thinking the same thing . . . you reckon you got more of that meat to spare?"

"Never let a man go hungry; that's my rule," David replied, knifing off a big dripping hunk and handing it to the man. "What's your name, if I might ask?"

"Moore. Ben Moore. Thank you for the meat. I'm obliged." Then he turned away and walked hurriedly back to his tent, the location of which David noted. Moore . . . the name wasn't familiar. But that face; he knew it, sure as the world, he knew it. But from where?

By the time David reached his own tent, nothing remained of the venison but a few bones and the single hunk of flesh he had reserved for himself and his mess mates. George Russell handled the roasting, and the cooked meat was unceremoniously divided and eaten, along with some rough hoecakes made from some of the parched corn, ground to a meal between two stones. Each man could have eaten twice what was available, but no one complained; at least they had enjoyed meat with a meal that otherwise, as David himself put it, would have been "bland as an old maid Presbyterian."

When the meal was done, David rose and walked back through the camp, heading toward the tent he had seen Moore enter. The mystery of the man's familiarity was heavy on his mind, and there was nothing to do but put it to rest. Moore was outside the tent, scouring out a cook pan with sand, when David strode up.

"Mr. Moore, I'm still pondering where I might have seen you before," he said. Moore was startled; he hadn't noticed David's approach. Standing, he dropped the pan and looked back at his visitor with an odd expression. Good Lord, David thought. He looks for all the word like he's scared of me!

"Mr. Moore, I'm wondering if maybe you might have spent some time at my father's inn. He was—"

David's words were chopped neatly off by a burst of recognition. For several seconds he stared at Moore, verifying to himself what he had just realized. Then, beginning to grin, he reached into his pocket and pulled out the little pouch he still carried, and from it produced the silver nugget his uncle Jimmy had given him so many years before. He held it before Moore's eyes.

"Take a look at that! You recognize it, Mr. Moore? Or should I say Mister—"

"No!" the man said in a sharp whisper. "Don't say it!" With his expression withering into one of great dismay, Moore grabbed David's arm and pulled him aside, away from all potential hearers. He leaned close and spoke in a very soft voice.

"I figured out who you was right after you give me that meat," he said. "It's been so many years that it took me a minute."

"Well, Ben Kelso, it has been a right smart spell of years at that."

"Don't call me Kelso, please. I . . . I got into a bit of trouble some years ago, and I been going by Ben Moore ever since. If I was to be known as Ben Kelso, there's places here and there where I might face the noose. I'm at your mercy, Mr. Crockett. I hope you ain't a man to carry hard feelings from years past." He glanced at the silver piece in David's hand and winced at the memory it evoked. "I treated you bad, I know, but I was just a boy with a mean spirit of bedevilment about me. You won't reveal me, will you, David ... Mr. Crockett? You won't hold a grudge on me ... will you?"

David pocketed the silver piece and rubbed his chin thoughtfully. "Time's a healer, Ben Kel—I mean, Ben Moore." He grinned. "Besides, there wasn't no real harm done, I don't reckon. It was right funny, putting that silver piece up that cow's bung. I didn't laugh at the time, but I can laugh now."

Moore said, "I was mean-spirited. I had a bad raising that rendered me sour."

"What's past don't matter," David said. "I'm glad to see you again, after all these years."

Kelso's worried expression melted into one of joy. David had never seen a man look so relieved. It made him wonder what mortal crime Kelso had committed, and where, to make him fear identification so tremendously. Maybe it was best not to know, he decided.

Kelso's voice wavered with emotion. "You're a fine man, David Crockett. A fine man with the soul of a Christian. Ben Moore is glad to call you friend, if you'll allow it."

David put out his hand and shook Kelso's. "Friends, then."

"Friends. Yes sir, David Crockett. You are my friend, my friend to my dying day."

Chapter 35

It surely seemed to David Crockett as if providence had it in mind to make him look very fine in the eyes of his fellow soldiers. Finding and sharing the killed deer had been winning enough, but the next day, as the army camped near a wide canebrake, fortune dealt an even better hand.

Hunting in the cane, David encountered nearly a score of hogs rooting around amid the stalks. There was meat here to fill many a stomach, and so with great care he leveled his rifle, aimed, and fired, bringing down the fattest of them all.

What happened next should have been no surprise to David, who had been around swine all his life. But it was a surprise, because he had been concentrating so hard on killing that one particular hog that he didn't consider what the others would do when the shot sounded. They let out a loud, collective squeal and ran off as fast as stumpy legs would carry fat bodies. David was so startled he stepped back and tripped, falling on his rump as the herd ripped through the cane in the opposite direction—heading directly for the camp.

A grin split David's face when he heard the shouts of surprised men, followed by a great eruption of gunfire and, in tandem, terrified porcine squeals. Rising, David reloaded his rifle, shouldered up with difficulty the hog he had shot, and marched out of the canebrake and into the camp. He was met by a cheer.

"I should have knowed it was you, Crockett!" a man yelled. "You're one caution of a hunter, I do reckon! It ain't many who can send meat a-running on the hoof right to where it's needed!"

There was pork in abundance, no question about it. David's shot had sent the hogs barreling right into the camp, where many of them had been shot down as soon as the startled soldiers could react to the porcine invasion. There was even a fresh-killed cow; it too had been grazing in the cane, and had been driven out by the shot and stampede of swine.

That night's mess was the best the men had enjoyed since the campaign began, and all around the camp sated soldiers extolled Crockett of Tennessee. David Crockett was now a famous and admired man within that limited little world, and he liked the feeling very much. He basked in it, thinking that a man could surely get used to admiration. It was better, headier, than the finest spirits John Crockett had ever sold back at his tavern inn.

The next day's march brought them to a town of Cherokees; here, they discovered, were the owners of the hogs and cow that had been killed and consumed. The officers signed out a United States government payment warrant in compensation for the livestock, and continued the march. After another night's camping, the volunteers met again with the regular army from which they had earlier divided. The combined force went to the farmstead of Radcliff. This was the white man, with the Creek wife, who had hosted and fed David's team of scouts earlier . . . but here, under interrogation from the officers, new facts about Radcliff emerged, and when they made their way back to David, he was deeply angered.

It was Radcliff, it seemed, who had sent the runner into the friendly Creek camp that night to warn David and his scouts of the Red Sticks crossing the river, ready to attack. This was the message David and his men had raced back to camp to give Coffee, only to have him ignore it. That remained a sore spot with David; it rubbed all the sorer when he discovered now that Radcliff's story had been a fabrication in the first place. There had been no

Red Sticks, no threat of immediate attack. Radcliff had made up the story simply to get David and his scouts out of the way. So in an ironic way, Coffee had been right to ignore his information—though when the same story had come via Major Gibson, he had certainly danced a different step.

Radcliff's place was searched and various provisions found; these had been hidden by Radcliff. Ire was hot against the man, and his two sons were forced into military service to make up for his deceptions.

The army advanced to a new camp; there, Colonel Coffee was promoted to the rank of general, and a captain elevated to colonel in his place. Afterward the army went on to the Coosa River and established a fort at the Ten Islands, from which scouting companies sallied forth, scouring the countryside in search of Creeks. Several prisoners were taken.

Word arrived of a force of Creeks some miles away in a town named Tallusahatchee, and plans were laid for attack. After many days of false alarms, false starts, fruitless reconnoiters, and small-scale forays, the first major fight was about to take place.

Silently and in long, narrow lines, two bodies of soldiers snaked in along the sides of Tallusahatchee, then closed their lines together at both ends, surrounding the unsuspecting Creek village. With a dry throat and nervous fingers, David Crockett fidgeted and waited to hear the first gunfire. It would come at any time now.

A ranger company under a Captain Hammond was even now advancing toward the town. They would deliberately expose themselves to the Indians in order to provoke a chase that would lead the Creeks out of the town and into the range of the rifles of the surrounding army. And then the squeeze would begin, soldiers moving in on all sides, driving the Creeks back into their town, crushing them as if in a great fist, forcing them to surrender or die fighting.

David glanced to his left, then his right. Persius Tarr

was beside him, eyes glaring and intense, tongue snaking out again and again to wet his lips. He looked fierce and eager. David turned away, looking straight ahead again; he did not want Persius to speak right now. He did not want to hear him again voice the hungry anticipation with which he claimed to regard the approaching slaughter.

Yells, screeches, then shots . . . David crouched lower behind the log that hid him and peeked carefully over the top of it. It had begun.

Moments later members of the ranger team came rushing into view. David lifted his rifle, laid it across the log, and clicked back the hammer. The rangers came on, then past, rushing through the lines of hidden riflemen. Tensely the seconds passed; war cries resounded in the trees—and then they saw them. For the first time in his life, David Crockett beheld the fearsome sight of onrushing Indians, warriors who in moments would learn they had been baited into an ambush.

"Now!"

As one, scores of rifles cracked. Indians spasmed and fell, some silently, others with deathly screams. Smoke rose through the treetops. For a moment there was near silence, broken only by the sound of men reloading, and then fully shattered by the crack of Indian rifles and the whiz of arrows sailing above, thunking into wood, smacking against rock.

Now the Indians turned and raced back toward their town. With a yell the soldiers left their cover and advanced, closing their circle. Now that the first shots had been fired, the tension of anticipation broken, David felt very different than before. A sort of wild eagerness for battle came over him, and a thoroughly inexplicable sense of invulnerability. He had survived the first round of fire, so why not the second, the third, the tenth, or twelfth?

They soon came into the very borders of the town itself. By now the Creeks had realized they were surrounded and had nowhere to flee, and many made signs to indicate they wished to be made prisoner. Those who surrendered their weapons were captured and spared.

But not all the Creeks were ready to give up. Moving

through the town, David saw a large house; into it a steady stream of warriors was pouring. "See that?" he said to a man at his side. "There's treachery in that, I'll wager!"

"You wager right, David," Persius Tarr replied. David was surprised; he had not realized it was Persius with him. "I've counted upward of thirty going through that door already, and that's shy a few I missed."

Other soldiers were about and also perceived the situation. A new string of warriors appeared, rounding another house and heading for the same larger one that held the others. Men gave chase, opened fire. Two Indians fell, but at least five made it in safety to the door.

David and Persius and some thirty other soldiers had now focused their full attention on the house that hid the warriors. "I say burn it down!" Persius declared. "Roast 'em alive!"

Only an hour earlier David would have found the suggestion repulsive. But now the fire of war was hot in him; no cruelty seemed unthinkable. "Fire would do it," he said. "We can't shoot them through the walls."

"Look there!" shouted a familiar voice. It was Kelso, alias Ben Moore. "There's a granny woman come to protect them red coons! Ha!"

An elderly squaw had come out of the big house and stood just outside the doorway, holding a bow and arrow in hand. She was withered and stoop-shouldered, with keen little eyes peering out of a shriveled, angular face. David found the sight of her unnerving, out of place here in a situation of war. "I wish she'd move," he said. "Otherwise she'll get herself killed."

"I'll kill the old harlot!" Persius said, raising his rifle.

But a form intervened between him and the woman, who had now seated herself cross-legged in the doorway, her face a mask of stoic, fearless disdain. It was Kelso, laughing loudly, advancing toward her.

"C'mon, you old bag of bones, you old rutting she-dog, you!" he yelled. "Draw back that bow and shoot me, if you think you got the strength!"

The old woman straightened her legs and laid the bow across her feet, so that the wood of it curved around the bottoms of her feet and the string was above them. As Kelso danced and taunted her, his scornfulness giving way to the obscenity that had been his mark when David knew him in boyhood, she nocked the arrow on the string, pursed her lips with determination, and lifted her legs so that the bow leveled. With both hands she pulled back the string, her scrawny body all in a strain, and let the arrow fly.

Kelso stopped his taunting in mid-sentence, looked down at his chest, and whimpered loudly. "Oh, Lord, she's shot me!" he said. He turned, pointing at the arrow piercing his chest. "She's shot me, boys. Put an arrow right through me. This thing will kill me, sure as the world, and me so young." He choked some, then spat up blood. "I ain't ready to die, fellows. I'm going straight to hell ... don't want to go to hell ... I want—oh, it's hurting now—I'm—" Abruptly he quit his babble and fell over dead.

The hag in the door cackled in glee, proud of her achievement. Something like a living, devilish spirit swept over the astounded soldiers, and more than a score of rifles rose and fired with ear-slamming concussion. Most of the shots hit their target, striking the old woman at the same moment, in the ugliest explosion of blood and flesh David Crockett had ever seen. It should have been sickening, revolting, but at this moment he was immune to such feelings. The fever was upon him, and on all the others. He looked into Persius Tarr's face, saw in it the bitter fury and blood thirst that had gripped him. He didn't know it, but had he been able to see his own face he would have seen that same fearsome expression.

They reloaded as quickly as possible. A warrior appeared at the door above the shattered body of the old woman. A soldier raised his rifle and shot him dead. The others, finishing their reloading, advanced to the door. Crowding together, vying with each other for position and cursing when they were outjostled, they fired through it again and again, killing the Creek men inside so that the floor became thick with gore. David joined in without hesitation; at the moment it felt to him no different than as if this was a slaughter of mad dogs.

Persius Tarr knelt by the dead woman and pulled a gorget from around her neck. He slipped it over his head as a trophy.

They set the house ablaze with the forty-plus warriors still inside, all of them now dead or wounded. The fire raged hot and fierce. All around, the battle went on. David stepped back and watched Persius Tarr shoot a boy of about twelve who showed himself in the door of a nearby house, holding a rifle. The boy made not a sound as the ball broke his thigh. He fell, then got up, hobbling on his good leg toward shelter, but veering toward the burning house in his state of mounting shock. Another man fired at him. This time the ball passed through the boy's arm, shattering it as well, making him drop his weapon. Still silent, the boy fell and lay unmoving.

David moved away, circling around, hungry for more battle. He found no one to shoot at; all the Indians within his view were already dead. Coming close to the burning house again, he saw the twice-shot Indian boy was still alive and now was crawling, trying to get away from the nearby fire. The heat of it was so intense that his skin was blackened and blistered—and still he made no sound, did not even show the torment on his stoic face.

Somewhere in the callus that had built itself around David's mind, a tiny opening suddenly appeared. For a moment the true horror of what was happening here, and the revolting fact that he was part of it, broke through to his consciousness. He was sickened, but then the window closed again and he went on as before.

The soldiers took prisoners in abundance, some eighty of them. Whenever they encountered resistance or the appearance of it, they killed. This was devastation beyond anything David had anticipated; surely the horror of Fort Mims itself, the tragedy they ostensibly were responding to, could have been no worse than this.

When the battle was done, David stood alone beside the dead body of the boy he had observed earlier. The youth had made it perhaps thirty feet before his wounds got the best of him and ended his life. Scattered across the battlefield or burning inside the flaming houses were nearly two hundred other corpses. It had become a place of gore, of horror, the harvest field of the very reaper himself. He had enjoyed a rich gathering-in today.

David thought of Ben Kelso, who had died declaring his dread of hell. Perhaps Kelso had come into hell in the end. David couldn't know. But he did know this: without question, hell had come to Tallusahatchee, and he had helped bring it.

A wrackingly painful process began inside him. His battle spirit began to fade, softening his heart and mind so that he could see this scene through his usual eyes again. What he saw horrified him; the fact of his participation made him feel like retching.

He felt a sense of disgust at himself, his companions . . . and particularly Persius. Persius, who had seemed to derive such a vicious pleasure from the killing, even the killing of a brave little boy. Persius became a monstrous, murderous being in David's mind, and he hated him for it, hated him—because it was easier to hate Persius than to hate himself.

Chapter 36

At that most inopportune moment, Persius Tarr walked up to David, grinning brightly. "Look at that Injun boy! Roasted like a chicken gizzard! The buzzards will be eating cooked meat today, eh, Davy?"

Persius's bright, cheerful voice and demeanor struck David like blasphemy would strike a priest. He wheeled on Persius, face reddening, emotions boiling. His momentary hatred of him surged and intensified.

"You think there's something to make jests over in all this? At least that little Creek boy didn't hide himself beneath a pile of corpses while his own kind were massacred!"

Persius stiffened as if stabbed between the shoulders. "What did you say to me, David Crockett? What do you mean, my own kind?"

"You heard me. You ain't deaf. It ain't suiting for a man who hid himself beneath corpses to save his own skin to be laughing over the death of a boy who at least had the manhood to fight for his own people instead of turning against them, and to die without a whimper! That boy you slaughtered was more a man than you'll ever be! Persius Tarr, the coward of Fort Mims! The man who hides under corpses to save his self while women and children are slaughtered all around him!"

"I didn't hide myself under no corpses, damn it! It just happened! I was knocked senseless."

David's turbulent emotions had found their focus now. All his fury, his rage, his sorrow were narrowing to a point and aimed straight for Persius Tarr. There was no controlling his words; the dam had broken and the waters gushed out. "Maybe you were, but you said yourself that you came to and witnessed the killing. Did you rise to try to save the life of a single child, Persius? Hell no! How many women did you watch having the life hacked out of them, while you lay there grateful for the dead who hid you? Tell me that, coward!"

Persius balled his fists. "I don't let no man call me coward, Crockett. No man. Not even you."

The confrontation was drawing attention. Other soldiers began gathering around the pair, some grinning, some very serious. David glanced at the encircling faces, and knew from what he saw that these men would take his part of this. His rifle had provided them meat. They had not forgotten. He heard mutterings pass from man to man: What was that Crockett had said? Something about Persius Campbell hiding himself while women and children were massacred at Fort Mims!

The spirit rising inside David was ugly and vicious— but yielding to it was far too gratifying for him to resist it. "You make me sick to the pit of my stomach, Persius! I regret the day I talked you into joining this army—I never thought I'd see a man pleasure himself with killing and dying the way you have here! Bloody hell, you're no better than any savage yourself!" David was too wrought up to realize that, having just chastised Persius for having been too eager to avoid war and slaughter to begin with, he now condemned him for having become too fond of them. It was very nearly a contradiction, but it passed unnoticed.

"Don't you preach to me, Crockett! God! I seen you do your share of killing, and I didn't see no tears in your eyes for the savages you laid low!"

David jutted out his chin and shoved his face close to Persius's. "At least I didn't kill my own kind, half-breed! You ain't no better than a savage because you *are* a savage! Half your blood is redskin blood! Ain't nothing to marvel at, what you did at Mims! The savages was as much your own kind as them they butchered!"

"You lie! You lie like hell!"

David's steam grew even hotter. "I'll tell you what I'm saying, Persius *Tarr*!" He yelled the last name, and looked at the men gathered around. "That's right—his name is Tarr, not Campbell. He's a half-blood Creek his own self, the bastard son of a trader and a squaw! I heard it straight from the mouth of John Haynes, who knew Persius Tarr's pap in his Injun trading days! This half-breed here watched women and children murdered at Fort Mims, and he's killed his own people here today!" David reached out, yanked the gorget from around Persius's neck and held it high. "See that? He took it off a dead woman who might have been his own granny, for all he knows! That's the kind of man Persius Tarr is! He's a savage, and he comes by it fair and square! But he don't just kill red-skins. He kills white folk too—he's wanted for murder in Jefferson County!"

Persius roared and drew out a knife. He made a lunge for David, but others stepped in and grabbed him, wrenching the knife from his hands.

"Let me go, damn you!" Persius shouted, struggling vainly. "He's a damned liar! I ain't no redskin!"

"It's you who are the liar, Persius," David said. "If anybody doubts the truth of what I'm saying, let them ask Haynes! Yes sir, you've lied aplenty in your time. You've lied here about your name, and you're lying about the blood in your own veins! And tell me this, Persius: Were you lying too about them men who threw you into that cave along the Clinch River? You said you let them be, but that ain't the truth, is it? You killed them, that's what you did—and it was the killing of them that shook you so bad you tried to turn Quaker . . . ain't that it? I can see from your face that it is. You—a Quaker! Pshaw! You weren't fit on your best day to touch the boots of a good Quaker like old John Canaday! You're naught but a murderer, a liar, a half-breed bush baby who's carried sorrow and trouble with him everywhere he's gone. You're a—"

Persius jerked free from those who held him and

pounded David hard in the jaw. David fell back and
Persius threw himself atop him, hammering blow after
blow against David's face and head until the others managed to pull him off. David had been beaten into a stupor.
By now the hubbub had attracted two officers, and after a
moment of interrogation of the witnesses, all of whom
soundly blamed Persius Tarr for the trouble, Persius was
placed under arrest, his hands tied behind him.

Hunger made David's stomach rumble. Supplies had
not reached the camp, so the men were on half rations tonight and suffering for it. But not David Crockett. He
hardly noticed his emptiness, nor even the pain of his
bruised face. His suffering was of a different and far more
severe kind.

He walked up to the weary-looking sentinel posted
outside a little tent at the edge of camp. Bleary-eyed, the
guard looked back at David, whiskered lips downturned,
shoulders stooped. "What you want?"

"I want to see the prisoner."

"Can't do that. Orders. He's to be kept alone until
he's took back to Jefferson County. He kilt a man there,
y'see."

"Yes. I know." David made a quick spy all around.
"Look here, I really need to see him. If you'll let me, I'll
give you ..." He faltered unable to think of anything to
offer.

"'Give me what?" From the man's expression and
tone, his openness to bribery was evident.

"Give you ..." David reached into his pocket and
pulled out a dollar coin. "... this. It's the best I can offer."

He knew the man wouldn't accept such a low payment for such a risky transgression of duty, and began to
turn away. The fellow surprised him by grasping his arm,
taking the coin, and nodding him into the tent.

Persius was chained to a deeply rooted post inside the
tent. He looked up at David silently. No feature moved except one corner of his lip, which twitched spasmodically
when his gaze met David's. The tent roof was so low that

David had to crouch on the balls of his feet, which put him uncomfortably eye-to-eye with Persius.

"Persius, I'm . . ." David winced; the words he was going to say sounded so hollow and futile.

"You look a sight," Persius said. "I pounded you up right good."

"I don't care about that. I earned the beating. Persius, I'm . . . I'm sorry. God, I'm sorry. I don't know why I did it. All them words just came tumbling out, and I don't know from where. I don't know how I could have done that to you."

"I do. You did it because you hate me." Persius spoke very matter-of-factly.

"Hate you? Lord, no! Persius, you been my friend since I first knew you. I don't hate you. Couldn't, if I wanted."

It astonished David that Persius didn't even look angry, not even sad. Just resigned. David would have preferred fury to this. Persius shook his head slowly. "Maybe you ain't hated me before, but you sure enough hated me today. David, I've sat here in this tent and thunk on the subject of hating, and I've ciphered it out. Take me. I hate Injuns. Purely hate 'em—and I've never really tried to figure why. Best I can come up with is it's because I got Injun blood in me, and it's like a black mark or some such, holding me back from ever being what I could be if my mother had been a white woman. I hate the Injun blood in myself, but I can't get rid of it. So it just makes me hate other Injuns, just for reminding me of what's in my own veins. That's the long and short of it. I hate Injuns because I hate myself."

"But I don't hate you, Persius. God above, if I hated you I wouldn't feel so regretful at how I got you in such a fix here. Out there today, it was like something in me just steaming and burning and making me say things I didn't mean. It was . . . I don't know. The way you talked about that poor little Creek boy . . . it made me mad. Kicked-dog mad. And so I just lit in on you."

Persius nodded. This time his tone was slightly sharper, definitely more intense. "You was mad at me because the same thing you seen in me, the thing that made you despise me, was in you too. Don't look at me that way—you know it's the truth. I saw you put your rifle ball through that old woman right along with the rest of us. And right on with the rest of us you shot them warriors inside that house she had guarded. Shot 'em like they was rats in a barrel. It's like I've got it figured about the Injun blood: I hate Injuns because they remind you of me, and out there today you hated me because I remind you of you. That's the truth and you know it."

David wanted to protest this, but there was no spirit left in him. Maybe Persius was right. Blast it all, he *was* right, hard though it was to face it. When he had turned on Persius, he was turning on the ugly side of his own nature.

Persius was in a philosophical frame of mind. "David, let me tell you a thing or two just for what it's worth, and while I've got the chance. You were right, what you said about them two on the Clinch River. I did find them and kill them after I crawled out of that bone cave. Cut the old one's throat, and threw the young one in alive like they'd done me—though I tied him up first so he couldn't get out. They was the first human lives I'd ever took, and it ate at me for a long time. You were right too about that being the reason I tried to turn Quaker." Persius chuckled heartlessly. "That *is* a caution to think about, huh? Persius Tarr, a Quaker! Hell, I'll never be good enough to be a Quaker or nothing else that's decent. You're right about me, David. Everything you said out there, it was true. And you know what? When I killed Crider Cummings, maybe it was murder. Sure, he come at me first, but even if he hadn't, I probably would have killed him, just to get him out of my hair. I reckon I've got a murderer's heart. So when they hang me back in Jefferson County, it won't be nothing I ain't earned fair and square. You can ease your conscience on that one."

David fingered his hair, shifting and posturing in ways that made obvious his rising anguish. "This is my fault . . . I'll go to the officers and tell them I was wrong, that you ain't really wanted for any murder. I'll tell them

I made it all up in anger over some past card game or woman . . . they'll let you go then."

"Too late for that. They rousted out another couple of soldiers here who had lived in Jefferson County before. They knew all about Persius Tarr and backed up what you had said. And that John Haynes told them I was the spitting image of old Mick Tarr the Injun trader. There was no point in denying the truth after that. I admitted it to them."

"You admitted to murdering Crider Cummings? Lord a'mercy, Persius, that was a fool thing to—"

"No, no. I admitted to being Persius Tarr, that's all. That's all. They want to hang me, they'll have to convict me first. And before they convict me, they'll have to keep me." He paused, eyes shifting, glittering meaningfully— and for a second David was back in Greer's store in Greene Courthouse, looking at the face of a swarthy little orphan boy freshly brought to town by John Crockett so he could be bound out through the Orphan Court. Suddenly David understood. Persius intended to escape. The comprehension gave him a wild, boyish thrill. Escape! That was the answer for Persius . . . and for David Crockett. If Persius got away, then there would be no removal to Jefferson County, no trial, no hanging. David's conscience could be left in peace.

The conversation from here out took place in even softer whispers. "But how, Persius? They've got you under guard."

"Guards can be bribed—as you being in here suffices to show. Or they can be conked on the head."

"You're chained. How will you get out?"

"The guard has the key. And from time to time he has to take me out to the woods for a piss or a squat. I'll find my chance."

An idea came. David reached into his pocket and pulled out the old silver piece.

"Here . . . bribe him with this. Tell him it's Creek silver, just part of a whole potful you found during the fight today. Tell him that if he'll let you go, you can take him to where the rest is hid. Then lead him off just west of camp, down in that little hollow beneath the sandy bluff.

I'll be there to help you. I'll go there soon as it's dark. We'll get you loose, Persius, or I'll give my life trying. I owe it to you, for it's my fault you're here."

"Well, to large measure, I reckon it is. Of course, the life I've lived has contributed its share to my situation too." Persius grinned. "Thank you, Davy. I ought to break your neck for what you've done, but I've never been able to hold a grudge on you for nothing, whether it's gathering a crowd to watch me poot worms, or trying to put my neck in a Jefferson County noose. I swear, one of these days you'll be the death of me, Crockett!"

"Don't say that," David replied. "It ain't funny. And Persius—no matter how you've got it figured, or what trouble my big mouth has got you into, I don't hate you. If I hated you today, it was stirred-up feelings causing it, and that's all. And I'll prove I don't hate you by helping you get away from here safe and sound. Tonight. I promise."

He went to the tent flap and whispered to the bribed guard that he wanted to slip out now. A few moments later the guard hissed the all-clear and David exited and left Persius alone.

Encumbered by his chains, Persius worked open the little pouch and removed the silver nugget. Closing it in his fist, he gave it a little squeeze for luck, and held it while keeping his eye on the base of the tent flap, waiting for daylight to fade. After it was dark he counted off the minutes until an hour was gone by, and called out: "Guard! You going to stand around there until a man's beshat his own britches? I need to go to the woods, and quick."

Gruffly the guard stuck his head through the flap, and Persius was surprised to see a different face than he had expected. The guard had changed—and this man might not be as open to bribery as the first obviously had been. Well, no matter now. He had already rolled the dice, and he would have to play the number he had received.

The guard entered and freed Persius's chain from the post. Taking up his rifle, he led his prisoner toward a line of trees, while all around, campfires sent sparks skyward and half-rationed soldiers complained about the gnawing emptiness of their stomachs.

Chapter 37

Before dawn the troops were up, still grumbling over their hunger. By the time their badly insufficient breakfast was eaten, something far more interesting than empty bellies dominated their attention. The story spread from man to man, and if any initially doubted its truth, the dark expressions of the officers and, at last, the sight of the draped corpse being carried into the camp verified the tale.

The dead man was a private who had been assigned as one of the guards of Persius Tarr. He had last been seen leading the chained prisoner toward the forest, probably to allow the prisoner to perform his private functions. The guard never came back. Evidence on the body showed he had been choked to death with the prisoner's chain. Afterward the key had been taken from the body and the chains removed. And one of the officers' horses was gone, probably stolen by the escapee.

No one was hit harder by this news than was David Crockett. Great fear came over him. Had he been seen coming or going from Persius's tent? The guard he had bribed for entrance was not the same one who had died. The original guard might reveal to the officers David's illegal visit to Persius. He might be suspected as an accomplice . . . and in fact he very nearly was. It was he who had encouraged Persius's escape attempt, he who had waited for several hours at the base of the sandy cliff for

Persius and the guard to show up. Persius never arrived. David had finally concluded that the guard hadn't snapped at the bait about the hidden Creek silver, and had sneaked back to camp and his bedroll.

David had hardly finished cleaning his mess dishes before he was called to come to the commanding officers' tent. When he entered, there sat the guard he had bribed with a dollar. The man's face was blanched; he looked thoroughly scared. David felt the color drain from his own countenance.

"Private Crockett, we'll come right to the issue. It is true, is it not, that you have been a companion of the escaped Private Tarr, and in fact enlisted in company with him, and made him one of your scouts when you were sent out to reconnoiter under Major Gibson?"

"Yes sir."

"And it was you who argued with Private Tarr loudly and revealed the murder charge pending against him in Jefferson County, Tennessee?"

"Yes sir."

"After which Private Tarr knocked you senseless, accounting for the bruises still visible on your face?"

"Yes. Yes sir."

"Private, did you make any attempt to visit or speak with Private Tarr during the time he was held under guard?"

David hoped his voice would not quake. "No sir."

"No attempt at all?"

"No." David's eyes flickered to the face of the bribed guard. He saw a look of relief. Praise be, David thought. That man has told the same lie as me.

He should have figured that to begin with. The guard wouldn't reveal him; that would show that he had taken a bribe.

"Are you aware of anyone else attempting to make contact with the prisoner?"

"No sir."

Silence, pursed lips, a conclusory nod. "Very well, then. You may go."

David left the tent, whistling nonchalantly. He walked

toward the nearest grove of trees, and disappeared into it. Once there, he sank to his knees, slumped over, eyes closed, and took deep breaths. For a few moments he had thought it all was over, that he had been caught in an escape conspiracy with a prisoner who had turned murderer. Thanks be to God, he thought—unnoticing of the irony of this prayer—that he was able to lie his way out.

And Lord, let that guard I bribed lie just as good as I did. Let him lie like the devil, Lord. In Jesus' name, amen.

It would be sometime later before he gave serious thought to the fact that Persius had killed another man. Murdered him outright. If there was still question about whether the slaying of Crider Cummings had been true murder, surely there was none in this case. Persius had choked the life out of an innocent man. But now he was gone. Thank God, he was gone.

Never again, David vowed to himself, would he befriend Persius Tarr, or let it be known, to any but those who knew already, that he was friend to such a man.

I wash my hands of him, forever. I was a fool to have ever entwined my life with his. I'll not make that mistake again, from now to my dying day.

Later in the morning, the troops marched back to the smoldering ruins of Tallusahatchee. Horrific sights met them: dead bodies, already being picked over by carrion birds. A sickly stench, combining the smells of charred wood, burned flesh, and bodily decay, hung like a cloud over the town.

David was drawn to the large house where the forty-plus warriors had died. Nothing remained of its walls now, so the heaped corpses were clearly visible. They had been mostly consumed by the flames, but not entirely, and what remained was sickening to behold. David could not look for long.

From a little Indian boy found roaming amid the horror, the troops learned that beneath the long house was a cellar full of potatoes. Despite the horrific heap of charred corpses, several men probed into the remains of the house and found a hole leading to the cellar, and as the boy had said, there were potatoes in abundance there, roasted by the heat of the fire.

David joined the feast with the rest of the army, eating the potatoes like they were apples. They tasted fine, like they had been stewed in fat . . . and suddenly David's stomach did an unpleasant turn as he realized that these potatoes had been roasted in the dripping bodily juices of more than two-score burning Creeks just above the cellar. He almost brought up what he had already eaten, but managed to squelch the heaves. Well, he certainly would eat no more. He was ready to throw away the last half-eaten potato . . . but no, he couldn't. Revolting or not, this was food, and he was still ravenous. He finished the potato, trying not to think about what he was doing.

It was one of the lowest days in the life of David Crockett. The matter of Persius and the murdered guard, his own self-protective lies, and now this disgusting eating of food cooked in the same heat that cooked human corpses . . . how much further could a man fall?

David Crockett wished he had never come to war.

But more war remained. From Tallusahatchee the troops marched to rejoin the regular army, where for several days they continued to suffer from insufficient provisions. Then word reached General Jackson that hostile Creeks had laid siege on Fort Talladega, which was occupied by Creeks friendly to the whites. A march toward that Coosa River fortification began at once.

The fight at Talladega didn't fall out quite as smoothly as the devastation of Tallusahatchee. Failure of communications and some yielding of ground by panicked troops forced Jackson and his army to withdraw to the protection of another fort, with seventeen men lost. Even so, the hostile Creeks, caught by the hundreds in a cross fire during part of the battle, fared much worse. Estimates of those killed ranged between three and four hundred.

Later in the month, the prospect of a negotiated peace

presented itself, only to be destroyed when more failed communications resulted in some troops from David Crockett's old home region of East Tennessee attacking friendly Hillabee Creeks in their towns. Jackson had nothing to do with this, but the Creeks who had just agreed to negotiations perceived it as treachery and withdrew, stretching out the Creek War much longer than it might have gone otherwise.

Unhappiness was rampant among Jackson's troops, and at one point an attempt was made by some disgruntled soldiers to "mutiny" their general—but Jackson called the bluff and prevailed. David took no part in the mutiny attempt, but he felt sympathy for those who did, and shared their resentment of Jackson when he successfully stood his ground against them.

Just before Christmas, David Crockett's term of enlistment ended, and he headed home, weary and eager to see his family. He had heard nothing more of Persius Tarr since his murderous escape from the camp. In fact, he had actually managed by the force of hard will to push Persius almost entirely out of his mind. The very thought of the man was enough to make him shudder and fill with a sense of regret and something like scarcely controlled panic. He thought often of the murdered guard, and felt partly responsible for his death. He hadn't wanted anything like that to happen when Persius escaped. He had just wanted to atone for having gotten Persius into trouble in the first place. How could he have known Persius would do what he did?

He dreamed sometimes about the murdered guard, and about heaps of charred corpses inside a burned Creek house. Sometimes he would wake up sweating, and imagined he could detect the faint taste of roasted potatoes on the back of his tongue. He could hardly bear it, and a time or two it made him sick outright.

Polly held him in silence for a long time the day he reached home again. He knew from her manner that she had feared he would never come back at all.

All was well at home. The boys had grown far more than David had anticipated. His enlistment had been only for ninety days. It seemed more like a year. He was astounded at how much his military service had exhausted him and drained him of the fighting spirit that had prompted his volunteerism in the first place. As far as he was concerned at that point, he would remain a civilian forevermore, if possible.

For many months he was to live the life he had known before, and gradually become his old self again. News of the Creek War continued to drift in, and he followed it closely. In March, Jackson defeated the Creeks at Horseshoe Bend, news that crackled at lightning speed across the nation.

In early summer Polly became pregnant and voiced a hope for a girl. David would have been happy to have another son—the idea of a houseful of strong young men appealed to him—but if a girl it proved to be, that would suit him just fine. Whatever made Polly happy.

August brought a treaty negotiation between Jackson and the Creeks, in which the Creeks ceded the lands above Fort Jackson, which stood near the confluence of the Coosa and Tallapoosa, all the way to Fort Armstrong. But full peace didn't follow the accord. Some Creeks refused to live by the treaty, and these recalcitrants were given aid and sanctuary by the Spanish in the port area of the Gulf of Mexico. The British had put their hand in the game as well, harboring ships with the Spanish and sending some three hundred troops to join themselves with the Indians.

It was outrageous affrontery, in the view of most Tennessee frontiersmen—and by now David Crockett had sufficiently forgotten the horrors of war and his earlier weariness and desire to remain free of military life. The fever was on him again, and in September, with Polly very unhappy about it, he enlisted with the Separate Battalion of Tennessee Mounted Gunmen, under Major William Russell.

They took no part in the battle at Pensacola, arriving too late for that. They found Jackson the victor and the British ships beginning to withdraw, but Fort Barrancas was destroyed, having been blown up by the British to keep Jackson from seizing it. Meanwhile, the Creeks had vanished into the wilderness.

David was among troops ultimately assigned to roust out and destroy these fugitive Indians in the swamps of West Florida. It was rugged, trying work, and here David saw anew how bloody war could be. But he was older, more hardened, and at one point even accepted the invitation of some Choctaw allies to take coup on the severed heads of some Creeks they had killed. Taking up a war club, he joined in striking the battered heads, and when the Choctaws gathered around him, chanting "Warrior! Warrior! Warrior!" he felt that the life of a combatant had its own fierce rewards after all.

With Russell, Crockett took part in a fight at an Indian camp where several warriors were killed and women and children were taken prisoner. Soon after, the regiment crossed the Florida panhandle, passed over the Choctawhatchee and headed east. They suffered the usual lack of provisions, but again Crockett's rifle brought down game, though not nearly enough. At long last the mission ended and the troops returned to the Coosa River and Fort Strother, established during Crockett's earlier term of service. On the way to Fort Strother they passed through the Fort Talladega battlefield and observed the skulls and skeletons of Indians killed there, still lying unburied in the open.

Seeing that made Crockett realize he was weary once more of military life, and longing for his Tennessee home. Near Fort Strother he chanced to meet a body of East Tennessee troops en route to Mobile, and among them were many of his old boyhood neighbors, and his own brother Joseph, a handsome young man who had reached his midtwenties. The brothers' reunion was a happy one, and David caught up on news of home and family—making him all the more eager to get back to Tennessee.

From Fort Strother he began his homeward journey, though he still was subject to call-up for more than a month. He reached home and found Polly again relieved, maybe even surprised, to see him again, having readied herself for life as a widow in case he should not return. He had been home only a short while when orders came in for him to return to service to scout for Indians along the Black Warrior and Cahaba rivers.

Polly was crushed. Would he be gone yet again, after having only recently gotten home?

"Not this time," he told her. "There's nary an Indian left there to be found, and I won't waste my time with it. I'll go into town and find me a substitute and pay him my last month's wages. I intend to be here when our baby is born."

Finding a substitute didn't prove too hard; soon he located a young man eager for such service, and struck the bargain. David returned home. His life as a fighting man was finished, as far as he was concerned, and that suited him perfectly.

Not long after, Polly gave birth to the girl she had hoped for, and they gave her the formal name of Margaret and the nickname of Polly, the latter in honor of her mother. David delighted in bobbing the newborn up and down in his broad hands, grinning into the crimped little pink face. And he could sit in perfect contentment watching the little one suckle at her mother's breast.

But he was worried too. His wife had recovered quickly from childbirth when the boys were born, but this time she seemed unable to regain her strength. For many days after the birthing she remained in bed, too weak to rise for more than a few minutes at a time. She rallied some after that, much to David's relief, and seemed on the way to a full recovery when one day she collapsed, bleeding from her vagina, her face as white as milk.

David called for help from neighbor women, who did all they physically could to stanch the flow of blood, while the eldest of them, a withered old woman who stood just over four feet tall, opened the family Bible to the sixteenth chapter of the book of Ezekiel and read a verse that many swore would stop even the worst bleeding: "And when I passed by thee, and saw thee polluted in thine own blood, I said unto thee when thou was in thy blood, Live; yea, I said unto thee when thou was in thy blood, Live."

A few minutes later the issue ceased and Polly slept. David cried out of happiness. She would surely get well now.

But for the next two weeks Polly Crockett didn't rise from bed. Her strength, already mostly gone, drained even further. Soon she lost her milk and David had to call in a local Indian wet nurse to keep the baby nourished.

He was nestled close beside Polly in their bed the night she died. There was no murmur, no stiffening, no evident pain. He felt her life pass from her like a faint breeze against his cheek. There was no need to examine her and verify her death; he knew it as soon as it happened, without a moment of doubt. He did not move, but held her body close the rest of the night. David was not given to frequent prayer, but he prayed now, thanking his Creator for the time he had enjoyed with Mary "Polly" Finley Crockett, and for the children they had brought into the world, and for the memory of her, which he would always carry with him, no matter where he went or what he did. Only after his prayer was done did he shed the first tears.

The next morning, eyes red and heart hollow, he walked into the woods and dug Polly's grave with a spade, and there laid her in the earth, covering her resting place with a cairn of stones.

Part 5

GENTLEMAN FROM THE CANE

Chapter 38

Aboard a Cargo Boat on the Mississippi River, Spring 1826

The mood of resignation that had held an exhausted David Crockett in its gentle hand for the last ten minutes shattered with a most literal jolt. Amid the sound of splintering timbers, he pitched sideways from off his stool, landing so hard on his side that the breath was knocked from him. Ash and smoke from the fire by which he had been warming himself scattered across the wood planking and onto him as well, making him howl in pain and surprise. Flailing at the embers, he rolled onto his back just in time to see the hatchway that led up out of the cabin collapse inward. The boat began to tilt beneath him.

David scrambled up, trying to keep his footing against the increasing tilt of the boat. He realized what must have happened. The boat had struck a sawyer, or run upon a bar of land or rock, or hit one of the clumps of escaped lumberyard logs that floated in this part of the river.

A hot panic gripped him. Not only was the boat tilting, but it seemed to be making a steady downward slide as well. It was sinking—and he was below deck! David lost his footing and slipped down the slope as water began gushing in a heavy, powerful jet through the cabin hatchway. He knew he had to get out very quickly, or he surely would drown.

For a minute or so he struggled to reach the hatch, but the water pounded him back. It was futile to compete with the strength of the inrushing river water. Half submerged, and with water rising by the second, he looked around the darkening cabin for some other way of escape. There was only one other possibility, that being a small opening through the cabin wall on its far side—now the upward side, considering the slant.

He heard footsteps above and shouts of alarm. David sent up a yell: "Hallooo! I'm down here—help me! Help!" And then he began working his way with tremendous difficulty up the sloping, water-slickened planking, making for the little opening.

By the time he reached it, the boat had slid even deeper into the river, and the tilt had grown as steep as the pitch of a typical house roof. To his dismay, he found the opening upon which his life depended was too small for him to squeeze his entire body through, but he did manage to get his arms and head out. He yelled and waved with all the volume and vigor he could muster, as the water rose beneath him, reaching his thighs, his waist, his stomach.

Meanwhile, his mind was frantically talking to itself. *So this is how the life of David Crockett comes to its end. Drowned like a bug in the bottom of a boatload of staves, doomed never again to see the light of morning or the faces of my family. And all because I wanted to make money in New Orleans.*

Indeed, this venture had been conceived as a promising means of making money, though now it appeared he wouldn't be earning, but paying, very likely with his own life. This lumber venture had seemed a fine idea last fall, when he had invested in building two sizable boats and hiring a crew of men to cut some thirty thousand staves to be shipped for sale in New Orleans.

David knew little about boats and water travel, his best chance at becoming a nautical man having vanished long ago when his ship boy's berth to London was snatched away by the treacherous Myers. But he had felt lucky and confident when the twin vessels pushed out along the Obion toward the Mississippi. Within two hours all such confidence had faded, and he learned that luck was no substitute for skill.

The problem lay in guiding the overloaded boats, which tended to drift sideways no matter what the crew did. David finally ordered the boats tied together, but that didn't help, and the boats caught in the current and went sailing along, as rudderless as driftwood, until darkness fell and the last light of hope flickered out. All attempts to steer, even to ground, the bargelike boats failed. In the pre-dawn hours, David surrendered his fate to the river and descended below deck to warm himself by the fire—and then whatever calamity it was that had shivered the vessel had occurred, and now here he was, trapped in a sinking boat, struggling to save himself against all odds.

Hands groped down to him and grasped his wrists. "We'll pull you out, Colonel!" A couple of his crew members had seen his waving hands. Thank God! He had feared no one would detect him, that no one would realize he was gone until it was too late.

He grimaced as they tugged at his arms. His body moved a little farther into the opening, then wedged like a cork.

"You won't fit through, Colonel!"

"Pull!" David shouted back. The water was lapping his chin now. "Pull even if you tear my arms from their sockets—otherwise I'm a dead man!"

He closed his eyes as they gave one more tremendous heave. Pain wracked him; he felt the fabric of his shirt tearing away. He gave out a pantherlike cry of pain as his body was pulled through the hole, leaving every scrap of his clothing behind, and a goodly portion of his hide as well.

He passed out for a few moments. When he came to, he was lying atop a wide, slimy log that was part of a huge tangle of sawyers and driftwood lodged against a small island. He was naked and cold. He sat up, groaning and shivering.

"What the devil happened to us, boys?" he asked.

"The boats run against these damn logs, Colonel," came the answer. "There's an island here, you see, and it had caught the logs. The current just shoved the boats down underneath it, like a dog diving under bedclothes."

"So that's why the boat tilted on me like she did," David mumbled. He looked around and now saw the grim results of the accident. Both boats had lost their cargoes, and looked ready to break free of the log tangle at any time and head on down the river unmanned and unloaded. They were stranded in the middle of the river, wide expanses of water separating them from the land on either side.

"Look at it," David said. "More planks in this river than Egyptians in the Red Sea. We've lost our cargo, boys. Every deuced penny, gone to ruination!"

"Yes sir. Mighty sorry."

"Anybody got a scrap of clothing to spare?" David asked, wrapping his arms around his naked, abraded body. "When that sun comes rising and we get ourselves rescued, Lord willing, I don't fancy parading my bare hind end before the whole blessed city of Memphis."

But when the morning came and a boat appeared to give rescue, David Crockett was still almost as naked as a newborn, because there had been no clothing to spare beyond a ripped shirt that he managed to use as a makeshift loincloth. Every man had left only what clothes he wore; all else had washed away with the staves, or sunk to the bottom of the river in the boats.

David welcomed the blankets and hot beverages the rescuers offered, and accepted their invitation to carry him and his crew on to Memphis, which was in sight of the wreck, and where they could surely find some sort of refuge and help. The name of one Marcus Winchester, merchant and prominent citizen, was spoken a few times. A generous and helpful soul, they said. David decided on the spot that he would look up this Winchester. At the moment, he needed a generous and helpful soul as badly as ever a man could.

•   •   •

The talk about Winchester's generosity proved true. Once again David was clothed, as were all his men, and if his purse was still empty, at least his belly and his glass were full. Winchester had gladly given aid to the hapless men—especially when he learned the identity of David, whose name had become quite well-known in the State of Tennessee during the years that had intervened between Polly's death and his freshly concluded misadventure as a boatman.

David sat across a table from Winchester in the latter's parlor, sipping from his glass from time to time as he told his life's story. Not only David himself, but his crew, had been given lodging by the good man, but at the moment only David shared Winchester's company, the others having retired.

Winchester was openly fascinated with his guest's biography and sat in rapt attention, frowning in concentration, asking the occasional prompting question. An hour or more of talk behind, David had just recounted Polly's death, and now he paused. Even though much time and change had come about since her passing, the subject still was difficult for him to discuss.

"What a tragic thing, losing one's wife at so young an age, and with children in the home," Winchester said. "What happened to you after that?"

"For a time my younger brother Joe and his own brood lived with us," David said. "They were a help to me, no question, but nothing seemed right, not with Polly gone. I struggled to do what I could for my young ones, working hard, trying to farm. And hunting. I hunted a lot, for meat, for pelts to sell. . . ." He paused, tapping his finger on his glass and looking wistful. "And mostly for my own sake. Just to get away, to be alone. I'd roam the woods with my dogs and talk to Polly, just like she was there." Now David glanced up, embarrassed. He had revealed more of his inner self to Winchester than he was comfortable showing. He blamed the liquor, but took another sip anyway.

"And now you've married again."

"Yes, yes. It didn't take me long to see that I couldn't

raise a bunch of children proper without a mother in the home. So I commenced to looking for a good woman."

"And you found one, obviously."

"Yes sir. Elizabeth Patton was her name, though I call her Betsy, same name as one of my sisters. Betsy's a big-boned North Carolina gal. I married her a year or so after Polly's passing. It was a providential union. She was widowed by the Creek War, you see, and left alone with her own children, as I was with mine. We had that in common and it drew us together." David paused a moment, then smiled. "The day we was married—it was in her house—a pig come walking in on the wedding, grunting and such. It was a pet of Betsy's. I booted it out and told the folks that from then on, it would be me and not that pig doing all the grunting thereabouts."

Winchester laughed. "I'm glad you found a good wife, David. Few men were made to make it through life without a helpmeet."

"I believe that's true, sir." He chuckled suddenly. "But you know, after I married Betsy, I come near leaving her in the same situation we were trying to get out of by marrying. I came nigh to joining Polly in the life hereafter."

"What? You were hurt or something?"

"No, it was illness. It happened while I was away from home too, and there ain't no sickness worse than the one that strikes you on the trail."

"Where were you?"

"Down south. Alabama country. After remarrying, I was struck with the wanderlust and took a good long trek into Alabama, looking for land to move to. I had a few neighbors with me. When some of our horses took off, I took chase after them a whole day, and never come across them, and that night I put up for rest in a house—and by the next morning I was sick as a dog, sick nigh to death. They brought in a man to bleed me, and before long I went looking for my fellows again, but the fever just gripped me all the harder and I fell out by the road. Some Injuns come along and helped me get to another house for rest, and by some circumstance or another my old partners came by there and took me on to another man's place and left me to die. They bought horses and rode home to give word of my passing. But I reckon I surprised them. Two weeks later I was quite a lot better, and hitched me a wagon ride home again. When I got there, Betsy thought I was a ghost, having been told I was gone from this world. And I reckon I did look like a ghost; up until that time I'd always had two bright streaks of color in my cheeks, and I ain't seen a sign of them since."

He told Winchester how the next spring he moved his family westward into Lawrence County, Tennessee, settling on Shoal Creek in territory recently obtained through treaty from the Chickasaws. There he and Elizabeth—who had brought some minor wealth of her own into the marriage—began to build up a sizable distillery, powder mill, and grist mill, all standing together on the bank of the creek. And there the fires of political ambition that had begun to flicker some years before finally broke into flame. David was made an unofficial local magistrate, then a state-appointed justice of the peace. He affiliated with the state militia as well, and through election gained the rank of colonel, a title he attached proudly to his name. He would no longer be merely David Crockett, or even Mr. Crockett. He would be Colonel Crockett, a title with the kind of dignity and authority he valued.

"I involved myself in politics," he related, a look of pride slipping onto his face. "I was elected town commissioner in Lawrenceburg right about that time. I had begun thinking about politicking while I was still in military service during the war. There was little enough government there at the time, so the people come together and set one up, and I had the pleasure to be part of it. And I'll confess to you, sir, I enjoyed holding office, and it began to grow in my mind that I might be suited for higher things yet."

"You were beginning to think, I assume, of your legislative run?"

"Yes sir. By the first of the year of 1821, I had settled on it firm. I laid aside my commissionership and put my hat in the ring for the state legislature. It was the grandest enterprise I had ever put myself upon, and I did my best

at it. But I knew I had an advantage, if I can be so bold
as to claim such a thing."

"What do you mean?"

David's eyes grew brighter and he spoke with even
more vigor. This was a topic he had thought out in detail.
"My advantage is that I understand the people, Mr. Winchester. The common people, I'm talking about. Poor folk,
folk who have to scrape and fight just to survive. Folk
who care more about a man's character than about his
schooling or how many big words he can toss out from a
stump. And I'll tell you something else, though I may
sound the braggart for it: since the days I was a boy, I saw
time and again that folks just ... well, *liked* me, took to
me. There was many a time when people offered me work,
and them hardly knowing who I was. There was a sea captain once tried to talk me into sailing to England with his
crew, and he had only just laid eyes on me when he made
the offer. I believe it's a gift providence has given me, Mr.
Winchester. There's something about me that draws people, at least some of them. I don't know why it is. But I
know it surely helped me when I made that first campaign
for the legislature."

"I've heard some word-of-mouth about your campaign style, Colonel Crockett. Colorful, I suppose you
could call it."

"It's common sense, that's all. A man running for office has to present himself in his best lights. And mine
ain't as a speaker, no sir. Me, I'm more at ease with a joke
or two, a little jab at myself and then a deeper one at my
opponent, and then winding it up by offering to buy every
man in shouting distance a good stout drink. Let me tell
you, that'll earn you the vote of a Tennessee stump-
grubber quicker than the finest words you try to sparkle
his ears with." He grinned and winked.

"You're a clever man, Colonel."

"Just a man who knows the people, and himself."

"And your majority was impressive in that first race,
I believe."

"Double my opponent's vote, with nine more to
spare."

"You are a man of great potential, Colonel. There are great things ahead of you."

It seemed to David that there was something more than mere politeness in Winchester's last statement. But he left the matter unprobed when Winchester went on to question him about details of his legislative career. David was struck by Winchester's knowledge and his perceptiveness of the issues that he had centered on. Winchester knew that David had voted against double taxation of delinquent landowners, had promoted various steps to ensure fair land issuances and surveys, and had supported efforts toward a constitutional convention much needed by western district settlers. An impressive show of concern for the welfare of the common man who he so extolled, Winchester declared it, and once again David puffed with pride.

"I'll tell you, sir," David said. "I soon had personal reason to look out for the concerns of the western district. There was a fierce bad flood on Shoal Creek, just as bad, or worse, than one that swamped out a mill of my father's back in Greene County when I was small. Every bit of what Betsy and me had worked for got washed away, clean as you please. Three thousand dollars worth of loss—that's what we faced. Betsy, bless her soul, just took it in stride, and declared we would just pay up as best we could, take our family and make a new start."

Winchester looked appalled. "How the devil did you deal with such a load of debt?"

"At great personal loss," David replied. "And it hurt, mighty bad. We turned over lands and slaves and every bit of property we had left, to cover our debts. I guess you could say we invited them who we owed to sue us, and didn't fight paying all that we could. But it wiped us out. We couldn't stay thereabouts no longer after all that. I turned my eyes west. To the Obion River country."

"Beautiful country."

"Yes. We settled in to try to make our way as best we could, which as often as not was from me selling wolf scalps and pelts and such. I had no notion of running for the legislature again—then I'm shot if somebody didn't go and put an announcement in the newspaper saying I was in the ring again. It was a joke, I reckon, but it got me hot, and I decided to see it through just to turn the laugh back the other way, you see. I made myself a shirt of buckskin with big old pockets, and carried a bottle of whiskey in one of them and a good twist of tobacco in the other, and every man I met, I'd offer him a swallow and then a chew to replace the one he had to spit out to take the whiskey. So he was better off when I left him, you see, than he had been before. And I was running against Dr. William Butler, you may recall, who had married one of Andy Jackson's nieces. I made hay over old Butler's money, of which he's got plenty, reminding voting men that their own wives had to wear worser cloth on their persons than old Butler wiped his feet on in his big fine house. Oh, I gigged Butler like a frog!" He drained his glass and refilled it.

"I hear you once gave one of Butler's own speeches word for word before his chance to give it himself. Is that true?"

David guffawed. "Yes sir. He had to make him up a replacement right on the spot. I won that race right handy, I can tell you." He sloshed his drink, and a splash of liquor spilled onto his shirt, soaking through and touching alcohol to one of the many abrasions he had suffered while being pulled from the sinking boat. The sting brought an abrupt end to laughter and talk.

Winchester stood, pacing the room and rubbing his chin thoughtfully. At length he turned and faced David. "Colonel Crockett, I must say I am deeply impressed with you," he said. "And I have a proposal to put forth to you, one that comes with my pledge of support, and which I hope you will take with the utmost seriousness."

"What's that, sir?"

"Colonel Crockett, the hand of destiny is upon you. I see it clearly. There are higher things in store for you than what you have yet achieved."

"Higher things?"

"Indeed. I'm talking of the Congress of the United States of America. You, Colonel Crockett, would make a most excellent congressional candidate, the kind of candidate who could most certainly win."

David smiled rather sadly. "But you know I've already tried my hand at that . . . unsuccessfully." The unpleasant memory of a failed effort to enter national politics the prior year made David shift in his chair, suddenly restless.

But Winchester waved his hand as if to brush off the subject. "A first race means nothing. Most first efforts for major office fail. You must not give in. Next year's race can be yours, Colonel. I'm convinced of it."

David mulled it. Had he thought of this himself, he wouldn't have given it much credence, but coming from Winchester, it had a believable sound.

"There is one thing I must ask you, however," Winchester went on. "Is there any event from your past, any scandal, or indiscretion, or unseemly past associate, who could scuttle your reputation in the heat of a national race, or once you are elected?"

David paused, eyes lowered; his mind flashed back to a military camp, the body of a guard choked to death by a prisoner's chains, desperate lies told in haste and fear. . . . He had made no mention of Persius Tarr to Winchester. In fact, he had put Persius so far from his mind over the past several years that he had nearly forgotten his existence. And maybe Persius didn't exist anymore; for all David knew, he was dead. Even if not, he was as good as dead to David Crockett.

He looked up. "No sir," he said. "There are none."

"Excellent. Excellent. A pure reputation is a boon, virtually an essential, for a successful candidate. Colonel Crockett, you will take my suggestion seriously, I hope?"

David tried to picture it in his mind. David Crockett, member of Congress . . . a man fulfilling his destiny in the very center of national power. Try as he would, he couldn't quite see it. The memory of his prior defeat was still too fresh.

And yet . . .

He smiled tightly at Winchester, and lifted his glass in

salute. "I'll think on it, sir. I reckon it can't hurt to think on it, can it?"

Winchester smiled. "No sir. It can't."

Glass touched glass, and they drank.

That night in his bed, David thought on it until he fell asleep. When the morning sun through the window pried open his eyes, it was the first thing that came to his mind—thought of even before he remembered the great economic loss the river had brought him, even before the first wave of a terrible hangover washed sickeningly over him.

He was still thinking about it—and talking about it with Winchester—when the sun set that evening.

Chapter 39

M any times before the thought had come to her, and now it came again: *He makes it easier for me to smile.*

For Elizabeth Patton Crockett, that counted for a lot, because life had not always given her much to smile about. Certainly the Carolina girlhood of increasingly distant memory had been a happy time, as had been the day she wed James Patton, the husband who had brought her to Tennessee. But much sadness had come her way as well, the greatest being James Patton's death in the Creek War. It was in the dark time afterward that she had discovered the ability of David Crockett, no stranger to bereavement himself, to bring light into the gloom. He had a way about him, a kind of inner sparkle shining through his dark eyes, that gave her a sense of hope . . . and made it easier to smile. That was the main reason she had married him and borne him children even though she had thought her married life was over and her childbearing years were past: he could always make her smile; and she loved him for it.

She had managed to smile even when the Shoal Creek flood washed away their mills and distillery—businesses that she couldn't help secretly regarding more as hers than his, considering that much of the money behind them had come from her pocket. She had smiled when David had gone down in defeat in his first race for

Congress, and now she was managing to smile again, despite her sense of shock over the two pieces of news David had delivered to her.

The first concerned the loss of the boats and staves. They were fully gone; after leaving Memphis, David and a companion had traveled as far as Natchez, hoping to retrieve the vessels, which had broken free of the log jam and headed downriver as expected. The effort was for naught. After months of planning, labor, and investment, all designed to lift them from the financial pit into which the Shoal Creek disaster had thrown them, they were again wiped out, and every day new lawsuits were being filed against them in connection with their prior loss.

That was jolt enough—but David had delivered another in its wake. He had just announced to her that he intended to run for Congress a second time. And this time, he declared, he could win—*would* win.

"The first time around all was against me," David said. "Colonel Alexander"—his opponent in that prior race—"had the advantage of high cotton prices at the time, which he could claim was because of his old tariff bill. And he had the benefit of being already in office, of course. But that will work against him this time, I'm convinced, and he surely can't claim that cotton prices are good now! Best you can get is eight dollars per hundredweight. It was about twenty-five a hundred in the last campaign.

"And this time, Betsy, I've got money backing me, out of Memphis. Major Marcus Winchester is going to give upward of two hundred dollars for me to use as I need it. And I'm a little older and wiser, and my name is known better than before. It will be different this time than the first. I've made you no fortune, Betsy, but in Congress I can make you proud, and maybe find a way to better our situation. I want to do it, Betsy. What do you think of it?"

She had never seen him show such eagerness in his expression. He was a man who had been dealt harsh personal blows in the mill and river disasters—but the possibility of political success obviously gave him hope. How could she do anything but support him?

"Davy," she said, "if it's Congress you want, then go and get it. You'll have me standing behind you all the way, win or lose."

He smiled and put his arms around her. "There'll be no losing to it, Betsy. I'm going to win this one; I can feel it. Before long you're going to be the wife of a United States congressman. You can be proud. You can hold your head up high."

"I've always held my head up high," she replied, and it was true, because she had always been a canny, practical, and self-reliant woman. And a little forward, at times, as she was right now. While David began to turn and slip away from her, she grasped his shoulders and firmly turned him toward her again, and kissed him on the mouth so forcefully he almost stumbled backward.

Dusk was falling and the torches were already lit near the platform at the edge of the clearing. Off to an adjacent side sat a wagon with a big whiskey barrel on it and the tailgate lowered and stacked with an assortment of cups and mugs. Already the clearing was filled with men, and more arrived every moment. Elizabeth Crockett stood in the shadows, deliberately keeping out of view, and watched her husband move among the crowd, shaking hands and joking and generally looking as if he was having the finest time of his life meeting the voters.

She smiled privately, proud of him. An intelligent woman, she realized her husband's limitations, his lack of education, his near illiteracy, his sometimes oversimplistic understanding of the world and of political matters, his too-short temper. Yet among the kind of backwoods constituency gathering now in this clearing, he fit in where the typical finely dressed, practiced, schooled politician did not. The men recognized that he was one of them, that when he put out his hand and shook theirs, no condescension or pretense marred the gesture.

Her eyes shifted to David's two opponents. One was Colonel Alexander, the incumbent he had faced before; the other was General William Arnold. Both men were residents of the city of Jackson, and cut from a different sort of political cloth than was David. They were silk, and he was sacking; they no doubt believed they held the advantage because of it. But Elizabeth knew what David knew as well: silk might be finer to look at, but sacking was a devil of a lot more useful.

As darkness fell, the campaigning began. This was the first such event Elizabeth had attended, and she watched with interest, and then mounting irritation, as first Alexander, and then Arnold rose to speak—and with snobbish deliberateness presented the campaign and the voters' choice as if this were a two-man race. David was being ignored, treated as a nonentity. No references were made to any of his positions, no points were addressed by either Arnold or Alexander other than those raised by one or the other of those two. As Elizabeth saw the strategy being played out, dark anger filled her. How dare they treat her husband with such contempt!

But David didn't look worried, she noticed, and when a flock of guineas came walking into the clearing, raising their usual racket and causing Arnold to have to pause in mid-speech to request their removal, she saw her husband's eyes sparkle mischievously.

At length the two pomposities were finished with their presentations and it came time for the backwoodsman to make his effort. Arnold and Alexander sat back, refusing even to look at Crockett, and feigning a few yawns as he began to speak. There was no polish on David Crockett's voice, no affected style or ten-dollar words. The Crockett that stood before the crowd to seek their vote was the same Crockett they would find if they were trading horses or swapping jackknives.

"Now gentlemen of the cane—as I was once called by an uppity and biggity sort of puffball in the state legislature, a man who didn't rightly appreciate us folk of the backwoods—you've surely heard some fine speechifying done by my two fine opponents here this evening. I was particular impressed by the ability of Colonel Arnold"— and at that Arnold twitched and frowned, for his militia rank was not colonel, but general—"to speak the language of the fowls."

David paused a moment. Men in the crowd glanced at one another. Language of the fowls? What could that mean?

"Now, the good Colonel Arnold is a polite man, so polite he didn't even risk offending me by calling my name even once during his entire speech. Why, he was so polite that even when my little bird friends, the guineas, come walking in here, calling 'Crockett, Crockett, Crockett,' he was so fearful I'd take offense that he even had *them* shooed away."

A great roar of laughter rumbled through the crowd. General Arnold turned ruddy and shifted unhappily in his chair, while off to the side, Elizabeth Crockett crossed her arms in satisfaction and smiled.

David's speech beyond that was brief. He mentioned the fact of cotton's price decline despite Colonel Alexander's tariff policy, threw in a few more jokes and jabs, then pointed a finger at the whiskey wagon.

"Gentlemen, I believe the time has come not only to elect David Crockett to the United States Congress, but to do so with properly wetted whistles. I'm ready for a cup, and all who'd like to share one, come with me."

A shout of approval rose through the treetops, and as a mass the men surged toward the whiskey. David grinned, turned and winked at his opponents, then descended from the platform and joined the tide toward the liquor wagon. Alexander and Arnold looked at each other with expressions of concern, and Elizabeth Crockett saw it and was gratified.

David Crockett, gentleman from the cane, might just win this campaign after all.

October 1827

David's oldest son, John Wesley Crockett, was no child anymore, but a strapping man about two decades old who dropped a hint from time to time that more than one

Crockett might turn to politics before all was done. He had accompanied his father extensively throughout the campaigning, and was with him now, along with stepmother Elizabeth, as the three made an autumn journey east, heading back through David's old territories and toward Elizabeth's original home grounds as well. This was a quiet, personal tour, yet also a celebration, because Colonel David Crockett was now Congressman Crockett of Tennessee, having won his race with a margin of almost three thousand votes.

They stopped at numerous places, meeting new people and visiting old friends. One of the latter was his former neighbor, James Blackburn, who was hosting a corn-shucking party when David showed up. Having a newly elected congressman in their midst brought much pride and pleasure to the frolickers, and David was made very welcome, but joined in the shucking with the others to make sure all knew he had not become conceited with his new important status.

He and his family went on the next day, but Elizabeth was worried. David didn't look well—she could always tell when he was growing ill—and sure enough, by the next afternoon he was feverish and weak, sweating even in the cool autumn breeze. This was a recurrence of the same illness he had suffered during his exploration of Alabama years ago.

They reached Swannanoa with David in very poor condition, and there they remained for many days until his health could return. A doctor was called in to bleed him, the usual treatment for almost any illness, and when he learned that David was bound soon for Washington to begin a term in Congress, he wrote a name on a piece of paper.

"Look up Dr. Campbell Ibbotson when you arrive in Washington," the doctor said. "He's an old fellow student and friend of mine, and quite a fine doctor with a good practice in Washington City. And he's a Tennessean, so he'll be particularly pleased to know you. Should this sickness recur on you there, he's the man you'll want to treat you."

November came, and David was still weak, but much better than he had been. Congress was to convene on the third day of December, and thanks to David's illness, there was no time for him to return home before departing.

He kissed his Betsy good-bye, turned her over to the care of John Wesley, and watched sadly as they began the long westward trek home. When they were out of sight, he paused, took a deep breath, and wiped a tear from the corner of his eye.

Then, fighting the fatigue left by illness, he mounted his horse and began his own journey, toward Washington.

Chapter 40

A Few Months Later

Sweeping off his hat as the door opened, David nodded a greeting to gray-haired Dr. Campbell Ibbotson. This meeting occurred on the external but covered landing outside the second-story entrance to Dr. Ibbotson's living quarters, comprising a suite of modest rooms above his office and clinic. The neat, smallish brick structure stood on a narrow side street that led onto the wide dirt thoroughfare of Pennsylvania Avenue; it had been home to the widower physician for five years.

"Well, if it isn't Colonel David Crockett! Come in, come in!" Ibbotson stepped aside and swept his hand back in invitation. "I'm happy you were able to come."

"Thank you, Campbell." David entered, looking around and sniffing the faint scent of medicines that always permeated these rooms, wafting up through the creaky floorboards from the clinic. It was an odd but not unpleasant smell; even so, he didn't like it because he associated it with being bled. He had arrived some months earlier in the capital city still weak from his recurring malaria, and had come here for treatment. He had found Ibbotson to his liking. A transplanted Knoxvillian, Ibbotson was acquainted with some of the families David had known in youth and enjoyed talking with David over matters and memories of their common home state. The doctor-patient relationship lasted only an hour or so, to be replaced by one of friend to friend.

Twice David had come to Ibbotson's quarters to play cards, share a bottle, and talk of this new and strange life of national politics in which he found himself. David was out of place and knew it. His manner was not that of a city man, but of a backwoodsman. His diction was that of an uneducated western southerner; his clothing, while not hunting garb, was of cheap cloth and styling. He had detected the stares and whispers that shadowed him, and caught fellow members of Congress giving him sidewise, amused glances many times.

Sometimes he had been embarrassed by this—but not tremendously so, especially since Ibbotson had counseled him that it could actually play to his advantage. "You are not merely one of the usual crowed," the old doctor had said. "You are different. You catch the eye and the ear, and have about you an air and manner that some might think is simple and illiterate, but which, if properly shaped and used, can equally be perceived as the rugged wisdom of the American common man. There is already talk about you, you might wish to know, to the effect that you claim the ability to wade the Mississippi River, whip your weight in panthers and fellow congressmen, and carry steamboats on your back."

"I've never made any such claims," David had replied. "Though there's not a thing you've said that ain't the gospel."

David tossed his coat and hat onto a newspaper-heaped sofa and seated himself at Ibbotson's table as the doctor fetched cards, glasses, plates of cheese and biscuits, and a bottle. For several minutes they played, ate, and drank in near silence, each comfortable in the presence of the other, until at last Ibbotson asked David about his latest impressions of Congress.

"I'm a right smart befuddled and dismayed," David said. "I've come to believe some of your early warnings about the slowness of activity among the lawmakers were right after all."

"Indeed they were. I've been here long enough to know, my friend. They all come in the first time like you did, expecting to see their pet bills passed in two days and put into effect in a week. Oh, it's a hard lesson that they face, but an essential one! The government's mills grind more slowly even than God's, David Crockett. And usually to much less effect."

David grunted, thinking of his own favorite measure that he had placed before Congress within days of his own arrival. This was a bill that sought to give West Tennessee squatters ownership of the federal lands they had settled upon. In Congress the issue was already a concern for a Tennessee congressman who had been in Washington since 1825, James K. Polk. It was an old and complex matter, arising out of North Carolina's 1796 cession of its former lands, which became Tennessee in that year, and certain stipulations involving recognition of prior Carolinian land laws and bounties of property paid to its Revolutionary War veterans. The upshot of it all for David Crockett was a desire to protect the best interests of West Tennessee squatters, who he believed would be threatened and impoverished if vested East and Middle Tennessee landholders had their way and the public lands were sold to fund public schools.

If there was any particular issue that Crockett perceived himself as championing, it was that of squatter's rights. It was primarily to deal with this matter that he had come to Congress in the first place, and he wouldn't consider himself a full success unless he pushed his bill through in some acceptable form.

Ibbotson and Crockett's discussions seldom failed to get around to the vacant land issue, and such was the case tonight. David was in a quiet mood, talking mostly about James Polk and the mutual cooperation they were extending to each other on the lands issue. But David was growing frustrated; it seemed that there were so many with vested interests in slowing the bill that it was being talked into oblivion.

"I had hoped to have the matter settled by the end of my first session, but now I'm deuced uncertain about it."

"Keep trying, David. It's the only way. Keep trying, and remain true to your principles. And compromise. Always be willing to compromise, or you'll succeed in nothing in this town."

"I don't see how a man can stay true to his principles and compromise at the same time. Let a man talk out of both sides of his mouth enough, and before long he'll be singing duets with hisself at the meeting house."

Ibbotson chuckled. "The fact is, compromise is necessary in this town. Those who don't learn to use it don't last."

"Well, a man can only compromise so far. Be sure you're right, then go ahead. That's my motto, and that's how I plan to handle this congressman business I've got myself into. My land bill is right, and I'll see it through, hell or high water."

Ibbotson smiled and took a sip of his liquor. "We shall see."

"You're blamed right we shall."

The Crockett Cabin, Gibson County, Tennessee,
Early 1828

Elizabeth jerked awake very suddenly, making a faint vocal sound in the back of her throat. Looking around the room, she found herself confused. It was dark, and the fire had burned low. The last thing she could remember, she had built up the blaze and sat down in her favorite rocker to enjoy a cup of hot tea before retiring. The rest of the family had already gone to bed, and she had enjoyed the solitude. But she hadn't intended to fall asleep in her chair.

Something nibbled at the corners of her consciousness; she felt a vague, undefined sense of disquiet. Why had she awakened like she had? Something she had heard . . .

. . . outside the door. She stood, remembering. A little cry, like a mewling cat or whimpering puppy. And a knocking sound—a rap on the door? Drawing her shawl tightly around her shoulders, she went to the door and looked out through the little window. It was cool and drizzly outside; she could see little. Then her gaze descended and she let out a gasp.

"Oh Lord! Lord have mercy!"

One of the children appeared in the room behind her as she scrambled to open the door. "Mama? I heard a knock. . . ."

Elizabeth jerked open the door and knelt, lifting the wooden crate that had been left outside it. The crate was half filled with dirty flax, and nestled down in it, wrapped in a filthy and tattered shirt of homespun linsey-woolsey, was a thin and sick-looking baby girl.

"Mama, is that a baby?"

"Yes, yes it is . . . oh God, who would leave a child out on such a night? And why did they bring it to . . . oh, this child looks ill and weak." She put a finger out and touched the face; the baby rooted toward it hungrily, found it, sucked on it, then made a displeased face and let out a feeble cry. This was the same sound that Elizabeth had heard in her sleep.

"Mama, did somebody leave her there?"

"Yes, yes, obviously so!"

"But who was it?"

"How should I know, child? Milk, that's what we need. Some warm milk, and a rag. This child looks nigh to death—see the pallor of her? What shall I do if she dies?"

John Wesley Crockett had come into the room by now, and gaped in astonishment at the amazing sight of his stepmother holding a skinny baby he had never seen before. "What the devil—"

"John Wesley, I don't understand this," Elizabeth said, talking rapidly and excitedly. "Someone has left a child here, and she looks like she could die at any moment, and she's just as sickly and weak as she can be, so much she can hardly cry, and—"

"Let me hold her," he said, seeing that she was becoming overwrought. He couldn't fault her for it; certainly this was a most disturbing, oddly frightening, development.

The child felt like little more than a cold clay doll in his hands. Instinctively he knew this was a seriously ailing baby. Whoever had left it must have been desperately seeking help for the child; perhaps they had believed that the family of a congressman surely would have some means of providing for the child's care.

"This old shirt stinks," John Wesley said. "Let's fetch a clean wrap." He removed the tattered garment from the baby and was shocked, and slightly repelled, at the thinness of the miniature human form now unveiled. Wadding the shirt in one hand, he tossed it into the fireplace . . . and only half noticed the object that tumbled out of the upturned cuff and onto the hearth. Only later would he recall, retrieve, and examine it.

They wrapped the baby in clean cloths and fed it as best they could on milk fetched from the springhouse and warmed. The infant, though acting hungry, would scarcely suck the nourishment from the rag. "What this baby needs is a wet nurse," Elizabeth said. "Come tomorrow, we must seek one."

But it was not to be, because the next morning the strange little infant, origin and name unknown, had closed its eyes and slept, and while sleeping, had left the world of the living.

David had never known such frustration. Despite his best efforts, despite cooperation and interplay with James K. Polk, all attempts to push through the vacant lands bill had come to nothing, and the congressional session was soon to close.

The issue, which seemed so simple at heart to him, had become increasingly complicated by the machinations of other representatives and the competition of various interests. John Bell had arisen in favor of using some of the vacant lands designated for educational usage as an endowment for the University of Nashville, a position that David fiercely opposed, believing that his poor constituents would benefit little, if any, from such usage. Better, he argued, to use the lands for common schools for the poor; most of the impoverished farmers who lived in his represented counties would likely never see the inside of a college. The sons of the rich would benefit at the expense of the poor.

He continued to work in alliance with Polk, though he sensed a growing tension between them on details of the debate. Still, when Polk argued that an insufficient number of land parcels had been set aside to fulfill the educational usage requirements laid out by an 1806 compact, and that in order to remedy this and aid the common school fund, certain lands should be sold by existing state land offices, David rose to his aid, helping defend his positions against opponents.

"I am a plain and unvarnished man," he told his fellow lawmakers. "I have not had the advantage of an education, and from that lack I know the value of what I've missed. That's why I'm wanting to be sure the poor boys that follow after me have their fair opportunity at schooling."

But in the end all the argument led to nothing. The bill was tabled, the session closed, and David Crockett headed home for Tennessee with no land bill in hand to show his constituents. He was surprised; he had honestly expected to be able to push the bill through in one legislative session.

Campbell Ibbotson wasn't surprised at all; he had been a congressional observer for a long time, and knew how matters really worked and how little idealism counted for. He felt sorry for his new friend's disappointment, but not too sorry. Crockett of Tennessee was learning the lessons that needed learning, and already Ibbotson could detect growth in the man. He was still uncouth, still poorly spoken, still so nearly illiterate as to require ghost-writing of almost every document he produced (Ibbotson himself secretly provided some of that service)—but he wasn't *quite* as uncouth, as poorly spoken, as illiterate as before. Even his choice of clothing showed improvement.

Dr. Ibbotson was a man who prided himself on judgment, and in his opinion, David Crockett was a rough stone that just might polish up into a diamond, or at least a ruby—*if* he had a little help, the right kind of nudging, support, and behind-the-scenes direction.

Well, Ibbotson decided, that he'll have, courtesy of himself. He'd see David Crockett rise to his potential yet, or count himself a failure. There was greatness beneath that rugged surface, Ibbotson thought. Destiny had its hand on that man, and he'd see if he could prod it along. Who knew how far David Crockett might rise in this world?

He poured himself a drink and sat back, entertaining a thought that seemed simultaneously farfetched and intriguing: it would be an interesting thing to be personal physician to a President of the United States.

In the dim light of dusk David strolled up Capitol Hill toward the massive building that never failed to give him pause and turn his gaze upward in sincere awe. The Capitol building—stately, vast, wood-domed, the very symbol of national power—caused him to catch his breath whenever he drew near it. Even now it was hard to believe he was really here, that he was really a part of the very power structure of the nation. Not all that long ago he had barely understood how the nation was governed; at one time he had actually believed that a president was equivalent to a king, his wishes automatically carried out by decree.

The Capitol building had a new look to it, accounted for by the fact it had been substantially rebuilt after being burned by the British in 1814. The fire had gutted the interiors of both the north and south wing. Repairs had been done, and construction of a central portion of the building began in 1818, and had been completed only recently.

It seemed that there was a bustle of activity around the Capitol at almost any hour, but at the moment all was relatively quiet. David entered the building and experienced the same somber feeling one receives upon entering a great cathedral. He swept off the broad white hat that was a typical part of his Washington garb.

He explored the dark recesses and hallways, and made his way into the great chamber where the House of

Representatives met. Looking around, he smiled. After weeks of feeling like an alien thrust into a world he knew nothing of, he was beginning to feel comfortable in these surroundings. It was not the first time he had made this kind of unheralded personal visit to the Capitol. By coming here at off hours, he accommodated himself to the place, made himself feel more at home. He looked about the empty chamber, remembering the impression it had made on him the first time he had taken his seat in a full session. Important-looking men had been all around him, shuffling papers, laughing easily, freely talking among themselves, even when business was being conducted from the chair—the circuslike atmosphere had put him in mind of one of his campaign appearances before a crudely mannered crowd of his own constituents—except few of his constituents dressed in the suits, cravats, and cambric ruffles that were the uniform of the typical United States congressman.

Returning to the front entrance, he looked out across the city of Washington. It wasn't a large city in comparison to the major cities of the nation, but to a man accustomed to little frontier towns, it seemed the epitome of civilization, as settled and firm as some ancient European capital. The monuments, the big buildings, the patterned layout of the town—it was enough to choke a man with astonishment and admiration. The world was indeed a much bigger and more astonishing place than David Crockett the frontiersman had ever known.

He was glad to have learned the world was as lofty as it was. In such a world a clever and capable man could ascend to dizzying heights. Or he could sure as blazes give it his best try. David Crockett intended to do just that. Maybe he hadn't made it very high in the world of commerce and business, but politics was a whole different climbing tree.

Looking into the night sky over Washington, David said aloud, "Betsy, you just watch me. I'm going to dig in tooth and toenail and climb as high as I can go. And this time I won't fall off."

"What's that, sir? Were you speaking to me?"

David wheeled. Two strangers had emerged from the shadows behind him and overheard him. He felt himself blush profusely and hoped the darkness was thick enough to hide it.

"No, nothing. Just jabbering to myself like granny in the still house, that's all. Evening to you." As usually happened when he was embarrassed, his Tennessee backwoods accent doubled its already substantial thickness and made his words all but indecipherable. Still blushing, he slapped his hat back on his head and made his escape as quickly as possible.

"You know who that is?" one of the men said to the other as he receded into the gathering dark. "That's Crockett of Tennessee. A member of the House of Representatives."

"You don't mean it! That backwoods pone eater? What'd they do, pull him out of a cornfield and force him into a suit and shoes at the point of a rifle?"

"That's substantially the tale I heard. And I understand the only reason he hasn't gotten out of the garments is that he hasn't figured out yet how to work the buttons." And they laughed.

Out on the walkway, David Crockett glowered. Snobbish educated fools! He'd encountered too many of their type already, and knew he'd have to deal with plenty more. They thought they were mighty smart, that breed— but they weren't even smart enough to know that a backwoods pone eater had keener ears than citified types. They obviously had thought he was out of earshot.

"You up there!" he hollered out of the darkness, enjoying it when he saw them start in surprise at the sound of his voice. "Yes, you two! Answer me a question, would you? Where in this town can a man find French Jane's Parlor of Delight?"

"What? I say, sir, that's a damned impudent kind of thing to be asking," one of the pair responded. "We're employees of the government, and not in the business of directing men of low repute to houses of sin."

"Oh, I ain't looking to be no patron of such a place," David called back. "I was just aiming on dropping in to say hello to your maw and sisters. Good evening, gentle-men."

Their walking sticks upraised like clubs, they looked for him for three or four minutes, but somehow he had managed to vanish like smoke in the darkness.

Chapter 41

One term in Congress had made David Crockett a relatively famous figure, and word of his return home preceded him. From a passing rider, John Wesley Crockett heard that his father was approaching. Keeping the information to himself, he discreetly saddled and mounted his own horse and rode out about a mile from home to meet the homecoming congressman.

David was weary, mentally and physically, and it showed. Son looked father up and down and shook his head. "They've wore you out up in Washington, Pa. They've surely wore you plumb out."

"That's the truth," David replied, thrusting out his hand to his son. "Good to see you, John Wesley. How are matters at home? Is Betsy well?"

"Yes . . ."

David caught the tentative tone and was alarmed. "What's wrong, John Wesley?"

The young man drew in a deep breath. "There was something that happened while you were away, Pap . . . there was a baby at the door in a wood box. Real sickly. She tried to save it, but—"

"Whoa! You'll have to chew that bite again for me. Did you say 'baby'?"

John Wesley slowed down and told the story in full. David was astounded, and asked why he hadn't been informed by letter. His son looked very somber, reached into his pocket and drew something out, which he presented to David. "Because of this, Pap."

David took it. It was the silver piece he had carried for so many years, the one he had last seen the night he put it into the hand of Persius Tarr in that camp during the Creek War. "How . . . what did . . ."

"I recognized it as your old silver chunk. It was in the shirt the baby was wrapped in—there on purpose, it seemed, from the way it was tucked in the cuff. I don't understand it, Pap. You said you lost that during the Creek War."

Lost it . . . yes, he had, though he had never explained even to his family just *how* he had parted ways with it. He couldn't very well admit he had passed it to a criminal prisoner for use in bribing his guard . . . a guard subsequently murdered.

"Well, I did lose it. I can't figure how it's come back to me in such a peculiar way." He paused, knitting his brows. "This baby, John Wesley. What did it look like?"

"I don't know. Just like a baby."

"It's color and such, I mean. Dark hair or light?"

"Dark."

"What about the skin?"

"Well, it wasn't no Negro. But it was on the darkish side for a white child. Why? You think you might know who it belonged to?"

David shook his head quickly. "No, no. Of course not. Just curious."

John Wesley lowered his voice; he looked very uncomfortable when he spoke next. "Pap, Betsy's got an opinion about who it belonged to. And partly I'm to blame for it, because when I found that silver piece by the hearth—it had rattled out of the baby's wrap and fell there—I told her it looked to be the same one you had carried when I was a boy. So now she's taken to thinking the baby is . . . well, yours."

"God!"

"Pap, it's hard to argue her down on it. I mean, it does look bad, you know. Why did whoever-it-was leave that baby at *your* door in particular, and how did they come by *your* silver piece, if they didn't know you already?"

"Is my own son accusing me of adultery?"

"No, Pap, no. I'm just telling you why Betsy is thinking like she is, and what she'll be saying to you when you get home."

David forced back the anger John Wesley's words had stirred. The young man deserved praise, not condemnation, for having forewarned him of the situation so frankly. David shook his head and sighed. What a homecoming this would be! He had been looking forward to seeing his wife; now he dreaded it. How could he explain this to her satisfaction, when he could find no explanation that gave him satisfaction himself?

They talked long into the night, with tears shed by both—and David virtually never cried about anything. But he argued so intensely and strove so hard to make her really know his innocence that his emotions involved themselves. He decided later that maybe it was the fact he had grown emotional that actually convinced her he was telling her the truth when he said he had been faithful and had no more idea than she about the origins of that unfortunate baby, and why it had been left at the Crockett door.

Now he lay awake, wondering if perhaps he *did* have an idea. It was Persius who had possessed the piece of silver; might the child have been his? A dark-haired, dark-skinned baby, John Wesley had said. That would likely be the look of a child Persius fathered. And if the child had been sickly, and something had happened to the mother, and Persius was close by at the time, and had known his old friend David Crockett lived hereabouts—he just might put the child on the Crockett doorstep.

The next day David went to the place the baby was buried and puzzled over the mystery some more, fingering the piece of silver in his pocket. It was a gnawing, nagging thing, not knowing the truth. It could be he would never know. At least the incident had been kept quiet, and if it *had* been Persius who abandoned the baby, at least he hadn't shown himself. As a congressman, David Crockett didn't need the likes of Persius Tarr in his life anymore. The man was trouble to the core, and he spread it everywhere he went.

Days passed, and David forgot the little grave and the odd return of the silver nugget. It was good to be home, away from the pressures of Washington. Not that there weren't troubles of other kinds at home. Finances were still difficult, and the losses he and Elizabeth had suffered at Shoal Creek continued to plague them. He had purchased land in Weakley County several months before, but was unable to pay the taxes on them. And he was going to be sued again by another creditor, according to all indications.

In the summer, he was appointed to mark a road from Weakley County's Dresden to the Gibson County line. Then there was the usual farming and family activities, along with background work toward the next legislative session and meeting with constituents, with whom the subject inevitably was the land bill. When he had the chance, he took his bear dogs, Tiger, Rattler, Death Maul, Whirlwind, and Thunderbolt, and spent time with them roaming the woods and hunting. Weeks rolled quickly by.

By winter the Twentieth Congress was in session and David was back in Washington, pushing his land-related efforts again, and more determined than ever to succeed. Ibbotson noted a difference in his friend this session and knew it came from experience. Crockett was still rough-edged and uncouth, but he was no longer naive. He knew what to expect, what not to. And he was beginning to develop a notion that his Tennessee colleagues were far more tied to the power structure within the state than he wished to be. His constituency was the impoverished western squatter, he declared to Ibbotson, not wealthy landowners and the state legislators who lived in their pockets. Differences between him and Polk began to emerge; David Crockett was becoming an increasingly independent political entity, and former allies began whispering and writing in private letters that he was "associating with our political enemies," and had begun offering to alter his vote on other projects in return for support for his own pet bill.

Ibbotson found his companion fascinating to observe. He sensed that his own relationship to David was becoming one of advisor and mentor, not to mention occasional speech crafter and writer of letters on his behalf. Ibbotson sought neither remuneration nor recognition for this; in fact he insisted that his dealings with David be kept entirely private, not wishing to be seen as factional. As a physician with an active practice in the political community, he could not afford to be boycotted by members of any party out of political retaliation.

Some of the battles he helped David fight from the background involved overcoming simple misperceptions. In one widely published newspaper story, David was presented as putting on an unforgivable display of crudity and boorishness at a dinner hosted by President John Quincy Adams. The story spread far, even appearing in Crockett's home region, and it required the writing and publishing of letters by others in attendance at that dinner to refute the charges. David was stung badly; he determined to improve his manners, dress, and speaking abilities—and the inevitable result was for him to turn more than ever to the guidance of Dr. Ibbotson.

By the time of the 1829 congressional campaign, James K. Polk and the "Jacksonians" had broken fellowship with Crockett. They worked to see him defeated, pitting Adam Alexander against him once more, but Crockett was popular at home, and soundly won the election despite some very hostile campaign tricks against him.

When the victorious Crockett of Tennessee returned to Congress late in 1829, he did so with his old Creek War leader, Andrew Jackson, in the White House. Toward Jackson, David held ambivalent feelings, for both personal and political reasons. From the time he had watched Jackson put down the "mutiny" attempt against him in the Creek War, he had held a private grudge against the man, though politically he had supported him, at least in public, during his first days in Congress. But privately he had begun to turn on Jackson and his cronies in the congressional session that had begun in 1828. As Jackson's time in office stretched out and certain of his presidential actions began to disappoint some of his former supporters, David found himself shifting gradually into a faction becoming known as Southern Whigs—purportedly loyal to Jackson as a person, but disdainful of the "direction" being given him by those around him.

As David's months in Congress passed, he became ever more solidified in his opposition to Jackson. He opposed him more and more vocally, while at the same time declaring that it was Jackson who had changed, not he. "I am yet a Jackson man in principles, but not in name," he said. "I shall insist upon it that I am still a Jackson man, but General Jackson is not; he has become a Van Buren man."

Then, in his second term, rose an issue that would create more controversy for David Crockett than any he had yet faced, and exact a higher personal price. When the vote came, out of all the Tennessee delegation, David Crockett would be left standing alone.

"I am concerned, David," Ibbotson said, his bushy brows moving toward each other as his eyes narrowed. "You are an idealistic man, and a man of principle, especially in view of your devotion to the 'common man'. . . ."

"There's a 'but' coming right about now," David said, grinning.

"Yes, yes. 'But'—you must be sure that your ideals don't lead you away from common sense. Life *does* involve compromise, David. Sometimes one must give up a portion of an ideal in order to win the greater part . . . do you understand?"

"Of course I do. I reckon I've done that aplenty. I've offered to trade my vote more than once."

"Yes, well . . . but a trade of votes, that smacks of giving in too much sometimes. . . ."

"Hold up here—which sin am I guilty of, holding too hard to my ideals or not holding hard enough? Make up your mind, Doctor."

Ibbotson pursed his lips and shook his head. "Never mind it, then. But let me ask you something, in confidence: How do you plan to vote on Jackson's Indian removal policy?"

The playful flicker in David's eyes went out like Ibbotson had puffed away a candle flame. After a pause David said, "Reckon I'm obliged to vote against it."

"Against it . . . when you know that the common men of your district would probably support the Indian removal to the last man?"

"Yes. I can't help it, Campbell. You have to understand that the Injuns"—catching the wink of the eye of Ibbotson, ever vigilant to correct the frontierisms of his speech, David paused—"the *Indians* as I know them now ain't the savages we fought in the Creek War days. Not all of them, leastways. Most of the Indians of West Tennessee are living in communities, farming, taking part in life with the rest of the folk. They're common men too. Neighbors, you see. I can't see the right in just uprooting them and pushing them out. I wouldn't be treated that way myself, and I don't see how I can support Jackson's bill."

"You'll pay a political price for such a stand," Ibbotson said.

"Well, then I'll pay it. They didn't send me to Washington to vote against my conscience, I don't figure."

"No . . . unless yours doesn't agree with theirs. Ask yourself, David—is it worth it, voting against a popular measure, when there's no chance of a majority taking your side? Jackson's bill will go through, however you may vote."

"That may be. If it is, I'll live with it."

"Your mind can't be changed?"

"Nope."

"You're far too stubborn, David Crockett."

"You think so? Next thing you'll be telling me is I ain't stubborn enough. That's the way with you, Ibbotson. I hope you don't practice your medicine the way you give me advice. You'd never decide what it is you're trying to cure and what you're trying to keep."

•   •   •

Unusual silence held in the great hall where the representatives sat gathered, and all eyes were on Crockett of Tennessee as he advanced to the podium. All present had a good idea of the gist of what he was going to say, and from the looks David saw on most of the somber faces looking back at him, he knew that his words were not going to fall on welcoming ears.

He paused, clearing his throat, looking around the distinguished assembly. For a couple of seconds a cold panic struck him, and more even than that first time he had set foot inside the Capitol, he felt out of place. What was he doing here, dressed in a fine black suit and cravat, his longish dark hair neatly combed back behind his ears, his feet shod in uncomfortable shoes of stiff leather instead of the old-fashioned moccasins he still often wore when he was home? He was a coot among peacocks, a cur among fox hounds, a mule among racehorses.

He fought back the panic, knowing it would be fatal to his credibility if he showed fear, and reached inside his coat to pull out a few folded sheets of paper. Spreading them, he looked down at the neat handwriting of Dr. Ibbotson, and felt a warm burst of gratitude toward his secret aide and mentor. Even though Ibbotson was convinced that David was making an error in publicly standing up against one of Andrew Jackson's most popular measures, he had sat down with pen and paper and helped David draft out as good and thorough an explanation of his position as he could. David was sure he could have never put together his thoughts so well on his own. Thank God for Campbell Ibbotson.

David coughed into his fist a couple of times and cleared his throat. Opening his mouth to speak, he coughed again. Glances and smiles passed subtly between the many members of the body who found Crockett to be little more than a walking joke, a coonskin congressman representing backwoodsmen. A little flurry of anger stirred through David, and it was to his advantage, because his nervousness immediately disappeared.

"Mr. Speaker," he began, "and distinguished members of the House of Representatives, it might be expected that a man with so humble a speaking manner as myself might content himself to cast a silent vote on the matter before us. But considering the place I stand in relation to this matter, and the place you stand, I believe it is my duty to explain the motives behind my vote.

"Other gentlemen here have already discussed the issue of treaty-making power, and I'll not attempt to do better than they have already." He lifted his eyes from his paper; now that he had begun to talk, he was at ease enough to begin mixing his own words with those Ibbotson had prepared. "All I intend to do here is explain the reasons for the vote I'm going to cast. I don't know if a man within five hundred miles of my home in Tennessee would cast a similar vote, but the fact is that I know I must give my vote with a clear conscience. I'd love to please my constituents as much as any gentleman here, but someday I'll have to make my accounting before the bar of my God, and what my own lights tell me is the right thing to do is the very thing I will do, consequences be *damned* . . . consequences being whatever they may be." With that slip, he glanced back down at the paper to regain his bearings.

"Gentlemen, I have always viewed the native Indian tribes of our country to be sovereign peoples. It's my understanding that they have been recognized as such from the foundations of our government. The United States government is bound by treaty to protect these people, and indeed it is our duty to do so.

"And as for the question of putting American money toward the removal of the Indians in the manner proposed, well, I cannot support that. I can do only what I can answer to God for, and if the people oppose me, that by comparison can be of no importance, satisfying as it is to have the pleasure of the constituents.

"Now, I've served for some years now in the business of legislation, served from the time I didn't even know what such a big word as 'legislation' meant." A mild titter of laughter ran through the assembly. From somewhere in the back, an anonymous, just-audible voice asked if

Crockett even yet knew what the word meant. He ignored the heckle and went on. "In all the times I have entered the legislative halls, I've never paid any heed to which party was doing the legislating, and God forbid that ever I should. I want to do only what is good for the country, and though I wish to work together with my colleagues in the West and the South, I'll never let a party govern me on a question of such consequence as this one."

"Get to the specifics, Crockett!" someone shouted.

"Well, sir, I shall," he replied. "I have many objections to this bill. First off, I don't like putting half a million dollars into the hands of the executive branch to be used in a manner nobody can really foresee and which we as Congress will be unable to control. Secondly, I don't want to see us depart from the manner we've set up in dealing with the Indian nations from the beginnings of our government. The Injun . . . the *Indian* as he lives today is nothing but a poor remnant of a group of people who were once strong and big. The only chance for help these people have today is from us, the Congress, and if we turn our eyes away from them and close our ears to their cries for help, well, gentlemen, all that will come to them, in my candid opinion, is misery and sorrow."

He paused, looking around the assembly and studying the expressions turned back at him. There were frowns, looks of skepticism and impatience—but they were all listening. David picked up his papers and stepped out from behind the podium, his fire rising.

"I'm reminded many times of the remark made by the famous Indian Red Jacket in this very building. You remember that story, don't you? How old Red Jacket was shown the big picture hanging in the"—he looked down at the written speech to pick out that blasted architectural word he could never remember—"the rotunda, showing the pilgrims meeting with Indians, and a chief handing them an ear of corn to show friendship? When Red Jacket saw that picture, he said, 'That was good.' He said that white men and red men both came from the same Great Spirit, and were willing to share the land with his brothers from across the water. But then they showed Red Jacket the picture of Penn striking his treaty with the Indians, and he said, 'Ah! All's gone now!' He knew what had come of treaties with the white men, and there's a great deal of truth in how he felt. This present bill is as prime an example as you'll find of what he was thinking about.

"Four counties of my district, gentlemen, border the Chickasaw country. I know many of that tribe, and there's not a thing I can think of that would make me consider trying to push them west of the Mississippi. I don't know what kind of country is to be given to them there. Now, I'd gladly vote to send smart folks to examine that country and see what it was like, and come back and make a fair and free treaty with the tribes, and if they desired to move after that, I'd gladly vote to put up whatever money was needed to help them do it. But until that has been done, I can't in good conscience vote for one cent.

"This bill before us is a consternation and a confusion. It seems to aim toward removing every kind of Indian east of the Mississippi in any state where there is federal land. Now I know there are many suffering and neglected Indians. There's plenty of them in Tennessee. No one would be more glad to see these folks removed to better stations than me, but only if they wanted it theirselves ... themselves. I know personally there's plenty of Cherokees who have said they'd rather die than be moved. 'Let them come and tomahawk us here at home; we are willing to die, but never to remove.' That's the very language you'll hear from some of the Cherokee."

He returned to the podium and leaned on it. He was smart enough to know he had persuaded no one, but at least he had their attention and—he hoped—their understanding.

"Gentlemen, I know I stand alone here, none of the other representatives of my state agreeing with me. I can't help that. I'll go home again with a glad and light heart. I wish to serve my constituents honestly, but in light of my conscience, and the minute I exchange my conscience for party views, may God no longer suffer me to exist. I may be the only member of this House that votes against this bill, and the only man in the United States who disapproves it, but I'll vote against it still and rejoice about it. I care nothing for popularity that isn't gained through being upright.

"I've been told by many here that I don't understand good English grammar, and that's true, I've had only a few months' schooling in all my life. But I wasn't willing to let that take from me my right to speak from this floor as a representative of free men. I've been charged with not representing the will of those who voted me in on this matter. Well, if that's true, the error is in here"—he touched his head—"not here." He touched his heart. "I've never had great wealth or learning, but I do have an independent spirit, and I hope to prove it by voting no on the bill before us."

He gathered his papers and returned to his seat. For a moment there was silence in the hall, and then someone applauded, then a few others. It never rose to much of a swell before petering out, but David appreciated it for what it was worth. He had spoken out for what he believed. Spoken out for a young Creek boy who had died with fire-blistered skin while a white army destroyed his town, spoken out for an old Indian woman who had drawn a bow with her feet and fired an arrow through the body of Ben Kelso, then paid for it with her life.

It was the best he could do for them. He knew it wasn't much, just a lone cry in the midst of a babble of dissent, but it had been an act from the heart, and David was glad he had done it.

Chapter 42

Hoping that nobody was close by to see him putting on so odd a display, David lifted his arms and stretched them toward the late May sky, then twisted his torso from side to side, waiting for the welcome popping in his back that would signal his spine was once again lined up properly. Beneath his breath he cursed the bed he slept on in his rented Washington rooms. It sagged in just the right way to make his back go out on him almost every night. It got so bad sometimes he dragged the blasted thing out onto the floor itself and slept on it that way. He should have done that last night.

He leaned backward now, bobbing his body, then leaned forward and touched his toes. When he arose he was smiling. His back had popped and the pain was gone—at least until another night came and that cursed bed twisted him up again.

He drew in a deep breath, enjoying the wet scent of the broad Potomac. Occasionally David enjoyed coming to the riverside for the fresh air and the simple pleasure of being near water. He had always loved rivers; he figured it was because he had been born beside one.

He seated himself cross-legged beside the water. Today he was wearing very casual clothing: boots, well-worn wool trousers, a baggy cotton shirt, a floppy felt hat. He was glad for this day of respite from the usual bluster of lawmaker activity. Since delivering his speech and casting his vote, he felt drained and weary, in need of a rest. So today he had said to devil with duty. Davy Crockett was going to be a boy again. He was going to play hooky just like he had on old Kitching so many years ago.

He was at the narrow portion of the Potomac where it passed Washington City some blocks from the White House. He found it remarkably ironic to be playing the child again in the very shadow of the city that represented duty and power. This wasn't something he would do often—but today it was downright fun.

He was tossing stones into the water when he heard a carriage rumble along the road behind him. At first he thought nothing of it and didn't even glance back, but then the carriage halted and his name was called. He turned. The sun was up in the eastern sky, silhouetting the carriage and blinding him so he could not see who had called him.

He cupped his hands over his eyes. "Who calls me?"

There was no answer, but in the blur of light and shadow, he saw the carriage door open. A tall, lean figure descended and came striding toward him. Even before David made out the face, he knew just who it was.

"By the eternal days," he muttered, "it's old Hickory-face Jackson hisself!"

He straightened his shoulders and took off his hat, regretting his terribly inappropriate state of dress. Who would have anticipated encountering the President of the United States at such a time and place as this? How could he face him? And then he chided himself. This might be the President, but he was also his political foe. Why should he feel ashamed before Andrew Jackson, of all men?

"Hello, Crockett," Jackson said, extending his hand.

"Mr. President." David shook Jackson's hand; it was lean and strong. Despite the advance of years and struggles with his health, Jackson's grip was still firm. The grip of a leader.

"Taking a rest from duty, Crockett?" Jackson asked,

the faintest smile tugging at his lips. "I had to look hard to be sure it was really you down here."

There was no point in denying the truth, and David didn't. "Playing hooky, sir. Nothing important to be done today, and the truth is, I think I'd be a better servant of my constituents if I gave my mind some time to clear."

Jackson nodded. "I'm not rebuking you, Congressman. The fact is we all need time away to clear our heads." That faint smile returned again. "But let me say something about your representation of your constituency. It seems to me that you have passed up a fine chance to represent them by going against the wishes of your own people in the Indian matter."

It was David's turn to smile. "I voted my conscience. My reasons were laid out plain enough in what I said."

Jackson shook his head, much in the manner of an exasperated father trying to deal with a wayward son. Seeing that made David's blood run hot, but he retained his smile.

"I'm glad I chanced upon you here. Walk with me, Crockett, and let's have a much-needed talk," Jackson said.

"I'd be tickled to, Mr. President."

Jackson called up to his driver to wait for him, and that no, he didn't need accompaniment other than his chosen companion. David slipped his hat back onto his head and dug his hands into his pockets. In contrast to the nicely dressed President, he looked like some good-for-nothing riverside slouch, without job or home.

"Crockett, there's no point in denying that you've been a disappointment to me," Jackson said. "As a fellow Tennessean and your former commander in the Creek War, I had hoped to have your support—indeed I thought I did have it there at the start. But bit by bit you've turned away from me."

"Mr. President, the fact is I believe it's you who have done the turning. Pardon me for saying it, sir, but you ain't the man many of us thought you would be. You've sung a different tune than we hoped."

"Blast it, Crockett, you seem determined to be a bane

to me! This Indian vote of yours is only part of it. Look at the record! In the time you've been here, you've opposed me on the lands issue—"

"Only because you've seemed to cast your lot with the enlightened yeomanry of our state 'stead of the common man you were supposed to represent."

"—on the matter of West Point, which you seem to want to actually close down—"

"It's the rich and the 'elite'—there's a new word I've learned here in Washington, Mr. President—who are served by West Point, while the poor and common man's taxes pay for it."

"—and you've opposed me on the Indian removal—"

"For reasons I've made plain."

"—and you've supported the Maysville Road bill, which I have vetoed."

"Now, there's a prime case showing the changes that bad advice has made in you, Mr. President. Back in the Senate you supported federal road improvements for places like our own home state, and now when you're in the White House, you've gone and given such a bill the boot. You see, President Jackson, all I've done is what's right and gone ahead with it. You, you've been listening so much to bad counselors that I don't believe you have a clear notion of what right *is* anymore."

Jackson stopped and faced Crockett. For several moments all was silent except the quiet music of the river, the singing of birds, the rustle of trees, and the farrago of noises made by city and waterway. At last Jackson drew in a deep breath and let it out in a long sigh. "I'll never draw you into the fold, will I, Crockett?"

"I've never left it, sir. It's you who've done that."

"Words, words! Endless words! You play with them, shift them here and there, like a boy playing with tin soldiers. Hear me, Crockett. I'd appreciate your support. Appreciate it more than you could know. Give it to me, and your political future is assured. Deny it, and . . ."

"And what, Mr. President?"

Just then, as chance would have it, a large beetle came scuttering from beneath a loose board lying amid trash along the river. It passed between the two men, and Jackson reached out his foot, caught the beetle beneath it, and slowly, deliberately, audibly, crushed it. Crockett watched, then lifted his eyes to look squarely into Jackson's.

"Do you understand, Crockett?"

David smiled slowly. "It's been a pleasure walking with you, Mr. President. We'll have to do it again sometime."

"Where I need you to walk with me, Crockett, is in the halls of Congress."

"I'll do it gladly, sir, when I see you walking the right road. Otherwise, I reckon I'll have to content myself with having walked with you here today."

Jackson eyed him coldly a couple of seconds. "Goodbye, Crockett. I wish you a pleasant summer—as you try to explain to your constituents why you voted against the Indian measure that they surely approve to the man."

"And a happy summer to you too, Mr. President. And may your conscience be as clear as mine will be when we see the results of this measure you love so well."

Without another word Andrew Jackson spun on his heel and strode back to his carriage. As it rumbled away into the city, David waved. Then he glanced down at the crushed beetle.

"Move over, friend," he said. "If that man has his way, it appears I'll be joining you."

Gibson County, Tennessee, Summer 1830

There were no more than a score of men in the crowd gathered before the porch of the feed store, but to David they looked like a hundred. The angry expressions accounted for this. He stood as tall as he could, pulled his shoulders up and his increasingly paunchy stomach in, and smiled in a friendly way, trying to inject a little goodwill into the dour-faced group.

"Well, what do you have to say for yourself, Colonel Crockett?" a man at the front asked.

"In regards to what?"

"In regards to this!" The man slapped at a newspaper he held. "Did you give this speech in Congress?"

"Yes, I did." David knew exactly what was in the newspaper. It was a copy of the *Jackson Gazette* from a couple of weeks or so before. The newspaper had printed the Indian removal speech he had made to Congress, explaining his vote. He wasn't glad at all the speech had received such a public airing in the press. In a concession of principle to expediency, David had arranged to have the speech left out of the congressional *Register of Debates*, but someone had leaked a copy to the newspapers anyway. Since the speech's publication, David had been accosted everywhere he went. It was enough to make him wish Congress were still in session and he was in Washington City rather than Tennessee.

"And you actually voted against the Indian removal?"

"Yes. I was the only man in the Tennessee delegation to do so. You know my motto, men: Always be sure you're right, then go ahead. You'll notice it don't say nothing about being sure the way you're going is the way everybody else is too."

"Well, this is one time you should have goed with everybody else. We appreciate what you've tried to do with your land bill, Colonel—but you're dead wrong on this one. Dead wrong."

"Well, I knew there'd be aplenty thinking that way when I cast my vote."

"How do you defend yourself!" someone else yelled.

"Have you read the speech, friend?" David answered. His naturally short temper was burning pretty hot inside him, but he was managing to hide it—a skill political life had given him.

"No." From the humble, mumbled tone of the answer, David figured the man probably was illiterate.

"Well, sir, let me summarize my reasons." And briefly he outlined the same arguments he had put forth in explaining his vote to Congress.

"Hell, let them redskins be moved out and damned, for all I care!" a voice yelled. "One of them red coons killed and scalped my pappy, and cut away his privates just to spite him as he lay a corpse!"

A rumble of outrage and agreement passed through the crowd. A man beside the first speaker took a step forward. "Colonel Crockett, you was elected to represent the people who voted for you. The people don't agree with what you done."

"I know that, sir. I've tried to stand with my constituents at every place, but this was a time I had to listen to my conscience. I'd rather make an error of politics than an error of the heart. Even if you can't agree with my vote, I hope you can understand that."

"The truth is Colonel, I've been growing right weary of several things about you. I don't like the split with the Jackson men—and there's no point in you denying it, because the papers are full of the proof of it—and I don't like all the broken promises about the land bill. I ain't seen diddly nor squat of that yet, after all this time and talk."

"I haven't broke my promise," David replied. "I'm still fighting for the land bill, and I intend, by the eternal days, to see it passed!"

"More talk! That's all we get from Washington! Talk and jabber! I say the hell with it!"

"Many's the time I've felt like saying the same thing myself. Men, I wish I could take every one of you into the congressional hall and let you see what a fight it takes to get even the smallest bit of good done. It's a shameful thing, and I battle it every day."

"Well, battle a little harder, and next time, you vote the way your people want!" a man yelled.

"And stand with Andy Jackson!" another man added. "I'm an Old Hickory man, and proud of it!"

"That's fine for you, friend, but around my neck you won't find a collar bearing the name Andrew Jackson and the words 'My dog.' Jackson's party wanted me to wear such a collar, and I refused. As a result, they banished me from their midst. I'll stand with Old Hickory at any time he meets one condition, that being that he's in the right. I'll not stand with him when he's in the wrong. The folk of Tennessee merit better than that."

"Old Hickory!" the man yelled. "Long live Old Hickory!"

David opened his mouth; his temper was really up now. But he held back his words, closed his lips and smiled. "Good day to you, gentlemen. Good day."

He walked away, leaving the men to talk among themselves. His ears burned from his knowledge that it was he they were chewing over. To the devil with them, he thought. I did what I thought was right, and that's the end of it.

The frightening thing, though, was that it also could mean the end of him as a political figure. Next year's election would tell the story; he could only hope he wouldn't end up crushed like a beetle beneath a Jacksonian foot.

Winter 1830

Elizabeth Crockett shivered in the icy wind as cold-hardened pellets of snow stung against her face. This was just a peppering of snow, not enough to lay, but three days before, a seven-inch snowfall had blanketed the land, and here in the shady woods most of it remained, even though it had mostly melted off the open roads and fields a day ago.

"Are you really sure you want to see it . . . her?" John Wesley asked. "There's no real need for it."

"Yes. Don't worry about me, John Wesley. Whatever it looks like, I'm sure I've seen uglier sights. Are they sure it's a woman?"

"No doubt about it. Long hair, wearing a dress. And there's enough of her left to even tell a little what she must have looked like."

The snow on the trail was much disturbed here, reflecting the abundant movement of men in this area since just after dawn. A pair of hunters had found the shallow grave by the first light of day; they would have passed over it entirely had not wolves or dogs dug into it, exposing a skeletal arm. The hunters had gone to the nearest house and given word, leading to a big party of men heading out and excavating the grave. Most of them were still there, talking seriously but excitedly, and standing around in postures of importance, as men will do at such times.

"Mrs. Crockett, howdy," said a tall fellow with a long and very thin beard. This was Joe Baggett, one of the hunters who had found the body. "Have you come to see the corpse?"

"Yes."

"It's no sight for a woman."

"It's as much a sight for a woman as a man, I would think. Especially since the body is a woman. And this is Crockett property she was found upon."

"Whatever suits you, then. The corpse is yonder under that blanket. We're still waiting for the sheriff to come."

The blanket lay nearly flat, indicative of the degree the body had decayed. John Wesley walked with Elizabeth to the blanket, took a breath and held it, then knelt and flipped back the cover of the cloth. Elizabeth stared without expression on the leathery face, drawn back tight over the skull, with bone showing through at the cheekbones, nose, and around the mouth. The teeth were strong and white, indicating, along with the dark and thick hair, that this had been a young woman.

She knelt and looked closer; unseen by John Wesley, her hand closed around something on the ground, then slipped to the pocket of her coat. She stood.

"Cover her back up now," Elizabeth instructed, and John Wesley complied with haste. He turned away, looking pale. Elizabeth had not lost her color; the gruesomeness of the sight meant nothing to her. Her concern was with the ramifications of this bizarre find.

"If the sheriff wants to talk to me about this, I'll be at my house," she said to Baggett. "Although there's nothing I can tell him."

"Yes ma'am. I'll tell him."

Walking with John Wesley the mile and a half back to the house, Elizabeth said, "I suppose she was murdered."

"I suppose."

"I don't know any other reason she would be buried in such a way, except to hide the body."

"But there was a clump of evergreen in her hands, and they was folded over her breast," John Wesley said. "Like she was buried with ceremony."

"That's strange, especially since whoever buried her must have been the same one who murdered her ... or maybe it wasn't murder." She paused. "I wish your father was here."

"Yes." He cleared his throat and brought up an uncomfortable matter. "Betsy, I'm thinking that she may have been mother to that baby that was brought to the house."

"Oh, I'm sure she was. I figured that the moment I heard she had been found."

"But why would somebody kill her and then bring her baby to a doorstep for rescue?"

"I don't know. Maybe she wasn't killed. Maybe it was a natural death."

That afternoon the county sheriff did call and ask a few questions, but he didn't seem to be holding out any suspicions toward the Crockett family. The younger Crocketts, children of David and Elizabeth and jokingly called the "second crop" by their father, crowded around—Matilda, Sissy, Elizabeth Jane, Robert, these ranging in age from nine to fourteen. The sheriff talked to them too, but they had nothing to tell.

That evening, Elizabeth sat alone by the fire, examining the thing she had picked up from beside the corpse. It was a bracelet that had slipped from the bony wrist of the corpse. It had been easy to palm away unnoticed. Elizabeth wasn't sure why she had picked it up. It had been an entirely impulsive act. But it had given her information: the dead woman's name had been Matty. Probably short for Matilda, Elizabeth guessed. The name was etched crudely on the inside of the bracelet.

Rising, Elizabeth went to a nearby writing table and fetched paper, quill, and ink from a drawer. She sat down and began writing a letter of her husband, away in Washington City. He would need to know about the corpse found near his house. She would go ahead and tell him about picking up the bracelet, and about the name "Matty," but warn him to tell no one those details. She had withheld them from the sheriff, fearing she would be in trouble for disturbing the evidence, and she didn't want to be found out through anything David might say.

Chapter 43

A fire burned brightly on the hearth, the room was fragrant with the scent of the doctor's pipe, and the remnants of an excellent supper of roast beef, potatoes, carrots, and biscuits sat on two plates on the table, abandoned by two well-filled men. The atmosphere was warm and pleasant, but David's mood was somber.

Ibbotson put down Betsy Crockett's letter, which David had just let him read, and removed his spectacles. "Quite an event," he said. "A corpse, buried near your home ... my my. And you believe, I gather, that this unfortunate Matty may somehow be associated with this Tarr fellow you once knew?"

"Yes," David replied. It had been a big decision on his part to reveal the existence of and his association with Persius Tarr to Ibbotson, but after receiving Betsy's disturbing letter, he had been compelled to do so. He felt the need of Ibbotson's wisdom and advice on this very troubling matter. "I first met Persius when we were small boys. I was separated from him a number of years more, then ran across him again in my youth. And you can figure the kind of man he is from what I've told you."

"You're speaking of this killing in Jefferson County that you mentioned?"

"Yes."

"You think this Persius Tarr is a wicked man?"

"Not wicked, maybe. Just bedeviled. Trouble seems to follow him."

"How can you be sure that Persius Tarr has anything to do with that baby, or the buried woman? And how can you know the dead woman was mother of the baby at all?"

"I can't know she was the mother, but it would seem mighty unlikely that she ain't. I mean, how likely is it that a foundling baby and a dead young woman are going to turn up on the same little plot of ground without there being a tie between the two? And as for Persius, I believe he was involved because of the silver piece my son found in the baby's wrap. The last time I seen that piece of silver was when I gave it to Persius Tarr one night in camp during the Creek War. He's the one who had it, so he must have been the one to put it in that baby's wrap."

"Why did you give the silver to him in the first place?"

David tensed but tried not to show it. He had told Ibbotson about Persius's escape from the army camp shortly after the Tallusahatchee massacre, but he had not told about the slain guard or revealed his own involvement in the entire affair. He had told Ibbotson simply that a soldier from Jefferson County had recognized and identified Persius as a fugitive accused murderer. He had no wish for Ibbotson to know the whole story, particularly the part involving himself. "It was just a token. Friendship."

"Are you certain the silver piece in the baby's swaddling was the same one?"

"Yes. That silver was a gift from a deaf-and-dumb uncle who was held Indian captive for more than fifteen years. He mined it himself in captivity, and it was a prized possession for me. I know every little turn and twist of that silver chunk; it was the same one, no question."

Ibbotson scratched his chin. "This whole business is odd, very odd. And I can see why you have concern, your wife being there in Tennessee without you, and foundling babies and dead bodies turning up on her without explanation." Ibbotson leaned forward, looking intently at David. "Have you considered the possibility that this Persius Tarr might have killed the woman and buried her?"

"I've considered it. But I can't make it cipher out on those lines. Why would he kill her and then bury her all pretty and laid out, with an evergreen sprig in her hands? You don't pretty up corpses of folks you've murdered. And what about the baby? Why would he have laid it on my doorstep if he's a murderer? Why didn't he just kill the child too?"

"Even a killer can have his heart softened by a child."

"Maybe so. I can't picture Persius harming a baby. But why would he leave the silver piece? That was as good as signing his name. He had to know I would recognize it and figure out he had been the one to leave it. No, he didn't kill that woman. Maybe it wasn't murder at all. The letter says there was no mark nor wound on what remained of her. And if Persius had murdered her, he wouldn't have left the silver to prove it was him."

"Perhaps he didn't expect the corpse to be found. And we must consider, why did he abandon the baby? The fact that he left it and ran away, and this after concealing a corpse—assuming it was him who buried her—makes him look as if he had something to fear, something to hide."

"That may be," David replied. "Like I said, I can make no sense of it. But I'll tell you this, Campbell: I don't believe Persius Tarr killed that young woman. He's a hard man, but for the life of me I don't believe he would kill a woman."

"Well then, I accept that. A man must trust his instincts on such things. But there is surely a mystery here no matter how you look at it."

Ibbotson puffed at his pipe, but it had gone out. He put it on the arm of his chair and studied it, his eyes fixed on the ash-filled bowl, his thoughts on the matter under discussion. After several silent moments he shifted his position so abruptly it startled David, who had fallen into a similar brood. "Well," Ibbotson said, "it's an interesting question, but likely one of no importance. This Persius Tarr has never shown his face to you since that night he fled the army camp, and if he does have anything to hide, he'll probably show his face not at all. And that's a good thing, from the sound of him. A politician needs no fugitive criminals associating with him, and no rumors about foundling babies and dead young women."

"Amen to that. I've already had enemies try to accuse me of adultery and such—bloody liars!"

As always with David and Ibbotson, the conversation had drifted around to politics. "How do you feel about your situation in the coming election?"

David looked squarely at Ibbotson. "Poorly. I'll be shot if I don't believe I could be defeated this time around."

"Because of your Indian removal stand?"

"Partly. That and the public road question, the blasted impossibility of getting the western lands issue settled . . . and the Jackson business as a whole. Folks who are loyal to Old Hickory-face are, well, damned loyal. And I've got a passel of Jacksonite lawyers working against me in Tennessee. This past summer they'd set up 'meetings' where I was supposed to come explain myself on the Indian bill and defend turning away from Jackson—only trouble was, they never bothered to tell me about these meetings. So when I wouldn't show up, they'd say, 'See? Old Crockett's afraid to show himself to his voters, and can't defend his actions.' It's done me damage, no dispute. Old Hickory said he'd crush me, and danged if he ain't making a good try at it."

"Has the opposition selected a candidate to oppose you?"

"Yes. I learned of it only yesterday. He's William Fitzgerald, a lawyer from Dresden. Jackson himself is working hard against me on Fitzgerald's behalf. He wants me gone fearsome bad."

Ibbotson went to the hearth and knocked out his cold pipe. As he refilled it, he smiled almost coldly. "Well, we'll have to do all we can to see that he is disappointed, eh?"

"Yes sir," David replied. "We surely will."

David Crockett's campaign began in February of 1831 with the release of a lengthy "circular letter" to his constituents. These were the best such letters that had ever gone out bearing David's name, but not because of David. Ibbotson was the mind behind them, honing them until they sparkled.

The letter was sixteen pages long and virulently anti-Jackson, accusing him of being wasteful of government money, cruel toward Indians, and a crony of Martin Van Buren, politically despised by David. He attacked Jackson for his plans to run for reelection despite his own earlier statements that no man should serve as president more than four years. He accused him of ill will in his opposition to "internal improvements," such as road projects, that David supported:

> I thought with him, as he thought before he was President: he has altered his opinion—I have not changed mine. I have not left the principles which led me to support General Jackson: he has left them and me; and I will not surrender my independence to follow his new opinions, taught by interested and selfish advisers, and which may again be remoulded under the influence of passion and cunning.

The letter was historic in David's political career, for in it he brought his well-established opposition to Jackson into the open. In the meantime, another kind of campaigning had begun: the Southern Whigs were building David Crockett into a living legend.

It was a process that Crockett's personality and wit had already gotten started. Word of his unique campaign style and sense of humor had preceded him to Washington, and both friend and enemy had helped spread tales of his colorful personality. For example, almost everyone knew the story of how David had been standing one day on Pennsylvania Avenue, watching a farmer herd mules up the dirt thoroughfare. A representative from Massachusetts happened along and sidled up to Crockett. "I see some of your Tennessee constituents have come to town," he said, pointing at the mules. David turned to him and said,

"That's right—they're on their way to Massachusetts to become schoolmasters."

In April an event occurred that alone did more than all the Whig efforts to advance the legend of Colonel Crockett. The famed actor James Hackett had sometime back set up a contest for playwrights, seeking a play that would be the quintessential American production, providing some character to embody the very soul of the nation. The winning play, by one James Kirk Paulding, was called *The Lion of the West*, and featured as its central character a frontier wildman hero named Nimrod Wildfire. As soon as the play opened in New York City, almost all who saw it immediately linked the colorful Wildfire with the growing legend of David Crockett. Nimrod virtually *became* Crockett in the public eye, and David and his political cronies were sharp enough to play the association for their benefit. Colonel Crockett of Tennessee, whose major political successes were admittedly hard to find, became perceived as a man who could grin a raccoon out of a tree and eat an alligator for breakfast.

But even as the Crockett legend grew wilder and the tall tales taller, the real man faced serious political problems. And oddly, the famous sense of humor seemed to be fading. Crockett had always been one to take jabs at himself as he poked fun at his foes, but the campaign of 1831 showed a different man—sour, sometimes outright bitter, vying against his Jacksonian enemies with little sign of grace and goodwill.

It came to a head in Paris, Tennessee, during a campaign appearance with his competitor, Fitzgerald, who had begun making some slanderous personal attacks against Crockett's character. In times past, David would have found some way to turn the charges humorously in his own favor. This time he could not, or would not, and had sent out word that if Fitzgerald dared to repeat them, he would face a thrashing.

The crowd at Paris was large; many of David's supporters came out to see if the war of words would become a real brawl. Fitzgerald had first crack at the podium, and did something odd: he laid a kerchief-wrapped object on the table before him. There it remained as he spoke. Fitzgerald had a calm manner, and repeated the controversial comments unhesitantly.

All eyes turned to David, who rose from his seat and advanced toward the podium, eyes flashing fire. He was almost within reach of Fitzgerald when the latter reached down and picked up the wrapped object. The handkerchief fell away, revealing a pistol, leveled at David's chest.

"Return to your seat, sir," Fitzgerald said.

David, clearly stunned by what had happened, looked uncertain . . . then turned and slunk back to his seat.

There were many who believed the race was lost for him at that point. In any case, it was lost for him on election day—a narrow defeat by Fitzgerald, close enough that David contested it, but in the end a defeat.

The fears David had expressed to Ibbotson had come true. He was disappointed, but not surprised; in a letter written shortly before the election results were in, he declared to his correspondent that he would "rather be beaten and be a man than to be elected and be a little puppy dog."

It was a brave front, but the truth was that David Crockett was devastated. He had longed for prestige and power as a young man; in his prime adult years he had found them . . . and now they were gone.

Matters had fallen out just as Jackson had threatened. Crockett of Tennessee had refused to get in line, and like a beetle, he had been crushed.

Chapter 44

Now came days of introspection for David Crockett, days of change, dreams and journeying in mind and body. And of anger and regret as well, long days of brooding over his defeat and his place in the world.

Elizabeth worried about her husband, who would sit for hours at a time alone in his house, staring out the window, his chin in his hand. She hadn't seen him like this before; indeed he had never *been* like this before. Had his political life meant so much to him? She had known it was important to him, but had not realized he had invested so much of his private self into the public one.

That was how she had come to view her husband; as a man of multiple incarnations. There was the David Crockett she had come to love after her first husband's death, the one who could make her laugh with a wry look or smile with a gentle joke, the one whose hand she loved to hold, the one she sometimes called by his childhood nickname of Davy. Then there was the other David Crockett—Colonel Crockett, congressman, foe of Jackson, friend of the squatter and the Indian, representative of the common man. This was the public Crockett, the one who roamed the halls of Congress and politicked from the stumps and store porches of West Tennessee. She did not know this second David Crockett nearly so well as the first, nor did she like him as well. To her, this public

Crockett had always been something contrived, a role her husband played in public but put aside in private. Now she saw he had never really put it aside at all. The public man who seemed false to her had been overtaking the private one she loved, and she had been blind to the process.

And there was a third Crockett too, she had begun to realize. This was the Crockett of the growing public legend, Colonel Crockett as Nimrod Wildfire, Crockett as bear hunter, ring-tailed roarer, gouge-fighter, panther screamer, star catcher. This Crockett meant nothing to her; he was a fiction and wild-eyed exaggeration that fed the hunger of citified easterners for a romantic, superhuman vision of the American frontiersman. Let them have their mythical David Crockett, if they wanted, and even their political David Crockett; Elizabeth wanted the real man as she had known him before. When she thought about it selfishly, she had to admit she hardly cared that he had been defeated. Maybe she was even a little glad.

But she wasn't glad about what defeat had done to his spirits. She stood quietly in the doorway one morning a few days after his return from Congress, watching him brood, and worrying about it. She did not realize he was even aware of her presence until he turned his head suddenly to look at her and said, "I've got to go."

"Go? Where?"

"Anywhere. Maybe to the places I've been. The old places, where I grew up. Or anywhere. It don't matter. Places where I can think different thoughts, and forget all the strains, and the defeats."

"Oh."

"You don't wish me to do it, I can see."

"I didn't say that . . . will you go alone?"

"Yes."

It stung to hear that. Her eyes burned. *No, no, I won't let tears come for him to see.* "I . . . I should be happy to go with you."

"It's something I must do alone. I need time to think, to be away from everyone. I feel very pressed; it'll make a mash of me if I don't get out from under it, and away from everyone who is crushing me so."

He spoke in a gentle, weary tone, and did not seem to see the jolt his words gave Elizabeth. *So I am one of the ones who is "crushing" him.* Could he be so blind, so naive, not to realize how he was hurting her with such words?

"I see," she said. "Do what you must, then."

He rose and came to her. Wrapping his arms around her, he said, "I'll always love you, dear Polly."

She did not allow herself to react until he was out of the room. This was the hardest blow of all. He had called her Polly, and not even noticed it! The man she loved, the man who had fathered four of her children, was talking of roaming the haunts of his former life, and called her by the name of his former wife. He could not have stabbed her more deeply had he cut her very heart with a knife.

She wrapped her arms around herself, shivering like it was the dead of winter, biting her lip until it hurt. Then she collapsed in grief, full of weakness and despair, wishing that David Crockett had never even given a thought to public life and Congress. Kneeling on the floor, she leaned across the chair in which he had been sitting, crying like a new widow, while her husband strode across the yard outside, hands behind his back and his mind far away from this place. He had no notion at all of what he had just done to his wife, and she knew he had no notion. That made it hurt all the more.

He had no specific destination in mind when he left his home. All he wanted to do was travel, to be alone, to think. Now that he had been ousted from Congress, he felt like a ship adrift, having no plan or purpose.

He first headed east, into Carroll County, traveling that way until he hit a stage road that angled up out of the corner of Madison County and northeasterly into Huntingdon. He followed the road to the Tennessee River, and ferried over it. He had the pleasure of traveling a long distance with no one at all recognizing him. He went out of Humphreys County into Dickson, then Davidson, arriving at Nashville, where he checked into an inn and spent two days alone, mostly just sleeping, eating, and practicing his aim at the brass spittoon. When he left his room and ventured out to the local taverns, he made sure to strike up no conversations and to leave as soon as he suspected someone was beginning to recognize him.

Leaving Nashville, he traveled into Rutherford County to Murfreesboro, then to McMinnville in Warren County and up to Sparta in White. There he followed a network of dirt roads in a generally southeasterly direction until he came to the Cumberland Mountains, and beyond them, Walden's Ridge, which he crossed to reach again the Tennessee River where it sliced southwest toward the Alabama line, just missing the northwest tip of Georgia. He rode upstream as far as Knox County, and by now he was a new man. He was weary, to be sure, but weary from physical travel rather than mental stress. He grew eager to return to his family—he was missing his Betsy very much, and becoming aware as his mind cleared that maybe he had left her in a state of unhappiness. He had been so self-preoccupied at that time that he hadn't really noticed, merely tucked the awareness away in some unused corner of his skull to be noticed only now.

In Knoxville he wrote her a long and loving letter, and posted it west. He would not be gone much longer, he wrote; he had only one more place he felt compelled to go before the journey home, and one person he really wanted to see.

The oddest thing about him was how little the years had changed him. "Dumb Jimmy" Crockett was quite an old man now, living on land owned by the rugged Middle Tennessee frontiersman "Coonrod" Pile, who along with the Clemens family owned a big piece of this county. Jimmy Crockett was well-liked by his neighbors but, naturally enough, cut off from them somewhat by his handicaps. David wondered if the old man would recognize him. He did. David came upon him stringing a fish line across a wide creek, and as soon as their eyes met, there was no question that Jimmy Crockett knew him. He approached slowly, being too old and stiff to move any other way, and put his arms around David. His thin shoulders quaked and tears streamed down his face.

"My boy," he mouthed out in tones lower than a whisper. "My good nephew boy Davy."

David looked into his face and talked slowly to make it easy for him to read his lips. "How are you, Uncle Jimmy? Good?"

Wiping at his tears, the old man nodded. "Good. Good." He tugged at David's sleeve, nodding toward his little house.

Inside, he winked at David and went to a little locked cupboard. He fumbled in his pockets and brought out a key, which he inserted in the lock. As he swung the door open he grinned and winked again. The cupboard was filled with bottles of some dark liquor, apparently home-made. Selecting one, he worked the cork out and handed the bottle to David, who sniffed at it.

"Blackberry wine!" he said. "And it smells fine, Uncle Jimmy. Very fine!"

It tasted fine too, though it was much drier than David had anticipated. He sipped his slowly, watching Jimmy dig through a pile of old newspapers, letters, and general papers. He had been at it for two or three minutes, which puzzled David. Finally the old man found what he was seeking, greeting his success with several guttural grunts.

He turned and laid a paper on the table before David. It was a Whig cartoon that David had seen before, showing a scepter-bearing Andrew Jackson in a king's robes, a haughty look on his face as he trampled a copy of the United States Constitution beneath his feet. Jimmy wagged a long finger at the illustrated Jackson face and made motions and sounds as of spitting.

David grinned, recognizing that his uncle was doing this to show that, like his famed nephew—most likely *because* of his nephew—he too disliked Andrew Jackson. As had been true of so many aspects and gestures of Jimmy Crockett, David found the show of family solidarity quite touching. Jimmy was a simple, unspoiled man; cut off in many ways from the world, he had not been sullied by it, and his actions came from the heart.

"I reckon you've been reading about me in the papers," he said, then caught himself wondering if Jimmy could read at all. He couldn't remember. However it had happened, Jimmy obviously had picked up knowledge of the rift between President Andrew Jackson and Congressman Crockett of Tennessee.

"Hickory . . . bah!" David could barely make out the mouthed words.

David laughed. "That's right, Uncle Jimmy. Bah on old Jackson. But right now he's whipped me. I was voted out of office, Jimmy."

The old man grinned and bobbed his head up and down; David knew he had not understood. It didn't matter.

"This is good wine," David said, lifting his nearly empty glass.

Jimmy did understand that, and poured his glass full again. When that was gone, he repeated the process several more times, until finally David's head was spinning. Jimmy Crockett made a strong wine.

David stayed the night with Jimmy. The first part of the night he slept hard, but as morning drew near, dreams started. He was back at the Crockett tavern, digging that blasted well he had slaved at in boyhood. There was Jimmy, as he had been at that time, and above were his brothers and father, hoisting up the buckets of dirt and rock he filled. Then he felt the burst of sickness that had struck him low at that time. He knew he was dreaming . . . but for a dream, this burst of illness had quite a realistic feeling.

When morning came he truly was sick. His malaria had flared up again. As he descended into the fever and delirium common to that disease, one of his last lucid thoughts was of the irony that once again Jimmy would care for him through the fever, just as he had so many years ago.

David lost the ability to keep up with time as he tossed, burning and then shivering, suffering greatly. His fevered delusions were extremely unpleasant and incoherent, following no pattern except for one recurring dream: Uncle Jimmy's face, appearing before him and speaking with words sounded in perfect clarity but undecipherable in meaning: "You'll know the glory only when the glory-time comes. Go into the shining, David Crockett, and shout your hallelujah!" David would ponder the oddity of hearing a dumb man speak, and puzzle over the crazy words he had said, then would come a snatch of distant music, familiar but yet unknown, and Jimmy's grinning face would vanish into the hellish flux of a meaningless, boundless malarial delirium. Then sometime later the cycle would repeat, always the same.

Jimmy Crockett treated David with a mixture made from ingredients including Virginia snakeroot, cone flower, various other herbal extracts, and dogwood shavings. Other Crockett kin lived in the area, and when David finally emerged from his illness, there was a houseful of kinfolk to greet him. He spent another three days resting up, hearing news of the family—and details about Uncle Jimmy he hadn't known, such as Jimmy's propensity to take off back toward the Indian country in search of his lost silver mine, and how he had once gotten lost right in his own home region, wandering around in a hollow thereafter known as Dumb Jimmy's Hollow.

On the day he was ready to go, David was approached by Jimmy, who with noises and gestures inquired about the piece of silver he had given David years before.

"I've got it still," David replied, pulling it from his pocket. "I've never let it out of my possession from the day you made me a gift of it." It was a lie, of course, considering the years it was in Persius Tarr's possession, but Jimmy seemed pleased to hear it.

Still weak, David traveled slowly, and eventually sold his horse and took to the stagecoach for the bulk of the journey home. As he rode, he engaged in deep thought. His time of travel had done him good. His mind was clearer now, and he began thinking toward the future.

In Nashville he sat alone at a table in a dark corner of a tavern, and overheard a conversation that gave his thoughts even more focus. Two other men in the tavern, oblivious to his identity, were talking over the contents of a ragged and outdated New York newspaper that had been left on the table by some traveler who had since gone his way. David only half listened to their talk, until he overheard his own name mentioned. He snapped to attention, unnoticed by the conversationalists.

"Nimrod Wildfire, my granny! Call him what you will, that's old Crockett, that's who it is! My half brother in New York has seen the play himself, and says it's Crockett they're portraying, and everybody knows it. They shout Crockett's name from the audience, and make jokes about old Jackson! If ever I get the chance, I'll go see that play."

The other man sat back and puffed out his chest. "I've knowed David Crockett personally."

"What? No! You're a-lying!"

"No, no I ain't. It was many a year ago and he was but a child, but I knowed him, and was of help to him when he had been cheated and harmed by a man not worthy of the surname of Myers. It was as much out of pride in my name that I give young Crockett aid."

David all but leapt out of his chair. The speaker was none other than Henry Myers, the wagoner who had befriended him after Adam Myers stole his money and barred him from going to sea besides. Myers was far older now and had managed to lose his left eye somehow or another, but there was no question as to his identity. David gaped at him from the shadows, heart racing. He had an impulse to go to Myers and identify himself, and a simultaneous contrary one to leave matters exactly as they were. There were others here, and he didn't want to become the center of a crowd's attention today, not looking as weak and pallid as he did right now.

"Myers, I don't feel inclined to believe you, except I know you for an honest man," the other said. "Where was it you met him?"

"On the road in Virginia. He rode with me some and I was able to collect a bit of money for him to go home on. I've always felt prideful of that. I never had no notion I was helping a fellow bound for fame."

"Well, I'll be! If I was you, I'd brag about that to everybody."

"I ain't the bragging sort, you know."

"No, you ain't. I'll say that for you, Henry Myers. You ain't the sort to brag."

David left that tavern without ever revealing his presence and identity to Henry Myers. Somehow it seemed best that way. As he rode in the rumbling, lumbering, westering coach, he mulled over the fact that Henry Myers had once again been of help to David Crockett, though he had no idea of it. His and his companion's conversation had reminded David of his own prominence, and had made him realize that, despite being out of office, he was still very much a man in the public eye, a man people were proud to know. He was in reality what Nimrod Wildfire was in make-believe.

He nodded resolutely, a decision made. He might be out of Congress now, but there would be another race—and in that race, by heaven, he would prevail! David Crockett would rise again . . . he would "go into the shining," just like Uncle Jimmy's dream-image had directed in his delirium. Who would have thought he would decipher meaning from a fevered dream? Sometimes a man's destiny revealed itself in odd ways.

He whispered the words to himself. "Go into the shining, David Crockett." Just as, with the most appropriate natural symbolism, this coach was rattling west toward the splendor of the setting sun. *Into the shining*. He liked the sound of that very much.

Chapter 45

The Crockett Cabin

Elizabeth Crockett took a sip of her tea, which had grown tepid and tasteless in the cup. She had brooded too long over it, leaving it untouched as she sat by the front window, looking out on the cold, snowy day, feeling miserable as she thought about the political comeback David had been planning since his lone journey east a year and a half ago, in 1831.

She couldn't help feeling the way she did, even though she believed she shouldn't. After all, David was happy again, excited about life. Even now, he was off with John Wesley on what he called an "Indian-styled bear hunt," just for the fun of it, knowing that soon he would be too busy with electioneering to enjoy many such diversions. What right did she have to begrudge his hope of re-election to his beloved congressional post? A wife had duties, after all, including the duty to support and submit to her husband, just like St. Paul himself taught right in the Bible.

She sighed and slumped in her chair like a melancholy child. St. Paul and wifely duty notwithstanding, she *did* begrudge David his anticipated victory. The prospect of him once again holding a time-consuming office, once again being distracted from home and family and away for long months in Washington—this was hard to abide. She had grown accustomed to having him home. Her father had recently died, and the loss had been easier to bear simply because David was close by. She even found a kind of solace in the fact that David had been named co-executor, with her brother, of the Robert Patton estate.

Now the coming election loomed like a shadow in Elizabeth's mind. She hoped David would lose it . . . yet she believed he would not. It was just an intuition, but a persuasive one. David had the same anticipation, though of course he held a much more positive attitude toward it. He was so confident that he was quite literally banking on a win. Just this morning Elizabeth had seen a copy of a letter he had written earlier in the month to a cashier of the Second Bank of the United States. He had asked for an extension of a loan, and reminded the banker that as a congressman he had voted in favor of the bank charter, and planned to do so again once reelected.

Her mind jumped ahead to the next year at this time. She pictured herself alone, with David off in Washington City. The image was dreadful.

Making it even worse were rumors that the Whigs had even bigger long-term plans for David than a mere congressional seat. There were whispers that he would be good material for a presidential candidate, perhaps as early as the next election. President! Elizabeth simply couldn't imagine her husband in that role, any more than she could imagine herself First Lady. The very thought made her shudder, even as it obviously tickled David's hungry ego.

Well, she thought, I might as well resign myself. David has said many times that he believes he is destined to be remembered through the ages. If that's true, then I mustn't stand in his way, mustn't . . . the devil with it!

She stood, tossed the tea from her cup right across the floor—a major domestic offense had one of her children done it—and slammed the cup down on the table so hard it chipped. Putting on her coat and shawl, she walked out into the gray, snowy afternoon. It was a day perfectly matched to her state of mind. Huddling against the cold, she began walking with a hurried stride, even though she had absolutely nowhere to go.

David Crockett had made his name as a bear hunter while still a young man. In the days he had been married to Polly Finley, he spent as much time as possible hunting bear. When politics had overtaken so much of his life, he was forced to cut back his hunting. He had missed it dearly, particularly when he was in Washington City and could most use the diversion.

Today he and John Wesley were taking advantage of the winter's day to hunt bear in a way David seldom did. Normally he hunted bear when they were active, using his hounds to sniff them down and corner them for the kill. But today he and his son had decided to follow the old method of the Cherokees and Creeks, who did most of their bear hunting in the winter when their quarry was hibernating. David had it in mind to fetch in a good bearskin this trip, and turn it into a rug for Betsy's floor. And there would be plenty of good use to make of its oil and meat too.

"Look there, Pap," John Wesley said, pointing toward a rotted log that lay on a nearby creekbank. "There's bear hereabouts for certain."

They approached the log and examined it. The rotted wood looked as if it had been burst apart from the inside, but what it really evidenced was a shredding by bears digging for grubs. This log had been pulled open sometime in the autumn.

Scouting about farther, they found more evidence that bears had passed this way, including a mud-and-hair-plastered tree that was also lined with claw marks. It was a habit of bears to mark certain trees in this way; David believed it was a way the animals actually communicated with each other about the terrain.

They headed into a wooded ravine and found a few old bear tracks and a beaten-down path leading toward a big hollow tree on the side of a ridge. David looked up at the tree and grinned. "There's our bear tree, John. What you want to bet?"

"Bet you're right."

They advanced to the tree, David sniffing the air. There was a musky scent hereabouts of hide and hair, and on the tree were claw marks. Circling the tree, he examined its structure. This was just the kind of tree a bear loved for a good winter's sleep. From evidence and intuition honed by experience, he felt certain that a healthy she-bear was hibernating up inside that big hollow trunk right now.

"Check your rifle, and look about for a good perch in case we have to make for one, John," he directed in a soft voice. "I'll get the cane ready."

David tossed down a bundle of dry cane he had been carrying on his back, and pulled flint, steel, and punk from his pouch.

When they were sure they were ready, they backed away from the tree. David put his hand to his mouth and made a very peculiar noise—an imitation of the sound of a distressed bear cub. He kept it up several minutes, and sure enough, a stirring noise began inside the tree and a bear's snout poked out through a hole high up in the trunk.

"There she is, Pap."

"I see her. You up to climbing, John?"

"Light the cane. I'll run her out."

David struck the flint and steel and set fire to the punk. Quickly, he set the cane to smoldering, and handed the smoking bundle to John.

"I'll boost you up."

John clambered capably up the trunk, careful to check the strength of each limb before putting down his weight, as this was a rotting and weak old tree. At last he neared the place where the bear had shown itself. By now it had withdrawn back inside.

Finally the climber was near the top of the tree and the cane was putting out heavy smoke. Clinging hard to the trunk, John Wesley shoved the smoking cane into another hole in the tree and pushed it down toward the bear beneath.

His intent was to scurry down before the bear was driven out of the tree, but this time the bear had a surprise in store. She surged out so quickly, she actually ruptured part of the trunk and almost knocked John Wesley from his perch. He let out a howl. The she-bear growled and swiped at him with her right paw. John howled and launched himself off the tree, falling feet first into a tangle of brush.

The bear began descending, and David lifted his rifle, took careful aim—and missed. He lowered the smoking weapon, disbelieving. He had hardly ever missed a bear in his life, even when the shot was difficult. But he had missed this time, with the bear in good open view.

"Grab your rifle, John!" he yelled, scrambling to reload while backing away at the same time. The bear, its fur scorched by the cane and its demeanor threatening, was almost to the ground.

"I'm stuck!" John yelled. He was thrashing about in the middle of the thicket, unable to get out.

David made a lunge for John's rifle, which he had left leaning against another tree when he started his climb. The bear reached the ground at the same time. David grabbed the rifle, swung it up, cocked and fired—and missed again. It was astonishing! The bear came directly for him. Meanwhile, John finally disengaged himself from the brush.

It was fortunate for David that he did, because his motion distracted the bear and made it divert toward John. He saw it coming and lurched clumsily to the left, barely missing another swipe of the paw. He dodged over to a young maple and climbed desperately until he was out of reach of the bear. Then he sat there, praying the bear wouldn't climb up after him.

It didn't. Instead it turned back toward David, but by now he too was up in a tree. Fortunately, he had managed to bring up John Wesley's rifle with him. His own lay on the ground where he had dropped it in haste.

Now to reload—but he couldn't. He had his own shot pouch, and it contained rifle balls too large for John's smaller-bore gun. He sat there, feeling ridiculous while the bear paced back and forth beneath the trees, keeping both men trapped.

"Throw me your shot pouch, John!" David yelled.

John lifted the pouch strap over his head and tied it around the pouch itself. "Here she comes!" he hollered, and tossed it—short. It landed beneath David's tree, and the bear immediately ripped it apart, scattering lead and shredded leather in all directions.

David and son looked at each other, and smiled sadly. What else could they do? Neither felt any urge to go down and take on the she-bear with a knife or hatchet.

"John, I believe we're going to have to sit tight for a spell," David said.

"Believe we are, Pap."

And there they sat as the day went by and the evening came on. By dark the bear seemed bored with its double catch, and both Crocketts rejoiced when at last it wandered away. Descending their trees, they gathered up their goods, stretched cramped limbs, and headed toward home.

"We ain't much at Injun hunting, are we? By the by, there's no need to tell this tale to nobody, John Wesley," David said. "It ain't the kind of story I want getting out."

"Don't worry," John said. "I'll claim you dropped down and chewed the dang bear's head off if you want me to."

David actually thought about it a few moments. "No, no. Better not. I ain't got no bear hide to show for evidence. We'll just keep this one to ourselves, huh?"

"So we will, Pap. Sometimes even a Crockett gets whupped, I reckon."

"Sometimes," David agreed. "But he don't stay treed for good. He always comes back, every time."

David cleared his throat. "Listen to this one, Betsy: 'And it came to pass in those days when Andrew was chief Ruler over the Children of Columbia, that there arose a mighty man in the river country, whose name was David; he belonged to the tribe of Tennessee, which lay upon the border of the Mississippi and over against Kentucky. . . .' "

"Heavenly days!" Elizabeth said. "It's a mockery of the holy scripture itself, that's what it is. I don't want to hear another word of it."

"The holy scripture! It ain't the holy scriptures he's making fun of! It's old Davy Crockett, your own dear beloved husband! Listen to this, farther down in it some . . . yes, there." He cleared his throat again; his face was growing red, the way it always did when he got seriously worked up. " '. . . and it came to pass' . . . ah, forget that part, let me jump ahead, here . . . 'Andrew and the wise men and rulers of the people were assembled in the great sanhedrin . . . David rose in the midst of them saying, men and brethren, wot ye not that there be many occupants of the river country on the west border of the tribe of Tennessee, who are settled down upon lands belonging to Columbia; now I beseech you give unto these men each a portion for his inheritance, so that his soul may be glad, and he will bless thee and thy posterity.' Hear that, Betsy? Mocking my land bill work, that's what it is."

"Well, I don't like to hear it. You needn't read more on my account."

David didn't even hear her. He began reading again. " 'But there were other "wise men" who objected, saying that the central government should give the land to Tennessee, who should in turn deal with the occupants—thus giving all Tennessee politicians, and not just David, the glory for ever and ever. But David became angry at their resistance to his scheme and vowed vengeance.' " He slammed down the paper. "God! It makes my blood boil!"

"Then for heaven's sake, quit reading it!"

Again he ignored her. "Listen to this part—they've got me talking to 'Daniel, surnamed Webster, a "prophet of the Order of Balaam" ' . . . here it is: 'And David lifted up his eyes and wept, and said, O Daniel! live forever. If the wise men and rulers had given my occupants the lands according to the manner I beseeched them, I could have been wise man and chief ruler in the river country for life. But if I join the wise men, and give it to the state of Tennessee, then they will share the honor with me, and the council of the State will give it to the occupants for twelve and one half cents per acre, and they will receive the honor instead of me, then the people of the river country will not have me for their wise man and chief ruler forever, and it grieveth me sore.' "

He stopped reading, to Elizabeth's relief, and lowered the paper. He drew in a deep breath and exhaled it slowly and loudly. "Hang it, it's hardly worth getting so mad over, I suppose. I'll be shot if I don't have to admit that old Huntsman has a bit of cleverness in his 'Chronicles.' But it's hard to take this kind of mockery in good spirit. The reeking old Jacksonians are seeking to make my motives look low and selfish. I don't see the humor in that."

"Don't lose the ability to laugh at yourself, husband. There are those who say one of the reasons you lost your last race was that you lost your good humor."

David glanced at her rather sharply; his loss remained a touchy subject even yet. He laid the satirical paper aside and grumpily mumbled something about "Huntsman the one-legged jackass" as he dug in his pocket for his tobacco twist and knife. When he had found both and settled a chew into his jaw, he pulled a crumpled letter from another pocket and began reading it silently.

Elizabeth was at work at her spinning wheel near the fireplace. As she labored she thought about the material her husband had just read. Written by Adam Huntsman, a Tennessee attorney, political wit, and avid Jacksonian, the simply titled "Chronicles" were clever political satires written in imitation of the King James Old Testament. Elizabeth had read them in private several times, and found them terribly funny. The real reason she had tried to make David quit reading them aloud to her just now was not that she was offended, but that she had feared she would chuckle at some of the portions, which David wouldn't like at all. In an odd way, Elizabeth had to appreciate the peg-legged Huntsman. If his satire succeeded, he might just keep David out of Congress and here at home with her. Of course, she could let nothing of this attitude show itself to David. He assumed she was just as supportive of him this time as she had been during the first congressional race.

She glanced up, watching him read the letter. She knew what letter it was. It had come in a week ago from David's Washington friend and mentor, Dr. Campbell Ibbotson. David had read most of it aloud to her; it was full of Washington gossip touting David's presidential possibilities, the ongoing Whig efforts to build up his reputation as the archetypal American frontiersman and common-sense representative of the common man, and of Ibbotson's own eagerness to see his Tennessee friend return to office. He had missed him much these past two years, Ibbotson wrote, and looked forward to evenings of whiskey and fireside conversation of the sort they had enjoyed before. Elizabeth resented this very much; what of *her* need to have David by *her* fireside? What of the time *she* would have to spend apart from him while he was miles away, warming a chair in Ibbotson's parlor?

Such things apparently didn't matter. They were "women's concerns," as she had heard it put. Why they should count less than men's was something she hadn't yet figured out.

August 1833

There was one trait of border men that David was keenly aware of: their resentment of all attempts to manipulate them. That stubborn trait, he believed, accounted largely for his success in the congressional race just finished.

The celebrations were done and David was alone now with Elizabeth. She had smiled often through the day and congratulated him, but it was all without vigor. She was of lower spirits than he would have expected . . . but what of it? Women were moody at times, and he had other things on his mind, in particular, his analysis of the successful campaign.

"I believe it was the matter of the districts that helped me, Betsy," he explained. "The people of Madison County aren't the kind to be toyed with, or shifted about like hogs or cattle in the market."

He was referring to a legislative action that had been clearly designed to hurt his chances for victory. The Ninth District had been split up, but Madison County had been left in the Twelfth—a clumsy gerrymandering obviously based on Madison County's history of voting against David Crockett. The trick hadn't worked; it was far too transparent, and enough Madison Countians had turned around and given a protest vote to Crockett to let him win. Or so went his analysis.

"I'm happy, Betsy," he said. "I'm on the verge of great things. You'll be proud of me before I'm done."

"I'm already proud of you, Davy."

He went to her and put his arms around her. "My Betsy," he said. "I've not always been the best of husbands to you—politicking, running off to campaign, or off to Washington when I'm in office . . . and never do you complain."

She smiled. "I do sometimes. You just don't always hear me."

"Do you? Well, if you do, it's in the softest and most gentle way. I love you, Betsy. I couldn't make it without you—whoa! Have I made you sad?"

"No, no. Just the opposite. I've needed to hear these things from you. I miss them when I don't hear them."

"I don't say them enough."

"Well . . . no. You don't."

He grinned broadly, eyes crinkling around the corners, the ruddy streaks that had colored his cheeks in boyhood revealing themselves again. He had the glow of health about him now, and a vigor he hadn't shown in two years. It came to Elizabeth that perhaps it was a good thing after all that he had won. Even though there would be time apart, might it not be compensated for if the time they did share was of heightened quality? When David was not happy, their relationship was not as good. There was distance between them that was almost as difficult to endure as physical distance.

She smiled at him, and with a deliberate inner act of

volition, yielded him up. It was nothing she had planned to do, but now that she had, she knew it had been inevitable and right. If there was a destiny for David Crockett, she would not resent him for claiming it. She loved him too much for that.

He kissed her. "I'd like to spend time with you tonight," he said. It was his standard, euphemistic way of expressing his intimate desires, a shy and almost boyish way of speaking that she found endearing.

"I want to spend time with you too."

He kissed her again. "I love you a mighty lot, Betsy Crockett. I wish I could just put you in a big old sack, throw it over my shoulder, and tow you off to Washington City with me."

"I wish I could go—even in a sack, I'd go."

"Maybe you can, sometime during my term coming up—not in no sack, of course." He chuckled, then looked deeply into her eyes and gave an excited little shiver. "Lord have mercy, Betsy ... 'my term coming up'—it feels good to be saying that! I get frustrated with Congress when I'm in it, but I know now it's exactly what I'm supposed to be doing. It was writ out for me before I was born, I swear it was. I can just tell it."

She laid a finger across his lips, nodding. "I know. I understand that. And I love you, Davy."

"I love you, Betsy. I love you dearer than anything else in this world."

She wondered if it was true. She hoped it was. Often she had suspected that she held third place in his affections, behind his love for politics and power, and his love for the long-departed Polly. Even now she suspected this burst of affection was spurred as much by his excitement over victory as it was by her presence.

But he had said the words she wanted to hear, and that was enough. She would not probe them too deeply, nor ask for more. Laying her head against his chest, she hugged him tight, loving him with a painful intensity and wishing she would never, never have to let him go.

Chapter 46

December 1833

In the cool of the evening David Crockett walked alone through the streets of Washington. He was in a reflective mood, out for no purpose but to reabsorb the atmosphere of this city of power, to reaffirm to himself that he truly was here again, and to mull what had changed and what had remained the same since he had last walked these avenues.

He reached the White House and paused, looking across at the official residence of his fellow Tennessean and greatest political enemy. Old Hickory had won his second term, to David's chagrin, and back on a bitter cold day in March had been inaugurated for four more years. The only consolation David found in the situation was his knowledge that Jackson surely had winced when he learned that Crockett of Tennessee had regained his own office and would be back to plague him. Sometimes a crushed beetle learned how to crawl again—and how to pinch.

David gave a contemptuous snort as he viewed the executive residence. Jackson's White House was much different than the one John Quincy Adams had occupied when David first came to Washington. In Adams's day the incomplete White House had been surrounded by workers' sheds built up against the very walls, and was frequently rung by the tied-up horses of clerks for the Treasury and State departments. The combination of horse and manure stench had done nothing positive for the ambience of the place. Adams's East Room had been substantially empty of furniture, and the wings of the house had been unfinished, leaving a building that was plain and downright unsightly.

Jackson had changed that, inside and out. He had built the North Portico and filled the house with chandeliers, gilded tables, expensive drapes and carpets, costly cutlery, dishware, and glassware. Throughout his first term he had hosted many lavish political and diplomatic dinners, catered by slaves brought up from his home in Tennessee and featuring meats such as turkey, partridge, and canvasback duck. The outer sheds had come down, and government workers had been told to find new places to tether their horses. Certainly Jackson's efforts had improved the White House's appearance and made it function in a more proper diplomatic fashion, but at the same time it had provided David and his fellow anti-Jacksonians much to point at when they made their common charge that President Jackson lived more like a "King Andrew" than a common man.

Jackson had given his critics little fuel for their fires in his second inauguration, though. From what David had read in the papers and heard from Ibbotson, those ceremonies had been extremely low-key and simple, quite a contrast to the wild celebration that had marked his first entry into office.

David had heard stories galore of the madhouse quality of that first-term inaugural, which Jackson had thrown open to the public at large. The openness policy had brought a rabble, a mob, crushing into the White House itself, stripping the East Room reception tables of cakes, flavored ices, punch, ice creams. The crowd of commoners had spat tobacco juice on the floor, along with plenty of chewed-out quids. They had climbed on the furniture in their booted, mud-coated feet. An estimated twenty thousand people, from the haughtiest dignitaries to the most humble representatives of the Great Unwashed, trampled the White House lawns and passed through the White House, where Andrew Jackson had to be shielded from his public by a circle of friends who linked arms to make a barrier around him. He had been a sick and weary man at that time, and indeed a few weeks before the inauguration was rumored to have died, throwing the city into a short-lived panic. Jackson wasn't dead, of course, but was in poor health and a deep state of depression. His wife Rachel had died recently, her name besmirched by charges that she was a common adulteress and that her marriage to Jackson had been illegal. Jackson was devastated and furious, believing that the harsh campaign warfare waged by John Quincy Adams and his Secretary of State, Henry Clay, had been the cause of her death. Even so, he had borne up with typical strength through that first inaugural celebration, making his final escape through a window because the crowd was too dense to penetrate.

His second inaugural, not surprisingly, was closed to the public. But Jackson again was ill, and more weary even than he was during the first celebration. David had heard that he didn't even attend his own inaugural balls, but headed for bed very early, where he lay and read his late wife's Bible before falling asleep.

David turned and continued walking. It was darker now, and cooler. He had a quick deep chill that reminded him of his malarial attacks. *No, no, not again.* But the chill quickly passed and he was relieved.

After roaming another hour, he found himself nearing Ibbotson's office and residence. He hadn't planned to call here this evening, but now that he was close, he was tempted to stop by and see his old friend. Yet part of him was reluctant, for two reasons. The first was that Ibbotson had suffered an attack of apoplexy during David's two-year absence from Washington, and had not yet recovered fully. His speech was slurred; the left side of his face drooped. Sometimes he would drool without noticing it; all in all he seemed much older and more decrepit, and it disturbed David to see it. Ibbotson's decline reminded David of his own mortality, and that he was approaching a half century of life himself. It didn't seem all that long ago that he was romping with his brothers and sisters back in Greene County, and here he was now, growing old.

The second reason was even more personal, but also political. Ibbotson had developed a set of fears about David and his career. He continually warned David about the supposed perils of his current political pathway. David actually found Ibbotson's warnings insulting. According to the increasingly plain-spoken old doctor, he was naive, easily led by those who flattered him and made him promises. Such traits made him a man easily used, Ibbotson warned, but also one who could be easily thrown away like a broken tool if ever his usefulness ceased. Ibbotson had seen it happen to others before. "Be wary of your alliance with the Whigs," he had cautioned. "Whatever you do, don't let yourself become useless. Beware that they don't build your pedestal high, only to let it blow down in changing political winds."

David was irritated by such chatter from Ibbotson, and handily attributed it to senility and the effects of apoplexy. So Ibbotson thought him naive, thought that the Whigs were using *him*! Bah! He knew it to be precisely the opposite. The Whigs weren't using him; he was using *them*. Already they had promised to help him push through his land bill in turn for letting their press and propaganda machine bolster his reputation as a possible presidential candidate. What could be wrong with that? What was Ibbotson so worried about?

David turned on his heel and headed for his rented Washington quarters. He wouldn't call on Ibbotson tonight after all. In fact, perhaps it would be best not to call on Ibbotson as frequently as he had in prior days. Being with the man simply dragged down his spirits and raised inner doubts that were certainly not useful. David Crockett was on a rise. He needed no one grabbing at his coattails, trying to hold him down.

Returning to his rooms, he undressed for bed, then poured himself a glass of whiskey. Settling in a chair near the fire, he sipped slowly, looking into the flames. At length, with his glass empty and his body relaxed and warm, he lowered his head and began to slip toward slumber. At such times his mind ran free, random images and thoughts playing through his mind. The images were of one of the earliest incidents in his memory, when he was a very small boy still living in the cabin where he was born, beside the banks of the Nolichucky River. His older brothers and a neighbor boy had once taken a canoe into the river and gotten caught in the swift current near a small waterfall, and David had stood on the bank, watching the neighbor boy struggle vainly with the paddle, trying to turn the canoe to the bank. As small as he had been at the time, he had thought: If only he would let my brothers have the paddle, they could get the canoe to the bank. But the neighbor boy, though inept at canoeing, had refused to relinquish the paddle, and the canoe had continued to sweep closer and closer to the waterfall. A neighbor, plowing in a field nearby, had seen the impending accident and waded out into the swift river to the canoe, which he muscled back to safety. David had been greatly relieved.

He opened his eyes and jerked up straight. The empty whiskey glass clattered to the floor. Gazing into the fireplace flames, he gripped the arms of his chair and took deep gasps of breath. An inexplicable feeling of panic came over him; he peered around the room as if assassins lurked in the shadows of the corners.

God above, what am I doing here? Why did I ever leave my family and home? What am I doing, turning the paddle over to others who don't know how to row? Why am I putting myself in their hands, when all I really want is . . . is . . .

There his thought faded away. What did he want for himself? He wasn't at all certain. Since boyhood, certain images, certain human themes, had attracted him. He recalled the old frontiersman he had seen leading a pack train during his boyhood roaming days; he recalled how the fringe and beadwork on the buckskin jacket of the treacherous Indian trader Fletcher had seemed so appealing and beautiful when he first saw it. He remembered how pleased he had been each time he had brought in another bear or two in his many hunts in West Tennessee. "There's nobody can hunt bear like Davy Crockett," people would say, and it gratified him deeply. Gratified him . . . how often had politics done that? Almost never. Generally it had left him frustrated.

Maybe all I ever was cut out to be was a man of the backwoods, a "gentleman from the cane," a frontiersman like that pack train driver. I should have never come back here. I should have stayed in Tennessee with Betsy and the young ones, and been content with what I had.

The thoughts came in a whitewater rush, overwhelming while they lasted. But then they passed. David stood, went to the fire, poked it up. Then he slumped back in his seat again and exhaled long and slow. Shaking his head, he chuckled, and said aloud, "Davy-boy, you surely let the fear get to you right then. You do that again and they'll haul you off for scrap."

He poured himself another whiskey and drank it a little too quickly, but when it was down, he felt much better, though a little confused. He had never before experienced a burst of panic like that. What did it mean, if anything?

Nothing, probably. Most likely it was all this background talk of David Crockett as presidential contender that had him worked up. That and simple weariness. What he needed was a good night's sleep.

He went to bed. Lord, how he wished Betsy were with him tonight! Sometimes a man needed the company of his woman, just for the comfort of it. But Betsy was far away, in Tennessee. Back at home.

He wondered if she knew how much he loved her, how much he missed her. With the image of her face filling his mind's eye, he rolled over and fell asleep.

David's evening of panicked doubt left its mark, but not permanently. For the two days following, he was nervous and unsure of himself. Several people asked if he was ill, and he made up excuses. He considered asking Ibbotson about what had happened, thinking maybe there was some medical cause behind it, but he finally decided not to. Ibbotson would only find some way to link it to his continuing warnings about letting the Whigs take control of his political destiny. So David threw himself into his work, and by the end of the third day had become so embroiled again in the busy life of a congressman that he all but forgot about the disturbing episode. When he did remember it, he laughed it off and attributed it to fatigue, cheap whiskey, and Ibbotson's gloomy counsel.

About a week later an event occurred that erased the last traces of his self-doubt. *The Lion of the West*, featuring the famous James Hackett, was playing at the Washington Theater, and he received an invitation to attend. His friends urged him to go. What a great scene it would be, Colonel Crockett face-to-face with Nimrod Wildfire!

Wearing his best clothing—much finer garb than he had ever worn in the initial days of his first term—he made his way to the theater on the appointed night, and found well-dressed ushers awaiting him. With the theater management leading the way, he was led into the crowded auditorium . . . and the audience came to its feet, cheering and applauding. His name rose all around him, mixed with applause and whoops of delight. Despite a strong effort to maintain a modest expression, he could not restrain a broad smile. He was popular; his mere presence here was an *event*. Turning, he waved at the crowd, then seated himself in the reserved front-row seat.

The lights fell; the curtain rose. But the usual opening scene—an apartment at the home of the New York merchant character, Mr. Freeman—did not present itself. Instead, James Hackett, wearing the buckskin garb and wildcat-skin cap of Nimrod Wildfire, the Kentuckian, stepped into the glow of the footlights and strode over to a position directly in front of the guest of honor. Doffing his hat, he made a slow, deep bow.

David came to his feet and bowed in like fashion, and behind him the crowd burst into a frenzy of cheers and applause that surpassed what had come moments before. Turning again to face them, David beamed.

You'll know the glory only when the glory-time comes. Go into the shining, David Crockett, and shout your hallelujah! Jimmy Crockett's words from that odd, malarial dream ran through his mind, and he wondered how he could have ever doubted himself. He belonged here. This was his city, his place, his destiny. Hand above his head, he waved for a full minute to the roaring crowd.

No room in him for doubt and panic now! This must be the glory-time; this must be the shining. He had been born for this, and from here on out it could only get better, and better, and better still.

Chapter 47

Early January, 1834

Thomas Chilton was a likable man, about ten years the junior of David Crockett and cut in some ways from the same cloth. Born in Garrard County, Kentucky, he knew the same breed of common people David had grown up among, and had a good grasp of backwoods speech. Like David, he had cut his political teeth in the legislature of his state, then had moved up to the United States Congress, serving one term but failing to win reelection to another. However, he had made a Crockettesque political comeback of his own and had been elected to the Twenty-third Congress. He was a staunch Whig and dedicated lawmaker. He was significantly more educated than David, having gone through the common schools and into the study, then the practice, of law. But most importantly to David Crockett and his fellow Whigs, Chilton was a capable, quick writer, and this above all had qualified him for the important task of ghostwriting an authorized, official campaign "autobiography" of Colonel David Crockett. It was a task David might have insisted should go to Campbell Ibbotson, if not for the distance that had developed between him and his former mentor.

At the moment, Chilton was sitting on a couch in David's quarters, notebook across his lap, quill and inkstand on a table beside him, a copy of *The Life and Adventures of Colonel David Crockett of West Tennessee* in his hand. He was very weary. It was late at night and the room was illuminated only by lamplight, so he frequently rubbed his eyes as he scanned the volume. His voice, lively and crisp-toned early in the evening, had declined to a soft, low rasp, and he asked many fewer questions than he had when this long work session began. He was ready to put this aside and call it a night.

David, on the other hand, seemed as full of vigor as ever. Since the pair had finished their supper hours ago, David had paced the room, airing his complaints with the contents of *Life and Adventures*, and instructing Chilton in detail about how he wanted his autobiography to vary from it. Chilton was doing his best to form David's comments into a semblance of an outline, but weariness was beginning to get the best of him and he was growing confused by the barrage of details. One thing there was no confusion about: David Crockett had a boundless reserve of energy. Chilton wondered how he did it.

And another thing was abundantly clear too: David was not at all happy about the *Life and Adventures* volume. Not that he could rightly put much blame on its author, since most of the information in the book had come from David himself, a fact David didn't deny to Chilton. Of course, he did plan to deny it to the public, right in the preface of his ghostwritten autobiography. The more distance between himself and the earlier biography, the better.

But certainly David did know the *Life and Adventures* author, just as Chilton himself and every other congressman knew him. Behind the pseudonymous name on the copyright page was Mathew St. Clair Clarke, House of Representatives clerk, who had published the book out of a Cincinnati publishing house in 1833, after interviews with David. The book had grown very popular both in its original form and in a version that had come out sometime later under the new title of *Sketches and Eccentricities of Colonel David Crockett of West Tennessee*.

Despite his complicity in the book's production and the flattering interest in him it had generated, David

Crockett disliked the way it presented details of his life that he felt were not politically attractive. And despite a talltale tone of voice, the book was sometimes a little too honest about such matters as David's sometimes strained relationship with his father back in boyhood.

Chilton rubbed his eyes yet again, and laid the notebook aside. Exhaustion overcame pride. Standing, he stretched and yawned. "Colonel, I'm afraid my energies fail me," he said. "I'll be of no further use to you tonight."

The Tennessean turned, looking surprised, then smiled apologetically. "Mr. Chilton, I'm afraid I've been right thoughtless, rattling on to such a late hour. I've put a lot of concern in this book of ours. But you're right. There's a time for work and a time for sleep."

Chilton gathered his materials. "I'm determined to make this as good a book as we can put together at such a hurried pace, Colonel. The sooner we can get it onto the market, the sooner we can begin reshaping the public perception of you as a more, shall I dare say, *presidential* figure. It will be essential to get you reelected in 'thirty-five if the party is to do greater things with you."

"Yes. Yes."

"Good evening, Colonel Crockett."

"Good evening, Mr. Chilton."

Late night was far colder than early evening had been, and Chilton shivered badly as he strode down the dark street. He wasn't fond of walking in Washington late at night. He was a sensitive-hearted man, and the beggars and stragglers that haunted the shadows roused his sympathy and made him feel powerless. How could one man help such unfortunate souls? It was partly to overcome this sense of helplessness that Chilton had turned his eye toward politics.

His eye caught a movement to his left. He shifted his gaze that way and saw a man approaching, wrapped in a heavy cloak. He was bearded and wore a broad-brimmed hat that drooped low over his eyes. A beggar, surely—or a street robber. Chilton steeled himself, just in case.

"Good evening to you, sir."

"Good evening." Chilton noted to himself that the

man had spoken with a rough backwoods accent much like Crockett's.

"There's something I'd like to ask you, sir—"

Chilton reached for his money purse. "How much do you need?"

The man, whose face remained hidden in the darkness below the front brim of his hat, shook his head. "No, no, it's not money I want."

Chilton was surprised. He had never encountered a beggar wanting anything else. "What, then?"

"Information. I'm seeking the residence of Colonel Crockett of Tennessee."

Immediately Chilton felt wary. Who was this man, and what was his business? Crockett was to some a controversial figure, and there were people in the world radical or senseless enough to assassinate politicians who offended them. Certainly this cloaked, shadowed figure perfectly fit the stereotype of the assassin.

"Are you a friend of Crockett's?"

"You might say that. A friend from young days."

"Oh."

"Do you know his living place? I'm thinking it might be that building you came out of."

Chilton decided he couldn't chance telling the truth to this man. "I'm sorry. I can't help you."

"That's not his place?"

"You'll have to ask someone else."

The dark figure held silence a moment, then turned away.

"Sir!" Chilton said.

The man looked back over his shoulder, his face still shadowed. "What?"

"If I should chance to ever meet Colonel Crockett, might I tell him the name of the man looking for him?"

"Yes. Tell him Persius Tarr has come to call. I'll find him, sooner or later."

"Persius Tarr. Very well."

"Do you know Crockett?"

"I've seen him. I've seen most members of Congress. It's a small enough city, after all."

The dark man grunted agreement.

"Well . . . good evening to you, Mr. Tarr."

"Evening."

The dark figure walked away, vanishing into the night. Chilton shuddered and huddled in his coat, then went on his way at a faster pace, unnerved and tense. He had an impulse to go back to Crockett and tell him what had happened here, in case the man was a threat. But he was eager for the safety of his own residence, and if Colonel Crockett had ever known this Persius Tarr, it must have been a casual and unimportant association. Otherwise the odd name would have been mentioned in *Life and Adventures*, or in the colonel's own biographical dictations.

Chilton hurried on, feeling guilty about not returning to warn his colleague, but not guilty enough to stop. Next time he talked to Crockett, he would mention this Persius Tarr, just in case. That would be good enough.

He reached his boardinghouse. Within ten minutes he was in bed, sleeping soundly and dreaming his way through the life of Colonel Crockett.

"Tarr?" David said. He frowned and shook his head. "Tarr . . . no, no. I have no recollection of such a name, and it's not the kind of name I'd likely forget."

"No, it isn't," Chilton replied. "Well, sir, I don't know whether to be relieved or concerned. There certainly is a man in this city who claims that name, and he's making an active search for you. I mistrusted him enough that I didn't give him any indication that this was your residence. The trouble is, he already had that information from elsewhere."

David frowned and rubbed his chin. He was putting on a display of mild concern, but in truth he was straining not to shake visibly. Persius—here in Washington! It was a terrible development. He had no desire to see Persius at all, and much less of a desire that his past friendship and association with him should come out. Persius was a murderer, a deserter, the kind of man who could ruin a rising politician.

"I admit a bit of worry about this," David said. "But I have to wonder why he hasn't shown up here between the time he spoke to you and now. That was two nights ago."

"I don't know, Colonel. Maybe he's shy a few bricks up here"—Chilton tapped his head—"and has just wandered off. You're a famous man now; there's a lot who would like to claim friendship with you."

"I suppose." David paused, then said, in as careless a manner as possible, "Mr. Chilton, are there rooms available in your own boardinghouse? I haven't been pleased with these here quarters anyhow, and if there's some madman roaming around and asking about me, maybe it would be the sensible thing to move. Besides, it would make it right easier for us to get together on this book of ours."

"Well, there are some rooms vacant, I think. I could inquire. . . ."

"Would you do that? I'd be grateful to the backbone."

Chilton grinned at that typical kind of Crockett expression. "I'll ask today."

"Very good, Mr. Chilton. You're a prime sort of man, you are, even if you do hail from Kentuck. I tell you what—I'll give you a signed draft, and if the rooms are clear and look good to you, go ahead and sign in whatever amount they name, long as it's within reason, and I'll make the move right off."

Chilton left and was back within two hours, informing David that the transaction was complete. David was already mostly packed, having few possessions of his own here. The furniture came with the room.

Chilton and David made two treks from one boardinghouse to the other, and that was all it took to make the move. David was generously grateful, even offering Chilton money for his help, but Chilton declined it, and headed into town toward the Capitol for a meeting for which he was already late.

He pondered the situation as he walked. It had seemed to him that Crockett had reacted when he first mentioned the name of Persius Tarr, but had striven to cover it up. Certainly he was more nervous about the man than he had let on. Why else would he actually change residences on such short notice? There was something very odd about this, something the colonel was hiding. It roused the curiosity of Chilton as biographer—but Chilton as loyal Whig had a different view. If there was some dark secret in Crockett's past involving this Tarr fellow, perhaps it was politically expedient that it remain secret. This curious behavior of Crockett's couldn't derive from mere fear of an unknown potential assassin. Colonel Crockett had his faults, like any man, but Chilton knew that cowardice was not among them. Crockett was as fearless a man as he had ever known.

Yet he had been shaken by the very name of Persius Tarr. Why? Was there a chance that Crockett might explain the matter, if he was questioned in just the right way and with promises that the answer would be kept confidential?

That raised a new thought. Maybe the Whigs *did* need to know what was going on here. If there was some scandal from Crockett's past that this Tarr knew about, it could do great damage to Crockett and the Whig cause. Perhaps this mysterious man was a blackmailer! Perhaps he—

Chilton shut off his thoughts and chuckled at himself. One mysterious night meeting with an odd man on a Washington street, and he was building up notions of conspiracies and scandal and blackmail. His imagination was getting the best of him. Chilton decided to put the matter to rest. If Crockett had something to say about Persius Tarr, he would say it. If not, then it wasn't anyone else's business. That was how Thomas Chilton resolved to look at it from here on.

David sat up in bed, confused and unsure about what had awakened him. Then he heard it again: a hammering on his door. He cranked up his low-burning bedside lamp and glanced at the watch lying by the lamp. Three o'clock in the morning! He slid open a drawer and removed the little flintlock pistol he always kept handy. Rising, he crept toward the door.

*God help me, it's Persius out there, I know it is. Who
else would come at such an hour?*

"Who's there?"

"Officer William Keener, sir, policeman. Have I
found Colonel David Crockett?"

The voice certainly wasn't that of Persius Tarr. David
slid back the latch, turned the lock, and cracked open the
door. A wall-mounted lamp burned dimly in the hall, illu-
minating an apologetic-looking uniformed policeman.

"Colonel? I'm very sorry to disturb you, sir, but do
you mind if I come in?"

"No . . . but hold up a minute and let me put on some
clothes. I'm naked as a hop-toad."

David closed the door and quickly dressed himself in
trousers and shirt. He put away the pistol, lit a second
lamp, and ushered in the policeman.

"Is something wrong?"

"Well, sir, not really, not for you, at least. There's a
man we've arrested, sir, for cutting a man in a tavern
brawl a couple of nights ago, and he's been calling for you
to come. He declares he's your friend, odd though that
sounds."

"What's his name?"

"He gives the name of John Canaday, sir. He's about
your age, maybe a bit older, with dark hair and a long
beard, and very swarthy skin."

Persius! It had to be.

"What does he want from me?"

"I don't rightly know. He just asks for you to come.
Maybe he believes that you, being a congressman, can
help him out in some way. There's no bail for him; he's a
rover, you see, and the judge figures he'll simply run out
before his trial if he's let free."

David yawned and brushed back his hair with his fingers. "Why'd you come calling at three in the morning?
Couldn't this have waited until tomorrow? And hang it,
you've had him two days or so already, ain't you?"

"Yes sir. I'm sorry about this, and I'll take the blame
personally. The fact is, sir, we've ignored his calls for you
until now, but the prisoner has took very sick, and is liable

to die. I made the decision myself to come fetch you up, Colonel. It came to me that maybe he really was a friend of yours, unlikely as it seemed, and I thought how bad it would be if he died without us ever letting you know. I'm sorry about the disturbance, sir. Like I said, I'll take the blame personally."

David sighed. The policeman was young and very sincere. He didn't fault him. But his message was most unwelcome. He had hoped Persius would just fade away and no longer be a part of his life, particularly not the public life he lived here.

On the other hand, if Persius was not going to conveniently fade away, perhaps this way was best. In a jailhouse there would be privacy, secrecy. No one need know.

"Don't fret, young man. You done the right thing coming to me."

"You know him?"

"Suffice it to say I've been associated with a John Canaday in the past."

"Well, this makes me feel better, sir. This may in fact be the same man."

David knew it wasn't, of course, but there was nothing gained in letting the policeman in on that. "Let me finish dressing," he said. "I'll come with you and meet your prisoner."

David wondered what Persius would ask of him. Maybe he wanted money. Maybe he simply wanted to talk to a past friend. Whatever, he would settle this unwelcome affair quickly, thoroughly, and discreetly. David had no intention of any further involvement with Persius Tarr. Crockett of Tennessee was a man of ambition, a man with a future, and by no stretch did he intend to see that future ruined by an old, bad memory after all these long years . . . if Persius even lived through whatever illness had him down.

He dressed quickly and headed out into the streets of the sleeping city with the policeman at his side.

Chapter 48

Wiping sleep from his eyes, Campbell Ibbotson rose, white hair mussed into a tangle, his pale, thin legs extending from beneath the hem of his long blue nightshirt. He peered at the clock on his wall. It was five-thirty in the morning. Whoever was jangling his bell must have come on a medical emergency. Never conveniently timed, those things. Throwing a robe around himself, he shuffled to the door.

"David!" he exclaimed after swinging the door open. The word was slightly mutilated by the lingering effects of his apoplectic attack many months before. "Are you sick again?"

"No, Campbell, not me. But there's a man being brought here for a bleeding. He's a man I knew years ago, the one I told you about. Persius Tarr."

"Tarr . . . my Lord! *The* Persius Tarr?"

"Indeed. He's been in the jail here for stabbing a man in a tavern, but I've worked it out for him to go free. The fellow he had stabbed was locked up there too, just a common type, and I paid him off to drop the charge against Persius. It's a story I can tell you fuller later on. The point of it all is that Persius is sick, nigh to death, and he needs a bleeding or some such in the worst way. Campbell, I'm sorry, but I've took it on myself to bring him here. I hope you don't mind it."

"Of course I don't. I'm a physician, am I not? And for you, David, I'll do anything I can, as you should well know. Where is he?"

"Being brought here by a couple of trusty prisoners from the city jail. They had to lay him out on a door to cart him, him being so sick."

Ibbotson tugged David inside and closed the door. He went to the basin in his bedroom and splashed water on his face and hair. He combed his hair back and dressed himself while David Crockett paced in the outer room. Ibbotson sent his mind back to the conversations he and David had held in the past concerning Persius Tarr. Since his sickness, it was harder to remember the details of such things, but after a few moments he had sorted it out. By the time Ibbotson was fully dressed and the trusties were knocking at his door, Ibbotson had entirely refreshed his memory on the Persius Tarr matter. Clearly a new chapter in the story was developing. He was curious to find out what it would yield.

David was already hustling the trusties into the room when Ibbotson emerged. The door upon which they had carried the ill man was too wide to fit through Ibbotson's doorway, so they were carrying the fellow bodily, his arms dangling, bearded head lolling to the side, his rump nearly dragging the floor. David directed them into Ibbotson's spare bedroom and had them place Persius Tarr on the bed.

"Why did you bring him up here?" the old doctor asked David irritably. "You know my clinic is downstairs."

"This one has to be hidden," David replied. He flicked his eyes toward the trusties. "I'll tell you more in a minute." He handed the trusties a coin apiece, which surprised and pleased them tremendously. They left in a cheerful mood, treading back toward the jail.

Ibbotson turned to David. "He must be hidden, you say? Why?"

"Because I don't want it known that Congressman David Crockett has anything to do with this man," David replied. "That ain't no deacon of the Baptist Church you've got lying in yonder. I don't need his reputation

ruining mine. I'll be fortunate if word don't get out
through the police or the other prisoners."

Ibbotson went to the bedside and lit the lamp. He began examining his unexpected patient. The smell of
Persius's unwashed body filled the room. His beard was
filled with grit and burrs and dried, crusted rheum, and the
abundant wrinkles lining his dark face were filled with
dirt, sweat, and general grime. Persius's hair and beard
were both overlong; all in all he looked like a man who
had lived in the poorest of conditions for a very long time.

Ibbotson examined Persius at length, lifting his eyelids, looking in his throat, ears, nose, feeling along his
neck and groin and midsection, where he lingered longest,
probing his hand deep to feel the size and shape of the internal organs. Finally he said, "I believe this man has
something in common with you other than past association. He's suffering the same affliction I've bled you for—
that or something very similar."

"I'll be shot! Is that right?"

"Yes. Now if you'll pardon me, I'll go downstairs and
get my bleeding equipment."

While the physician was gone, David stood looking
down at Persius and marveling at himself for what he was
now doing. What could be more ironic? The last thing he
had wanted was any further involvement with Persius
Tarr—and yet here he was, springing him from jail, paying
off his victim to drop the charge, and now bringing him
for medical care. It was a fool thing most assuredly, but
what else could he have done? When he looked into that
cell and saw the pallid form of a man who once had been
a close friend, he couldn't simply walk away. David
Crockett might not be a saint, but neither was he a devil.
It was his duty to help Persius.

But it was a risk to do so, and that concerned him.
While giving his life's story to Mathew St. Claire Clarke
and more recently to Thomas Chilton, David had carefully
avoided any mention at all of Persius Tarr. No reader
could even guess such a man existed, based on what information David had preserved. Who could have supposed
that Persius himself would suddenly reappear after . . .

how long had it been? David counted back the years to that night he had talked to Persius in the prison tent. Good Lord, that had been right about twenty years ago! Where had the years gone?

Ibbotson came back in with his gear and set about bleeding Persius. David watched the operation, noting how slow and feeble Ibbotson was now. And old, doting man. It was sad to see. Ibbotson's condition, combined with the awareness of the past that Persius roused, made David melancholy. How quickly a man's life sped by, to be gone before he even noticed its passing! And he could never know how much time he had remaining. It was enough to sober anyone who pondered on it.

Persius certainly didn't look any better for his bleeding. He was more pallid than before, his tightly closed eyes more sunken. He looks dead as a beached shad, David thought. He stood over Persius, wondering if he would die. The calculating, political side of him couldn't help but consider the convenience of it if Persius did die; the human side of him felt appropriately shocked at such a thought. Of course he didn't want Persius to die. They weren't friends now, but they had been friends before. As a child he had looked up to Persius even more than he had his own older brothers.

Ibbotson sat down on a chair at the far side of Persius's bed. The sun was rising now, spilling light through a window behind him. "I certainly don't see much of you anymore," Ibbotson said. "I fear I've run you off with my warnings about the Whigs."

David saw little point in trying to deny the obvious. "I suppose that's the straight-out truth of the matter. After a while I got weary of hearing how gullible old Davy Crockett was, and how the Whigs were going to chew him up only to spit him out like a husky quid when they'd drained the juice from him."

"Forgive me, my friend. I was only trying to be forthright. I had no intention of driving you away."

David grinned. "Well, I've sure come running back, now that I have need of you. I hope you won't think ill of me for that."

Ibbotson waved off the suggestion. "Glad to be of service to you, even if only by helping Mr. Tarr here. But I must ask you: What do you want me to do with him? Keep him here until he is well?"

David was glad Ibbotson had been the one to actually bring up that idea, which was precisely what he did have in mind. He told the doctor as much.

"Very well," Ibbotson said without a falter. "If that's what you wish, you'll have it."

"I'll pay the costs, of course."

"Fine. My fee is a revival of your visits to me, just as it was before. I pledge to you I'll offer no more unsolicited advice."

David grinned and leaned over the bed, putting out his hand. Ibbotson shook it. "Consider it a bargain," David said.

David remained by Persius's bedside the rest of the day. By midday Persius had come around some, but was in no better shape to communicate. He was delirious and fevered, thrashing in the bed and babbling. David felt a chill of recognition when he picked out the words "Matilda" and "Matty" from Persius's jabber. Matty . . . the very name inscribed inside the bracelet that Betsy had taken from the corpse found on their property. Together with Uncle Jimmy's silver piece found in the baby's wrap, that provided strong evidence in favor of David's suspicion that the woman had been Persius's wife or companion, and the baby had been his as well. It gave David a pang when he realized that Persius might not yet know what had happened to his child. . . .

And with that thought, David realized why Persius Tarr must have gone to the trouble of venturing all the way to Washington City to find him. He had wanted to learn what happened to his baby girl.

David began to dread the moment that Persius came out of his sickness. He could not predict what it would do to his ailing old companion when he found out that the child he had given over to the Crocketts had not survived.

• • •

Persius remained in substantially unchanged condition for three more days. David had to come and go because of his congressional obligations, but at every opportunity he slipped to Ibbotson's rooms to be at Persius's side. He didn't bother to notice the change that was taking place in him simply because Persius was nearby. He was spending much less time dwelling on himself and his political destiny. He had twice excused himself from book-writing sessions with Chilton, giving feeble and undetailed explanations that obviously left Chilton confused. David could understand the confusion; it was he who had been so preoccupied with making progress on the autobiography before.

On the morning of the fourth day, David was roused from his bed by a street boy sent by Ibbotson to fetch him. "The doctor says to tell you he's awake," the boy said, obviously not understanding the message he was bearing. But David understood, and dressed in a hurry, rushing straightaway to Ibbotson's.

Persius was sitting up, sipping on a cup of hot broth. When David entered the room, he smiled feebly. For several moments the two men stared at each other. Looking Persius in the eye swept the years away from David; he felt like a boy again in his presence.

"Howdy, Colonel Crockett."

"No colonel to you, Persius. Just David."

"I hear I come near to dying."

"You did. I could tell it. I was at your bedside through a lot of it."

"That's what the old man told me. I do appreciate it—and you fetching me out of that jail. I would have died there, sure as the world."

"It wasn't nothing. You'd have done the same for me."

"No. I wouldn't have been allowed to. A congressman has what they call 'influence.' " Persius took a trembling sip of broth, downing it with smacking lips. "I'm proud of you, David. I was proud of you when I first heard you'd gotten in the state legislature. When I heard about you turning congressman, it was right hard not to brag on you outright. But I didn't. It wouldn't do no good for your reputation for folks to know you had been a friend of mine."

Hearing his own frequent thought returned to him from Persius himself embarrassed David. "Pshaw!" he said. "I don't reckon you could hurt me."

Persius smiled. "Don't try to spare my feelings, Davy. I read your storybook, and noticed I wasn't in it."

"That wasn't really my storybook. Another fellow wrote that. I'm writing my own right now."

"Will I be in that one?"

David reddened, lowered his head. "No."

"There! You see it just like I do. Don't go hangdogging on me about it, Dave. I don't mind it, really I don't. I had dropped the last of my pride before I sprouted my first whisker." He lay back and closed his eyes. "Wears me out, talking so much."

"You need your rest."

Persius looked at David again. "Not until I find out one thing. There was a sickly baby left on your Tennessee door a few years back, left by a man whose wife had just died, and who was running hard from folk who would kill him if they caught him. David . . . did that baby live?"

David's throat was dry and tight. "No, Persius. I'm sorry. My Betsy did her best, but it just . . . I'm sorry."

Persius closed his eyes again and clamped his mouth tightly shut. For several moments there was no sound but the ticking of the grandfather clock in the corner and the sound of Ibbotson's muffled voice filtering up from the office below as he talked to a patient. A tear slipped out from beneath Persius's right eyelid, and he wiped it away with a callused finger.

"I'm mighty sorry," David said. "I had already figured it was your child. Because of the silver piece."

"I hoped you'd find it. There was no time for me to do anything else to make you understand. They were close upon me; I had to run."

"She was buried like a Christian, Persius."

"I'm glad. You reckon babies go to heaven, David? I

heard there's some say they don't, unless they've been water-sprinkled."

"I figure they all go to heaven, Persius."

"So do I. So she's all right now. She's happy."

"I'm sure she is. What was her name, Persius?"

"Rebecca. After your mother, who was so kind to me."

That news caught David by surprise, and touched him too. "I'll be sure to tell her," he said. "She'll be pleased."

"So your mother is still living?"

"Yes, and my father too, though they're both well up in their years."

"Still at the tavern?"

"No. They're West Tennesseans now, just like me. The Crockett family always seems to move west."

"I'm glad they're still alive."

"I want to hear about your wife and child, Persius, if you've got the strength to talk."

"Not now," Persius said. "I'm feeling weak and right sad. Later I'll tell you everything."

"That's fine. You sleep now. I'll be back this afternoon."

David left and went down to inform Ibbotson that Persius was resting. He left the office and took a long walk. Glad as he was that Persius was regaining strength, he felt very depressed, mostly out of sympathy with Persius's grief over his lost child. And also he was beginning to worry again. Now that Persius was recovering, would he want to remain here with his old friend? That was out of the question. The situation had the potential to become very delicate indeed. David began to feel wrought-up over the possibility, until he remembered that Persius himself had expressed his own understanding of the need to keep their association secret. Surely that meant he didn't intend to remain around. David hoped so—and then felt guilty for it.

Near evening David returned and found Persius awake again and looking stronger. Before, his pallor, combined with the swarthiness of his skin, had given him a sickly, almost olive color. Now he had a ruddier look, and was sitting up taller in the bed. He greeted David pleasantly. David noted that age and weathering had accented Persius's swarthiness. From some angles he looked Indian, from others almost Mexican.

They talked over polite trivialities for only a few moments before Persius settled down to telling his story, picking up at the place David and he had last been together: the soldiers' camp in the Creek War.

Chapter 49

"I appreciated your notion of helping me escape that night," Persius said, "but I knowed I couldn't involve you in it, David. So instead of luring that guard to the place you said, I had him take me into the woods, and I got the chain around his neck and choked him senseless. He had the key on him, so it was easy to get loose from my chains, steal a horse, and take on out of there.

"I headed north and then east, all the way into North Carolina. I wound up in the town of Wilmington and found me some work in a warehouse. Stayed at it about a year, and then the wife of the man who owned the place left him and he went out of his head. He went into the warehouse in the middle of the night, set the place afire around him, then shot hisself through the noggin. Well, there was no work left for me there after that, so I went on up to the Chesapeake Bay and found work on the docks. I was there for a good five years, working under a different name than my own, and putting money aside in a strongbox I hid beneath the floorboards of a little house I rented. I met a woman and she moved in with me for about six months, and said she'd marry me. The landlord of my little place got wind I had took in a female, and Lord he got fearsome mad! He was a righteous sort, and told me she would have to go right off, or marry me right off, or out I would go. I was ready to marry, and she pledged to do the same, but while I was out scouting for a justice of the peace to do the job, she took my strongbox from under the floor and lit out with it, leaving me flat broke and jilted besides."

"That's a hard blow for a man to endure, Persius."

"Made me furious angry. I headed out to find her, and discovered she'd had a man on the side all that time and it was him who had talked her into stealing my money. He was a peg-legged man, so it wasn't hard to find folks who remembered seeing him."

"I've had my problems with peg-legged folk myself," David mumbled, thinking of the "Chronicle"-writing Adam Huntsman.

Persius went on. "I followed them two all the way across Virginia, and when I at last caught up with them—I should say caught up with *her*—he had took the money from her and dumped her off like a sack of bad feed. She was repentant as a harlot at the gates of hell, begging me to give her another chance, to forgive her, take her back, all that kind of thing. I wouldn't do it. I might be simple-headed gullible from time to time, but not *fool* gullible. I bid her good-bye and went out looking for Mr. Peg-leg and my money.

"By the time I found him, I'd gone all the way to the Falls of the Ohio, and he'd spent every cent. Gambled it off mostly, or spent it on women. I whupped up on him until there wasn't an unbroke bone left in his face, then dumped him off in a pile of smuts and rubbish and headed out to find some other way to rebuild my fortune. It was my fault, I know, for not taking better care of my money. I should have guessed that woman would steal it.

"For the next several years I did what I had to do, working mostly, stealing if it came down to that. After a time I got work on the river. Keelboating to begin with, then steamshipping. I was just a hand to start out with, but I had the right knack, and before long I was being trained to be a pilot. I've never been prouder. For the first time in my life I was going someplace. I was important.

"But they say a man's past always catches up with him, and mine surely did. That man who had took my woman and my money, he hit it rich gambling and showed up on the riverboat, fresh-married to the daughter of some fat mine owner living west of the Big Muddy. I had changed a right smart bit—fattened up some, and muscled, and I had no beard at the time, and short-clipped hair. But he knowed me right off, and to make a long story short, we had trouble. I knifed him deep and left him bleeding on the deck. Bled to death. It was a case of self-defense, just like with old Crider Cummings, but that don't make no difference when you're half redskin and half white-skinned trash. The dead man's widow put her rich pappy on to me. He hired men to search me down, just to make his widowed little girl happy, no matter what it took, no matter what it cost. He had a half-dozen men on my trail at one time. I didn't know a thing about it until they were nigh on to catching me, a good six months after I had fled the steamboat. I caught one of them in Memphis and made him spill out the facts to me at the point of my blade. He told me the whole tale, and that's how I found out I was being chased in a mighty serious way. I knew then I had bad trouble."

Persius paused to rest his voice. The exertion of talking was making him weaker. David sat silently, marveling that one human life could have been so embroiled in violence and trouble from its very beginnings. Persius had been a fugitive of one sort or another, or several sorts at once, since the time he fled his Orphan Court bonding back in Greene County in 1794.

"By the time I found out there was men on my trail, I had married me a girl I met in a rooming house in Memphis. That was my Matty, bless her heart. She was a lot younger than me, but had no kin, no schooling, no man, nothing but poverty and suffering ... but oh, she was a fine young woman, even if she was puny and ailing most the time. Finest soul I ever met. Even read her Bible and prayed for my soul, every day from the day she met me. I had never knowed anybody else so good. She was too fine a person for me, David; she deserved a lot better. But I was all there was for her, and she became my wife and really cared for me. She saw good in me where nobody else had, except maybe your own mother, David.

"I never had really loved nobody before Matty. She would've lived a better life before she met me if it hadn't been for a man forcing hisself on her when she was just a young girl. She bore a baby because of that, and folks wouldn't have nothing to do with her. It was like she was marked, you know. The baby was like Matty herself—on the sickly side. It didn't survive a year. She told me all about it, weeping all the while."

Again Persius briefly stopped talking, a distant, wistful look in his eye. He spoke again in a softer tone. "If I could have healed the hurts that woman carried around with her, I'd have cut off my right hand to do it. There's mysteries aplenty in this world, David Crockett, but no greater one than why good folks like my Matty have to suffer. I can understand a scoundrel like me suffering, but why her? I can't figure it."

Silence lingered. If Persius was looking for an answer to that question, David couldn't provide it. Persius cleared his throat and continued, his voice beginning to grow hoarse.

"After we hitched up, we were living in Memphis and I was doing warehouse and dock labor on the riverfront. Them rangers or detectives, or whatever you want to call them bastards that had been hired to get me, caught wind of where I was and come after me again. Matty was with child. They set our house afire and we had to flee. We almost didn't make it out of there. I killed one of the ones that done it; that was my only satisfaction.

"I didn't know where to go. Matty had no folks we could turn to, and I surely didn't. But in Memphis I had heard a lot about the famous Davy Crockett, congressman for Tennessee. Oh, I was proud of you, David. It was hard not to brag on having run with you, but I didn't want to bring down your reputation, like I've done told you. I knew where you lived, everything, and even played around with trying to visit you, but it never seemed the right thing to do. Then came the year of 'twenty-eight, right at the first of it in the bitter season. Matty had gave birth to baby

Rebecca in a cheap boardinghouse we had took a room in, and both of them were sickly. And later they caught up with us again, and put us on the run. I went for your place, David, not having anywhere else to go. Bad weather hit and Matty got sicker and sicker. She died on me not far from your house, and I carried her corpse on my shoulder until I found a place to lay her to rest. It was in a little gully close to your place. I laid her out, put a sprig of evergreen in her hands, and covered her as best I could. God, I wish I could have done more. I wish I could have buried her proper."

"Her grave was found later on, Persius. And she was reburied, in a proper grave with a cross atop it."

"I'm glad to hear it, Davy." Persius paused, swiping at moist eyes. He drew in a labored breath and went on. "Well, there I was, them men after me, rain and drizzle falling down and nigh turning to snow, and me crazy with grief over Matty. And poor little Rebecca, not more than three months old, hungry and needing her ma, yet so weak she could hardly cry. She was lying in her box of flax, the drizzle falling on her. I heard riders on the road and figured it was them hired detectives after me. I picked up Rebecca in her box and made for your house. There was no time to do nothing but tuck that silver piece in her wrap in hopes you'd recognize it and figure out she was my child. I hammered the door and ran. It was the last time I ever laid eyes on my little girl."

"God, Persius. What a sorrowful thing."

"Maybe I did the wrong thing leaving her. But you got to understand, Davy: I was being chased. I had just lost my wife, just buried her with my own hands. I was crazy with it all. Didn't know what to do, didn't know what was right or sensible. So I just left her there and ran."

"I don't fault you, Persius. You had stood up under more than most could bear already."

"The riders I had heard on the road . . . it wound up that it wasn't them detectives after all. Just travelers, that's all. I headed back to your house, but the baby had done been took inside. I stood there in the yard for the longest time, thinking maybe I should show myself ... but I didn't. I didn't know if you were there or off in Washington. One of your boys might have shot me. And there was something else too. I knowed that my little girl would have a better life in your home than ever I could give her. So I turned and went away. I've wondered ever since if I had done right by my daughter." Persius took another deep, slow breath. "Now I know it didn't matter anyways. She was bound to die. David, maybe it's my fault she died. Maybe her getting all wet and cold while I buried her ma made her take sick and ..." He trailed off and more tears came, silently.

David's heart went out to Persius. The fact was, he had been thinking the same thing, but Persius had nothing to gain by chastising himself for a tragedy long past. "What's done is done, Persius, and it's a page you can't turn again."

"I know it. God, I wish I could turn it again."

"What happened to you after that?" David asked.

"I just kept running. Working, stealing, gambling. Living my life day by day. I headed east and managed to throw them rangers off my trail, and I never saw hide nor hair of them thereafter. But now that I was safe and alive, all the things that made being safe and alive worth something were gone from me. I took to drinking a hell of a lot. Some sort of sickness got hold of me and like to have killed me. I reckon this thing I just shook off was the same sickness, come back again."

"I've had the same kind of sickness. Doc says he believes skeeters spread it to me once when I was in Alabama," David said.

Persius did not comment, his thoughts still fixed on his story. He went on. "Many a time I'd think back on little Rebecca and wonder what had become of her, and think maybe I should go and find out if she had made it through ... then I'd see myself all drunk and filthy and know that if she was alive, it was best that she never know who her father really was.

"But it ate at me, not knowing what had happened to her. I drifted here, there, all about. Then one day, after I heard you had been elected again to the Congress, I figured it out: I could come to Washington City and look you up, without your family around. I could find out what had become of my girl, but she'd never have to see me herself. She'd never have to know her father was the kind of man he was. Of course, now I know it wouldn't have mattered. My little girl is dead." He stopped, brooding.

"And so here we are, back together like the old days," David said, trying to brighten the somber atmosphere.

Persius looked at him very seriously. "No. The old days is gone. There'll never be nothing like the old days again. We've split off in two different directions, me and you. You count for something. They say you might make president someday. Me, I don't count for nothing. Never have and never will."

"You count for something to me." David said the words and meant them—and then he recalled his own selfish concerns about Persius's return and felt shamed.

"No, David, I don't count for nothing, and you know it. If I did count, you'd have put me in your storybook. But like I said, I don't blame you for leaving me out. I understand why you had to."

David's sense of shame grew until it felt a little like anger. Persius's direct words had a way of stripping off the layers of pretense and rationalization with which he had veneered so many of his thoughts and attitudes. It was an uncomfortable kind of surgery to endure, and he suddenly resented Persius for putting him through it.

And perhaps in unconscious desire to give a sting of his own in return, he said, "Persius, there's some things you must know. You said you choked that guard in the army camp until he was senseless. You did more than that. When they found him next morning, he was dead. You had killed him."

"Killed . . ." Persius looked bewildered. "I swear, I never tried to kill him. He was breathing when I left."

"Well, then he stopped breathing after. What it amounts to, Persius, is that in the eyes of the army, you murdered that man."

"I never knew!"

"That's two murders the law holds to your name. First Crider Cummings, and then that guard." David decided forthrightness was in order. "You're right, Persius. I did try to distance myself from you after you killed that guard, for the very reasons you said. I've even worried that somebody who knew us both when we were young would up and say something about Colonel Crockett having been friend to a murderer in his young days. So far that ain't happened. I don't want it to happen now."

Persius looked squarely at David. "It won't. As soon as I've got my strength, I'll be gone. I come to find out what had happened to my baby girl, and now I know. All that's left now is for me to thank you and your wife for what care you gave her in the short time she lived, and to head out. You'll never see me again."

David might have thought that those words were just what he had wanted to hear. Now that they were said, he felt otherwise.

"No, Persius. I do want to see you again. I'm a public man, but surely there's room for private friendships."

"Even with a man the law calls murderer?"

Blast it all, why did everything Persius say have to unsettle a man so? David hardly knew how to talk to him. "You're no murderer at heart."

"There's several dead men that might say different, if they could."

"Hang it, Persius, just shut up about all such as that! You rest now, and I'll come back tomorrow and see how you're doing. I've got business I've got to attend to tonight."

David left, and spent the evening with Thomas Chilton, working hard on the autobiography. Throughout, he was painfully conscious each time he omitted or disguised the person of Persius Tarr in his story, but made sure he gave no hints of it to Chilton. He went to bed late, and didn't sleep well.

Congressional concerns occupied him all the next day, from breakfast until well past supper, and that night he received an unscheduled visit at his rooms from Whig strategists putting together a grand tour for the famed Colonel Crockett, to take place in the spring. By the time they were done, it was too late to go visit Persius, despite his promise. He retired, pledging to himself that calling on Persius would be his first order of business the next morning.

He rose with the dawn, washed and dressed, and headed for Ibbotson's. When he got there the old doctor was already up and about.

"He's not here, David. When I went in to see him this morning, he was gone."

"Gone . . . where?"

"I don't know. Just gone. I'm not surprised. He seems the wandering type. Come and go without word to anyone. I regret he's gone, oddly enough. You'll have to tell me more about him. I know he is quite the ruffian, but I find I rather like him, somehow. I'm not sure just why."

"I know what you mean," David said. He felt dejected and sad, remembering Persius's comment that they would probably never see one another again. "I like him too. More now than I ever did before, strange to say."

"You think you'll run across him again?"

"He said I wouldn't. But I hope I do. I really hope I do."

Chapter 50

Days of intense, slavish labor brought the biography into being at last. It was entitled *A Narrative of the Life of David Crockett of the State of Tennessee, Written by Himself*, and published by E. L. Carey and A. Hart of Philadelphia and Carey, Hart & Company of Baltimore. Its form followed the standard autobiographical pattern laid out by Benjamin Franklin in his famed literary self-portrait. David Crockett thought his book was as fine a volume as he had ever seen, right up there with Franklin's in quality.

The story it contained came almost entirely from David himself. The language was a combination of David's and Thomas Chilton's. David had put the final touch on the volume by writing a preface in which he stated, "The whole book is my own, and every sentiment and sentence in it. I would not be such a fool, or knave either, as to deny that I have had it hastily run over by a friend or so, and that some little alterations have been made in the spelling and grammar; and I am not so sure that it is not the worse of even that, for I despise this way of spelling contrary to nature."

He concluded with a declaration that the book is "truly the very thing itself—the exact image of its Author," and signed his name at the bottom.

At that point Chilton had breathed a sigh of relief. For a book in which David Crockett had supposedly written "every sentence," the representative from Kentucky had certainly spent a lot of hours with pen in cramped hand and eyes glazing over from labor. But he did not mind the anonymity of his contribution. This book was designed to add to the glory of Colonel David Crockett for the sake of the Whig party. It was never intended to be a vehicle for Thomas Chilton.

David's declarations that his book was complete and always reliable were, of course, not fully true. In its pages he presented himself as more unsophisticated than he truly was, for the image of an unsophisticated man of native wisdom was attractive to those who mistrusted educated, silver-tongued politicians. David had played to such perceptions quite successfuly in the past, and now, thanks to Nimrod Wildfire and an abundance of colorful newspaper anecdotes about "Canebrake Davy," the picture of Crockett as the Unschooled Everyman was all the more exploitable.

For similar motives, subtle changes had been made in the *Narrative*'s presentation of David's Creek War military record. For example, he failed to record some of his advances in rank. After all, for a man who was "common as a coon spoor in a barley patch" (not to mention a congressman who had supported the elimination of the highbrow military academy at West Point), it simply sounded better to portray himself as nothing but a common soldier, first to last. And since he was a well-known opponent of Andrew Jackson, it had seemed expedient to alter the record of the length of time he had volunteered for Creek War service and to present himself as a participant in, rather than a mere observer of, the "mutiny" attempted against Jackson by some of his disgruntled volunteer troops. David and the Whigs liked the notion of presenting the protagonist of the *Narrative* as a man unwilling to bow before "King Andrew" from the days the Fates had first thrown the two together. There were other little shifts of facts as well, all designed to give the reader the impression of Crockett as a hardworking, humble soldier who had done his duty, yet without letting General Jackson lord over him.

One matter that David would not allow to be fully distorted or softened, despite the pleas of his political advisors, was the horror of the massacre at Tallusahatchee. Even though minor expunging was done at editorial insistence, he resolved that the worst of the horrors he had witnessed should remain. And they did, in gritty, unsoftened detail. He wrote of the old woman who had fired the fatal arrow from the doorway, only to die with "at least twenty balls blown through her"; and the Indians who were slaughtered "like dogs" inside the house she had guarded; and the wounded young Indian boy who had crawled beside the burning house with "the grease stewing out of him" from the heat; and the hungry soldiers eating potatoes baked in the cellar below that same burning house, potatoes that had cooked in the "oil of the Indians we had burned up on the day before" and which looked like they had been "stewed with fat meat." David Crockett knew very well the hideousness of war and despised what had been done to Indian women and children in particular. He would not let the account of such a massacre be perfumed with rosewater and pawned off as a Sunday school picnic. He had stood up for the Indians on the floor of Congress; he would not cease to do so now.

There were, however, plenty of matters having to do with individual personalities that David did not hold sacrosanct at all. Persius Tarr, of course, was absent or disguised throughout. And David portrayed his occasionally tense relationship with his father in a less truthful way than had Clarke's *Life and Adventures*—though the episode of the drunken chase with the hickory pole remained intact. Clarke's book had made that adventure too famous to be ignored.

Then there was the matter of names. Many were left out either because they were forgotten, or seemed irrelevant, or simply because of a quirk in David's personality that made him reluctant to publish them. He named few of his siblings and childhood companions. Absent also were the names of Amy Sumner and Margaret Elder, his first loves. More remarkable still, nowhere in the book did he call by name either of his wives, or any of his children by either marriage.

Chilton had gently suggested that such omissions might seem astonishing and inexplicable to some readers, but David would hear no such arguments. He declared that his instincts told him it was right to leave the names out, and whenever he was sure he was right, by heaven, he always went ahead. It was his very motto, printed right on the frontispiece of the *Narrative*. Chilton shrugged and did it Crockett's way, though he could still not see any sense in leaving out the names.

Despite such trivial disagreements, both men were generally pleased with the book. Certainly it was sometimes uneven in its style, sometimes skipped several years in its chronology, had a few errors of dating and such brought on by the haste of its production, and included quite a few misspellings—David's beloved old Quaker mentor John Canaday having become John "Kennedy," for example—but as a political volume, it was an improvement over *Life and Adventures*, and because it was an autobiography, would surely supercede that earlier volume in popularity and authority . . . all the better for the Whigs.

The *Narrative* done and off the press, David turned his attention to the next phase of the great Whig campaign of status-building: the Great Tour of the North and East.

On the surface it was a simple promotional tour for the *Narrative*; in fact it was more a promotional tour for David Crockett himself. Plans were afoot for another book, shaped by Whig political interests, to be published the next year detailing events on the tour, and certainly the tour itself would expose the colorful and entertaining "Gentleman from the Cane" to many potential voters in the next presidential election. There were other books in consideration as well, to be written by others and credited to Crockett; a satirical, biting "biography" of current vice-president Martin Van Buren being one. Van Buren, despised by David Crockett, was expected to be the man upon whose shoulders Old Hickory's mantle would fall.

David was concerned that the tour would start while Congress was still in session. His absence from the floor would cause him to miss votes and certainly would be used as propaganda against him. "Don't worry," the Whig strategists reassured him. "The tour will be so grand, so splendid, that people will scarcely notice." So he didn't worry. When it came down to it, David Crockett was an overly trusting man, trusting to the point of being naive— just as Campbell Ibbotson had so often tried to warn him.

He left Washington on April 25 with his entourage and traveled to Baltimore's Barnum's Hotel, dining there with some fellow Whigs before spending the night. He set out on the next day, dressed in gentleman's clothing, his dark hair neatly parted in the center and combed back to expose whiskers grown down the sides of his face in the style that would later be called sideburns. He traveled by steamer across the Chesapeake, disembarked and took a train to Delaware City, returned to a steamer to travel up the Delaware River and on to Philadelphia.

At each stop he had made, he was met by cheering crowds. He could tell that some were surprised to see the figure of a nicely clothed, fine-featured gentleman rather than a real-life, buckskinned Nimrod Wildfire, but if they were disappointed, their accolades didn't indicate it. In Philadelphia he regurgitated one of the speeches prefabricated for him by Whig writers, then was driven to the United States Hotel, very heartened, and eager now for the rest of his tour.

While in Philadelphia he made stops at prominent places such as a mint, asylum, waterworks, Navy Yard, school, theater, and the exchange, and delivered a fierce speech against Jackson. He was given a watch-chain seal engraved with his famed motto, and informed that he would later be presented with an excellent, ornamented rifle, courtesy of the Philadelphia Whigs. Very fine, he declared. A man from the cane always needs good weaponry.

On April 29 he sailed up the Delaware, railroaded across New Jersey to Perth Amboy, and then ventured on to New York City. Ensconced in the American Hotel, he remained in New York until the afternoon of May 2, making speeches, greeting crowds, meeting dignitaries, and visiting important spots, including the Stock Exchange, where he fired off another rousing oratorical discharge of Whig propaganda.

On May 1 he felt fatigued and sick to his stomach, making only a brief appearance at the Bowery Theatre. Had the event not been advertised in advance, he might have passed it up altogether. He returned to his room and took some extra rest, fearing his old malaria was about to recur. But the next morning he felt much better, and jumped heartily back into action. He traveled to Jersey City to participate in a rifle shooting exhibition before heading back to New York to catch a steamer for Boston.

Crockett and company stopped in Newport and Providence, and made it the rest of the way to Boston by stagecoach, arriving the afternoon of the third. Once again he was swept through tours and meetings. He was given a hunting coat in Roxborough, before heading to a Whig banquet that evening for another harangue against Jackson.

For the next few days he continued touring the area, heading into Lowell for more gifts, banqueting, and speaking, returning to Boston on May 8. There he visited the home of the lieutenant governor, made a theater appearance, and on the ninth headed by stagecoach into Providence, Rhode Island; then shortly afterward to Camden, New Jersey. There he spoke to a large group, then boated to Philadelphia for another appearance there. On the thirteenth he was back in Baltimore, and after another public appearance, hopped on a Washington-bound stage. The tour was not over; it was merely in respite. When Congress concluded its session, David would head out on the final leg.

He was tired but happy as he rode back into Washington. Long gone from his mind was the memory of his brothers, caught in a canoe on the Nolichucky River with the oar in the hands of someone else. So what if Whig leaders were steering his political canoe? They seemed to be doing a good job of it. Based on his reception at each stop, he was convinced that his popularity and potential were greater than he had previously thought. And gone was any sense of restraint in his attacks on Andrew Jackson. He had been speaking before receptive Whig audiences for days, and their vigorous cheers at his sallies against the President had rendered him fearless.

Too fearless, some Whigs began to say. Too fierce a polemic against Jackson might blow up in their faces. But David didn't listen. He was soaring now. There was no reason to descend.

With a sense of reluctance, he returned to finish the session of Congress, and during the same period sat for a portrait by John Gadsby Chapman. He wasn't much pleased with the initial version, a standard bust-type portrait that he said made him look like "a sort of a cross between a clean-shirted member of Congress and a Methodist preacher." What would Chapman think about painting him as he might look on one of his bear hunts back in West Tennessee? That would be a picture worth looking at. The painter was pleased with the suggestion, and David set about looking for the right props and accoutrements.

To Chapman's surprise, David managed to scout out a dingy linsey-woolsey hunting shirt as well as leggings and moccasins—no small feat in the sophisticated city of Washington. He also rounded up what he called the "tools" of hunting: butcher knife, rifle, powder horn, bullet pouch, hatchet. David was insistent that his tools be placed in precisely the right order on his person: butcher knife in easy reach of his right hand, along with the horn and pouch, the hatchet placed on his left hip, shoved in handle first and placed far enough back not to interfere with the handling of his rifle. Posing full-body at semiprofile, his rifle cradled across his left arm, his wide-brimmed flop hat nestled on his head, with his long, dark locks flowing out from beneath it and down the back of his neck, David made an impressive sight—even if the years had added a few inches to what in youthful years had been a lean midsection.

But as the full-sized painting progressed, Chapman

grew unhappy with it, yet could not say just why. David himself unwittingly provided the solution when he strode in one morning to pose and, in a show of high spirits, let out a loud whoop, raising his hat and waving it in the air. Chapman immediately realized what was lacking, and at once set out revising the painting to show the hat uplifted in David's right hand. The result, with hunting dogs painted in around Crockett's legs, was a grand-looking portrait with a cheery quality—Colonel Crockett in his element, looking grandiosely into the distance, hat uplifted as he greeted his future. It befitted the cheerful spirit David was showing these days. His fame was mounting, his prospects brightening, and the *Narrative* was already in its sixth printing.

On June 29 the tour resumed. David rode by stage-coach for Baltimore, arriving that evening. On the next day he was in Philadelphia, having traveled there by boat, and was put up again in the United States Hotel.

The next evening he was presented with the rifle pledged to him on his first visit. It was a beautiful, octagon-barreled rifle, one he promptly dubbed "Pretty Betsey" to distinguish it from the rifle he actually used, simply "Betsey." He also received various accoutrements for the rifle, a gleaming butcher knife, and a shining silver tomahawk with his name engraved in script on the head. He made a gracious thank-you speech and was given a cheer in response.

The next day he traveled to Camden, New Jersey, and there fired off his new rifle a few times. When July Fourth came, he was in Philadelphia with a slew of senators, including the famed Daniel Webster. At the Music Fund Hall he joined other speakers, raging about the "tyranny" of Andrew Jackson. Later in the day he spoke again at another gathering, and at an even later theater appearance was called on to speak a third time. He did so with gusto, raging against Jackson at full boil until his voice was gone.

On the fifth, David took his rest and received more

gifts: gunpowder and a china pitcher. The next day he rode the train across Pennsylvania. His voice was still weak and hoarse, and when at one stop a glass was put in his hand and he was called upon to make a toast, he lifted the glass and rasped out: "God bless you, for I can't." But then, somehow, he managed to croak out one more speech.

At Pittsburgh he boarded the *Hunter* and traveled down the Ohio river. By July 12 he was in Cincinnati; the next day he was on the move again, toward Louisville. There he stayed several days, making visits and speaking. Going into Indiana, he spoke at Jeffersonville Springs, and after embarking on the steamer *Scotland*, reached Mill's Point.

His son William was there, awaiting him, and they journeyed together toward Gibson County and home.

The Great Tour was over. By now David was glad it was done, because he had grown very weary. *But hadn't it been grand!* He had to smile when he recalled the cheering throngs, the famous hands shaking his, the gifts and flattering comments.

Surely David Crockett's glory-time had come. The future he surveyed ahead of him was a landscape bright with glory and fame, and across its broad distance, becoming ever more visible through the haze, loomed the image of the White House, home of his despised fellow Tennessean Andrew Jackson. Not for long, though, David told himself. Before long it would be the home of another man from Tennessee. David couldn't picture it falling out any other way.

Chapter 51

In the fall of 1835, old John Crockett breathed his last, and David was made administrator of his will. Through his youth, David's relationship with his father had been like a river that was smooth and tranquil at places, rocky and swift in others. Sometimes it had seemed to David that all he could remember were the rocky stretches, but now, with his father's body laid under the soil, he remembered more of the good times: their hunts together, his father's hands demonstrating the skills necessary to backwoods living, and the times John had actually bothered to praise one of his boyish achievements. He recalled the tears his father had shed the time he worked off the debt to John Canaday on his behalf, and the way in recent years that John had bragged to all who came within hearing distance about his famed congressman son. Now that John Crockett was gone, David wished he had taken more time to be with the old man in his later years. There had always been so much to do, so many distractions ... no matter now. The past couldn't be changed. John Crockett was gone, and David was going to miss him. He took comfort that his mother was still alive, living now about five miles away, with one of his sisters.

Pondering his father, David wondered what was left of the man in his own person. He could see much of John Crockett in his brothers, but he had seldom thought much about what aspects of his father were incarnated in him. Did he have much of his looks, his temperament? Sadly, the one common characteristic he could think of was a depressing one: both he and his father were lifelong companions to poverty. Fame and congressional power had done little to erase David's debts. Even now David had to turn to a friend, William Tucker, to borrow about three hundred dollars before his return to Washington in November.

Back in Washington, he was soon drawn into an effort to halt Andrew Jackson's plan to make Martin Van Buren his political successor. A more popular name among the Tennessee congressional delegation was that of Knoxville's Senator Hugh Lawson White, a handsome and dignified man held in esteem by the people. The effort, initiated by Jacksonian Democrats who didn't favor Van Buren, eventually expanded to involve the Whigs as well, when Jackson held firm and would not relinquish Van Buren. White was thrust into the race as an independent, and Democrats who were secretly disgruntled with Jackson supported him. Meanwhile, members of the Massachusetts delegation put out Daniel Webster as another alternate candidate, and the Whigs rubbed their hands in glee at this dividing of Democratic forces, hoping the result would be loss of a Democratic majority in the presidential race, throwing it to the House of Representatives.

David stayed busy in the anti–Van Buren effort, helping create a humorous parody letter that mocked Van Buren while pretending to praise him. And he turned attention as well to concerns of his constituents back home—Ibbotson having reminded him sternly that by becoming so distracted by political squabbles with the Jacksonians, he was on the verge of neglecting the duties he was actually elected to perform.

David entered a resolution for the improvement of various Tennessee rivers, arguing that this would be important to national defense should any force ever invade the United States by way of New Orleans. The measure was promptly voted down, adding to his troublingly long list of lawmaking failures.

David turned to his old battle standard, the West Tennessee land bill. He struggled to have the measure debated again on the floor, but despite some assistance from other West Tennessee representatives, the rest of the Tennessee delegation would not cooperate. David began to worry about his chances for reelection. His hopes for an eventual presidential nomination depended upon his being returned to the House—and yet he had little by way of success to show his constituents back home.

January of 1836 brought David a double blow. The first was confirmation of longstanding rumors that his opponent in the next congressional race would be the clever Adam Huntsman, who was said to be telling one and all that he had toured virtually the entire congressional district and found evidence that David's popularity was greatly declining. "I begin to believe I can beat Davy," Huntsman had written to James K. Polk. Success with his land bill would give David an advantage, Huntsman said, but otherwise "the conflict will not be a difficult one."

This kind of talk inevitably filtered back to David, and began to unsettle him. His great tour of the prior year might have bolstered his confidence of national popularity—yet what good would that do him if his own neighbors decided to evict him from Congress? He realized he might have been better served to spend less time symbolically battling Andrew Jackson and company, and more time seeing to the practical needs of his constituents. Hadn't Campbell Ibbotson said a thing or two about that before? David hadn't listened.

And then the second blow fell. In mid-February, Ibbotson suffered another stroke, far worse than the first. He lived only two days. David lingered at his graveside in the snow long after the other mourners had left. He felt very alone now, and realized how much he had relied upon the practical-minded old doctor for advice and support. Ibbotson had become his family away from home, his chief unofficial advisor, aide, and mentor.

But there was too much at hand for David to spend

an inordinate time in grief. Huntsman posed a tremendous challenge, and he knew it. Even Huntsman's wooden leg, about which David was sorely tempted to make jokes, was a political advantage. He had lost his real leg during distinguished service in the Creek War, and its wooden replacement was like an eternally visible reminder or badge of his military sacrifice. Furthermore, Huntsman was clever, witty, and well-liked by the abundant West Tennessee supporters of Andrew Jackson.

The short session of Congress ended, and David turned his full attention to getting reelected. Meanwhile, the Whigs put out two books under his name, one of them the aggrandized account of the prior year's tour, the other a scandalously insulting "biography" of Martin Van Buren. Crockett had very little involvement in either volume other than gathering newspaper clippings to be rewritten for the tour book and allowing his name to be placed on the Van Buren volume.

More interesting and amusing to David himself than either of the official Whig publications was an almanac that had burst upon the scene late in 1834 and spread widely throughout 1835. Published in Nashville by a firm that—with tongue firmly in cheek—billed itself as Snag and Sawyer, the wildly illustrated volume was entitled *Davy Crockett's Almanack of Wild Sports of the West and Life in the Backwoods, Calculated for all the States in the Union*. At the top, in quotation marks and above pictures of a wolf and dog, were the words "Go Ahead!" abbreviated out of David's famous motto, "Be always sure you are right, then go ahead!" In the midst of the 1835 date printed in huge type at the bottom center of the cover was a caricature of a black, rod-toting fisherman with a top hat, a pained expression, and a fish hanging by the mouth from his left little finger. That image pretty much set the tone for the contents. In some respects it was a typical almanac, featuring planting tables, astronomical data, moon phase forecasts, weather predictions, sayings, recipes, jokes, and the like. But mixed throughout were wild tall tales and anecdotes of which Crockett was the hero—the screamer Crockett; the half-alligator, half-panther Crockett; the wild-man Crockett cast in the Nimrod Wildfire image. David found it all very funny, but worried some about it as well. He wondered if the wild, tall-tale renderings of himself did all that much to advance the fortunes of the real man.

He campaigned hard through the summer, staying so busy that he gave only scant attention to another matter of great national interest taking place in the Mexican possession called Texas, home to many transplanted Americans. The dictatorial president, Santa Anna, was gradually tightening his grip on all of Mexico. Relationships between the American Texans and the Mexican ruler had become so strained that in June a young, tall, somewhat moralistic native South Carolinian named William Barrett Travis had raised a company of volunteers who captured and disarmed a Mexican garrison at Anahuac. Many predicted that more such militaristic activities would take place in Texas before the antagonisms were settled.

In less pressed times, David had thought about Texas. There was reported to be good land there, available in quantities of more than four thousand acres per settling family, at only a few cents per acre. The Mexican government itself, now independent of Spain, had been encouraging Americans to come in. Depending on how governmental matters fell out, it was a land with a future. The kind of place a man could go and build a fortune if he was savvy. From time to time David had thought half seriously that he ought to make a journey to Texas, especially if his political fortunes turned sour. But of course, that wouldn't happen. His destiny was the White House itself.

Or so he had thought, until the advent of the current campaign against Huntsman. Now he wasn't so sure.

In the summer, David was jolted by yet another personal loss when his mother died. This struck him even harder than the death of his father. How many times had he lay awake at night as a small child, wondering what would happen to him and how he would make it through if his mother died? He had not had to endure that kind of loss as a boy, and was thankful for that. But now, even as a man—a man so reputedly superhuman that it was widely rumored he was going to wring the very tail off of Halley's Comet as it passed through the 1835 evening skies— the loss of Rebecca Crockett made him a boy again. He cried quite a lot, always in secret.

Meanwhile, Huntsman and the Jacksonians continued to batter him politically. Jackson himself allowed Huntsman to use his franking privileges to send copies of the pro-Jacksonian Washington *Globe* to post offices throughout Crockett's congressional district. David brought this to the attention of the press, but the clever Huntsman replied, truthfully, that David had used his own franking privileges to steadily flood his district with anti-Jackson material, a full twenty thousand pieces of it. Surely what was sauce for the goose was sauce for the gander as well.

David resorted to more serious charges. The Union Bank, he declared, was offering twenty-five dollars to any voter who would pledge for Huntsman. Huntsman's reply, and the bank's, was that if the esteemed Crockett intended to make such charges, let him present the evidence of its truth. And then Huntsman offered up the reminder that he, unlike his opponent, had never paid for a vote with gifts of liquor. It was a cutting and effective comment in a constituency of voters who knew that Crockett had greased his political skids with gifts of liquor, tobacco, and the like.

As the summer passed, David felt his confidence slipping. Hammered by deaths of family and friends, surprised by a vigorous Huntsman campaign, and dismayed by mounting evidence that his constituency was not overwhelmingly behind him, he waited for the August vote with a trepidation he dared not show.

David Crockett lay in bed, listening to the soft snoring of Adam Huntsman, who slept in the same room. He marveled at how odd a situation politics could put a man into. He rolled over on his side and looked across toward Huntsman's bed. The lawyer's wooden leg leaned against the wall near the head of the bed. David peered at it, resenting it for the political advantage he believed it gave his opponent.

Who wouldn't be impressed with a man who had literally given part of himself in battle, yet who retained intelligence, charm, wit, political capability? And to make it all the worse for David, women clearly thought Huntsman was quite a specimen, even if he had only five toes between him and the earth. David had noted the way they gazed adoringly at the man when he spoke. And he had heard the stories about Huntsman's alleged reputation as a ladies' man.

Drat it all, David thought. It's hard enough to have to share the stump with that joke-cracking jackass, much less have to sleep in the same room with him! It was enough to rob a man of what good humor he had left.

The situation in which David found himself had come up naturally enough, and was actually common in country politics. He and Huntsman had been traveling together, debating one another and presenting their standard speeches, and this night, in a farmhouse near Memphis, they had been put up by the same farmer, who lodged them in the same room. Huntsman seemed quite comfortable here— and well he should be, David thought resentfully, given that their common host clearly had cast his support to Huntsman. He had been cordial and impartial in his hospitality, but his talk had made his political leanings very clear.

David was drifting toward sleep, half-closed eyes still gazing at the moonlight-illuminated outline of Huntsman's wooden leg, when the thought came that it would be a fine, satisfying thing to somehow rob Huntsman of their host's vote. Then an inspiration struck that wiped away all weariness, and David sat up in bed, grinning.

His mind went back to what his wife had said after his last political loss, something about David Crockett having lost his famous sense of humor. . . . Well, this night he would show that nobody could rightly make that charge in *this* campaign!

Rising silently, careful not to waken Huntsman, David reached over and gently laid the wooden leg on the floor beside the bed, arranging its straps to make it appear it had been hurriedly tossed down. Then he tiptoed across the room, picked up a straight-backed wooden chair, and held it to himself as he slipped through the door and out. He carefully, silently, closed the door behind him.

He was on the back porch of the farmhouse now. On the other side of the porch was another door, leading into another bedroom—the bedroom of the young, unmarried, breathtakingly beautiful daughter of their host.

David crept to the door, took a deep breath, and then loudly rattled the latch, bumping his shoulder against the door as if trying to force his way in. He heard movement on the other side of the door. He bumped it again, and a loud scream of pure feminine terror erupted from inside.

Turning, David put one foot into a rung of the chair and held it so that only one chair leg touched the wooden porch. Then hurriedly he hobbled back toward his own room, using the chair to make a noise precisely like that of a man wearing a wooden leg.

Good timing was essential now. David entered his room and quickly closed the door behind him. He gingerly set the chair back into its place and slipped into his own bed, as elsewhere in the house a tumult arose. The old farmer had heard the racket at his daughter's bedroom door and the noise of what had sounded for all the world like a peg-legged man rushing across the back porch.

David pulled the covers to his chin and squeezed his eyes tightly shut. He heard muffled voices—the farmer's, the daughter's. Then the farmer's voice again, louder, and swearing fiercely. Stifling the urge to burst into laughter, David began to snore.

The door all but burst from its hinges. The farmer, wearing a long nightshirt and holding a lighted lamp aloft, filled the doorway. David peeped out from nearly closed eyelids. He hadn't seen a face showing that much fury since the time his own father had chased him with a hickory pole.

"Adam Huntsman, you peg-legged dog, you womanizing child of Satan, I'm a-going to kill you dead, here and now!" the farmer bellowed. Huntsman, jolted from a deep sleep, gave a sort of spasm beneath his covers and sat up. "I'm going to beat you to death with your own leg, you tomcat, and enjoy doing it!" He hove into the room and rounded the foot of David's bed.

"What's wrong?" Huntsman asked in a scratchy voice. "I don't understand . . . *waaaauuugh!*"

The farmer had grabbed the wooden leg from the floor and was raising it aloft like a club over Huntsman. Meanwhile, David had sat up, pretending to have been awakened by the noise.

"Whoa, whoa, now!" he yelled, throwing off his covers and jumping out of bed. He grabbed the wooden leg as it began its downswing. The farmer cursed and tried to pull free, but David was stronger and wrested the leg from him.

"I'm a-going to kill him, I am!" the farmer bellowed to David. He was trembling in fury. "He tried to bust in on my little girl!" He aimed his finger at Huntsman. "I don't stand for that, not even from you, Adam Huntsman! You think that because you have my vote—*had* my vote, I ought to say, because you surely don't now—that you can ruin the honor of a pure young woman?"

"I don't know what you're—"

"Don't go playing the saint with me, you footless scoundrel! I heerd that leg of yours, knocking on the boards of the porch."

"I swear, sir, I don't know what you mean."

"Easy now, everyone," David said. "I believe we'd best let some tempers cool. Sir, I'm sorry for what my opponent here has done. I believe perhaps the loveliness of your daughter got the best of his judgment. I promise you I'll keep an eye on him the rest of the night, and come sunup, we'll go our way and leave you and your daughter in peace. You can count on David Crockett, sir."

"Well, I—the devil! I ought to kill him!"

"That'd do nothing but bring you trouble; more than Mr. Huntsman is worth. I promise: I'll keep him penned the rest of the night. You've got the pledge of Colonel David Crockett on that, and my pledge is better than a paid bond."

The old man calmed himself. "Very well. That's good enough for me. And you, Colonel Crockett, have my vote—and the vote of every other man I can turn away from that stump-swinging scoundrel a-lying yonder!"

"I do appreciate that, sir. I'm proud to have your support."

When the farmer was gone, Huntsman said, "What in heaven's name was that all about?"

"Just forget about it, Adam. It's late, and we both need our sleep. Good night."

David closed his eyes, warm with satisfaction, and enjoyed the best night's sleep he had experienced in months.

Late August, 1835

Elizabeth Crockett walked quietly into the bedroom. David was there already, lying on his back in the bed, hands behind his head and eyes fixed on the ceiling. A lamp burned dimly on the bedside stand. The window was open and a warm breeze blew through the room, making the lamp flame flicker in the bowl.

She walked to him slowly, her dress rustling softly, and sat down on the foot of the bed. Reaching out, she laid her hand on his knee.

"You fought it well, husband," she said. "You can be proud of the fight, even without the victory."

He said nothing for a moment. Then, "It was so close, Betsy. Forty-four hundred votes for Crockett . . . but forty-six hundred fifty-two for old Peg-leg. I'm lying here and wondering what I could have done that would have made the difference. Defeated by two hundred fifty-two votes! God!"

"You did all you could, and there's nothing to be sorrowful about. We're still living. We still have our home, our children. Each other. What did you lose that really matters?"

He sat up so abruptly she gasped. His brown eyes flashed angrily and he put his hand on her wrist, gripping it painfully tight. "What have I lost? Any reasonable chance to ever be President of the United States of America! God in heaven, woman, you don't believe that really matters?"

Eyes wide, lips parted, she stared at him like he was a stranger. As she watched him, his lip trembled and his eyes grew wet with tears. His grip on her wrist loosened, then released.

"Betsy, I'm sorry, I'm sorry. Forgive me, please. I didn't mean—"

He sobbed aloud and turned away to hide his face. He was still as ashamed of tears as he had been while a boy.

"David . . . it's all right. My words were poor-chosen. Of course it matters. Of course it does. I was just trying to tell you that not everything is gone. That's all." She touched his quaking shoulder. "Oh, Davy. My Davy."

"I'm ashamed for you to see me now," he said in a choking voice. "Go away from me, please. Leave me alone for a little while."

For a moment she remained, about to speak, but then she closed her lips and rose without words, blew out the lamp and left him alone in the dark room.

Part 6

HELL AND TEXAS

Chapter 52

October 1835

Elizabeth Crockett's attempt at a smile was valiantly performed but unconvincing. David looked at her keenly and said, "You don't favor the idea, I can see."

"Why do you say . . ." She faltered away to momentary silence. "You've always seen clean through me, ain't you, husband?"

"Don't you see, Betsy? It's a fine opportunity for us. They say the land is good there, and easy to obtain. It's an opening country, the kind where a man like me can set an early foothold and then climb. There'll be towns growing, governments forming. I could go far there, and get out of this debt and trouble that has plagued us so."

"It's so far away, David. Texas!"

"Not as far away as Washington City. And it would be only an exploration, like the one I made that time into Alabama. If the prospects look good, then we could put our names down for land and move on in."

He paused, waiting for an answer. She gave none.

He gave a snort of mild but growing exasperation. "Well, tell me this, Betsy: If not Texas, then where? You believe our fortunes will improve if we stay rooted right here? I'm ready for new country and new starts. This old state is a well that's run dry for the Crocketts. We need to sink a new one."

"I don't know what it is, David. The very name of Texas strikes a fear into me. I suppose it's because of the trouble there."

"There's always trouble when you've got colonists from one land shifting in under a new government. Such affairs will be settled in time. It's a chance for us to plant our stake in something that's going to grow and turn rich."

She said nothing, her face set in a frown. There was no point in trying to cover her true feelings any longer. He saw it and glowered.

"Hang it, Betsy, I'll be shot if I can understand a woman! Can't you see the sense in what I've been saying?"

"Of course I can. A woman has a mind just like a man."

"Well, if you see the sense in it, why do you stand there looking so unhappy about it?"

"Because there's something fearful in it, no matter what you say, and I can't put a finger on what it is."

"If you can't put a finger on it, why worry about it?"

"I can't help it."

"You know my rule, Betsy. Always be sure you are—"

"Yes, yes, yes, God knows I know your rule! Don't I know I've had to put up with aplenty of hardship because of your 'going ahead,' regardless of what anybody else thinks of it! And I know you'll 'go ahead' to Texas, whatever I may say, and so why do we stand here wasting our words? Go on with you! Go to Texas! There's nary a thing I can do to stop you!"

He glared at her bitterly, turned on his heel and stalked away. She heard the door slam. Thank God there was no one here at the moment but David and herself. She didn't like the family witnessing this kind of squabble between them. It was only too bad that she and David had such a history of them.

She went to the table and sank listlessly into a chair. Idly, she picked up a gourd dipper someone had left on the table rather than returning it to the water bucket by the stove. Looking around the room, she viewed the meager but personally precious possessions her life here had brought her. David's "Pretty Betsey" rifle, its barrel two inches shorter than originally, since David had cut it down to suit him better, hung on pegs on the far wall, with other relics of David's grand tour nearby it. A corner cupboard stood across from where she sat, its doors open to reveal an assortment of simple but attractive china and pewterware. A Revere lantern sat on a chest of drawers beside a clock that David had never gotten around to properly hanging on the wall, and off in the corner beside a chest was the rocking wooden cradle in which she had once laid her infants and now couldn't bring herself to part with. The old cane-bottomed high chair was there too, with a ratty quilt draped over it. On the wall hung samplers she had made on the many long nights David was far away in Washington, and on the bed was a big quilt comprised of pieces of cloth taken from countless worn-out pairs of breeches, scraps of petticoats, linsey-woolsey shirts, and even a piece from one of David's cast-off cravats. Much love and family heritage had gone into that quilt, not to mention countless careful stitches and a lot of eyestrain from the times she had worked on it by candle or lamplight. Yonder, beyond the sprawling rug made from the skin of one of the countless bears David had brought in on his hunts, stood her well-used butter churn, its long dasher handle smoothed and worn thin in the middle. Over by the bed was a nicely varnished washstand with basin and pitcher, with a couple of hand-embroidered towels hanging on the stand's built-in wooden rack.

Just common goods in a common house, but she loved them, and it. And long ago she had grown accustomed to debt and squeezing by from one year to the next. She could endure that, to some measure, indefinitely, as long as she had her home and a few personal treasures, and her husband close at hand. As long as David could hunt and as long as she could garden, they would have food for the table. And there would be good years for their crops, and opportunities to buy and sell livestock and such.

Bit by bit they could better their situation, just staying right here.

But David was David; he was not one to stay still for long. His mind and heart were set on Texas, and nothing a wife could do or say would make any real difference.

Sighing, she stood and carried the gourd dipper over to the water bucket. Then she brushed down her apron and left the house. In the yard she cupped her hand over her eyes against the orange light of the setting sun and looked for David. There he was, silhouetted against the sunset, slicing a quid of tobacco while giving the dogs a run. She strode toward him.

"Pretty sky this evening," she said.

"Humph."

"Davy, go on to Texas. It's all right. I'm sorry for acting as I did."

He looked at her evaluatively, as if wondering whether she really meant it.

"I admit that I don't feel happy about the prospect of moving so far away. I'm happy here. But if you believe it should be Texas for us, so be it."

His face brightened. "You really would go along with it?"

"Yes." She tried to put some spark into the word, but it still came out in a tone of resignation. David didn't seem to notice.

"Good, Betsy, good." He put away his knife and faced her, extending his arms and cupping her shoulders in his hands. "If we should go there, we probably wouldn't be alone. William and Abner are wanting to come with me, and Lindsey Tinkle too. We might find ourselves surrounded by friends and kinfolk. It'd be hardly different than being here."

So why go? Elizabeth thought, but did not ask.

"I'm pleased you've changed your mind, Betsy. I'll not be gone that long, and I'll be back with good news. It's in Texas my destiny lies. I know that it is."

His destiny. Once again he was thinking like a lone wolf, as was his habit far too often, in Elizabeth's book.

She put her arms around him and hugged him. *Don't go, David. Please don't go.* The thought was like a shout in her mind, but she didn't verbalize it. She had yielded outwardly to David's plans, knowing that she really had no choice, but her heart remained unpersuaded. The thought of Texas still made her heart race unaccountably in fear.

Perhaps David's intuition was that Texas held his destiny. Hers was that it held nothing but trouble. There was no way she could see how both could be right.

Three Days Later

Even as a defeated congressman, Colonel David Crockett still could draw a crowd—this kind of crowd in particular. He was seated on the porch of a small general store, cup of cider in one hand and hunk of cheese in the other, while a gaggle of rough-hewn backwoodsmen with whiskers overhanging their lips and shreds of tobacco from yesterday's last chew still filling the gaps between their coated teeth, were gathered around. This was a far cry from the besuited, cravat-wearing congressional crowd David had moved among in Washington, or the nicely dressed, dignified city folk who had cheered him during his northern tour—but a crowd was a crowd, and this one suited him fine. He had grown up among this breed of men, had herded cattle and hauled cargo with them, had seen countless numbers of them eat and drink in his father's tavern in Jefferson County. Among such he could relax and be fully himself, with no pomposities around to sniff at him for it.

"What you going to do down there in the Texas, Dave? You going to sire you some half-Mex young'uns?"

"Lord, no, Jimbo. Betsy'd make a gelding of me, sure as the world, if such a thing happened. No, I'll ride through and pick me a fine spot, plant me a coin or two in the earth, then come back home and fetch the family. By the time we got back to Texas, we'd be rich."

"How you figure that?"

"Good soil down there along the rivers, they say. Good enough to grow a coin into a money tree."

"Well, I'm going with you, then."

"Come on then, Henry! We'll take you. 'Cept in your case, I expect you have it in mind to plant that good-time gal you hang about with and grow you a harlot tree."

The men laughed. David bit off a hunk of his cheese and washed it down with a swallow of cider. He was happy today, happier than he had been since Huntsman took him down politically. All his plans to visit Texas were falling into place very nicely. His brother-in-law Abner Burgin and his nephew William Patton, along with a neighbor named Lindsey Tinkle, were all planning to join him on the journey. He anticipated an interesting, diverting jaunt over new country. He was told that Texas was quite a different kind of place than Tennessee. Though much of it was reported to be green, fertile and well-watered, other parts were by comparison almost devoid of plant life, and what plants did grow were such dry-country plants as prickly pear and mesquite—botanical strangers to David Crockett, whose travels had always centered in the lush landscapes east of the Mississippi.

"Davy, did you ever get that comet tail wrung off?" one of his audience asked.

"No sir, Jack, no sir. I clumb the mountain to do it, but the dang thing just swung off the other direction soon as it saw me. But I'm thinking I might try to grab that tail again, should old Halley make another run close by, and let it haul me to Texas."

More laughter. David crossed his booted legs, finished his cheese and cider and chewed some tobacco. It was getting into the afternoon now, his wagon parked nearby, laden with the supplies he had come here to purchase, and he needed to be heading toward home. It was hard to hurry, however, considering that he had such a fine group of companions, most of whom he might soon be saying good-bye to for the last time. If he did wind up moving to Texas, he doubted he would make many social runs all the way back to Tennessee.

"Well, gentlemen, I believe the time has come for me to go. I bid you ... Lord have mercy, what's that? A cat in a churn?"

All the others, except the oldest and deafest ones, had heard it too. It was a high-pitched, whining sound, vaguely musical. As David cocked his ear to pick it up better, he surmised that it was indeed music, or an attempt at music, and it came from the half-open window of one of the rooms in the hotel across the street.

"That's somebody scratching on a fiddle," he said. "Phew! That fiddling's so bad you can smell it!"

"I believe somebody's skinning a cat," one of the others said.

"Men, I'll take my leave. I hope to see you again sometime or another."

"When you leaving for Texas?"

"First of the month."

"Good luck to you, Colonel."

"Good travel to you, Davy."

"Burn up that Texas trail, Crockett."

David shook hands all around. He was eager now to get this done, not being fond of partings. Whistling to cover a rising emotional discomfort, he walked briskly to his wagon, climbed aboard, and threw off the brake. He pulled out into the middle of the street, waving at his friends. He winked mischievously at them, then twisted on the seat and shouted up at the hotel window: "Can you come fiddle for my poor departed grandpappy's wake tonight? That noise ought to be enough to rouse him back from the dead, and if you could do that, Granny would be mighty beholden to you!"

The men on the porch laughed heartily. The fiddle music stopped. David turned and snapped the lines, lurching into motion again. He heard a man's hoarse voice from the window, cussing at him, but then the voice broke off and whoever it belonged to went into a fierce fit of coughing, loud and long and painful coughing that made David wince to hear it.

"God, friend, I'm right sorry I jawed at you. I believe

you're terrible sick at the lungs," David muttered beneath his breath. Still the hacking, consumptive coughing continued. With his boisterous mood suddenly lessened, David gave a final wave to his friends. The wagon rolled on down the street and out of town.

Chapter 53

November 1, 1835

As he rode out from his home, David Crockett was in a far more reflective mood than he had expected to be at this moment. Betsy had seemed in a sad, strange frame of mind, gazing at him closely in a way he had never seen her do before. Not with anger, not with intent to dissuade him from an adventure he had already firmly determined to undertake, but with . . . he didn't really know. Intensity. Sadness, perhaps. Her manner, like her parting kiss, had been unexpectedly unsettling.

His sober mood didn't linger for long. Once they were a mile or so along the way, the familiar surge of excitement that the anticipation of this Texas journey had stirred in him came back in an exhilarating rush. No longer anticipation, but the reality! He was on his way into a new life. Texas was land, freedom, opportunity. He'd find rich land to settle on, make his presence known, befriend and charm the people just like he had befriended and charmed so many Tennessee border men through the years. Before long he would be as deeply involved in Texas politics as he had been here at home. He could hardly wait.

He was dressed in the clothing he liked best: plain trousers, hunting shirt, flop hat, woolen coat. He had packed no gear that couldn't be fit into his saddlebags, along with his rifle "Betsey"—his older, well-worn hunting weapon, not the fancy engraved rifle given to him by the Philadelphia Whigs. There was nothing in his appearance at the moment to suggest he was a man of prominent reputation. He looked like any West Tennessee bear hunter—except perhaps for the glittering watch chain that stretched across the front of his shirt, linked to the excellent gold pocket watch he had brought with him.

With him were Tinkle, Patton, and Burgin. All along their route they encountered friends and neighbors who hooted greetings at them and invited them in for meals or drinks, several of which invitations they accepted. David enjoyed such attention. He might have been voted out of office, but there were still plenty about who loved Colonel Crockett! And as for those who had voted against him—well, maybe they had done him a favor without intending to. Let Huntsman have Congress; Texas was better for David Crockett.

Their first goal was Memphis, where David intended to visit with his old friend Marcus Winchester, who had spurred him and financed him in that first successful congressional race. David was eager to reach Texas, but not so eager that he didn't intend to have a fine time along the way.

On the outskirts of Memphis they were met in the road by a very old man who must have heard that the famed Colonel Crockett was coming this way. He waved down the group and approached David.

"Colonel, I'm privileged to meet you, sir," he said, looking up at the mounted David. "I've been a follower and supporter of yourn right from the start, and if it was up to me, I'd make you President of the whole durn United States nation, which I myself helped fight to create in the big war against the English."

"Thank you, sir. I'm moved through and through."

"I've brung you a gift, Colonel, if you'd be willing to take it. Made it myself." The man held up a fur cap, made of a fox pelt with the red tail hanging down in the back. "I hope it'll fit your noggin."

David accepted the cap. Removing his hat, he deliberately put the cap on backward so the tail hung over his nose.

"Well, I don't know about this, friend. I believe this hat might make me sneeze a right smart."

Grinning, the man said, "Try 'er hanging down backward, Colonel."

David shifted the hat around properly. "Fits like a glove on a hand, good citizen. I'm shot if it ain't the finest cap I've ever had between me and the sky. I thank you for it, and make you a gift of the one I been wearing."

The man accepted David's old flop hat solemnly. He looked at it as if it were a sacred relic. "I'm honored to own it, Colonel. Thank you, sir." He looked up suddenly, back down the road along which they had traveled. "What's that?"

David looked back over his shoulder. "I don't see nothing."

"No sir, it's a sound. Right odd one, like a bird or a squealing baby ... well, I don't hear it no more. I've always been keen of ear, Colonel Crockett, and I swear that since I've got old I hear keener than when I was a boy."

It's just the wind whistling in your ear hole, old partner, David thought. There's nothing to be heard.

"Thank you for this here hat, Colonel."

"Thank you for this one. I'll wear it proud all over Texas."

They went on. David hadn't worn fur caps like this often, not liking the feel of most he had tried on, and preferring a brim to keep the sun off his face, but now that it was autumn and the sun's rays weren't so glaring, a brim didn't matter so much, and this fox cap would keep his head warmer when winter came on. So he was satisfied.

"You look fine in a fur hat, Davy," William Patton said.

"Thank you, nephew. It couldn't fit better had the old gentleman laid a measuring string around my melon. Now let's get a few more miles behind us before we eat a bite. I'm hot to get to Memphis. Old Marcus Winchester knows every good whistle-wetting establishment in the city, and I'm in the humor to pay call on every deuced one."

It had been a wild night so far and promised to be wilder yet before it was through. They had started early and now it was late, and there were no signs of a letup.

David's anticipation about Marcus Winchester had proven true. He had led the band from one drinking establishment to another, and now all were well-fueled with alcohol. Already there had been several fights among members of David and Winchester's party, though David had tried valiantly to be the peacemaker. He didn't want his reputation sullied by tavern fighting here at the end of his Tennessee career.

They were in the bar of the Union Hotel now, and David was in high form. For the last hour he had told tale after tale from his colorful past—and quite a few from an even more colorful past that existed nowhere but in his imagination. With senses of humor lubricated by liquor, his audience of friends and hangers-on gave a gratifying response to every joke and anecdote he related. For the last little bit he had concentrated on unflattering stories about "King Andrew" Jackson and his cronies, exaggerated for effect. These stories seemed particularly entertaining to his listeners.

Eventually, one of the drunker and more verbose members of the crowd stood and said, "Colonel Crockett, there's some of us gentlemen here who'd like you to commentarize on the last election, which so scandal-o-faciously has wrested your esteemed and honorable self from your rightful chair in Congress and given it over to be filled by a peg-leg. When you occupied that chair sir, it was to the good of all men, noble and otherwise, of the great State of Tennessee."

"You are saying," David interrupted, "that when I was in my chair, my chair was an asset?"

Thunderous laughter went up, though only after the couple of moments it took for David's subtle play on words to sink in.

"Indeed it was, Colonel. Indeed it was. Now in this chair sets an ass of a different breed, an ass of the long-eared jack variety. Now, to our sorrow, this chair is filled by a scoundrel who must hop from his bed to his privy, a man who without a whittled prop lacks even the ability to kick a stray cur without crashing bodily to the earth, and whose only skill of merit is the ability to trim the nails of his toes in half the time it takes the average man. Your thoughts on this, Colonel!"

David stood, lifting his glass. "Gentlemen, I'll answer this fine request for comment with a toast, addressed to all the former constituents of mine who have so foolishly turned me out to pasture. My toast is this: if you had elected me, good citizens, I would have delighted to serve you to the best of my ability. But since you have chosen to elect a man with a timber toe to succeed me, you may all go to hell, and I will go to Texas!"

The men cheered in delight, drained their cups, and hammered them on the table. "Crockett! Crockett! Crockett!" someone began chanting, and others picked it up until soon it rang so loud that it rattled the barroom ceiling. David beamed. Truly, this kind of adulation was greater than any victory would have brought him. He never would have thought it before, but there were occasions when to lose brought more satisfying rewards than to win.

Half an hour later, the celebration still going strong, David slipped out of the barroom and hotel and headed for the nearest private alley. Behind him a shadowed figure moved and followed. He half sensed the presence but thought little about it, his sensibilities numb from drinking. At the end of the alley he relieved his bladder. When he turned around again, he found himself facing a bearded man with a wide-brimmed hat.

"Hello, David."

A pause. David frowned. "Persius . . . Lord have mercy, Persius, is that you?"

"Yes." Persius's voice sounded weak. He turned his head to the side and coughed.

"Persius . . . why, I be shot, drawed, and quartered!"

David grinned. "Persius Tarr, right here in Memphis!" He stumbled forward, very drunk, and threw his arms over Persius's shoulder. But Persius pulled away, turned, and went into a severe fit of more coughing. Every hack seemed to wrench him deeply. Before the fit was done, Persius had sunk to his knees and seemed on the verge of wretching.

David was so bleary-minded it was hard to force out clear words. "Persius . . . you sick or . . . something?"

His voice was a whisper. "Yes. It's my lungs. Don't know what it is that's wrong with them." He hacked a couple of more times. "They hurt me a lot, and sometimes I swear I cough up little pinkish pieces of my own insides."

"Sounds right . . . bad."

"It is. I figure it'll kill me."

"Why, I'll haul you back to Washington and let you see . . . old Doc Ibbotson"—he paused, feeling confused—"except that he's dead, so he wouldn't do you much good. Sorry if I don't make . . . much sense, Persius. I'm heading for Texas and am drunk as a redskin in a vat of tater beer."

Persius stood. He seemed to have regained some of his strength and self-control. "I know about Texas. I been following you since right after you left home, Dave."

"Following me? I ain't seen you."

"Maybe you've heard me." Persius had a sack slung over his back, and he swung it around. Reaching inside, he pulled out an oddly shaped something David couldn't see very well in the darkness.

"What's that?"

"A fiddle. I been trying to teach myself to play it."

Something tugged at David's memory. "Persius, was that you fiddling . . . up in that hotel—and coughing?"

"It was. And I had no notion until I looked out the window to cuss you that it was David Crockett who had hollered up from the street. But I took to coughing and couldn't yell to let you know it was me, not until you were gone. I was sick in that hotel a little spell, and after I got out, I went toward your house, and a neighbor told me you had fresh set out for Texas. And so I followed you, and I been playing my fiddle along the way to amuse myself."

He coughed a little again, but managed to keep it under control. "Talking brings out the coughing sometimes."

"I never heard your fiddling, Persius. But an old man we met, he did. He said he was ... keen of ear, and I reckon he was."

"I want to go to Texas with you, David. I believe maybe in Texas my lungs might heal."

"Then come on. We'll make a play-party of it, Persius. I'm going to start me a new life there. Land. I'll get ... back into politics."

"They say there's trouble brewing there too. Lot of people talking revolution."

"I ain't seen no trouble yet I couldn't handle."

"Except in your last election."

"That would have been ... a sore spot, if you'd said it right after I lost."

"But it ain't now?"

"No. No. I'm set on Texas now. It'll be better ... in Texas." David burped loudly. "Lord, I'm drunk. There's a bunch of us in yonder ... you come too."

"No. I hide out from folks some now, because of my coughing. Folks get afraid they'll catch whatever I got."

"You don't need to hide from me."

"I'll stay out here. It's the way I want it."

"Where will you be? We'll be leaving for Texas to-morrow."

"I'll meet you at the ferry. Thank you for letting me ride with you, David Crockett."

"Glad you want to, Persius Tarr. Now I'm ... a-going back in there to get a mite drunker, so I can be ... in the best condition I can to travel." He paused. "Durn if I don't already need to spray again, Persius."

He went back to the far end of the alley for a few moments. When he turned back again, Persius had vanished. He staggered out to the street and looked around, but Persius was nowhere in sight. Shrugging, he headed back to the barroom to rejoin the revelry, and didn't give Persius another thought for the rest of the night.

Chapter 54

They headed to the landing the next morning, heads aching and faces puffy and blanched. For the sake of the townspeople who watched their processional, David did his best to look dignified and stately, toting his rifle and wearing his new fox-skin cap at a cocky tilt, but it was hard to face the morning light. Even with his hangover, however, he still felt excited about going to Texas.

At the landing he recalled his alleyway encounter and looked around for Persius Tarr. Their meeting last night was a fuzzy, imprecise memory—if it was a memory at all. He wasn't entirely sure he hadn't passed out in the alley for a few minutes and dreamed up the entire thing. Now he became even less sure, because there was no Persius to be seen. He hadn't mentioned the encounter to any of his other companions, and was glad of it. Most likely it had been a particularly vivid combination of alcohol and imagination.

"You looking for somebody, Davy?" Lindsey Tinkle asked as David made one last sweep of the area.

"No," David replied. "Just looking. Let's get on to Arkansas."

They led their horses along a gangplank and onto a lower-level stable area on the steamboat that would carry them downriver. The men boarded the upper deck and leaned across the railing, waving at those who had gathered to see them off. As the boat prepared to pull out into the water, a young man with a fresh face, big eyes, and a notepad raced feverishly to the edge of the landing and yelled at them across the distance. "Colonel Crockett, sir? A question for the newspaper? Is that a coonskin cap you are wearing?"

"Fox skin," David called back, as loudly as his pounding head would allow him, and that wasn't very loud at all.

"Beg your pardon, sir?"

"Fox, I said!"

"Coonskin, Colonel?"

David didn't feel like yelling anymore. Wearily he nodded his head. The young reporter smiled, jotted on his pad, and waved gingerly.

"Get the mush out of your ears, you citified little scribbler," David mumbled beneath his breath. "If you don't know the difference between a coon and fox, devil with you!"

The boat floated down the river, its hung-over passengers dozing where they sat for the first part of the journey. Time dragged on; the sounds of the river became a pleasant music, punctuated by the shouts of boatmen working on other craft, their voices amplified by the water. There were other sounds: the churning of the big paddlewheel, the shouts and occasional oaths of the boat's crew as they labored all over the vessel, and from the distant banks, the clang of a church bell, the shouts of boys playing along the water's edge, the barking of dogs.

Along the way, the boat pulled into shore at various communities, and at each David Crockett was greeted and applauded. The river eventually carried them to the mouth of the Arkansas River, and they followed that waterway all the way to Little Rock. There a delegation greeted them and led David into a banquet hall, where a fife and drum corps played "Hail, the Conquering Hero Comes."

From Little Rock they disembarked with their horses and rode to Fulton, in the Red River country. David was happy to be making real progress now. He was coming into the very country he was most interested in seeing.

They reached the little town of Lost Prairie, Arkansas, and paused there to spend the night. David was in need of cash, having spent far more than he should have during his Memphis escapades, and traded his gold watch with a resident named Isaac Jones. In return, David had taken Jones's lower-quality watch, plus thirty dollars in cash.

They continued along the Red River, which marked the northern Texas line. David was pleased so far with what he saw. This was good land, with lots of timber, rich springs, and abundant wild game, buffalo, and bee trees.

It was during this stretch of the journey that he began to fancy he could hear a strange, high-pitched musical sound from far behind them . . . like a fiddle. Many times he stopped and turned to study the landscape behind him, but he never saw anything. Oddly, none of the others seemed to hear the noise at all. David was bothered by this. Was he jittery and spookish without even realizing it? Was his mind beginning to play tricks on him? Or might it really be Persius back there, following at a distance?

They crossed the water and went into Clarksville, Texas. As they traveled across Becknell's Prairie some five miles west of town, they were met by two women on horseback, one of them the wife of James Clark, for whose family the town was named. Having heard that the famed Colonel Crockett had come through town and was heading southwest, they had decided to intercept and give warning to him that such a course put them at risk of Comanches, who were at the moment in a very warlike mood.

Crockett and company took up temporary residence in the home of a local family, the Becknells, diverting themselves in the meantime with a hunting trip under the guidance of a man named Henry Stout. While hunting, they met James Clark on the headwaters of the Trinity River. He concurred with the caution his wife had given them, and even advised them to stop the current hunt because of the Comanche danger. They did.

When David was back at the Becknell house, he was informed that a rider had come from Clarksville with a message. A man had ridden into town, asking after Colonel Crockett and his company. He was a swarthy fellow, perhaps Indian or Mexican, with a fiddle he carried in his sack of provisions. Did the colonel know this man, and wish to see him?

David nodded. Certainly he did know this fellow, and yes, he would return to Clarksville to see him. He thanked the messenger, who immediately rode back to give word of David's impending return. David ate a quick meal, borrowed a fresh horse from the Becknells, and rode back toward Clarksville, knowing now that his encounter with Persius had been no drunken fantasy, and worried that Persius had followed, alone, in a poor state of health.

Persius, now clean-shaven, was ensconced on a porch, passing his time plucking at his fiddle while awaiting David's arrival. He grinned as David rode onto the street and veered his horse over toward him.

"Howdy, Dave."

"Persius. I be danged! I didn't really believe you was coming."

"I told you I wanted to go to Texas with you."

"Yes, but you weren't at the landing come Sunday morning. I figured you had changed your mind." David didn't want to reveal that he actually had doubted the reality of the alcohol-hazed encounter in the alley.

"No, I hadn't changed my mind. But I was took worse sick about sunup and wasn't in no shape to make it to the river. So I let you go on, and later that day I paid my way onto another boat and followed. I been trying to catch up with you ever since."

"You paid your way? You have money, huh?"

"There some reason you think Persius Tarr wouldn't have money? By the way, I'm Ben Breeding to the world now. Too much law trouble attached to my real name."

"I'll try to get used to it, Per—Ben, I mean. I didn't mean you no offense about the money. I was just trying to say you must have done some good business somewhere along the way these last months."

"Since I left you in Washington I went to work at a

hotel in Nashville and made myself a good name with the rich old man who owned it by dragging out some of his family when a fire broke out in their quarters. I saved their lives, 'cording to him. When he died I found out he'd writ me into his will. A thousand dollars and this old fiddle. That was my part of it."

"A thousand dollars! That's a fine piece of wealth."

"More than I've ever had before or expect to here-after."

"You ain't coughing no more, glad to see."

"I believe this Texas air is already doing me good. Purging out my lungs like that wormweed your ma gave me purged out my bowels—you recollect that? For the last couple of days I've hardly coughed at all."

"I'm glad to hear it . . . Ben." David grinned. "It's going to take some getting used to, calling you by a new name."

Persius said, "A new name seems the right thing to have in a new country. I have to remind myself that this ain't even the United States. It's Mexico."

"I believe that before it's done, this will be part of the United States. From what I hear of the rebellion, all they're seeking is to get back the constitution that has been took away from them, but it's my private opinion that eventually they'll be part of the union. That's what needs to happen, and I might just see what kind of hand I can lend toward helping the process along. The Mexes got a president here name of Santy Anna, and he's a prime dan-dified scoundrel from the git-go, from what I hear. They say he has a gold snuff box and squats on a silver chamber pot. He's already put on some taxes that had been took away under the old president, and they say he's got a worser bullying and bossing way than old Andy Jackson himself. But he can be dealt with. This here is a fine land, ready to bloom like a flower. It's the garden spot of the world from what I've seen. And I want to see a lot more of it."

"Well, where you go, I want to go—if you'll have me."

"You're welcome to join me, Persius. Ben, I should

say. Though I ain't sure why you want to. I get plenty of attention, but the fact is I'm still a poor man. I've found you can't get much more than a free meal or two with fame, which is about all that's left to me at the moment. But you have money. You could buy a lot of land here and make a real place for yourself."

"Well, I plan to do that. But when I do, I want you in on it with me."

"I don't see what you mean."

"You remember once, back before we went off to fight the Creeks, you talked about fate or destiny or some such as that?"

"Yes."

"And I said I didn't believe in it. Well, now maybe I do, or at least have a suspicion of it. It's just a feeling. I got to thinking back on how we've come together, gone apart, come together again, and so on, and it just seems to me that if there's any such thing as fate, mine must be linked up with yours."

"That's all there is to it?"

"No. There's more. I don't want you to take offense at the words I'm about to speak, David."

"Offense? Just what are you getting ready to say?"

"That I want to help you get settled here, if that's what you want. I can do it, with the money I have now. It's the first time in my life I've been in a position where I can truly help out somebody else."

David took a step back. He was no stranger to receiving the help of others, but the idea of Persius Tarr offering him help seemed like such a reversal of roles that he didn't like the feel of it. He laughed uncomfortably. "What? I'm becoming your Christian charity case?"

"Now there you go—that's the kind of thing I figured you'd say. No sir, not by no stretch. You're no charity case and I'm no Christian. What you are is the best friend this no-count old half-breed ever had from the day he was born. You and yours have always done your best for me, more than anybody else.

"I think back on your family taking me in for a spell when I was orphaned. I recollect you doing your best to save my neck when Crider Cummings was after me that time I beat up on his brother in Jefferson County. You did your best for me again when you risked your own hide to find a way for me to escape from that army camp, your wife did her best to save my baby's life, and you got me care of a doctor in Washington City when I was sick. The best times of my life, beyond them that I spent with my wife and daughter, are them I had with you. You've done your best for me all my days, David Crockett, and now the time has come when maybe I can do my best for you."

David smiled, almost sadly. "Hearing you lay all that out reminds me how often I've tried to help you but never done you that much good. I've done my best many a time and failed. When my family took you in back in Greene County, I pleaded with my pap to make you part of the family, and it did no good—he sent you straight to the Orphan Court. And it was John Canaday, a lot more than me, who helped save your hide from Crider Cummings. As far as trying to help you escape from that army camp, you'll recall it was my mouth that got you arrested to start with. And however hard Betsy tried to save your baby's life, your baby died. Even in Washington, it was Campbell Ibbotson who really provided you the doctoring. When you line it all out, Persius ... Ben, you see that me and mine ain't really done that much for you at all. Maybe we tried, but trying don't pay for the beans."

"It pays for a durn good lot with me. Ain't no other man ever stood by me like you have, David. Let me join with you. Let me be your partner. We'll get land. I'll shake off this lung trouble of mine and get strong again. We'll make a new start in Texas, both of us, and put the past behind. Persius Tarr and his sorry ways will be dead and gone, and Ben Breeding will be a man of measure. And you won't be Crockett of Tennessee no more, but Crockett of Texas, a man who'll stand tall and have every kind of success in whatever he tries. There *is* such a thing as fate, or destiny, or whatever you call it, and for me and you both, it lies right here in Texas."

David peered deeply at his old companion. Persius's utter sincerity was clear to see in his face. Grinning, David shook his head admiringly. "Persius Tarr, I never heard so fine a stretch of speech-making in the very halls of Congress as what you've outed with today. You keep talking like that and you'll wind up president of Mexico your own self!"

"Not Persius Tarr—Ben Breeding. But Persius Tarr thanks you for the compliment."

David reached out his hand; Persius grasped and shook it.

"Partners," David said.

"Partners," Persius echoed. "Where to now, Crockett of Texas?"

"Nacogdoches," David replied. "We're going to swear our allegiance to Texas, and get on toward making that new life you been preaching about."

Chapter 55

From the beginning, Nacogdoches had attracted men from the shadowy borders of society—gamblers, thieves, confidence men, smugglers, absconded debtors, even murderers. Located within easy distance of the Louisiana border, it was the kind of town a man in trouble in the United States could flee to in a hurry when the homeland grew too dangerous. He could scurry to its gambling halls and saloons like a roach scurrying for cover in a rubbish pile.

And David Crockett took an immediate liking to the place as soon as he rode into the dusty street. This was the kind of town in which a gent could carouse and enjoy himself, with no one looking for him to set a shining example of excellent behavior. A man's kind of town, a wild, free sort of place.

As he had neared Nacogdoches, David's company had grown significantly. Not only was fiddle-toting "Ben Breeding" now part of his group, but several other would-be Texas volunteers as well, some of them, just like David, Tennesseans with an eye to a future in Texas. Word that one of the most famous sons of Tennessee, the famed Colonel Crockett, was making his way to Nacogdoches to put his name on the line as a Texas volunteer, had drawn them together, and plans were afoot for them to form themselves into a company of mounted volunteers under Crockett's command, just as soon as the oath was signed.

But oaths were better signed without the handicap of thirst, so the first order of business for Crockett and his companions was to visit one of the local saloons. They found an appropriately Mexican-looking dive on a side street, a stone building with thick beams holding up its ceiling, a massive stone hearth built on an elevated floor in the center of the single wide room, and big stone pillars here and there throughout the place, upon which candles stood in holders pegged right into the stone.

They drank to the health of each other and the future of Texas, and then David turned to make one more toast: To Lindsey Tinkle and Abner Burgin, whose Texas adventures were ending here. They would be heading back home again. The rough-cut group drank their health and wished them safe travel, then returned to their "whistle-wetting" with enthusiasm. Spirits were high; at the moment, the little group of men felt that if necessary, they could whip the entire army of the hated Antonio Lopez de Santa Anna all by themselves.

When they had drunk their fill, David wiped a sleeve across his mouth, walked toward the door and picked up his rifle, which he had leaned there upon entry. Raising it above his head, he said, "Men, let's go pledge ourselves to the cause of Texas!"

With a yell of assent, the company surged to the street, mounted their horses, and with whoops and shouts made their way to the office of Judge John Forbes, led by those of the group who had been awaiting David Crockett's arrival before going through the oath ceremony.

Forbes greeted the group with calm dignity. Though they looked like nothing more than a horde of criminals, dirty from the trail and smelling of freshly consumed liquor, Forbes did not blink. His time in Nacogdoches had accustomed him to dealing with what might be called interesting folk. Texas had such in abundance, with more swarming in by the day. And in Texas, appearances were deceiving. For all Forbes knew, some of the ill-smelling ruffians standing before him might be the most respectable of men in their home environs.

When Forbes learned that the fox-skin-capped leader of this particular gaggle was none other than the celebrated Colonel David Crockett himself, he bowed respectfully and put out his hand to his famous visitor. "Colonel, I will write out the oath and present it to you and your men to sign. Texas is honored to have you as a visitor and supporter, and soon, we hope, as a citizen."

"I'm much appreciative," David replied. "Now get that paper writ out—I'm eager to set my hand to it."

Forbes sat down and wrote out the following:

> I do solemnly swear that I will bear true allegiance to the Provisional Government of Texas or any future Government that may be hereafter declared, and that I will serve her honestly and faithfully against all her enemies and opposers whatsoever, and observe and obey the orders of the Governors of Texas, the orders and decrees of the present or future authorities and the orders of the officers appointed over me according to the rules and articles for the government of Texas. So help me God.

"There you are, Colonel Crockett," Forbes said. "This is the standard oath, and I'm sure it meets your approval."

David looked over the oath and handed it back to Forbes. "No sir, it does not."

Every eye turned to him. Forbes cleared his throat. "I beg your pardon, Colonel?"

"That thing has me swearing to uphold any government that might arise in Texas. I won't do that. What if some tyrant takes the place over? I wouldn't support a Texas tyrant no more than I would support King Andrew back home. You change that to read *republican* government, there at that 'any future government' part, and I'll sign."

Forbes smiled thinly. "You are a perceptive and deep-thinking man, Colonel Crockett. I haven't had a man yet to raise that issue with me, and I confess that such a thought hasn't come to my own mind until now. You are right, sir, and I'll change the oath gladly." He took up his pen again and inserted the word "republican" as Crockett had requested.

"There you are, sir. If you wish to be the first to sign, I'm sure no one would—"

"No," David cut in. "I'm no more than the rest of you, just a man pledging his support to good Texas government. I can wait my turn. Let them closest to you sign first."

"Very well."

Carefully, and with varying degrees of penmanship, the volunteers put their names on the paper. The name of David Crockett was nineteenth on the final list, but even so, it managed to stand out above all the others. He was a famous man. He had a reputation. And signing up to support the Texas cause was just the way to live up to it. He knew that when the battle for Texas was done, the people here would not forget the Tennessee volunteer who lent his famous name and rifle to their cause.

By the ninth of January, David Crockett and his companions were in Saint Augustine. His family back in Tennessee was on his mind, for even though he had very cavalierly declared to a woman back in Lost Prairie that he had set his family "free" and they must now "shift for themselves," the truth was that they were frequently in his thoughts, and he was eager to get on with the business of obtaining land and settling himself so he could begin bringing his kin to join him.

He sat down in the quiet of the evening, away from all the others, and wrote a letter to his daughter, Margaret, and her husband, Wiley Flowers.

He greeted them warmly and wrote of his "high spirits" and "excellent health," and of being "received by everyone" in Texas with friendship and even ceremony. "The cannon was fired here on my arrival and I must say as to what I have seen of Texas it is the garden spot of the world. The best land and the best prospects for health I ever saw, and I do believe it is a fortune for any man to come here. There is a world of country here to settle."

He described the ease with which land could be obtained, the abundant timber and fine streams, and how he hoped to settle in a "pass where the buffalo passes from north to south and back twice a year, and bees and honey plenty."

He continued: "I have taken the oath of government and have enrolled my name as a volunteer and will set out for the Rio Grand in a few days with the volunteers from the United States. But all volunteers is entitled to vote for a member of the convention or to be voted for, and I have but little doubt of being elected a member to form a constitution for this province. I am rejoiced at my fate. I had rather be in my present situation than to be elected to a seat in Congress for life. I am in hopes of making a fortune yet for myself and family, bad as my prospect has been."

He requested his daughter to show the letter to others in the family, and urged her to "do the best you can and I will do the same."

Almost as if in afterthought, he wrote: "Do not be uneasy about me. I am among friends. I will close with great respects. Your affectionate father."

And then, with the characteristic disdain for "spelling contrary to nature" that he had noted in the preface of his autobiography, David Crockett closed his hurried letter with a single word, not noticing how oddly final it was in tone.

"Farwell."

The next days were taken up with travel. David noted that Persius seemed to be feeling at least slightly ill again, and his cough had come back, though not as badly as before. He fiddled as the company rode, drawing many complaints from his fellows and making David swear that surely the old belief that the fiddle was the devil's instrument must be true, since there could surely be nothing godly about the kind of screeches being inflicted on them now. But the truth was that nobody really minded the fiddling much, partly because it was diverting to hear the music improving, bit by bit, in quality.

Moving southwest, David and his company covered some 150 miles over a period of a few days, reaching Washington-on-the-Brazos by the final Tuesday of the month. There he signed an IOU to a man who gave him and some of his company help.

Washington 23rd January 1836

This is to certify that John Lott furnished my Self and four others Volunteers on our way to the army with accomodations for our Selves & horses The Government will pay him $7.-50 cts-
David Crockett

They went on, heading for San Antonio de Bexar, a town that had until short weeks ago been occupied by a Mexican general named Martin Perfecto de Cos, who, under the mounting threat of revolution, had fortified an old mission that once had housed a Spanish colonial company from Alamo de Parras. The Texas colonists from America now simply called the old mission the Alamo, for short.

General Cos had lost control of the Alamo and San Antonio de Bexar back in December under attack from Texas forces led by an old frontiersman named Ben Milam. Milam's men had actually forced the Mexican general to begin negotiations. On December 10 General Cos had agreed to withdraw past the Rio Grande and to leave alone the Texans in San Antonio.

Unfortunately, further military excursions by fired-up supporters of the revolution had caused much of the military supplies in San Antonio to be removed elsewhere, and even as Crockett and company advanced toward the town, one Colonel James Neill was struggling to fortify the Alamo mission with only a relative handful of volunteers. It was no easy task, especially in light of reports that

President Santa Anna was furious at the rebel seizure of San Antonio and didn't intend to let it stand.

An atmosphere of desperate unease overhung the approximate three acres covered by the old mission, with its four-foot-thick walls and roofless chapel. It would not be long, Neill and others were convinced, before San Antonio would again be a place of battle.

Chapter 56

February 1836

An old, crumbled-up-looking place if ever I seen one, David Crockett thought as he rode at the lead of his Tennessee Mounted Volunteers and through the gate of the sprawling compound once known as the Mission San Antonio de Valero, now commonly called El Alamo.

A horse or two behind him, Persius Tarr scratched out a rough version of "Hail, the Conquering Hero Comes," which David had taught him by whistling the tune until Persius finally got it. Now it seemed to be Persius's favorite number, perhaps because it was one of the few tunes he could play from start to finish with no gaps.

Sitting tall in his saddle and wearing his most prideful expression, David showed nothing in his looks but haughty confidence. From the great tour of his congressional days and his ceremonial stops along the way to Texas, he had learned much about making a grand entrance. This one proved as gratifying as most; as soon as he was on the big inner plaza, he was greeted by an uproar of cheers as if from a thousand throats. No more famous man had passed through that portal.

He lifted his cap and waved it above his head, looking around with a big grin on his face. Once again the expression hid the great burst of concern rising in him. A thousand throats? Hardly. David looked all about and saw maybe two hundred men at the most, and that was putting a stretch to it. Was this meager group actually expected to hold this place, should it come to a fight?

Persius evidently had similar thoughts. Glancing around, he muttered, "Which way back to Tennessee?" David pretended not to have heard.

"Screamer Crockett, by Christmas!" some backwoodsman in the crowd bellowed. "Ol' Mexes'll have to run clear to South 'Meriky now that ol' Canebrake Davy's come with his rifle-gun!"

Amid other such rough-toned heralds of welcome, David dismounted, and with the instincts of the experienced politician made for the nearest facsimile of a speaking platform, in this case, an empty crate. He stepped up on it and lifted both hands above his head.

"Gentlemen of Bexar, I greet you as friends and companions!" he said. "I come here to join myself to you, and to stand by your side as no more than a simple private soldier. I have traveled far from my home state of Tennessee, and have come here in company with good men, who like me, come to throw their hats in your ring."

More cheering. He looked at the faces of those who had come with him. Familiar faces like Persius's—who looked very concerned right now as he cast his eyes about the place—and those of others who had aligned themselves with him along the way: a Kentucky lawyer named Daniel Cloud, a Pennsylvania physician named John Purdy Reynolds, and fellow Tennessean Micajah Autry, who was expert on the violin and so had suffered more than anyone else under Persius's supposedly musical assaults. Good men ... men who were walking with him into a situation that was more sobering than he had anticipated. He was proud of them all for being here, and proud of himself ... but the danger was worrisome. No wonder Persius looked as nervous as he did.

Now, however, was not the time for such thoughts. David saw that his mere presence here brightened spirits around this dusty place. He launched into some of the standard old anecdotes he had used in his various political campaigns, describing how he had once traded a pelt for liquor with which to buy some votes, sneaked the pelt out from under the bar and traded it to the same barkeeper again, and again, and again. He gave a humorous recounting of the time his father chased him with a pole for laying out of school, and topped it off with some blatant lies that were far more entertaining than any truth he could have related.

Meanwhile, he noted a dignified, light-haired young man striding across the plaza from one of the various buildings that lined the inside of its thick walls. With clear but sad eyes, a somewhat long nose, and thin, expressive lips, this was a man with an air of authority, even though, if David took his best guess, he would place this fellow some years shy of thirty. The fellow stood somewhat to himself, a patient but serious look on his face. He smiled at some of David's jests and stories, but did not join in the guffaws. David could tell that the man was waiting to see him.

Only after the impromptu speech-making was done and David's shoulders had been slapped sore by scores of callused hands did the young man approach. David put out his hand, and the man took it.

"Colonel Crockett? I welcome you to Bexar, sir. I have heard much about you for years now, and it's an honor to meet you at last." His voice had the pleasant drawl of the South Carolinian and was touched as well with Alabamian inflections. "My name is Travis, Colonel William Barret Travis. Please excuse my lack of a uniform. I had ordered one for shipment to me but had to leave for this place before it could reach me."

"Are you one of the head men of this garrison, Colonel? If so, there is quite a lot I need to learn from you."

"I have been sent here by the governor, and though Colonel Neill remains in command, it appears he may soon leave us. I'm only newly arrived here myself, but there is much I can tell you. Come with me; we can talk better in private."

•   •   •

By darkness, some hours later, David Crockett walked about the old mission, examining it closely and wondering just what would finally happen here. Thanks to the time he had spent with Travis in the afternoon, he had a much clearer conception now of what was going on in Texas and at San Antonio de Bexar. He knew now that much had taken place here during the same period he was conceiving and undertaking his own Texas pilgrimage.

Early in the fall of 1835 there had been a fight at Gonzales, an American settlement about seventy miles east of San Antonio de Bexar. Mexican troops had attempted to take a cannon from the colonists there. They had fired the cannon at the troops, killing several and driving the others back. Afterward the Mexican fort at the coastal town of Goliad was taken by the rebel colonists, and another rebel army set out to take San Antonio. A Tennessee-born former Louisianian named James Bowie, now a resident of and military figure in San Antonio de Bexar, had led his advance force to victory near the Concepcion Mission, and finally the impatient old frontiersman Ben Milam had led the successful siege of San Antonio de Bexar, driving out the Mexicans. Thus the town and the old mission had fallen under the control of American colonists.

Winter had been hard on those occupying the Alamo. With two hundred of their number gone off—taking most of the good provisions and arms with them—on a mad attempt to take the port of Matamoros some three hundred miles away, and with no money or decent clothing to be had, the cold winter was a torment. By mid-January, Colonel J. C. Neill had been left with only fourscore or so men to hold the place, the rest having drifted back to their homes.

Since then, Travis had arrived with some regular army troops, and volunteers such as David's own group had also come in, but even so, the place was sadly undermanned. At least the Mexicans had themselves done much toward making the place defensible, digging ditches, building gun emplacements, adding palisades and thickening the walls with earth. The Americans had further strengthened the place, and had converted the old mission buildings to new functions. Along the east wall, a row of flat-roofed, joined houses, a former *convento*, served as barracks for artillery-men and infantry; across from them on the west wall were the officers' quarters and headquarters. The chapel held the powder magazine. At strategic locations around the fortress, cannon were emplaced. Travis was most proud of a strate-gically important eighteen-pounder that commanded the southwest corner.

So far the rebels holding the old compound had not been called on to use their artillery. But the garrison had gone through one major scare: a false report in January that a Mexican attack was imminent. Neill, Bowie, and others had known that they were hardly ready for any kind of fight, but defiantly sent word that they would "die in these ditches" before giving up the Alamo to the foe.

Travis seemed a man of similar spirit. Ordered to the Alamo only recently, he had brought with him almost thirty members of the Regular Texas Army. David was fa-vorably impressed with the young officer, who confided in him that he expected to be placed in command here after Neill left. Among his qualifications, Travis noted, was his abundant prior service to the Texan cause, and his fluency in Spanish.

Provisions were still very scarce, and Travis was try-ing to obtain more. Beef and corn were about all the food there was, and this with no salt to flavor it. Any man wanting a cup of hot coffee to wash down his mundane meals was out of luck.

Yet it was odd, David reflected as he paused near the north wall: every man he had talked to today seemed de-termined to stay here, to hold this isolated outpost should it come to a fight. Such resolve was hard to explain, yet as David looked around the old compound, which dated back more than a century, he felt the same kind of stirring in himself, as if some valor-loving spirit of the place was whispering encouragements in his ear. He hadn't come to Texas looking for a fight; he hadn't come expecting to ex-pose himself to danger . . . yet here he was, doing just that.

And if there was to be a fight, chances were it wouldn't be a small one. For weeks now, David had learned from Travis, intelligence had been reaching the Alamo from sympathetic Mexicans who told of Mexican troops amassing south of the Rio Grande. Travis had seemed quite confident about his knowledge of the size and strength of Mexican forces within striking distance of the Alamo.

A sound caused David to turn. A familiar figure approached him.

"Hello, Persius."

"Ben Breeding, durn it! I ain't Persius no more, remember?"

"I can't get used to that. Besides, there's nobody close by to hear."

"Well, it don't matter anyways, I don't reckon." He lowered his volume. "The fact is I won't be here to be called by any name."

"You won't . . . you're leaving? Running out?"

"I got a bad feeling about this place, David. There's going to be trouble for us if we stay."

"Maybe a fight, sure. But we've fought before. I believe that behind these walls we could hold out here against a devil of a lot larger army."

"But why? Why hold out at all? Why the bloody hell should me or you risk our hind ends for Texas?"

David laughed in mirthless astonishment. "What happened to the man who was talking just days ago about building a new life in Texas, and Texas being hope and a future? We want to be part of Texas, we might have to put a few cents' worth of effort into making it a place worth being part of. You know that as well as I do. You have more reason to stand up and fight here than you did to go fight in the Creek War. You were fighting against your own in that one!"

"Yes, and the only reason I fought in that war at all was because you talked me into it—and then you turned on me because you thought I was too bloodthirsty."

The subject brought a stab of pain. "That was an ugly time, Persius. I was shook by that war. I said things about you I shouldn't have said. I regretted the trouble it caused you so much I tried to help you escape."

"I know, I know. That's past, and I put it behind long ago. Hell, I didn't even hold no grudge against you then, if you care to remember! The point now is there's no reason to make the same mistakes twice. I don't like war. I'm leaving, Davy. And if you're the smart man I believe you are, you'll come with me."

"You're deserting, Persius. You've already took the allegiance oath. You've already put your name on the muster sheet."

"What's a muster sheet but a list of men soon to die? And what's an oath but a piece of paper? I ain't yet seen the piece of paper worth dying for."

"It's your word. Your bond."

"You're forgetting something, David Crockett. Persius Tarr is a rogue and scoundrel, and the word and bond of a rogue and scoundrel is so much dirt." Persius touched his hat. "It's been a good ride, and I hope to see you on the other side of whatever happens here. The truth is, I hope to see you before that. I hope you get the good sense to light out of this place before the Mex army makes a hell out of it."

"I've vowed I'll stand up to the fodder rack, and I'll be shot if I don't intend to do it or die, Persius. I'm a man of my word."

"And I ain't. Fare you well, David Crockett. And if you make it through, I'll see you again and we'll buy that land we talked about."

"No."

"What?"

"You leave here, and there's no more partnership between me and you. I'll not have a thing to do with you again if you turn coward now."

Persius broke into a sudden spell of coughing right then, and conversation ended for almost two minutes until he was in talking condition again. Obviously his health was beginning to take a serious decline once more.

In a hoarser voice he said, "A living coward still sees the sunrise and tastes the whiskey. A dead brave man, he just rots away and is gone. You want to turn your back on the best chance you'll ever have to be free of debt and trouble, then fine. Go ahead and do it. I can spend my money on some pretty Mex good-time gal just as easy as on land for you!"

David's temper boiled up. "If you see it that way, damn your hide, there's no more to be said to you. Get on with you! Get out before I take my rifle butt to your skull bone!"

Persius looked at David as if he were a man to be pitied. It was infuriating to David, who realized then that there remained a fundamental difference between him and Persius, a difference time hadn't changed, and which all the healing words they had recently spoken couldn't change either. There was no true honor in this man, no sense of duty to any but himself. David knew he had been a fool to think that he and Persius could again be the friends they had been in the days of their youth. Persius might have declared his old self dead and gone, but the man standing before him right now was no different a Persius than ever. Indeed he *was* a rogue and a scoundrel, and would never be anything else.

"Good-bye, David."

David turned away and began to stride off.

"I left the fiddle for you, in the barracks," Persius called after him. "It's good to while away the time with. I'll bet you can learn to outfiddle me in no time."

David ignored him, and kept on walking until he was swallowed by the darkness. He circled the big enclosure, working all the way back around to the big, distinctive front of the roofless chapel, whose black windows stared like empty eye sockets across the plaza. In the darkness the place had an ominous appearance. He looked around the grounds for Persius and sought him in the barracks as well. No sign of him. He really had gone off, just like he said.

For the first time since he had come to Texas, David felt alone. And as much as he hated to admit it, afraid as well. Persius's grim talk of dead heroes had put a bigger fright into him than anything Travis had told him.

But he wouldn't show it. He was Colonel Crockett, the man who grabbed comets by the tail, rode alligators for fun, and dropped coons from tall trees simply by grinning at them. Such a man didn't run from danger.

He made for his sleeping place, missing his wife and family very much, and wishing that Persius hadn't gone away.

Chapter 57

Northern Mexico Mountains

The soldiers who struggled through the howling blizzard were a diverse group of human beings, though they were being driven as if they were no more than animals. They included uniformed senior officers, infantrymen in white cotton fatigues far too light for such weather and with shakos on their heads, dragoons in breastplates, and even some Mayans from the Yucatan. The Mayans were dying more quickly than the others; their bodies lay where they fell, cooling in the snow, finally buried while the others trudged past, ignoring them.

With the soldiers were the *soldaderas*, women and children who always trailed after the Mexican army, generally getting in the way, slowing down progress, diminishing supplies, distracting the troops. But they kept the soldiers happier and less prone to desert, and so were tolerated by the otherwise stern officers. Behind them, forcing wagons and two-wheeled carts and pack mules through the thickening accumulation, was the supply train, along with scores of independent sutlers. When their wagons and carts bogged or broke down or their pack mules fell to rise no more, their goods were confiscated by others, piled onto new conveyances or pack animals, and hauled on. The supplies would be needed when the army reached the San Antonio River and the old forted mission that stood beyond it. If there was a fight, medicines and such would be needed as well. Too bad virtually none had been brought along.

Not that the siege, if there was one, would take all that long. There were reportedly only a handful of men inside El Alamo, too few to make much of a stand. Even so, the troops had marched a long way with insufficient food and medical supplies, sometimes living on little more than berries and mesquite nuts they found along the way. They were far too weary to want even a small battle once they reached their destination. They hoped that their numbers alone would be enough to bring about a surrender of the little Texan garrison. With any luck, they might not even have to fire off their aging *escopetas*, which kicked like *diablos*, bruising the shoulder, and had a range of only seventy-some yards.

Possibly the lone exception to this prevailing discontent was embodied in the arrogant and extravagant man in command of the army, General Antonio Lopez de Santa Anna. Bitterly angry at the nagging Texan rebels who had already made his troops in Texas look so weak and inefficient, he was leading this foray himself. Not that he had any intention of suffering the same want that his troops had to endure. Wearing his ornate silver-draped uniform and a sword worth more money than many poor Mexicans might see in their lifetimes, he traveled far ahead of the main body, followed by a carriage carrying his personal fine china, foodstuffs, tea supplies, and silver chamber pot.

They would soon be through the mountains, and after that the travel would be much easier. Santa Anna could hardly wait to smite the upstarts in Texas. He would give them a single chance for surrender, but he hoped they would resist, at least for a little while. Then, facing the inevitability of their defeat, they would throw down their arms and run up the surrender flag. They would beg for mercy, plead for their lives, grovel before him. And it would make no difference. Already he had decided that if there was any early resistance, there would be no later mercy. He had brought with him his red flag and had made sure his trumpeters were well-practiced in the Deguello. Both the flag and the song carried the same meaning: no quarter for the enemy. All who are captured will be killed.

Perhaps the rebels would fight all the harder once they knew there was no option for surrender. There might be a few more Mexican casualties because of it . . . but no matter. He, Santa Anna, would be safe, and triumphant, and as for common soldiers, was it not their lot to die? He had not climbed the ranks of Mexican authority and become military dictator by being overly scrupulous about the welfare of others.

Ignoring the snow, the general spurred a little more speed from his tired horse. He was eager to reach the Rio Grande and Texas. The Texans would never expect that a Mexican army this large would advance so far in the winter; they would be expecting no attack before spring. Santa Anna could imagine their surprise when several thousand soldiers appeared on the horizon.

He could scarcely wait. The battle that was almost certain to take place at the old Spanish mission was going to be the most fun he had enjoyed for a very long time.

San Antonio de Bexar, February 23, 1836

Persius Tarr rolled over, coughed spasmodically a few times, and opened his eyes. He reached to the other side of the rumpled, dirty bed and found it empty.

"Rosa?" he said, and coughed again. He sat up, running fingers through his hair and his palm across his stubbly face. He had last shaved four days ago, and the whiskers were just now starting to grow back in.

Another coughing fit hit him; he hacked into his hands, and when he looked at them afterward, they had been stained with a faint spray of blood. He wiped them clean on the bed linens and mumbled a curse. Obviously he was a sicker man than he had first thought. The improvement in his health he had enjoyed after first entering Texas had been only a respite, not a healing.

"Rosa!" he called again. No answer. Grumbling, he

stood. His trousers hung over a chair; he slid his legs into them and slipped the galluses over his shoulders.

Sun spilled in through a window to his left. He went to it and peered out. He was in Rosa's second-story room above the cantina where she worked serving liquor and tortillas and the like; she also worked in a different way here in this very room, selling herself for money.

Persius had been here since the night he left the Alamo. He hadn't planned to remain in town at all, not with the rampant rumors that Santa Anna himself was leading a massive force up from deep in Mexico to mount a surprise attack on the isolated Alamo. The opinion of the locals was mixed concerning these rumors; it appeared that many doubted the veracity of them, as the Alamo garrison reportedly did. Such tales had been frequently heard since the rebels had taken over Bexar. Nothing had come of any of them. Besides, Santa Anna surely wouldn't try to advance an army in the winter.

Whatever the truth about the rumors, it really made no sense at all to remain here and take a chance with his safety. Had he not deserted the garrison because it didn't seem sensible to play the odds? Yet here he was, living for the last several days with a Mexican prostitute, finding every excuse in the world not to leave town.

He had told himself it was Rosa who kept him here, but that was not the truth. She was fat and plain and of no real interest to him. She liked his money, that was all. He was staying because . . . because . . . he really didn't know. He had tried to leave a couple of times, and both times had returned, puzzled at his own behavior.

There seemed to be an unusual amount of hurrying about in the streets. Wagons, laden with furniture and food and families, rumbled by in a hurry. Many people were on foot, carrying bundles and *bambinos*, racing along like the devil was chasing them. A woman carrying a bundle and draped in an oversized coat—*his* coat!—cut across the street below. It was Rosa.

He shoved open the window. "Rosa!"

She stopped and looked up at him like he was a stranger, then turned and went on.

"Rosa! Wait!" he yelled.

Without even slowing her pace, she called back to him over her shoulder in her thickly accented English. "You'd better run, amigo! Santa Anna, he has come! He will be in these streets before the sun sets!" She scurried on around a corner and was gone.

"God!" Persius declared, pulling back into the room. "Santy Anny! It's really starting to happen!"

He took off his trousers again so he could put on his long underwear and shirt. His head throbbed from the effects of last night's liquor; he coughed even more than usual, and his fingers fumbled at their work. He could feel his heart pounding unusually hard against his ribs, and fright rippled through him. Santa Anna was here! Why hadn't he had the good sense to flee earlier?

As his pants dropped around his ankles he happened to glance at an open cabinet in the corner. Rosa had substantially emptied it, yanking down clothes that now made up that bundle she carried—all this while he slept drunkenly on her bed, ignorant of the danger descending on the town. Persius fumed. You couldn't count on Mexican women for any kind of human kindness, at least not Mexican women of Rosa's ilk! He was very glad he had at least awakened on his own before afternoon. It would have been a rude awakening indeed to have opened his eyes and found Mexican soldiers surrounding his bed.

It was even more maddening that she had taken his coat. Likely he'd freeze to death now. His eye was drawn again to the open cabinet. He went to it and dug through the heaps of clothing at the bottom of it, and found some Mexican-style white cotton fatigues and a loose-fitting Mexican shirt. He pulled out the clothing and examined it. It appeared to be about his size. "Well, this will just have to do," he mumbled, and coughed.

He put on his long underwear, and the fatigues over it. The extra layer would serve to keep him warm in the wind, even without his coat. Glancing up, he saw himself in the mirror. Rosa was right in a comment she had made: with his swarthy skin, he could be taken for a Mexican as quickly as for an American.

Atop the fatigues he managed to get on his own clothing. His rifle and gear stood in the corner; at least Rosa hadn't stolen that. Taking it up, he headed downstairs, hoping fervently that no fleeing San Antonian had taken his horse from the livery.

He was fortunate; his horse was still there. He paid the liveryman out of the fold of money he kept inside a special leather pocket inside his boot lining, a pocket whose existence he had prudently concealed from Rosa. He saddled the horse and swung into the saddle. The exertion brought on a new fit of coughing; he tasted blood on his tongue. This here sickness is going to kill me, he thought. It ain't getting better at all.

He didn't like thinking that way, and pushed the matter from his mind. He rode out of the stable and along the central street to the far side of town, across the little wooden bridge spanning the San Antonio River, and onto the road that led to Gonzales.

The Alamo loomed on his left. There was great activity at the gate, cattle being herded inside, men swearing, shouting, looking back over their shoulders as if expecting to see Santa Anna right upon them. He forced himself not to look toward the old mission. Then a short distance up the road, he reined his horse to a stop and turned. He stared at the crumbling old walls and felt the most unexpected impulse. An insane one, the kind that would surely get him killed if he gave into it.

All he had to do was turn again and keep riding, but he didn't do it. He just kept sitting there, gazing at the Alamo.

David Crockett was fooling around with Persius's handed-down fiddle when the news had come from the town. A lookout posted in a church tower had seen something glittering on the horizon, like sunlight reflecting off armor or weaponry. Since then, everything has been a mad scramble. Some men of the garrison had raced into town, looking for any kind of provisions and food they could round up to carry into the Alamo. To their dismay, they found the populace in flight and most of the provisions already taken. By the time Santa Anna's advance force was nearing the town, only some thirty beeves and a bit of corn had been gathered in to supplement what was already on hand.

David checked his Betsey once again to make sure she was in firing order. It was hard to believe that the Mexican army had actually come. Santa Anna must have driven them through hell itself to get here before spring! He could not know how very nearly on the mark that thought was. The advancing Mexicans had suffered drought, deserts, famine, and blizzards to reach this place. Only Santa Anna himself had traveled in relative comfort.

David had been given command of one of the fort's weakest points, a gap in the original enclosure that had been filled with palisades and earthen embankments. Here the best marksmen were stationed under his command, armed with long rifles. It would be up to their accurate, long-range weapons and marksmanship to make up for what protective qualities the palisades and earthworks lacked. They would be doing their fighting directly in front of the roofless chapel building that was the Alamo's most distinctive feature.

David was giving a final examination to the palisades when he heard his name called. Turning, he found himself looking into the face of Persius Tarr.

"Persius? Is that really you I'm looking at?"

"It's a damn fool you're looking at, Davy. It appears I've come back."

"You're going to help us fight?"

Persius had a very disgusted look on his face. "So it seems. Likely I'm just going to get myself good and dead." He coughed, very hard. "Maybe it don't matter. These lungs of mine are bound to kill me before long anyway."

"We're not here to die, not unless it comes down to it," David replied. "I don't get into fights planning to lose them, but I'll be shot if I run from one either, no matter how it goes." He grinned and put his hand on Persius's shoulder. "Glad to have you back, Persius. Or should I say, Ben?"

"I don't care what you call me. I don't think it matters a bit anymore." Persius looked around the compound. "Looks stronger than when I last seen it. Has anybody give thought to what we'll drink if they block the stream?"

"There's a well been opened up over yonder," David said. "See it?"

"Yes. Good. If it gets too fearsome here before long, maybe I'll just run and jump down it." He coughed some more, and spat blood onto the ground.

"You ain't the only man sick at the lungs here," David said. "Jim Bowie is getting worse by the day."

"I don't know him."

"He's commanding the volunteers, with Colonel Travis commanding the regular soldiers. There's been an argument between them, and no love lost on either side. But no time to chew that fat right now, Persius. We may be fighting here before long, and I've got a world of getting ready to do."

In mid-afternoon the defenders of the old mission saw an ominous sight across the river. A bloodred flag hung from the tower of the San Fernando Church, which stood hard by the Military Plaza in San Antonio de Bexar.

"What's it mean?" one of David's men asked him.

"It means that the Mexican army is in town now. But more than that. I'm told a red flag is Santy Anny's sign that there'll be no quarter given to prisoners," David replied.

"Damn," Persius muttered. "I reckon I *am* a fool. I could have been a long way from here by now."

Chapter 58

February 24, 1836

The concussion hammered them so hard that their ears popped and their chests rattled, causing Persius Tarr to cough violently. Grit and shards of stone hit them like a rain of nails. When the dust had settled, the clump of men lifted their heads and began beating the dirt and grime off their hats and shoulders.

"That was the closest one yet," David Crockett commented. "I can see already I ain't going to like this kind of fighting, all closed in like a hen in a coop."

"Fighting?" one of the others asked. "We ain't done no real fighting yet, Colonel. You just wait till we do—there'll be plenty of dead Mex flesh to feed the buzzards, yes sir."

"That's right," David said. "We're going to drop them by the hundreds."

" 'Pears to me we'd best figure a way to drop them by the thousands," Persius commented. "Otherwise they'll swarm right over the top of us."

"You always did look for the bright side, Persius," David said. He had dropped Persius's alias of Ben Breeding, and to those who sought an explanation for the change of names, both Persius and David frankly explained that Persius had run into trouble in Tennessee and had used a false name for safety. No one was shocked; many men changed their names throughout life. And now that the group of less than two hundred was locked together inside this old stone mission, past affairs from the outside world didn't seem to matter to anyone anyway.

A cannonball sailed overhead and arced down into the livestock pens beyond the old chapel. Horses trumpeted and nickered.

"Bet that killed at least one of them," a man said.

David peered across the smoke-filled enclosure and made out Colonel Travis darting for cover near the northern postern. Moments later an explosion not far away from that spot rained dirt and stone all over the man. David was concerned; was Travis all right? Moments later he saw Travis stand and brush himself off, talking to another fellow nearby.

This enclosure was Travis's to command now; Neill had been called away from his post. Bowie had grown even sicker and was now lodged in a bedroom over near the main Alamo entrance, close by the place David and his marksmen huddled. Word was that Bowie was so sick he was unlikely to live long, even if he did survive this siege.

David rose and peered over the palisades. A blast of smoke and a boom that reached his ears a moment later revealed the release of yet another round of Mexican artillery. He ducked. The missile sailed far overhead and came down in the center of the plaza, leaving a big crater.

"Trying to wear down our courage, not to mention the walls," David said.

"The walls are holding up better than my courage," another said.

"We'll come through fine," David replied in a tone of forced cheerfulness. "Come spring there'll be flowers blooming on Mex graves from here to the Rio Grande."

But he wasn't really that confident. The size of Santa Anna's force was already staggering, and intelligence was that even more troops were on the way. And a messenger from Goliad had come in the evening before, saying that Colonel James Fannin, who had been expected to bring more than four hundred men to reinforce the Alamo, would not be able to come at all. It was grim, disheartening news.

David hoped the bombardment would cease soon. It was beginning to wear down the nerves of the defenders, and worse, there was no way to fight back in kind. Only seldom did any of the Alamo's cannon return fire. There was no powder to spare, and what there was would be needed far more badly when this prelude was over and the real battle began.

That night, Travis sent out a courier bearing the following message:

> To the people of Texas and all Americans in the world, Fellow citizens and compatriots—I am besieged by a thousand or more Mexicans under Santa Anna. I have sustained a continual Bombardment & cannonade for 24 hours & have not lost a man—The enemy has demanded a surrender at discretion, otherwise, the garrison are to be put to the sword, if the fort is taken—I have answered the demand with a cannon shot, & our flag still waves proudly from the walls—I shall never surrender or retreat. Then, I call on you in the name of Liberty, of patriotism & everything dear to the American character, to come to our aid, with all dispatch—The enemy is receiving reinforcements daily & will no doubt increase to three or four thousand in four or five days. If this call is neglected, I am determined to sustain myself as long as possible & die like a soldier who never forgets what is due to his own honor & that of his country—Victory or Death.

> P.S. The Lord is on our side—When the enemy appeared in sight we had not three bushels of corn—We have since found in deserted houses 80 or 90 bushels and got into the walls 20 or 30 heads of Beeves.

A few minutes after ten o'clock on the following morning, David had the pleasure of taking his first real shot at a Mexican soldier, and the gratification of seeing him grasp his chest and fall. Santa Anna had launched an infantry assault against the southern wall, bugles blaring as some three hundred Mexican infantrymen charged the walls, inaccurate smoothbore muskets in their hands.

David reloaded, grateful for his rifle. He could pick off a Mexican at two hundred yards, while the Mexicans, with their inferior weaponry, had to advance to within seventy yards for even half a chance of hitting anything.

At Travis's orders, the Alamo marksmen had allowed the Mexicans to come within easy range before opening fire. The effect was telling; some two hours later, at least eight Mexicans were dead and no one in the Alamo had been hurt, save those who were cut by flying stones during the earlier bombardment.

Furthermore, several of the huts that had shielded the advancing Mexicans were now in flames, set ablaze by a group of brave Alamo defenders who raced out from the walls with torches, then back inside again.

"That'll teach 'em," one of David's marksmen said.

"No, I'm fearful it won't," he replied. "We haven't seen a real siege yet. Santy Anny will take his time before he really hits us. He wants us to be as weary and scared as we can be."

"I ain't scared," one of the younger riflemen blustered.

"I am," Persius Tarr mumbled as he reloaded his rifle.

That night, Persius was among the soldiers who went to James Bowie's room to see how the man was faring. Most of those who came in knew Bowie personally and came out of friendship. It hardly mattered; Bowie was so sick he didn't seem to know them.

Persius hadn't come out of friendship, but because he was beginning to believe he shared the same disease as Bowie, and probably would share the same fate . . . assuming he survived this siege at all. When he saw the pallid, delirious man laid out on his cot, he was chilled. Soon, he thought, it will be me dying like that.

He left Bowie's room in a rush, and did not go back again.

February 26

Shoulders aching from the repeated slams of rifle recoil, David Crockett's marksmen kept at it, aiming and firing, swearing when their shots missed and cheering whenever they saw a Mexican fall. Though they were growing wearier by the day—Santa Anna kept up enough cannon fire to make sure no one inside the mission could get much sleep—there was a general sense of encouragement. So far, not one defender had died, and even though the Mexicans had managed to move gun emplacements nearer and nearer the ancient Alamo walls, they were paying a dear price for it. David's marksmen were excellent snipers, and the long range of their rifles kept the Mexicans hopping. No one had been able to keep an accurate count of Mexican casualties; David had long since quit trying.

Further encouragement came as rumor spread through the ranks that Colonel Fannin was on his way after all. Troops questioned Travis about this, but he could not confirm it. "We may hope and pray it is true," he said.

The weather was worsening. On the first day of the siege, the day had warmed significantly, but now a cold wind had swept in. There was little firewood inside the Alamo with which to counter the cold.

"Lost my coat to a harlot," Persius said to David as the cold night fell. "I'd be freezing half to death if I hadn't put on some Mex clothes she had."

"Mex clothes?"

"Yes, under my own clothes." He opened his outer shirt and showed the cotton shirt beneath it.

David asked, "Are the britches like the shirt?"

"Yes."

He leaned close and spoke in a low voice. "Persius,

in them clothes and with your dark looks you could be took for a Mexican. Some of the soldiers I've seen are dressed like that."

"Well, that's true, now that you mention it."

"You might be able to slip out of here. You could live."

Persius smiled subtly. "You encouraging me to desert, Colonel Crockett?"

Hearing it put out so plainly made David frown. "I'm just saying that . . . never mind it. It was just words." David looked away. "We're likely to die here, Persius. You know that. You're my friend. I don't want to see you die."

"What is it, David? You believe only a fine citizen like yourself deserves to have any glory?"

"Never mind it, Persius. Like I said, it was just words."

"I'm going to die anyway, Davy. Just like old Bowie's going to die. These lungs of mine are worse and worse. The way I see it, if I get killed here, at least for once in his life Persius Tarr can say he done a good and grand thing. I ain't never lived right. Maybe I can die right."

David studied the dark face of his companion. Maybe there was more to the man than he had ever shown before. His words had an iron in them David wasn't accustomed to hearing from Persius.

"Who knows, Persius? Maybe we'll make it through. Maybe Fannin will come with his men and save our skins. Then we can take that money you got and buy us the land we were talking about."

"Partners again, eh?"

"That's right. If you're still willing to have me."

"I am. But there's something I need to tell you about that money. It wasn't inherited. It was stole."

"Stole . . ."

"That's right. Robbed right out of a rich man's safe, right in his house. I was working for him in Nashville, and he was fool enough to leave it open. Even that fiddle is stole. It belonged to the rich man's house servant, an old darky. I took a shine to it and just carried it out with me."

David's spirit drooped. Why was it always this way

with Persius? Every time the man showed some spark of nobility, he would turn around and snuff it out.

"I wish you hadn't told me, Persius."

"It really don't matter now, David. There's not going to be any land, any partnership, any new life, at least not for me. Maybe you'll come through alive and make that new start for yourself and your family, but me, I'm going to die. Either here, or later on in some bed, coughing my life away like poor old Bowie in yonder room. I believe I'd just as soon do my dying here. There's nothing left for me, even if I do survive this."

"You sound like you're set on death, Persius."

"No. But I do believe death is set on me. It comes to us all sooner or later. We just have to face it."

They held silent a few moments. Outside the walls they heard the noises of busy Mexicans, taking advantage of the cover of darkness to move their gun emplacements even closer to the walls. It was a grim thing to listen to, grimmer even than Persius's soft-spoken talk of death.

"If I die and you live, Davy, I want you to have my money. I keep it in my left boot, in a pocket stitched into the lining. There's maybe six hundred dollars left."

"I can't take that money, Persius. I wouldn't feel right, spending stolen money."

"I reckon I shouldn't have told you, then."

"No, you shouldn't have."

David picked up Persius's old fiddle. He had brought it out of the barracks to while away time with during breaks in the fighting. He plucked the strings with his thumb, fingering out an old tune.

"You've learned to play that thing already, Davy?"

"Just a bit."

"I'll be. You're a better man than me even on the fiddle."

"I ain't a better man. Here I am, right up on fifty years old, and all I've got is a political career that went bust on me, a pile of debts, and a few thousand Mexicans wanting to send me to meet Jesus soon as possible."

Persius smiled. "Don't get low-spirited, David. This

here may be the end, but we can make it the glory-time if we want to."

David looked at Persius sharply. "What did you say?"

"I said, we could make this the glory-time, if we want to."

The dream-image of his Uncle Jimmy flashed across his mind. *You'll know the glory-time only when the glory-time comes. Go into the shining, David Crockett, and shout your hallelujah!*

God above! David thought. Is *this* the destiny I've been waiting for? Is this what my life has been leading up to . . . is this why my name will be remembered when I'm gone? Could it be that sometimes a man finds his real glory-time, his shining, only at the end of his days?

"Into the shining." He whispered the words to himself.

"Did you say something, David?"

"No. Nothing at all."

"I'm thinking I'm going to take that money out of my boot and throw it down the well yonder. I ain't going to need it no more. You sure you don't want it, Dave?"

"I don't believe I'll be needing it either, Persius. You go ahead, if that's what you want."

Persius dug out the bills. Looking at them, he sighed. "I never thought I'd come to the place of throwing several hundred dollars down a deuced well." He hacked and coughed a few moments, then rose.

"Well, here goes." He strode across the pitted, trampled earth and tossed the bills into the well.

"Lord have mercy," David heard him say. "Lord have mercy on a fool like me."

Chapter 59

There was one good thing that happens to men who are likely to die very soon, David Crockett discovered. It takes away some of their need to struggle so hard for survival. Oddly, it gives them moments of near fearlessness, moments when they stand ready to accept without resistance what fate has thrown their way.

Right now there was little evidence of fear on the part of anyone defending the Alamo. The cold wind had died down, and the light rain that came in its place was much easier to endure. As evening fell and the fighting lulled, David decided it was time to inject some fun into the atmosphere. He grabbed up Persius's old fiddle and bow and marched over to one John McGregor, a Scotsman who was one of the several Europeans among the defenders of this old mission.

"McGregor, you sorry old coot of a Scot, I'm an Irish fiddler, name of Crockett, and I can fiddle you into the ground while you try to squeeze a tune out of that dead cat or whatever it is you call a music-maker! I'm challenging you to a duel, you mangy son of men in dresses!"

"Ah! Is that so, you bloody Irishman? I'll fetch out me pipes and we'll see about who's the music-maker good and quick!"

"Go get 'em, highlander! I'll learn you quick how a tune ought to sound!"

McGregor trotted off to his barracks to get out one of the oddest items to have been brought inside the Alamo: a set of authentic Scottish bagpipes. McGregor was quite good at playing them and treasured them highly. In a few moments he was back out with them, blowing through the mouthpiece and getting his arm into position on the bellows.

"Play your best, Scotsman!" David shouted, winking at the weary men gathering around them.

McGregor began playing, the droning notes carrying far into the night, even over the Alamo walls. David grinned, imagining the puzzlement of the Mexicans who were close enough to hear. Well, they ain't heard a thing yet, he thought, and put the fiddle to his chin.

He dragged the bow across the strings and set into a ragged version of an old mountain fiddle tune. He couldn't play it fancy like good fiddlers could, but he did manage to make the tune recognizable. Never mind that it was not the same tune McGregor was playing, nor even in the same key. It made a wild ruckus of noise, and the men of the Alamo seemed to relish it.

"Saw that thing in half, Colonel!" someone yelled.

"Squish on that cat, McGregor! You can outplay old Canebrake Davy any day!"

"The devil he can! I'll put my money on the colonel."

"You ain't got no money."

"I got beauty. A pretty face the women dearly love to kiss on."

The banter made for much better music in David's ears than any of the tortured sounds he and McGregor rendered. Banter and lightheartedness were just what was needed right now. This was almost surely a doomed garrison—he knew it, and all the men here knew it. The latest emissaries to slip in through Mexican lines had reported that Fannin was indeed on his way, but by now it hardly mattered if he got here. There were far too many Mexicans surrounding the Alamo for any significant relief to get through.

And so Crockett fiddled and McGregor played his

pipes, fiddled and played defiantly in the face of impending death.

David had expected that there would be few or no encouraging developments from here on out, but he was proven wrong a few hours before dawn when Lieutenant George Kimball and some thirty members of his Gonzales Ranging Company of Mounted Volunteers were ushered through the Alamo gate. It was a stunning event, heartening beyond words, and if it meant little in terms of significantly strengthening the compound, it meant much in terms of symbolism and defiance of Santa Anna.

The intense darkness brought by the bad weather was what had allowed Kimball and company to make it through. Their arrival sent spirits soaring; even the usually serious Travis was so happy that he declared just a little of the increasingly precious gunpowder could be used to fire upon a particularly prominent target, a house on Bexar's Main Plaza . . . a house some declared was the very headquarters of Santa Anna.

They fired it off as the wind-whipped morning came on. It was a successful shot. A big chunk of the house blew to rubble, causing the Alamo defenders to cheer.

And then David's eye caught sight of a man in fine uniform running toward the damaged building. His heart raced. Santa Anna himself! Judging from the uniform and the way those around him acted, Santa Anna it surely had to be! He raised his rifle, lifted its sight above its target in hopes of sending the ball arcing down to hit the man, and fired. It was a vain shot, but worth the effort. He didn't consider it wasted powder at all.

Time passed, and the fate of the Alamo became more and more clear. Additional Mexican reinforcements swarmed into town; estimates now had about twenty-five hundred Mexican soldiers around the mission, and many more on their way. As time passed, the Mexicans moved their emplacements ever closer, and dug new trenches under the Alamo's very walls. David and his marksmen killed many who exposed their forms a moment too long, but by now the killing was almost symbolic. There were far too many Mexicans out there for any hope of defeating them. Even if every remaining rifle ball inside the walls found a heart as its target, there would be more than enough Mexicans remaining to wipe out the garrison.

On March third a courier made it through the Mexican lines and came in with grim tidings. Fannin would not be coming at all. The courier, an old friend of Travis's named James Butler Bonham, reported that Fannin's efforts to reach the mission had been thwarted by the high waters of the San Antonio River, which had broken up many of his wagons in the water. And by the time that problem had been overcome, Fannin had learned that a small band of Texans under Colonel Frank Johnson had been wiped out at San Patricio. He made for that place rather than the Alamo, believing it would soon be attacked again and that he could better serve the revolution at San Patricio. No one faulted him. It was a sensible decision, one Travis would have made himself had the circumstances been reversed.

There was no question now that the Alamo's fate was sealed. On March fourth the continuing Mexican cannonade paid off for Santa Anna when a large hole was knocked through the north wall. The Alamo defenders struggled to throw debris back into the gap, but the Mexicans hit them all the harder with mortar and cannon fire. The area inside the walls became so dusty that David and his riflemen could scarcely see what was going on elsewhere in the compound.

"I don't much like this being hemmed in, Persius," David said. "I believe I'd rather die out in the open."

"Dying's all the same, wherever it happens," Persius replied. "Be strong, David Crockett. Take as many of them with you as you can."

"I intend to. I intend to."

On the next evening, Travis called the men together. They made a motley, sorry sight—huddled together, caked in dirt and sweat and mud, clothes ragged and ruined, hair filthy and stringing down the sides of their whiskered faces. Only one of the number could not stand, and that was Bowie, who had been carried out on his cot.

Travis looked them over, face-to-face, then spoke.

"Our fate is sealed," he said. "Within a few days, maybe a few hours, we shall all be facing our eternity. This is our destiny and there's nothing we can do to avoid it. Our doom is certain.

"All we can do is die here in our fort and fight to the end, and sell our lives dear."

He drew his sword and with its end drew a clear line in the dirt. "Any man determined to remain here and die with me, let him step across this line."

For a moment there was no movement, then one man stepped forward, and another, and another. Bowie, more lucid today than the time Persius had gone to his room, had his cot carried across; if he and Travis had quarreled over authority before, the squabble was now forgotten. They were two men of one cause.

In the end all were across the line with Travis, except for one man, Louis Rose, a Frenchman with battle experience going back to the Napoleonic wars.

Bowie pushed himself up on his elbows. "Rose, you don't seem willing to go to the end with us."

David joined in, gently. "Old fellow, you might as well come die with us. There's no escape."

Rose shook his head. "No. I've seen enough of death and battle in my life. I'll not remain."

He turned and ran toward the wall. Clambering up with skill remarkable for an old fellow, he made the top, then dropped over. No one tried to stop him, nor did any look to see where he went, or if he made it far alive.

Travis thanked his men and dismissed them, and they scattered back to their posts to await the end. Persius happened to glance at David just as something slipped from David's bullet pouch and fell to the ground. Stooping and picking it up, Persius saw it was the silver nugget David always carried. He was about to yell to David and tell him he had it, but Travis called for David first, ordering him to come for a conference. Persius put the silver into his pocket. He could return it later, when David wasn't busy.

Later. Would there be any more of later to be had? He looked at the walls and sensed the thousands of antagonistic human presences outside them. The feeling was like being in the palm of a hand that was curling into a tight, crushing fist. Crushing steadily and slowly, like the pain that burned in his chest every time he coughed.

David was walking beside Persius an hour later when the fearlessness that had protected him vanished suddenly and panic took its place. This was cold, wrenching panic that swept him unexpectedly, just like the time alone in his rooms in Washington City when his nerve gave out and a sense of inadequacy overcame him. He gasped for breath and slumped to the side, hand against an adobe wall, and gazed wildly about.

"David, what's wrong with you?" Persius asked, putting his hand out to steady his friend.

David brushed the hand away. "Don't touch me! Get away from me—need to . . . breathe."

"David, you all right?"

David lurched off into a dark corner and sank to his knees, where he heaved his stomach empty. Rising, he stepped off deeper into the shadows. Persius followed. He found David leaning against a wall, palms flat against it as if he had been shoved up for a search. Persius put his hands on David's shoulders and felt him tense.

"Davy, Davy, it's all right. The fear has hit you, that's all."

David turned, shrugging off Persius's touch. Here in the dark it was difficult to make out his face. "I am afraid, Persius. I haven't been before . . . not like this, at least. We're going to die here. You understand that, Persius? We're going to die!"

"I know, Davy. I know. But there ain't no news in that. We're born to die, Davy, every one of us. Only difference between us and most everybody else is that we know when and where it's going to be. That's all."

"I'm afraid. Look at me, Persius! I'm shaking!"

"Of course you're afraid. I am too. Ain't a man here not afraid."

"I can't be afraid, not me. I'm Crockett. I'm Cane-brake Davy. I'm half horse, half alligator. The man who wrung the tail off the comet."

"I know you are, Davy. So do all these men here. That's why you're going to get past this. You're going to put that fear behind you right now, and walk back out there, and fight like the man you are." Persius stopped and coughed; he tasted blood and felt weakened a few seconds. With a great wrench of will, he forced the strength back into himself, then looked at his friend. "It's gone now, David. The fear's come and now it's gone, because there's nothing to be gained from it."

"Gone . . ."

"That's right, Davy. It's gone. No need for it any more. Just let it fly off, like a bird, way up in the sky yonder. Ain't no need for fear. This is our time, Davy. Our time."

"The glory-time . . ."

"That's right, David. The glory-time. There's men out there with their eye on you. You're the only thing keeping the fear away from them. You're joking and grinning and fiddling and such—it gives them courage they wouldn't have had without you. Maybe that's why you're here, Davy, to make the little men and the scared men into big and brave men. Hang on to your courage. You've always cared about the little men, Davy. Remember who you are. You're Screamer Crockett. You're the man from the cane. You're Crockett of Tennessee, and your glory-time has come. Don't you miss it. Don't you miss a bit of it, you hear?"

"I hear."

And strange as it seemed, after that David wasn't afraid anymore. He was sad, and thought frequently and fondly of his family back in Tennessee . . . but it wasn't fear that stirred his heart, only the love of a husband and father bound never to see his loved ones again. Why should he be afraid? This was the glory-time. This was the shining. This was the moment he had been born for, and he intended to meet it with dignity.

Persius was right. He was here to show how a man could face his death the right way. He was here not only as a man, but also as a legend. And it was his duty to live up to it.

And so his fear died. As did the last of any harsh attitude toward Persius Tarr. It seemed astonishing to him now that he had ever tried to hide his associations with this man. For years Persius had been the shame of David Crockett. Now he was his inspiration.

Persius Tarr was facing the end of his days with a courage that surprised and awed him. And if Persius could do that, by heaven, David Crockett could do no less.

Chapter 60

The end began with the first hint of dawn and was heralded not with gunshots, but cheers. Inside the north wall of the Alamo a sentinel halted his pacing and listened, with comprehension and terror rising simultaneously, to the harsh chorus of Mexican shouts.

"Viva Santa Anna! Viva Santa Anna!"

The sentinel clambered up an earthen cannon emplacement and peered over the wall. Just as dawn broke through in the east, he saw them coming in a great swarm, bearing ladders and pikes. Across the pounded and pitted earth, into and across the moatlike ditch, and toward the north wall.

"The Mexicans are coming!" he yelled, leaping back to the ground and darting toward the barracks. "Colonel Travis, wake up! The Mexicans . . ."

Travis was the first to respond to the call, but in mere seconds the grim news spread among the men, who sat up drowsy and cold, then rose, instantly awake and oblivious to the chill. Rifles clattered; there were muffled grunts and oaths and prayers as men pulled on boots, slid on shirts and jackets, slapped on hats.

David Crockett and Persius Tarr, who had jerked awake at the same moment, were among those in the scramble. They glanced at each other; the time had come for last words. But there were none. All that needed saying had already been said days before, months before, years before. They snatched up their rifles and headed out into the growing light.

A glance toward the north wall revealed ladder tops just now leaning into place above the wall's rim. David picked out Travis's voice amid the hubbub. "Give them hell, boys! Hurrah! Hurrah! Give them hell!"

"Look at him, Persius! That's an officer there, a *real* officer." David glanced down to check the lock of his rifle. When he glanced up again, Travis was firing a shotgun over the wall, aiming almost straight down. The Mexicans were immediately at hand now. "He'll give them hell, all right!" David continued, "And I intend to do the . . . God! He's shot!"

Persius had already seen it. Travis spasmed and pitched backward, his shotgun falling from his hands, a spray of blood exploding from his head. He had taken a bullet through the forehead. Now his body, dying as it fell, pitched off the cannon platform and onto the sloping earth built up against the inside wall. There he lay, legs sprawled, head bloodied and drooping to the side. For him, the battle for the Alamo had ended very quickly.

At the moment, the seige was focused on the northern portion of the enclosure, where columns of troops under General Martin Perfecto de Cos and Colonel Francisco Duque attempted to swarm the Alamo like ants. But the level of fire they encountered from the defenders was proving unexpectedly effective. Mexicans fell in appalling numbers, and their onslaughts withered. So far, the few Mexicans who had reached the walls with ladders and pikes had been killed or driven back, and two major thrusts had been turned away. But now the Mexican troops were being helped by their very own disorder. Columns of their troops mixed and surged forward together, an incredible mass of humanity, so many men that all the Alamo's guns firing accurately together would leave the vast majority still alive and charging.

They passed through the field of cannon fire, many falling, pierced by rifle balls and grapeshot, and then swarmed in close to the walls. But now that they were here, they were in a sense prisoners of their own success. Though the cannon could no longer harm them, the Texans could pick them off easily with rifles, and they were so cramped together that they could barely move, much less pick up the ladders that the Texans had pushed away from the wall after the first failed onslaught. Milling like cattle, they died in piles, sometimes unwittingly killing one another by their own wild and careless cross-firing.

Meanwhile, David Crockett took his bearings. At the moment, the battle remained centered at the north end, but already he could see Mexican troops beginning to sweep out in new directions. His assignment had been the defense of the palisaded southern wall, in front of the chapel. His troops gathered around him, checking their weapons, and then all made for that area. As he ran, David thought how odd a thing it was to be racing for the very spot where he would almost certainly stand his last on the earth. Everything around him took on a surreal aspect, like one of his disconcerting malarial dreams.

He stopped in his tracks, turning his head. Music . . . trumpeted and somehow frightening, like the music that had unsettled him so during the fever that Uncle Jimmy had pulled him through that time back at John Crockett's tavern.

"It's the Deguello," a Texan nearby him said. "The Mexes play it when there is to be no mercy given."

For a couple of moments David felt frozen in place, but he shook it off. "No mercy . . . no mercy given by *us*!" he declared. "Men, we're going to turn this ground red with Mex blood long before we spill our own!"

"Amen, Davy," a voice nearby him said, and David turned and looked into the grim but smiling face of Persius Tarr. David grinned back, taking courage from the mere presence of his old friend.

Before long the fight came to them in the form of a column of troops under a Mexican colonel named Morales. With yells and cheers they charged in, and David barked the order for the first volley. Rifles cracked and Mexican troops fell. David heard Persius laugh loudly, triumphantly, then give way to a fit of terrible coughing while he grabbed a new rifle and shoved his empty one to a young man assigned to reloading.

The defensive fire proved very effective. Morales's troops continued to shove toward the flimsy-looking palisades, but a second volley killed even more of them. On it went, assault and response, advance and retreat, until finally the Mexicans gave up and moved their attack to the southwest corner and the area swept by Travis's prized eighteen-pounder cannon.

Elsewhere, the inevitable had already begun. In the glow of morning, Mexican troops had swarmed up the walls, mounting the wooden redoubt built over a wall breach and clambering up the northern postern. Desperately, the Texans fought to hold back the flood, but a flood it was, and it could not be checked. The Mexicans paid a dear price for their success, but at last the way was cleared and they swarmed in easily, eager for blood.

And from then on it was all different. No longer was this a fight to keep an enemy outside the walls. That purpose was lost. Now it was hand-to-hand combat, men looking into the very eyes of other men they did not know but were trying desperately to kill.

Persius Tarr fired off a shot and then looked toward the southeastern corner. The Mexicans were over the wall there too, and even as he watched, they killed the last of the men manning the eighteen-pounder and took possession. Persius swore, picked up another rifle, and fired toward the closest of the Mexicans. He swore again when he missed.

At the north wall, the Mexicans had driven back the last of the defenders and came pouring in, bayonets flashing silver, lancing downward, then flashing red. The screams of the dying were terrible on all sides. Persius coughed hard and blood flowed down his chin. He wiped it with his sleeve and paid it no heed.

David, meanwhile, was the image of calm. He lifted his rifle, fired, watched a Mexican fall. Handing off the rifle for reloading, he raised a fresh rifle, fired again, and again took a life. The young man doing the reloading reached for the spent weapon, but took a ball through the temple and died on the spot. David glanced down, shook his head regretfully, and reloaded the rifle himself.

The Mexicans seemed to be everywhere now. Persius grabbed a fresh rifle, took a loaded pistol from the belt of a fallen companion, and waded into the thick of the fight. He fired off the rifle at point-blank range, sending a ball through the neck of a soldier who raced toward David with his bayonet ready. Another soldier came toward Persius himself, swinging a saber. Persius lifted the pistol and fired it into the man's face. He fell with a grunt and died.

But there were many more after him. They came at Persius with teeth gritted and bayonets aimed. Persius swung his rifle like a club and brought down one, then two of them. Turning, he ran to the side and missed being pierced. Now he fled wildly toward the barracks, as across the clearing other defenders did the same. This had been the plan all along, and the barracks had been strengthened for a final stand. But then Persius stopped and looked back. David was still fighting, swinging his rifle like a club, bringing down every soldier who charged him. They literally lay piled around him.

Persius knew he could not go to the barracks. His place was beside David Crockett, fighting to the last with the man who had been more a friend to him than any other human being except for the young wife he had loved so dearly. With a triumphant shout, Persius darted toward David, blind to all the carnage around him, blind to bayonets, sabers, rifles, blind to death that could come in a dozen different ways. He did not expect to live now. All he asked was to be at David Crockett's side when the end came.

Then a form loomed before him. A big Mexican soldier, grinning and ugly, his saber uplifted. Persius screamed at him to get out of the way, damn his soul, so he could reach David, but then the saber swung down and Persius felt his face laid open from eye to neck. He jerked back, feeling hot blood stream down his chest. The saber swung again and Persius's throat gave him a sting. He tried to shout again and found his voice was gone. Mild as the sting had felt, his groping fingers found a wet and gaping wound. Passing out, he fell in a heap.

The next thing he was aware of was crawling, mindlessly crawling, moving with no more speed than a worm toward David, who even now still fought with his shattered rifle, still alive despite all odds against him. Something caught at Persius's outer shirt—the tip of a musket bayonet sticking out from beneath the body of a fallen Mexican soldier. It had snagged Persius's clothing. He pushed himself up long enough to rip away the outer shirt, exposing the cotton Mexican shirt beneath it. He fell and crawled some more. He was nearly to David now, and astounded that he had made it so far.

Davy ... He had forgotten he could not speak. He moved his mouth but no sound came out. *Davy, I'm here now ... I'll stand by you, Davy....*

Then a crushing mass fell atop him, heavy and deadweight and fleshy. His breath was cut off. He found himself staring into the bloody face of a dead Mexican soldier. He struggled to push the body off himself, but yet another fell atop the first, putting him at the bottom of a heap of dead men. Straining for air, he managed to turn his body just enough to make breathing possible. *Davy, don't bury me beneath your dead ... I'm here, Davy....*

And then he passed out.

When he was next aware of his own existence, Persius thought he was back in Fort Mims at the massacre. He was buried in bodies and slick with blood. He opened his eyes and looked out through a red stain. The face of the dead Mexican soldier still looked into his from inches away. It was already turning black.

He remembered now that he was not at Fort Mims, but the Alamo. Listening for sounds of battle, he heard none. Just tramping feet, moans, voices talking in Spanish. The fight was over—and he was still alive.

He pushed his way out from beneath the corpses, a process that took several minutes. He lost his trousers in the process, literally squeezed out of them, so when he came out from under the pile at last, he was wearing only the cotton Mexican clothing he had taken from Rosa's cabinet. It was no longer white, but rusty with mud and drying blood. Exhaustion, loss of blood, and a burst of cool wind chilled him. He wrapped his arms around his torso, shivering, then reached down and removed a bloodied coat from a dead Mexican soldier at his feet. He threw it across his own shoulders. He didn't have the wits about him at that moment to realize what a providential circumstance it was that he now looked just like the Mexicans all around him.

There was activity some distance across the clearing. Stumbling around the heap of corpses, Persius blinked away more blood from his eyes. There was Santa Anna himself, standing haughtily in the midst of a circle of officers. Facing him were a handful of Alamo defenders—five, six of them. Persius couldn't tell. One of them turned his head exposing his face.

David! You lived, David! You made it through!

He tried to move forward but his feet gave way beneath him and he fell on his face. Slowly he pushed his way up again. If David had been captured, he would be captured too. They would go through it all together, like they always had, and if they came out alive or wound up dead, they would do that together too.

A Mexican in a general's uniform was talking fervently to Santa Anna. Persius couldn't understand the words, but he gathered the subject was the handful of prisoners.

David, look at me! I'm here, Davy! Here!

He was unable to shout, and it would have been foolish to do so even if he could. In the back of his mind he began to think how curious it was that he, one of the rebel defenders, was not being bothered. Suddenly he realized why. In the clothing he now wore, with his swarthy half-breed's skin, he was mistaken for one of the Mexican soldiers! It was so ironic he might have laughed. He was moving freely in the midst of men he had been doing his best to kill only a little while ago, and they didn't even notice him!

David turned; his eyes locked on Persius. He looked shocked, and Persius wondered why. Then he realized that

his clothing and laid-open face must have made him un-
recognizable. David peered at him more closely, trying to
see if maybe . . .

*Yes, Davy, it's me, it's Persius! I'll help you, David,
somehow or another I'll get you away from here. . . .*

Santa Anna turned his back. Moments later a group
of soldiers advanced upon the little band of prisoners. David was still looking toward Persius, who tried to scream,
tried to warn him, but could produce no voice except the
one that raged inside his head, vainly wanting to get out.

*Look out Davy—oh watch out, they have bayo-
nets. . . .*

He sank to his knees, beginning to pass out again.
The image before him swam and wavered—David, pierced
again and again by bayonets, taking the assault without an
outcry, claimed by his destiny, going to his glory-time like
the bravest of soldiers.

"Davy . . ." A whisper. It was all Persius could manage. He pitched forward, only dimly aware of the final
gory image of David's corpse being lifted on the points of
several bayonets.

*Farewell, David Crockett. I'm glad I've knowed you,
mighty glad I've knowed you.*

Then darkness came and Persius Tarr knew nothing
else.

He awakened with bandages on his face and neck,
and a Mexican leaning into the window of vision his one
uncovered eye provided. Words in Spanish chattered at
him. He closed his eyes and slept.

When he awakened again, he sat up. He was inside a
big room, filled with wounded, moaning, and, in some
cases, dying Mexican soldiers. *My God, they still think I'm
one of them.* He rose, dizzy, and walked out.

He was in San Antonio; he recognized the street. Like
a walking dead man, he staggered out into the thoroughfare. Someone cursed at him and yanked a wagon to a halt
to avoid running him over. Without even looking at the
man, Persius went on by.

He found Rosa's cantina and climbed painfully up the stairs. The room was empty, standing just as he had left it, though it appeared that perhaps some soldiers, probably officers, had taken up quarters here during the siege, because the bed had been moved and the cabinet door closed. Persius fell into the bed, and did not rise again for days except to rid his body of its wastes. No one found him. He was not disturbed at all. His bandages became stinking and foul, so he pulled them away and tossed them into the cabinet, and disinfected his wounds with a half bottle of whiskey he found tucked behind a shelf. The pain of the alcohol on his wounds made him want to scream—which he couldn't do—and so he drank the rest of the whiskey and slept when the sting finally died away.

For a long time he was sick, aching, and every time he coughed, his saber wound stung and hurt. He sensed that his life was in his own hands; with an act of will, he was sure he could yield himself up to death. But he didn't do it. There was one task yet before Persius Tarr was ready to leave the world behind.

One more task, for Davy.

Chapter 61

Near the Crockett Cabin in Tennessee, Early June, 1836

Despite the warm day, the dusk was cool enough to make Elizabeth Crockett throw a shawl across her shoulders before beginning her evening walk. These solitary outings had become her regular habit of late; the time alone was pleasant and gave her moments to contemplate, to cry on the bad days, to laugh at some happy memory on the good ones. Time to heal, or try to, from the wound of loss.

Perhaps she was making progress, because tonight she hummed to herself. It was the first time she had felt any impulse toward music since that news from Texas had reached her. The tune was that of a peppy march written a year before, but she hummed it slow as a dirge to keep pace with her unhurried steps. Oddly, she had never much liked the melody before. It had been a favorite of David's, however, for natural enough reason: The title was "Go Ahead; a March Dedicated to Colonel Crockett." A New York music publisher had brought it outright about the time of David's triumphant tour, when he was last running for reelection to Congress.

The irony still stung her when she recalled how secretly happy she had been when he had lost that last race. She had believed it would keep him home with her; she hadn't known he would go chase a dream to Texas. She hadn't known that he would turn soldier and in the company of scores face down an army of thousands, and then ... but no matter now. Yesterday was gone, and neither she nor her lost Davy could ever live it again.

She stopped, catching her breath. The exertion of her walk had gotten to her. Since her Davy was gone, she felt older. Not nearly as vigorous and strong as before. She wondered if her children ever noticed.

Digging into a pocket on the apron she wore, she pulled out a gold watch to check the time. Then she flipped it over and examined the engraving on the back: D. Crockett. David's watch, the very one he had taken toward Texas. A Mr. Isaac Jones of Lost Prairie, Arkansas, had recently sent it to her along with a letter telling how David had passed through his home area on the Red River, and had traded the watch with him for a cheaper timepiece, plus thirty dollars. Remarkably kind, Elizabeth thought, that Jones had sent it back. Not many would have been so thoughtful. Such a memento of the famed Colonel Crockett would be of great monetary value, but Jones had unselfishly surrendered it.

She slipped the watch back into her pocket and looked up. Approaching through the gathering dusk was a rider, slumped in the saddle and wearing a blanket across his shoulders. Strange, she thought. The evening hardly seemed cool enough to justify such a heavy covering. Stepping to the side of the road to allow him room to pass her, she examined him closely. His hat was pulled so low it almost covered his eyes. He coughed suddenly, a rattling, painful-sounding cough, and Elizabeth realized why he bundled himself so. He was ill.

He pulled his horse to a stop near her. Lifting his face, he looked at her with weary, watery eyes, the eyes of one whose health is nearly gone. A long, fresh scar ran down his left cheek, into his beard, and across his throat.

"Good evening, ma'am." His voice was deep and very soft, so soft she had to strain to hear it, just as he seemingly strained to produce it.

"Good evening, sir."

"Ma'am, I'm wondering if you might be acquainted

with the wife of the late Colonel Crockett. I know her house is yonder, but there is no light in it and I fear she might be gone."

"I am Elizabeth Crockett."

He sat up a little straighter; his brows lifted over those weak-looking dark eyes. For a time he said nothing more at all. Then he reached up and removed his hat, and nodded respectfully at her. "I'm truly honored to meet you, Mrs. Crockett."

"Is there something I can do for you, Mister . . ."

"No ma'am, except to accept a thing I've brung to you. It's a small thing, but I believe you'll want to have it." He dug beneath the blanket and brought out something in his hand. He held it out to her. "Take it, ma'am. It should be yours from now on."

It was a small box, the size of a ring case, wrapped crudely but tightly in brown paper with twine all around it. She was puzzled.

"Sir, I don't know if I should be taking gifts—"

"It's not a gift, not really. Just a thing you should have. No—don't open it yet. Later. When you're by yourself." He put the hat back on his head and coughed again, three times. Each time, he hunched his shoulders as if in pain. "I beg your pardon, ma'am. I been sick for a good spell now. I swear I believe it's liable to kill me soon. Good evening to you, ma'am."

He rode on past her and down the road. Elizabeth watched him round the bend and go out of sight, then her eyes fell to the little package in her hand. By the last light of the day she pulled away the twine and ripped off the paper. When she opened the box, she put a hand to her mouth and gasped. It contained the little silver nugget that David had carried with him all his days, the one his beloved uncle Jimmy had given to him so long ago.

For several moments she gaped at it. How could this man possibly have come by it? David had carried it in his pocket to Texas. . . . Had he traded it with someone, as he had his pocket watch? It seemed unlikely. He had always treasured it so.

She had to know more.

Gripping the nugget in her palm, she gathered her skirts and ran around the bend after the rider. "Sir! Sir! Please sir, wait!"

He was not far ahead. He stopped and turned in the saddle to see her, then wheeled his horse and waited for her to reach him.

"Sir . . . how did you obtain this?"

"It was dropped by Colonel Crockett in the old mission. It . . . come into my possession."

"But how? They all died there, all of them."

He lowered his eyes. "They say there was one who might have got out alive. He was a half-breed, I hear. A rogue and a scoundrel, no good to nobody, but treated well by your husband. Maybe it was him who brought out the colonel's silver piece."

She looked at him probingly, silent a couple of moments. "Yes, sir. Maybe it was."

"Ma'am, you may hear a tale that Colonel Crockett was took prisoner and put to work in a Mex salt mine, but I can tell you it ain't true. They took him, but they killed him before Santa Anna. He died well, and brave. He didn't bow before them. I know it for a fact. It's just that folks, they don't want to let him go. That's why they tell tales like that. Because they loved him."

She looked at the nugget in her hand again. It was growing very dark now on this shaded stretch of road; she was glad, because it hid the tears that had begun to slide down her cheeks. When she lifted her eyes to the rider again, his face was equally hidden in shadow.

"Who are you, sir?"

"Nobody who matters."

"Please, sir, it matters to me."

He said nothing for a time, and seemed to be looking past her, down the road. "Let's just say I'm a man who's knowed many a bad and evil thing in his time, but a few good things too. And now and again through his years, the best thing." He lifted the reins, ready to go on. His straining voice grew even softer. "Let's just say I'm a man who has knowed what it is to have a friend."

He turned his horse and moved slowly down the road,

disappearing into the darkness. Elizabeth heard his cough long after she lost sight of him, then even that faded into the distance and was gone.

She slipped the nugget into her apron pocket, with the gold watch, and slowly trudged through the thickening night, back to her home.

Afterword

*C*rockett of Tennessee is what can best be called an imaginative expansion upon the life history of Colonel David "Davy" Crockett of Tennessee. The facts of Crockett's life are included in abundance, but supplemented by imagination, the latter most strongly embodied in the fictional story line involving "rogue and scoundrel" Persius Tarr. It is this writer's hope that many who read this tale of Crockett as molded and expanded upon by a novelist will be spurred to go further and examine the fascinating real man whose life is behind the story.

Few public figures in American history came closer to achieving the status of "living legend" than did David Crockett, born where Limestone Creek spills into the Nolichucky River in Greene County, Tennessee, only a few miles from this author's home. Through the Nimrod Wildfire association to word-of-mouth popular anecdotes, from Crockett's own tales of himself to the wildly exaggerated stories in the *Crockett Almanacs*, Crockett was a bigger-than-life figure long before he elevated his name to heroic stature at the Alamo.

Passing years have only added to the Crockett legend. Obviously, the biggest contributor to the modern perception of the man was the famous Walt Disney movie and television series of the 1950s, which set off a Crockett craze that surely would have amazed and amused the real

Crockett. He probably would have recognized only a little of himself in his Disney incarnation, but I think he would have appreciated the flattering portrait and loved the attention.

As best I can see him, the real David Crockett was quite a character, sometimes great, sometimes mundane, sometimes gullible and ambitious, sometimes fully heroic. He overcame a lack of education with natural wit and intelligence. He was not as handsome as a young Fess Parker, but had an appealing face and undeniable charisma. He was politically slick enough to advantageously stretch the facts here and there in his autobiography, yet honest enough to sternly refuse to sugarcoat horrors he had witnessed in the Creek War. The same Crockett who admitted killing Indians "like dogs" at Tallusahatchee also voted against the Indian Removal bill in Congress, despite the tremendous unpopularity of that stand. The same Crockett who went to Texas to find land and new political power, readily put at risk his own ambitions to join the Alamo's defenders, among whom he fought and died so valiantly that it deeply impressed some of the very enemies who killed him.

In that *Crockett of Tennessee* combines history and fiction, it may be useful to help the reader distinguish between the two. Beyond the Persius Tarr story line, most of the fictionalization consists of imaginatively fleshing out characters and situations, occasionally incorporating fictional figures into historical situations, making minor alterations in chronology, or assigning names, personalities, and actions to some of the many persons Crockett mentions, but left anonymous or undescribed in his often terse autobiography.

Historical figures within the story include the various Crockett relatives mentioned, though the names and ages of David's siblings are disputed among genealogists; this novel follows the genealogy laid out in 1956 by Robert M. Torrence and Robert L. Whittenburg in their book, *Colonel "Davy" Crockett*. Other historical figures include the Canadays, Amy Sumner, the Finleys and Elders (though I did create the first name of Annalee for Margaret Elder's sister, whom Crockett left unnamed in his autobiography), most of David's various companions and employers during his "wandering boy" stage, most of the individuals named in the Creek War portion of the story, Thomas Chilton and the other political figures from his Washington days, and his fellow defenders at the Alamo, except, of course, Persius Tarr. Some very minor characters, such as McClure, the ship's captain who seeks to take young David to London, and Kirsten, who introduces David and Polly at the reaping, are historical persons whose roles and actions Crockett described but whose names he either did not remember or chose not to record, and whose identities have not been figured out subsequently by researchers.

Purely fictional characters, in addition to Persius, include the Cummings brothers, Saul Greer, Ben Kelso, Alonz Tidwell, Fletcher, Beaulieu, and a handful of others. The Dr. Campbell Ibbotson character is a fictional composite of real but unknown people who worked in Crockett's background during his congressional days, guiding and molding him as a public figure.

Was Crockett really called Davy within his lifetime? At times, yes, though he went by David in formal affairs. Supporters sometimes shouted "Davy! Davy!" at political rallies; his final political opponent, Adam Huntsman, referred to Crockett as "Davy" in a letter to James K. Polk; the first *Crockett Almanac*, published within Crockett's lifetime, called him Davy; and the Natchez, Mississippi, *Courier* mourned his death in a paragraph that began "Poor Davey Crockett!" Crockett researcher Joe Swann believes 'Davy' is a childhood nickname that Crockett was occasionally called throughout life, and I have followed that pattern in *Crockett of Tennessee*.

How about the famous animal-skin cap? Did Crockett ever wear one? Apparently not usually, but he was reported to be wearing one when he left Tennessee for Texas, and one of those who saw his corpse at the Alamo noted his "peculiar cap" lying nearby, something that wouldn't be said if the cap was his usual brimmed hat. And one of the Mexicans involved in the Alamo battle referred to a particularly effective American fighter in a "long buckskin coat and a round cap without any bill, made out of fox skin with the long tail hanging down the back." This might have been Crockett, a possibility that led me in this novel to put a fox-skin cap, rather than one of coonskin, on David's head as he heads for Texas.

How about the mode of Crockett's death? In *Crockett of Tennessee* he is presented as dying by execution at the order of Santa Anna after being taken prisoner in the fight, and there is abundant evidence that this may be what happened. Those interested in exploring the evidence for themselves are referred to the 1978 monograph called *How Did Davy Die?* written by Dan Kilgore, past president of the Texas State Historical Association. I personally think Kilgore is on the right track, though certainly the subject remains an open question, and a touchy one for some. Some Crockett devotees grow quite upset at the suggestion he died by execution, believing this minimizes his heroism. I don't agree; his heroism is established not by the mode of his death, but by the valiant way he fought to the end.

I owe thanks to many people for their help in making this project a reality. Thanks first to Bantam Senior Editor Tom Dupree and Editor Tom Beer, both of whom helped guide and mold this novel; to former Bantam Senior Editor Greg Tobin, who first conceived the project; to Tom Burke, editorial assistant, and to all the other fine people at Bantam Books.

Thanks also to the staffs of the Davy Crockett Birthplace Park at Limestone, Tennessee; the Alamo in San Antonio; the Lawrenceburg, Tennessee, Chamber of Commerce; Gary Crockett of Jamestown, Tennessee; the helpful folks at the East Tennessee Historical Society; and my agent, Richard Curtis, and his staff.

Most of all, however, I thank the two men to whom this novel is dedicated, Joe Swann and Jim Claborn. Jim has helped keep the Crockett legacy alive in East Tennessee by his work at Morristown's replica of John Crockett's tavern, where David spent his boyhood, and through his many appearances at festivals, schools, etc., as a buckskinned Davy Crockett imitator. I'm particularly flattered that Jim was already a fan of my novels before I contacted him during the planning stages of this book; he had written earlier to tell me that while working as an extra in the filming of the Michael Mann production of *The Last of the Mohicans*, he "died" in one scene with a copy of *The Overmountain Men* tucked under his British Redcoat uniform.

Jim steered me to Joe Swann of Maryville, Tennessee. I'm grateful he did. Joe possesses not only the thoroughly provenanced first rifle of David Crockett (now on loan to the Tennessee State Museum in Nashville), but also has collected very detailed information about Crockett's East Tennessee years. Joe freely shared his data with me, exceeding in generosity and encouragement anything I could have expected, and enabled me to include a few historical facts (such as Canaday's original ownership of the land where John Crockett built his tavern) that have never before been published, to my knowledge. I appreciate him greatly and look forward to the day his Crockett history-in-progress sees publication, an event that is only a matter of time, considering the quality of his research and writing. I can only hope that Joe will not mind the fact that I employed abundant imagination in my account of how David came by that first rifle.

And as always, thanks to Rhonda, Laura, Bonnie, and Matthew Judd, truly a great bunch of folks with whom to enjoy family picnics at the riverside place where a very young David Crockett once pranced about, by his own account, not only without shoes, but without "breeches" as well.

And thanks above all to you, the readers. You are indeed deeply appreciated.

CAMERON JUDD

Greene County, Tennessee
April 2, 1993

ABOUT THE AUTHOR

CAMERON JUDD is a former newspaper reporter and editor and the author of twenty published books, including *The Overmountain Men, The Border Men,* and *The Canebrake Men.* He lives near Greeneville, Tennessee, less than six miles from the birthplace of Davy Crockett. Cameron Judd is currently working on a novel based upon the life of Daniel Boone.

If you enjoyed Cameron Judd's Crockett of Tennessee, *be sure to look for his next novel:*

BOONE
A Novel of the American Frontier

He was a hunter and a trapper, a man who spent a lifetime traversing the American frontier, from Pennsylvania to North Carolina; as far south as Florida, and as far west as the Yellowstone River. Daniel Boone was a wanderer and explorer, torn between the family he struggled to raise and the great untamed wilderness of the Southeast. Fending off hostile Indian attacks, Boone bravely led an expedition through the Cumberland Gap into Kentucky, where he established Boonesborough, one of the first white settlements. But in Boonesborough, Daniel would face his greatest challenge yet: capture by a band of Shawnees who both despised and admired this intrepid white frontiersman. . . .

Turn the page for a preview of Cameron Judd's epic novel, BOONE, *on sale in summer 1995, wherever Bantam Books are sold.*

1

Early Summer, 1755

Crouched by the roadside, his face twisting in a grimace of pain, a wagoner named Nate Meriwether opened his mouth slowly, gingerly, and allowed a fellow wagoner to peer inside.

"Turn your head a mite, Nate—no, the other way, for the light. That's good. Pull down your lower lip." The sufferer complied, holding his posture awkwardly, head tilted back and mouth gaping skyward as the other leaned over him to closely eye a row of yellowed, long-neglected lower teeth. "Nate, that tooth's been let be as long as it can. It'll have to be pulled before it goes to poison."

Nate closed his mouth and looked very sad. "I feared it would come to this," he mumbled. "I dread it."

"Well, a pulled tooth hurts a little while, but a rotten one hurts without end," the other replied. "We'll take care of this here and now. You'd never be able to endure that pain all the way to the Monongahela."

The wagoner about to turn tooth-puller was named Daniel Boone. He pivoted on moccasined feet and headed for his wagon, which stood parked in a queue of assorted wagons and tumbrils that extended far back along the twelve-foot-wide road. Ahead of the wagons was a moving armory, a conglomeration of horse-drawn cannon, howitzers, and light mortars. Farther ahead still, and momentarily out of sight of the wagoners because of the swell of the terrain, were continental soldiers under the immediate command of Lieutenant Colonel George Washington. Beyond them were the soldiers of the British regular army of Major General Edward Braddock, chief commander of this campaign in the Pennsylvania wilderness. And at the very lead and far out of view, chopping away the brush and saplings that had grown on this wilderness route since the Ohio Company hacked it out three years earlier, were the engineers and axemen whose duty it was to sufficiently broaden the road, to erect crude but stout bridges over the many streams, and to pave marshy areas with logs laid side by side. The entire processional reminded Daniel Boone of a great, long worm chewing a westward course into the Alleghenies, a worm that chewed and crawled far too slowly to suit him.

Daniel's pale blue eyes glanced up the line of wagons, horses, and drivers. *Should have forgotten the wagons and used only packhorses and tumbrils.* He couldn't count the number of times he had run that same thought through his mind since this expedition began. Packhorses and tumbrils alone would have progressed more quickly and easily than these big wagons Braddock had commandeered from Pennsylvania farms, and would have required much less road-clearing to accommodate them. Horses bearing packs or pulling light tumbrils wouldn't have tired nearly as fast as big draft horses pulling more than their proper limit in weight. *Should have used only packhorses and tumbrils.* It was simple common sense ... but Daniel had already discovered that the decisions of General Braddock often had little to do with common sense. The man was courageous, dedicated, authoritative, and thoroughly trained—but he was as out of place on the American frontier as a crown prince in a swine pen.

Daniel loosened and pulled back a section of the heavy oiled cloth covering his wagon's cargo and fumbled around until he got a grip on the rawhide handles of a heavy, hand-made wooden trunk. With a grunt of exertion he pulled the trunk up and out, then sat it on the ground beside the wagon.

Opening the wooden latch, he flipped back the lid.

The trunk contained a seemingly random assortment of tools: farrier's hammers, chisels, beak irons, tongs of many varieties—hoop tongs, hammer tongs, tongs with round bits and square. These tools and others, particularly the wagon jacks, had been called into service time and again since the departure from Fort Cumberland many days ago, because some of the overloaded wagons had literally been jolted to pieces on the rugged, stumpy road. Each time it was essential to stop, unload the cargo, fix the damage, then load up again and go on until some other calamity caused a halt. Occasionally wagons damaged beyond repair would have to be abandoned altogether, their cargo distributed out to other wagons. *Should have used pack-horses.*

The wagons stood unmoving at the moment because the army ahead had halted again. None of the wagoners knew why, and there was little point in asking. Such stops had occurred with frustrating frequency since the expedition left Fort Cumberland days ago. If the wagons weren't breaking down and holding back the army from behind, the army was blocking the wagons from advancing, as now. It was jolting, monotonous, laborious work to move Braddock's army across the wilderness, and anyone with a head on his shoulders knew it would only grow more difficult the deeper they went into the mountains. Often the long processional moved so slowly that the gaggle of camp followers, a combination of prostitutes and wives and children of the soldiers ahead, almost outpaced the wagons.

Daniel Boone, like his neighbor and frequent hunting partner Nate, had joined this campaign as a volunteer militiaman from the Yadkin River country of North Carolina. Any who saw Nate and Daniel together inevitably received the impression that the latter had several years' maturity on the former, but in fact Daniel was only two years Nate's senior. Nate's boyish face and the seasoning effects of Daniel Boone's more extensive experience on the frontier accounted for the seemingly greater difference in their ages.

Daniel probed some more until he pulled out two tools, one a pair of long, flat-bit blacksmith's tongs, the other a much smaller set of farrier's pincers. Rubbing his chin, he studied both a few moments, then rose lightly and carried both tools over to the sorrowful-looking Nate Meriwether.

"Nate, I don't know which will give me the better pry of that tooth," he said. "I could wrench harder with the long ones, but these here pincers might bite in some and get me a stouter grip."

"God preserve me," Nate murmured. "I'm to be tortured like a captive of savages."

Daniel ignored him. Nate had a tendency to whine. He pursed the thin lips of his wide and slightly downturning mouth and nodded firmly. "The pincers," he said. "And if that don't work, we can always try the tongs."

Nate Meriwether looked like he might jump up and run away. Daniel eyed him sympathetically but sternly, then turned and called to another man still seated on his wagon about three vehicles back in the train from Daniel's, head lolling as he took advantage of the halt for a catnap. "John! John Findley! Come here—I need thee . . . need you." Daniel blushed, embarrassed that one of the old speech habits of his Pennsylvania youth had slipped back into his talk again. It still happened from time to time, even though his Quaker days were long behind him.

John Findley, a thirtyish man whose clever mind was masked by his humble-looking face but revealed in his sharp, intelligent eyes, lifted his head and tilted back his wide-brimmed beaver hat. He blinked, yawned, stretched. "Aye, Dan. On my way."

Findley leaped lithely down from his perch, his fluid body motion reminding Daniel of the manner of movement common to Indians. Perhaps Findley had unconciously picked up that manner while making his living as a Pennsylvania licensed trader years before in Indian country few white men had seen. Findley came to Daniel's side, yawned and stretched again, then fixed him with a curious expression, awaiting direction.

"I've got to yank out Nate's bad tooth," Daniel explained. "He's dearly suffering with it."

"What do you want me to do?"

"Hold his head tight. I doubt he has the gravel to hold still himself."

Nate frowned at Daniel's unflattering assessment, but did not dispute it. Now Findley grinned, his eyes brightening with mischievous delight; it made him look very much the native-born Irishman that he was. Like Nate, who hailed from Suffolk, England, John Findley was an American colonial by immigration, not birth. His Irish accent had faded substantially in the fifteen or so years he had lived in the colonies, but for Nate's aggravation he deliberately stirred it to life again. "Ah! A chance to enjoy the suffering of a bloody Englishman! What finer a pleasure for a man from the green isle, eh?"

"May you roast in whatever pit of hell the Almighty has reserved for the Irish," Nate replied. Even though he had been a colonial since age three, he still clung to his English heritage, a fact Findley had ascertained and had much fun with since this expedition had brought them together.

"Get a stout grip on him, John," Daniel directed, opening and closing the pincers to get the right feel of them. Findley moved around behind the squatting Nate, cracked his knuckles, bent, looped his right arm under Nate's chin, and fixed his left hand on his brow. "Open wide, Nate," Findley said. Then, with a wink to Daniel: "You know, these English always do have blasted sorry teeth."

Nate was about to respond, but Findley pulled back on his brow and closed in tight on his neck, cutting off words and most of his wind, and forcing his mouth open besides. Nate watched Daniel advancing with the pincers and squeezed his eyes shut as the cruel-looking tool descended toward his throbbing tooth. As soon as metal touched enamel, he let out a high moan. Tears streamed from beneath his tightly squeezed eyelids. Findley grinned like a cat.

Good thing it's a front-and-bottom tooth, Daniel thought, otherwise I'd never get these big pincers in there. He had never noticed before what a small mouth Nate Meriwether had. "Get ready, Nate, you're about to loose her," he said, and closed the pincers tight around the cavitied tooth.

Nate writhed and cried, tongue wriggling about in his upturned mouth like the head of a snake with its tail in the fire. Findley's strong arms clamped down as if he were trying to crush Nate's head like a walnut. Daniel closed the pincers so tightly they cut into the tooth, and began pulling up with a twisting, wrenching motion. The tooth didn't want to let go; he began wrenching harder. Nate's eyes opened wide and rolled back in the sockets so far that only the whites showed as a final hard twist pulled the tooth free. His mouth flooded with blood. Findley let him go, and Nate groaned and slumped to the ground, eyes still rolled up as if he were trying to see the inside of his own skull.

"Danged if he ain't fainted," Daniel said. He held up the bloodied prize. "And no wonder! The root of this thing must have run nigh to his chin."

Findley knelt beside Nate, turning his head to the side so he wouldn't swallow blood. Then he gently shook him, urging him out of his swoon. Nate moaned, opened his eyes, and pushed upright, spitting blood onto the ground.

"As courageous an Englishman as I've met!" Findley said, slapping Nate's shoulder. "Well done, Nate Meriwether."

Nate muttered an oath. Daniel trotted back to the wagon, stuck a hand into his rifle pouch, which lay on the seat, and returned with a couple of pieces of patching. "Nate, bite down on these until the bleeding stops. That tooth will be giving you no more pain now."

Nate's color was beginning to return. He bit on the patching a minute or so, then glanced up at Daniel and nodded his thanks. He pointedly failed to do the same for Findley, delighting the Irishman, who had found no greater pleasure along Braddock's Road than getting Nate Meriwether's goat as often and in as many ways as possible. Winking again at Daniel, Findley returned to his wagon, whistling an Irish tune. Moments later an official call came back down the line: The advance was resuming.

"Are you fit to drive?" Daniel asked Nate.

"I'm fine," Nate replied through clenched teeth. The bit of patching, very bloodied now, stuck out across his thick lower lip. His sparse beard, usually rich brown, now was rusty-red because of the bloody drool that had soaked into it during his tooth-pulling ordeal. But he grinned weakly, and Daniel knew that though Nate looked a sight, he already felt better.

"A tooth can kill a man if it gets bad enough," Daniel said, wiping the pincers on his trousers. "I seen it happen once. It's good we got it out."

The wagons ahead were already creaking into motion. Hurridly returning to the trunk that bore his blacksmithing tools, Daniel put the tools back inside, closed it, put it back into the wagon, and strapped down the cover. He launched himself back into the driver's seat and set his wagon in motion just as it was his time to roll out.

Ten minutes later, he was sniffing the air and noting that a marsh lay ahead, its muddy scent distinctive even in the overwhelming reek of the draft horses. Distinctive, at least, to Daniel Boone, who had spent his youth among the scents and sounds of the outdoor world and had become adept at distinguishing and interpreting them. In boyhood days he had roamed the hills and forests of this very colony, keeping watch over his father's cattle, and—until Squire Boone presented him with his first rifle at the age of twelve—hunting rabbits and other small game with a hurling club he had devised from the gnarly-rooted trunk of a sapling. He had gotten very good at this primitive hunting, just as he was very good at doing most anything having to do with life in the wilds. Even in youth he had known that he was unusually skilled at surviving, even thriving, in the wilderness. No arrogance grew out of this knowledge. It was simply a fact Daniel accepted like he accepted any other.

Daniel looked around him as he drove, thinking that by coming to Pennsylvania he had in a fashion come home again . . . but no, this wasn't home. He wasn't the kind of fellow who looked back once he had left a thing or status or place behind. Daniel preferred to look forward.

Even so, Daniel's memories of his Pennsylvania

Quaker boyhood were vivid and precious to him. He had enjoyed life in this colony, but he was old enough now to understand how difficult affairs had been for his parents in the old days. They had been affiliated with the Exeter Meeting of Friends, but difficulties had arisen: his oldest sister, Sarah, marrying a young man who was not a Quaker, and getter herself with child before the wedding besides; a brother, Israel, repeating the offense of marrying a non-Quaker, causing the Friends to come to Daniel's father, Squire, and demand that he discipline his wayward children. Squire declined to do so, and soon after had been expelled from the Meeting, as Sarah and Israel already had been.

Pennsylvania had seemed harsh, alien territory for Squire Boone after that. North Carolina called and Squire answered, moving south, lingering for a time in the Shenendoah Valley, then continuing on to the Yadkin River. Now the Boones were Carolinians, Pennsylvania Quakers no more. Life in Pennsylvania was part of an increasingly distant past, and Daniel's return here to join Braddock's march against Fort Duquesne was a journey of patriotism and adventure, not of sentiment.

He and Nate Meriwether had signed up in the North Carolina militia on the same day, and had headed for Fort Cumberland, Maryland, right on the border of Pennsylvania with no clear notion of what experiences military duty would bring them. Even without specific expectations, Daniel had been surprised by one thing: General Braddock, for all his arrogance and disdain for colonials, seemed downright inept at his job. He was particularly condescending to his young lieutenant-colonel, George Washington, who commanded the blue-coated colonial troops, a group Braddock clearly regarded as greatly inferior to his red-coated British regulars. Daniel knew that on wilderness soil, the opposite was true. Even Nate knew the same, despite his native British pride and the fact that one of Braddock's regulars was his own eldest brother, Frederick Meriwether. Ironically, Frederick was the only Meriwether brother who had not come with the family to the colonies, yet had been shipped here anyway on military assignment. The middle Meriwether brother, Clive, was a Pennsylvania farmer living west of Carlisle. Nate had talked some about wanting to see him while he was in the area.

Stories of Braddock's arrogance and incomprehension of the realities of wilderness campaigns had spread through the colonial troops even before they set out from Fort Cumberland. Ignoring the advice of Colonel Washington and Philadelphia's noted Benjamin Franklin, who had helped provision Braddock's force, Braddock insisted on a full supply train of wagons and on marching his regulars at the front of the ranks and placing the colonials—men far more familiar than the regulars with the terrain and Indian warfare—farther back. And he would give no heed to any notion that mere savages could prevail over his red-coated army. The Indians that the French had recruited to help them fight might be a threat to "raw American militia," Braddock informed Franklin, but against "the king's regulars and disciplined troops" it would be "impossible they should make any impression." As for Fort Duquesne, the French-held outpost Braddock was intending to capture, it would fall easily, in two or three days at the most.

The wagons rolled ahead, and Daniel's anticipation of a marsh proved true. He guided his team carefully onto the makeshift pavement of logs laid across the wet earth, and felt his teeth jar in his skull with every bump of the wagon. What a road! *Should have used packhorses.*

So far Daniel had held his silence about Braddock's ineptitudes. He was just a young wagoner, after all. His job was to move the baggage of an army, not to second-guess trained officers. But he couldn't help but worry about one thing: If Braddock was incapable of advancing an army through the wilderness in the most sensible way, would he do battle in the wilderness any better? Would he expect that Indians and frontier-savvy Frenchmen would fight by formal English rules of warfare? If so, the lesson he was bound to learn would probably be painful and bloody.

The wagons rolled on, trailing the soldiers deeper into the dark and rugged mountains.

2

That night John Findley talked about the Kentucky country, and Daniel Boone was transfixed. Three times before on this expedition he had listened to Findley's talk of that dark and rich land, where buffalo grazed in herds so vast a man had to look twice to see them all, where broad stands of tall cane gave evidence of the richness of the land, where beaver, otter, mink, and deer roamed in such abundance that a man could make himself rich with their pelts with hardly any effort at all.

But it was a dangerous land, too, prized and protected by the Indians. A man could gather wealth easily enough, but whether he could make it out with his wealth and his scalp still in his possession was another matter altogether. It was only because of such repeated calamities, Findley avowed, that he hadn't come out of Kentucky a rich man.

Daniel asked him if he would ever go back to Kentucky. Findley replied that he surely would, someday, and make another try at riches. Kentucky was a wonderful place, a virtual heaven except for the Indians. It just lay there spread out under the sky waiting for clever men to come pluck its treasures like so many ripe grapes. And if any didn't believe the word of John Findley on how fine a land Kentucky was, they could go seek out Thomas Walker, commissary-general of this very expedition, or Christopher Gist, Washington's scout. Both had seen the Kentucky country. And Walker had spied out a big gap through the mountains, the mountain notch the Indians called Ouasioto, through which ran the old Indian trail of

Athawominee, what the white men called the Warrior's Path. By this route a man could cross the mountains from North Carolina, or travel down the great valley from Virginia, and enter Kentucky by land.

Daniel Boone's eyes gave a keen flash as he listened to Findley's enticing words. Kentucky—accessible by land through a route not terribly distant from Carolina! Hearing Findley talk about it made it all seem much more accessible. Kentucky was a place he fully intended to see one day. It was a closed, virtually unknown, dangerous land now, but not forever. Someday it would be opened—and Daniel Boone would be there when that happened.

Or such was his dream . . . the dream of a young man at the moment no more than a wagon driver on a plodding military campaign.

That thought brought him back to his true situation. Before he could turn his attention to chasing dreams there were present challenges to meet . . . Braddock's road to travel, Fort Duquesne to capture. No point in getting stirred up by a momentarily unfulfillable wanderlust. Daniel Boone rose and left Findley's fireside with a sense of resignation and regret, resenting the immediate and mundane.

The next morning the march began again, and it was all as before, but worse: even more wagons breaking down, horses falling exhausted or injured or dying, carrion birds flying above like a grim omen, waiting to descend and feed on the fallen beasts. Time and time again the engineers found themselves facing obstacles too big to overcome. The army would divert onto a new course, winding along difficult and rocky trails, under massive cliffs, across waterways that threatened to wash away wagons and cannon. Exhausted, frustrated soldiers began to grow sick. Nate heard that his brother was among the ill but was still having to march, and openly cursed the name of Edward Braddock for having advanced this expedition to begin with.

They crossed the crest of the mountains and struggled on. George Washington, himself beginning to fall ill, complained to Braddock that their current course was hazardous. By the time they reached Fort Duquesne, the men would be weak and sick, unable to fight. For once, Braddock listened, and at Washington's request divided the force, taking part of it forward at a somewhat greater speed and leaving the rest as a rear division, to approach more slowly. But the end result made little difference, the advance force never reaching that far ahead of the rear group.

And so it went until the early days of July came, and the army at last neared the Monongahela River. George Washington was sicker than before and being carried in the bed of a wagon. Fort Duquesne was not far away, and barring a French surrender, soon the battle would be joined. From all indications Daniel Boone could see, Braddock still believed the fight would yield a quick and easy victory. What other notion could explain why the general was still marching the more experienced colonial troops to the rear of regulars who knew almost nothing of the frontier? Where were the scouts, the flank guards? Did Braddock not realize the dangers of this approach?

Then came the morning of July 9, and the shining Monongahela. And across the water, disaster awaited like a crouched catamount ready to spring and kill.

CAMERON JUDD

Writing with power, authority, and respect for America's frontier traditions, Cameron Judd captures the spirit of adventure and promise of the wild frontier in his fast-paced, exciting novels. In the tradition of Max Brand and Luke Short, Cameron Judd is a new voice of the Old West.